SCANDAL ON RINCON HILL

ALSO BY SHIRLEY TALLMAN

The Cliff House Strangler

The Russian Hill Murders

Murder on Nob Hill

SCANDAL ON RINCON HILL

SHIRLEY TALLMAN

Minotaur Books New York

SCANDAL ON RINCON HILL. Copyright © 2010 by Shirley Tallman. All rights reserved. Printed in the United States of America. For information, address St. Martin's Press, 175 Fifth Avenue, New York, N.Y. 10010.

www.minotaurbooks.com

Library of Congress Cataloging-in-Publication Data

Tallman, Shirley.
  Scandal on Rincon Hill : a Sarah Woolson mystery / Shirley Tallman.—1st ed.
    p. cm.
  ISBN 978-0-312-38697-9
  1. Women lawyers—Fiction. 2. Murder—Investigation—Fiction. 3. San Francisco (Calif.)—History—19th century—Fiction. 4. Rincon Hill (San Francisco, Calif.)—Fiction. I. Title.

PS3620.A54S33 2010
813'.6—dc22

                                                                        2009039823

First Edition: April 2010

10 9 8 7 6 5 4 3 2 1

In loving memory of our wonderful son, Chris.
We will always believe.

And, as always, to H. P.

ACKNOWLEDGMENTS

Many thanks to my niece, Melody Bennett, for being one of Sarah Woolson's most steadfast fans, and for inspiring the Melody Tremaine character featured in this book. What would I do without your loyal support, Mel, even if it's all too frequently accompanied by your outspoken opinion concerning which man should win Sarah's heart? Love you, sweetie!

CHAPTER ONE

The nightmare began early on the morning of Sunday, December 4.

Upon reflection, perhaps I ought to rephrase this statement. By *nightmare,* I do not refer to the frightening dreams each of us suffers upon occasion. Rather I am describing the horrific events which sent ripples of fear through the inhabitants of Rincon Hill—nay, through the entire city of San Francisco—shortly before Christmas, in the year of our Lord 1881. Unarguably, the murder which set the horror in motion that morning was a tragedy, yet none of us could have possibly foreseen the carnage which was yet to follow.

I had retired late the previous evening, and was in a deep sleep when I was abruptly awakened by an odd noise. I sat bolt upright in my bed, but it was several moments before my groggy mind comprehended the source of that sound; some fool was throwing rocks at my window!

Pushing back my bedcovers, I arose and, without bothering to pull on slippers or robe, hurried across the room to the window facing the west side of the house. I was reaching for the edge of the drapes when another handful of pebbles bounced against the pane. By now thoroughly awake, and not a little irritated, I angrily pulled up the sash.

Below me, a pool of light emanated from a kerosene lantern, held aloft by the dark figure of a man. Regarding him in some surprise, I realized he appeared to be wearing the dark blue frock coat (appearing nearly black in the dim light) of the San Francisco police department. I should have known, I thought, expelling a sigh of relief. The man peering up at my window was George Lewis, my brother Samuel's good friend and a sergeant on the above-mentioned force.

"George," I called down to him, "would you kindly explain why you are throwing rocks at my window? And in the middle of the night?"

"I apologize, Miss Sarah," he said in a loud whisper. "Your back fence prevented me from reaching Samuel's window. A body's been found in the Second Street Cut, and I knew he'd want to be the first reporter on the scene. Would you—could you please wake him?"

I thought for a moment I had misheard. "Did you say you found a body just two blocks from our house?"

"Yes, and I'm in something of a hurry. I have to return there as quickly as possible." His voice grew more urgent. "I hate to bother you, Miss Sarah, but would you please tell your brother?"

I made up my mind on the instant. "Yes, I'll fetch him right away!"

In my bare feet, and still not bothering with a robe, I left my room and padded quickly down the hall. The way was but dimly lit by several small sconce candles hung on the walls, requiring me to watch carefully where I stepped in order to avoid the squeakier floorboards. Samuel's bedroom was located at the rear of our house, overlooking the back garden. The gnarled old oak tree that grew just outside his window had for years provided my brother with a convenient method for coming and going without our parents being any the wiser. Even now I knew he occasionally utilized the tree for this purpose, especially if he were pursuing a newsworthy story.

Unknown to my mother and father, or any other member of the family, for that matter, Samuel—who had completed his legal education some five years previous—had invented endless excuses to postpone taking his California Bar examinations. In those intervening years, he had become far more interested in the life of a crime journalist, for which he had unarguably been blessed with considerable talent.

The reason for this subterfuge was because our father, the Honorable Horace T. Woolson, superior court judge for the County of San Francisco, nurtured a deep prejudice, not to mention mistrust, toward anyone in the newspaper business. It was Samuel's profound hope that Papa would never discover the real reason why he continued to avoid taking that last step en route to becoming an attorney. He had, you see, been busy forging a career in journalism under the name Ian Fearless, the noted San Francisco crime reporter much in demand by a variety of publications, ranging from the *Police Gazette* to the city's well-established daily newspapers. George Lewis was right. Samuel would undoubtedly do anything to scoop the town's other reporters when it came to a good murder.

Not stopping to knock, I boldly entered my brother's room and crossed to his bed. Samuel was an especially sound sleeper—it was a family joke that he'd even managed to sleep through several significant earthquakes—and I was forced to shake him by the shoulders before he could be roused from his slumber.

"What the hell?" he grumbled, pulling the bedcovers over his tousled head. "Go away and let me sleep."

"Samuel, wake up," I said, continuing to shake him. "George is waiting for you outside. They've found a body in the Cut. He thought you'd want to cover the story."

At this, he sat up, rubbing sleep from his eyes. "What time is it?"

By the faint glow of candlelight spilling through the open door to the hall, I could just make out the hands of his clock.

"It's a few minutes after two o'clock," I told him. "Hurry up and get dressed if you want an exclusive story."

Without waiting for him to agree, I scurried back to my own room. Hastily, I tore off my nightgown and pulled on the first dress that came to hand. Not bothering with petticoats or stockings, I threw on a pair of old boots and tossed a long, hooded wrap over my shoulders. I gathered my thick mop of tangled hair into a bun as I raced down the stairs and, grabbing hold of one of the lanterns kept at the ready in a downstairs cupboard, flung open the front door. Leaving it slightly ajar behind me, I joined a startled-looking George Lewis who stood waiting on the street.

"Miss Sarah," he protested, "you can't mean to come with us. The victim is . . . that is, it's not a pleasant sight."

"Never mind about that, George," I said, straightening my cape so that it covered me more securely. "You should know by now that I am not faint of heart."

Before George could find more reasons to object to my presence, my brother came flying out of the house, pulling on his topcoat with one hand, while attempting to balance a notepad and his own lantern in the other.

"I might have known you'd insist on coming along," he said, spying me standing next to his friend.

"I tried to tell her she should stay here," George said, regarding me unhappily. "Where I'm taking you is no fit place for a lady."

Samuel gave a dry little laugh. "Save your breath, George. You have as much chance of stopping her as you'd have holding back a wild boar." Striking a match, he lit both our lamps, then blew out the flame. "All right, my b'hoy, lead us to this body of yours."

George flashed me one more uncertain look, then silently turned and set off at a brisk pace toward the Harrison Street Bridge. This structure, which the noted author Charles Warren Stoddard referred to as "a bridge celebrated as a triumph of architectural ungainliness," had been erected to span Harrison Street across the gap caused by the infamous Second Street Cut. Many San Franciscans—my father and I included—considered the cut a greedy and ill-advised scheme, which had signaled the beginning of the end to Rincon Hill, until then one of the city's finest districts.

Tonight, the bridge loomed before us like a long, graceless serpent, barely distinguishable against the dark sky. A god-awful eyesore, Papa was fond of saying, and I must admit that I heartily agreed with this sentiment.

As we drew nearer, I spied a one-horse chaise parked to the right side of the road leading onto the bridge. A man I assumed to be the driver moved out of the shadows and signaled to us with his lantern, then turned and directed us to yet another light burning on the dirt slope below the bridge. Stepping closer, I could make out the figures of three men standing some thirty feet beneath us. The man waving the lantern up and down was wearing a police uniform. Two more dark forms stood off to the side, silently watching our approach.

"The men standing next to Officer Kostler are the ones who discovered the body," explained George. "They were crossing the bridge when they heard screams coming from below. They say they saw the figure of a man scrambling up the opposite embankment. When they investigated, they found the victim lying under the bridge with his head bashed in. They sent the driver to summon the police, then agreed to wait with the body while I fetched Samuel." In the lantern light, I could make out a wry smile. "Kostler owes me a favor, so I trust him to keep his trap shut about my little side trip to your house."

Admonishing us to watch our step, George picked his way cautiously down the eastern embankment of the overpass, a precarious, hundred-foot side hill prone to mud slides during the rainy season, and sloping steeply to the bottom of the "cut" and the redirected Second Street below.

About a third of the way down, I spied a dark, unrecognizable shape sprawled in the dirt, partly hidden by one of the concrete bridge supports. As George held up his lantern, it was possible to make out the line of a leg, and just above it, a hand. Drawing closer, and raising my own lantern, I could see that the victim was a man, and that he lay facedown, his arms stretched out as if attempting to ward off the blows to his head. His legs were flung out to either side of his trunk at awkward angles.

It shames me to admit to such squeamishness, but I confess that

I recoiled at the sight of the man's wounds. His dark hair was matted with blood, and the right side of his face had been battered in beyond recognition. As Samuel drew closer, the combined light of the three lamps revealed a three-foot section of a two-by-four lying half a dozen feet above the body on the steep slope. From the blood-soaked look of it, I concluded that this must be the murder weapon. George obviously concurred, although he made no move to pick it up, or indeed to move it.

"He hasn't been touched," Officer Kostler told his superior. "And no one else has come along, or even crossed the bridge, for that matter."

One of the two men standing apart from the policeman regarded George in some distress. His round, full face appeared very pale in the spill of lantern light.

"It's late and damn cold," he said, his voice none too steady. "Can we be on our way now? We know nothing more about this horrible crime than we've already told you."

"Just a minute," said George. He reached into a pocket and pulled out a pencil and notebook. After jotting down their names and addresses, he informed the two men that they were free to leave. "But we may want to speak to you again at a future date, so please inform us if you plan to leave town."

The men nodded gratefully, then scampered up the hillside as quickly as they dared, given the dim light and unsure footing.

When they were gone, Samuel moved closer and felt the man's face. "He's still warm, and this is a chilly evening. Most likely he was murdered within the past half hour."

"Yes," George agreed. "That skews with the witnesses's account. Too bad they weren't here a few minutes earlier. Might have scared off whoever did this, and saved the bloke's life."

My brother peered down at the sad figure who, a short time earlier, had been as alive as any of us standing here now. "Who is he?" he asked his friend. "Have you gone through his pockets?"

George nodded. "That was the first thing I did when I realized the poor sod was beyond mortal help. Whoever did him in took his wallet, but left his gold pocket watch and the two gold rings he's wearing. There were a few bills stuffed into one of his pockets. Of course it's hard to tell if anything else is missing until we speak to his family."

"So you think it was robbery then?" asked Samuel.

"Looks like it," George replied. "Probably a case of the poor bugger being in the wrong place at the wrong time."

"But, George, that makes no sense," I said. "Why would a thief leave behind cash and valuable jewelry?"

"That's easy enough to explain, Miss Sarah," George said with a cheerless smile. "The knuck sees this fellow crossing the bridge and decides to take advantage of the opportunity. He takes the mark's wallet, but before he can grab anything else, he hears a carriage on the bridge and the sound of voices. He very sensibly skedaddles off before anyone has time to see his face."

"I don't know," I said, still not convinced. "Why kill the poor man? Surely the thief ran little risk of being identified on such a dark night. Why not just render his victim unconscious, rob him, then leave before he came to? Surely there was no need to beat the man's head in, er—" Out of my side vision I caught a glimpse of the victim's battered upper torso and swallowed hard. "Like that."

"Who knows, Miss Sarah?" said George. "Sad to say, we see this sort of thing all too often. These rounders care little enough about their victims. Just as soon kill them as not."

I knew what he said was true, but I continued to be troubled by the excessively violent nature of the crime.

Before George could respond to these concerns, Samuel nudged my arm and nodded up the slope. Following his gaze, I spied a stout figure making his careful way down the hill with the aid of a kerosene lantern. As the light swung back and forth in front of his face, I was dismayed to recognize the newcomer as our father.

When Papa grew closer, I saw that he was wearing the old topcoat he kept on the back porch, along with the gardening boots which were also stored there. I suspected that beneath his coat he might well be wearing nothing more than his nightshirt. His hair was mussed, and he looked none too happy. I glanced quickly at Samuel, who shared my surprise at this unlikely addition to our group.

"Papa," I called out. "What are you doing here?"

My father did not immediately respond, seemingly busy saving his breath for the arduous descent. Even when he finally reached us, he spent several moments taking in deep gulps of air before endeavoring to answer my question.

"I heard the two of you leave the house," he said, once his breathing had steadied. "You made enough noise to wake the dead. Couldn't imagine why in tarnation you were stomping hell-bent down the stairs in the middle of the night. I managed to follow your lanterns, although there was no need for you to walk so blasted fast!"

His eyes fell on the crumpled body lying beneath one of the bridge supports, and he stopped short. "Who is this?" His voice was less strident as he regarded the unfortunate man.

George was the first to answer. "We don't know his identity yet, sir. Whoever did this made off with his wallet."

My father moved closer to the body. He appeared to be paying particular attention to the man's clothing and shoes. For the first time, I realized the victim was wearing evening dress; he had evidently attended the theater, or a soiree of some kind that evening.

"May I turn his head?" Papa asked George. "I'll try not to disturb anything else."

George nodded, but seemed puzzled why my father should make such a request. We all watched silently as Papa pushed up his sleeves and gently moved the man's head until he could more clearly see his face. Bringing his lantern closer, he studied the victim's features for several long moments.

"I think I know this man," he said at last, stepping almost reverently back from the body. "His condition makes it difficult to be certain, but I believe his name is Nigel Loran, no, wait, it was Logan, Nigel Logan. If I am not mistaken he is—*was,* rather—a botanist or biologist of some sort. My wife and I met him for the first time last night, at a party we attended in honor of the Reverend Erasmus Mayfield's twenty-fifth ordination anniversary. Mayfield is the rector at the Church of Our Savior."

"Do you happen to know where Mr. Logan lives?" George asked Papa. "It can't have been too far away for him to walk home so late at night, instead of taking a cab."

My father thought for a moment before replying, "I believe I heard someone say that he had a room in a boardinghouse on Harrison Street, several blocks beyond the bridge. I seem to recall that he taught science at the University of San Francisco. You know, the college run by the Jesuits?"

Indeed I did know. This renowned institution had been established in 1855 by the Jesuit fathers. Located on Market Street between Fourth and Fifth, it was now widely regarded as one of the city's foremost academies of higher education. If Mr. Logan had taught classes there, he must have been an accomplished scholar.

"Tell me more about the party you attended last night, if you would, Judge Woolson," requested George. "I've sent for some of my men and a wagon to transport the body, but while we wait I'd like to hear about this Logan fellow."

"I can't say that I know much more than I've already told you," Papa said thoughtfully. "In fact, the only reason I remember the young man at all is because of the argument he had with the Reverend Mayfield."

"And what argument was that, sir?" asked George, once again opening his notebook and moving closer to Samuel's lantern. Pencil poised, he regarded Papa with keen interest.

"It was just the usual folderol between the church and the scientific world, this time over Charles Darwin's theory of evolution." Papa harrumphed, displaying grave misgivings that the human race could possibly have developed from a lower form of animal species. "Logan began quoting from Darwin's latest epic, *The Descent of Man,* and not surprisingly the Reverend Mayfield took exception to this reference, as well he should. I'm sorry to say, the two of them went at it hammer and tong for some little time before our host managed to break them up." He chuckled. "I thought for a while the two might actually come to blows over the idiotic book."

"You said the Reverend Mayfield became upset?" inquired George, looking up from his pad.

"I'd say he was a damn sight more than upset," answered Papa, still smiling at the memory. Then, for the first time he regarded the younger man as if just now realizing where his questions were leading.

"Wait a minute, George," he went on. "What are you getting at? It's true that both men were agitated, but if you're trying to imply that the Reverend Mayfield was so angry he followed Logan and murdered him because he disagreed with his beliefs, you're barking up the wrong tree. I've known Erasmus Mayfield for fifteen years, and he's one of the few ministers of my acquaintance that I consider to be a true man of God." He nodded toward the crumpled body. "I assure you, sir, that the Reverend Mayfield is incapable of violence, much less the degree of brutality visited upon this unfortunate soul."

George raised a hand, obviously in an attempt to calm my father. "Please, Judge Woolson, I didn't mean to imply that I thought Mr., er, the Reverend Mayfield killed Mr. Logan. I'm just trying to collect information about the victim, particularly the time leading up to his murder. It occurred to me that maybe someone else, someone who overheard the argument, say, might have been so het up about Nigel Logan's support of Mr. Darwin's book, that he thought to teach the young scientist a lesson. And maybe that lesson went too far and the man accidentally killed the fellow."

I considered this highly unlikely, and said so. "Come now, George, churches have been railing against Darwin's hypothesis for over twenty years. I can't imagine anyone at the Tremaines' party becoming so distraught over Logan's argument with the Reverend Mayfield that he would bludgeon the man to death."

Samuel nodded in agreement. "Sarah's right. Excuse the pun, George, but the severity of those blows to Logan's head strike me as overkill. This attack has the feel of a more personal crime, as if the killer bore an intense grudge against the fellow."

"Maybe, maybe not," commented George, unconvinced by this argument. "I see cases like this every day, more than I care to recall. And I've come across many a rough who'll beat a man to death for the sheer love of the kill. Doesn't seem to matter if he knows the bloke or not."

Samuel seemed about to offer another objection, but was distracted by the sound of a police wagon clattering across the bridge. Papa, Samuel, and I remained standing by the body, while George and Officer Kostler went to meet the men. A few minutes later, they returned with three uniformed policemen, two of them carrying a stretcher.

Before George would allow them to move the body, however, he asked one of the new arrivals to sketch the scene, paying particular attention to the position of the corpse in relationship to the bridge support, as well as its rough distance from the top of the dirt embankment.

"This isn't exactly police procedure," he commented, directing a self-conscious look at my father. "But Fuller here has a good eye and does a bang-up job with a sketch pad. I find it helps me remember the condition of the body and where we found it. I've heard that some police departments back East have actually started to take photographic pictures of crime scenes, but so far we haven't been able to convince the commissioner that it's worth the expense."

"I think it's a wonderful idea, George," I said, regarding him with newfound respect. Ever since he had made sergeant earlier that year, he seemed to be developing into a fine detective. "Imagine how helpful it would be to have a true representation of a murder site, one that could be examined at a later date for missed or overlooked evidence?"

Papa looked skeptical. "Considering all the time it takes for one of these photographer fellows to get a halfway decent likeness of their subject, I can't see the process being of much use to the police for years to come, if ever."

With this somewhat cynical pronouncement, my father turned and commenced the laborious climb back to the top of the embankment. Samuel and I waited where we were until Fuller completed his sketch (which was remarkably good considering how quickly it had been rendered), then watched as the remaining policemen loaded the victim's body onto the stretcher. Given the steep grade leading up to the waiting police wagon, George and Samuel were forced to lend a hand in order to prevent the stretcher bearers from losing their precarious foothold and sliding down the hill, taking their heavy burden with them.

I followed this procession, steadying my lantern in an effort to see where I was placing my boots. Even then it became necessary for Samuel to take hold of my hand and pull me up the final half-dozen feet or so. As he did, I was dismayed to see a taxi pull to an abrupt stop by the side of the bridge. I recognized the man who exited the carriage as Ozzie Foldger, a crime reporter who frequently competed with Samuel for stories.

"Who do you suppose tipped him off?" murmured my brother, eyeing the short, tubby little man who had a well-earned reputation for the ruthless tactics he all too often employed in his quest to scoop other reporters. "Sometimes I think that man has a telegraph machine installed inside his head."

Foldger gave Samuel a mocking smile, nodded in some surprise to me, then blinked in astonishment when he recognized our father standing by the police van. The reporter acknowledged Papa's presence with a polite tip of his cap, then pulled out his own notebook and pencil and set off to corner Sergeant Lewis. George shot a helpless look at my brother, then with unhappy resignation began to answer Ozzie's rapid-fire questions.

With a muttered oath, Samuel kept a wary eye on his rival, as the stretcher bearers loaded the body into the police wagon. Seemingly using this as an excuse, George broke away from Foldger, bid my father and me a hasty good morning, and joined Kostler and their fellow officers for the ride to the city morgue. With another sardonic smile, Ozzie Foldger pocketed his notebook and got back into his waiting cab.

As Papa, Samuel, and I started for home, I was unnerved to see our father silently considering his youngest son, a perplexed look on his face. I could tell that Samuel, too, felt the tension which hung over our heads like a heavy swirl of morning fog. Indeed, the unspoken strain between my brother and father seemed to build with each step we took, until the short, two-block walk home felt closer to a mile.

It was a relief when we finally reached our house and were once again inside the quiet foyer. I headed immediately for the stairs, suddenly very weary and looking forward to the comfort of my bed. My brother followed closely upon my heels, eager, I was certain, to escape Papa's probing gaze. We had gone only a few steps, however, when we were halted by our father's voice.

"Wait a minute, the two of you," he said, his tone pitched low enough not to awaken the rest of the family, but with a sharp bite of authority. He regarded us levelly from the hallway below. "You must think me remarkably naïve to accept without question how my two youngest children came to be standing beneath the Harrison Street Bridge in the middle of the night, examining a brutally murdered young man. I heard no police bells or other sounds of alarm, and even if I had, I would hardly expect the two of you to rise from your beds at that ungodly hour and chase after them."

I glanced nervously at Samuel who stood a little below me on the stairs. His handsome face betrayed his agitation as he struggled to come up with some rational explanation for this admittedly *ir-rational* act.

Before he could manufacture an excuse, however, Papa sighed and gestured dismissively with his hand. "Oh, never mind. I'm too tired to listen to what are sure to be a litany of woeful excuses."

He used his thumb and forefinger to rub the bridge above his nose, a gesture he often performed when he was suffering a headache.

"Your mother and I plan to spend the day with friends in the country. I'm going to try to get what rest I can before it's time to leave."

He lowered his hand and stared deliberately at each of us in turn. "But don't either of you think for one moment that this marks the end of our discussion. I know you two are up to something, and I have every intention of finding out what it is."

CHAPTER TWO

Samuel and I spent Sunday afternoon creating—and just as quickly discarding—a number of mostly ridiculous reasons to explain our presence at a murder scene that morning. The simple truth, of course, was that we had no good excuse for being there. Short of telling Papa an outright lie, which neither of us cared to do, we were forced to admit that we had done a pretty thorough job of painting ourselves into a corner. To make matters worse, our father had always possessed an uncanny ability to see through our fabrications, a decided disadvantage for any child, much less an adult.

In a cowardly attempt to avoid Papa, Samuel spent Sunday evening at his club, while I judiciously retired to my room before my parents returned from their visit to the country. Although this was, strictly speaking, my brother's problem, we had long been (in Papa's words) partners in devilment, and I felt a certain sisterly loyalty. Despite the provocation, I vowed not to betray my brother's secret identity as the infamous Ian Fearless, intrepid crime reporter.

In a continued effort to avoid the inevitable confrontation, I set off for my Sutter Street office earlier than usual the following morning. I arrived to find my downstairs neighbor, Fanny Goodman, speaking to a strikingly lovely girl outside her millinery shop. The young woman was holding a baby in her arms.

"Ah, Sarah, I'm glad to see you," Fanny said with a welcoming smile. "This young lady has come to consult you on a legal matter." She made a soft, clucking sound with her tongue, and gave the girl a look of mild reproof. "I offered to take her inside where it's warmer for the baby, but she insisted on waiting for you out here."

I gave the young woman my full attention, and was surprised to realize that she was younger than I'd first assumed; certainly she could be no more than eighteen or nineteen. This observation alone was startling, since I could think of little reason why someone hardly out of childhood should seek my professional services.

"My dear," Fanny went on, "may I introduce Miss Sarah Woolson. Sarah, this is Miss Brielle Bouchard. And this little darling"— she tickled the baby under its chin until it gurgled happily—"is Emma."

I was well aware of my neighbor's fondness for children, an affection undoubtedly sharpened by the unhappy fact that she and her late husband had remained childless throughout their marriage. In this instance, however, I had to agree that little Emma was very pretty indeed, with pink cheeks, a button nose, wispy blond curls that surrounded her chubby face like a halo, and wide, amazingly attentive blue eyes. I judged the child to be no more than three or four months old, and was struck by her remarkable alertness.

Miss Bouchard smiled and bounced the baby proudly in her arms, as both Fanny and I made much of the tyke. Indeed, she appeared to be the most loving and solicitous of mothers, somewhat unexpected, I thought, for one of such tender years. At length, however, Fanny reluctantly excused herself and I led my prospective client up the stairs to my office.

Perhaps I should pause briefly in my narrative and explain how I came to acquire the above-mentioned workplace. I have already stated that I am a lawyer, having passed my California Bar examinations some eighteen months earlier. Since woman are still unfairly excluded from most of the country's law schools—California being no exception—I must thank my father for his evenhandedness in exposing his only daughter to the same quality of education he afforded my three older brothers, Frederick, Charles, and of course Samuel, whom you have already met.

For the first nine months of my legal career, I worked as an associate attorney for Shepard, Shepard, McNaughton, and Hall, one of San Francisco's most prestigious law firms. It was during this time that I made the acquaintance of Chinatown's most dangerous and mysterious tong lord, Li Ying. You may well wonder why I choose to call such a villain my friend, nay, my benefactor; I have certainly asked myself the same question innumerable times. Suffice it to say that Mr. Li is, in his own way, one of the most honorable and brilliant men I have had occasion to meet.

In fact, it was the generous fee I was paid for representing one of Li's countrymen that enabled me to leave Joseph Shepard's narrow-minded law firm, and take up quarters here on Sutter Street. While it's true that I cannot state with certainty how long I'll be able to maintain my two-room office over Fanny Goodman's millinery store, I have adopted as my motto, "sufficient unto the day," and try not to worry about the future.

It was into the main room of this small, second-floor suite that I led the young woman. Seating her on one of the room's three chairs, I removed my wrap and took a seat behind my fine old cherrywood desk. I frankly admit that I was curious to hear what had brought Miss Bouchard to my place of business. (Since I could see no wedding band on the third finger of her left hand, I was forced to assume she was unwed).

"Now, then, my dear," I said, assuming a reassuring smile. "How may I help you?"

Settling the baby comfortably in her lap, she looked me straight in the eye. Her gaze was uncomfortably direct for such a slip of a girl.

"I would like your help enforcing a contract which was signed by a gentleman and myself nearly two years ago," she stated without preamble.

Again, I was taken aback by the girl's poise and self-confidence. Her voice was well modulated and pleasant, and her speech pattern indicated that she had enjoyed a better than average education. Now that I had the opportunity to examine her muted violet gown, I could see that it was not only the latest Paris fashion, but that it perfectly fitted her slender but shapely figure. Her neat little black boots, lace reticule, and matching parasol complemented her dress. An abundance of soft blond hair was styled in shiny ringlets to frame a beautiful face, and was topped by a small black hat which she had tipped becomingly to one side. Her wide violet eyes, I was surprised to note, closely matched my own in color, if not in shape, hers being of a more oblong curvature than mine. Taken as a whole, I decided, Brielle Bouchard was an exceedingly attractive young woman.

My curiosity could no longer be contained.

"Miss Bouchard," I ventured, "please forgive me for asking such a personal question, but may I inquire your age?"

"Certainly, Miss Woolson," she replied without the least discomfiture, "I will be twenty next summer."

I gestured toward the baby contentedly resting in her arms. "And little Emma is—"

"Yes, Miss Woolson, Emma is my child. And no, I am not married to her father. He is, in fact, already married and the father of three children." She shifted her right elbow to rest more comfortably against the arm of the chair, the better to support the baby's weight. "I was his mistress for just over eighteen months. He arranged for me to live in a fashionable house on Pacific Avenue, where he employed a most adequate household staff, and provided me with a generous weekly allowance."

It shames me to admit that I was by now staring at the girl in astonishment. "Good heavens, Miss Bouchard. That means you were barely seventeen when—when you—"

"When I became a kept woman, Miss Woolson?" She regarded me with those lovely, far too experienced violet eyes. A brief smile curved her lips, revealing delightful dimples to either side of her graceful mouth.

"Please do not appear so mortified," she continued. "And do not attempt to prettify my profession. I know full well what I became then, and what I remain to this day. However, I must assure you that I was entirely an innocent when I agreed to become the gentleman's mistress. That was, in fact, one of my benefactor's conditions. He feared contracting a disease from any woman who had been with another man. He went so far as to have me examined by his personal physician, to ensure that I was telling him no less than the truth."

To my chagrin, I felt my face flush. This child was nine years my junior, yet she was able to discuss with perfect aplomb a subject abhorred, and as far as possible ignored, by polite society. Naturally, I was fully aware of the many houses of ill repute which flourished in San Francisco. Yet to hear it discussed with such casual abandon, by this angelic-looking creature, was astonishing to say the least.

"Miss Bouchard," I said, endeavoring to mask my discomfiture. "Perhaps if you were to relate the circumstances which led you to your present, er, occupation I might—"

"I think not, Miss Woolson," replied the young woman, quietly but with firm resolve. "My past can have nothing to do with the matter which has brought me to your office this morning. I read about you in the newspapers and, given the rather sensitive nature of my business, decided that I would prefer to be represented by a woman rather than a male attorney."

Her lips formed an attractive, if slightly crooked, smile. "I regret having shocked you, but any sort of prevarication would be counterproductive. As I say, this gentleman and I signed a contract, and I have faithfully adhered to the document in every detail. As long as I agreed to see no other men, and made myself available to him any time of the day or night, he promised to keep me in the manner we had agreed upon for a period of no less than three years."

"Miss Bouchard, if as you say you did nothing to break the contract, may I inquire what has persuaded you to initiate this lawsuit?"

She gave an ironic smile. "It was he who defaulted, Miss Woolson. We were well into the second year of our arrangement, when he discovered that I was five months with child. He immediately insisted that I rid myself of this *inconvenience,* as he put it. I refused, upon which he swore he had taken all the necessary precautions to avoid an unwanted pregnancy, and that the child could not possibly be his. He said that my own unfaithful behavior had rendered the contract null and void, and ordered me out of his house. That is the crux of the matter." The smile vanished to be replaced by a grim line of determination. "Now, what can you do to help me address this injustice?"

Really, I thought, this was without a doubt the most self-assured and blunt young woman I had ever met. I smiled inwardly, not a little amazed to realize that, despite her scandalous occupation, I could not help but admire my lovely visitor. Most of my friends and family considered me too outspoken for a woman. What, I wondered with some amusement, would they make of Brielle Bouchard?

I cleared my throat. "Before I can discuss the merits of filing a lawsuit, Miss Bouchard, I will need to see the contract you signed with this man." I started to go on, then realized I had no idea whom she wished to sue. "May I inquire the gentleman's name?"

"It's Gerald Knight." At my look of surprise, she went on, "Are you acquainted with him?"

"Not personally," I admitted, "although I believe I have heard of him. Is he the same Gerald Knight who owns and manages the *Daily Journal* newspaper?"

"Yes, that is correct." She smiled sardonically. "The very proper Gerald Knight, champion of the American family and all that is good and moral. I was his third mistress, Miss Woolson. If that were made public, I daresay the righteous Mr. Knight would have a good deal of explaining to do."

I knew Brielle was referring to Mr. Knight's frequent, and often zealous, campaigns condemning vice and depravity in our city. He had published one or two of Samuel's crime pieces over the past several years, and my brother had confided to me that he sensed something slightly off center about the man. I could not, of course, break client confidentiality, but I would have given a pretty penny to hear Samuel's reaction to Brielle's story.

"Am I to understand that the document was duly witnessed and signed?" I inquired, silently wondering if this case could become any more bizarre. I had never before heard of a man signing a legal contract with a woman of Miss Bouchard's profession; to the best of my knowledge it was without precedent.

"Two of Mr. Knight's employees were present when he and I discussed the agreement," she calmly replied, as if this sort of thing were an everyday occurrence. "Without actually reading the document, they each signed where Mr. Knight indicated."

"Did you bring a copy of the contract with you?" I asked, doing my best to match the girl's unruffled manner.

Moving carefully in an effort not to disturb the sleeping baby, my visitor reached into her oversized reticule and pulled out several sheets of paper which had been folded into a cylindrical roll and fastened with a black ribbon.

"Here, Miss Woolson," she said, handing me the document. "I was certain you would wish to see it."

I took the spool, slipped off the ribbon, and unrolled the papers. Quickly I scanned the amazing contents. To my considerable surprise, the contract appeared to be properly prepared and signed. What in the world, I wondered, would persuade a man of Gerald Knight's position to risk public censure if this document ever came to light?

"I'm surprised Mr. Knight allowed you to keep a duplicate of the agreement. If your relationship were to deteriorate in any way, your copy could prove embarrassing to him, to say the least. As you say, he's married with a family, not to mention his standing in the community."

A pink flush spread prettily across her cheeks. "Actually, Miss Woolson, the copy Mr. Knight gave me contained no signatures. He said it was simply to remind me of the terms of the contract. He placed the single signed document in a wall safe he maintained in my home."

I eyed her pointedly. "If the original contract is locked inside the safe, how do you happen to have it with you today?"

Miss Bouchard drew herself up in the chair as far as possible without disturbing the infant in her lap, and lifted her chin defiantly.

"I did not think it right for Mr. Knight to possess the only signed copy of the contract, while I had nothing but a few pieces of paper to *remind* me of the terms we had agreed upon." She wrinkled her small, slightly upturned nose. "As if I required a reminder! Fortunately, he kept other papers inside the safe that I assumed he preferred his wife not see, and was obliged to open it regularly. Each time he did so, I committed to memory at least one number of the combination. By the time I realized I was with child, I could open the safe on my own."

I decided not to comment upon this confession, at least not at the moment. "Who drew up the contract?" I inquired instead.

"Mr. Knight did, but I insisted upon several changes before I would sign it. He agreed to these modifications."

At that moment, the baby awoke and shook her tiny fists in the air, then screwed up her little mouth preparatory to a wail. With a series of soothing sounds, Brielle gently jiggled her daughter until the baby once again subsided into a peaceful slumber.

"I see." Again, I was taken aback to learn that Mr. Knight had allowed Brielle to effect any changes whatsoever in the document. What sort of power did this child wield? I asked myself. It came as no surprise, of course, that the newspaperman would do everything possible to insure that no one else ever read that document. All too many men in San Francisco kept a mistress, but it would hardly do to name names and broadcast the particulars to the entire city. Even San Francisco society had its limits!

"You must see why I was so determined to learn how to open the safe," she said. "It was the only protection I had against the very thing that has now happened."

"That was astute of you. You appear to have been unusually well educated, Miss Bouchard. Your parents are to be commended."

"Yes," she agreed, and for the first time since entering my office, avoided my eyes. "They were extraordinary people."

"You use the past tense. Am I to understand that they are deceased?"

Her head came up abruptly. Again those unwavering violet eyes stared directly into mine. "I cannot see what my parents could have to do with this business, Miss Woolson. I have been on my own for several years now, and take sole responsibility for my affairs."

"I apologize, Miss Bouchard. I did not mean to infer otherwise."

I stifled the urge to inquire why mention of her parents should illicit such a defensive reaction. Had she left home because of family friction? I wondered. Yet she could not bear her parents too much animosity if she did not hesitate to characterize them as extraordinary. Most peculiar. But then there were more than a few things about Brielle Bouchard I found tantalizingly curious.

Unexpectedly, the young woman shifted the baby's weight in her arms and stood. "I'm confident you will require a day or two to study the contract," she announced matter-of-factly. "If it is agreeable with you, I shall return on Wednesday morning and we can discuss the matter at greater length."

Startled, I regarded her in surprise. "That won't be necessary, Miss Bouchard. I can look the document over right now and we can—"

"I would prefer that you make a thorough study of it." Once

again, she reached into her reticule with her free hand, this time drawing out several bills and placing them on the desk. "I am prepared to offer you forty dollars as a retainer. We can settle on the remaining balance once you have had an opportunity to examine the papers." She closed her reticule and turned to leave.

I swiftly rose to my feet, perturbed and not a little taken aback that I had somehow lost control of the interview. "Please, Miss Bouchard, wait. What address may I use if it becomes necessary to contact you?"

"I doubt that need will arise," she replied coolly. "As I said, I shall return here the day after tomorrow. At the same time, shall we say?"

Before I could answer, the young mother swept to the door, then, once again shifting little Emma in her arms, turned the knob and was gone.

I spent the next hour studying the contract Miss Bouchard had signed with Gerald Knight. The document itself was easy enough to comprehend; the subject matter, on the other hand, was irregular to say the least!

The contract read much as Brielle described. Gerald Knight agreed to support Miss Brielle Marie Bouchard for a minimum of three years, on condition that she remain his exclusive and devoted mistress. It went on to promise that Mr. Knight would maintain Miss Bouchard in a house on Pacific Avenue, with adequate servants and a generous monthly allowance, again on the condition that she entertain no other gentlemen, or in any way prove unfaithful to him. Finally, the document specified that Miss Bouchard must hold herself available to Mr. Knight at any hour of the day or night, according to his convenience.

After perusing the agreement for the third time, I sat back in my chair, frankly amazed. The girl was astonishing! Not only was she one of the most exquisite young women I'd ever seen, but she possessed a clever mind and an abundant measure of audacity. I could not bring to mind a single woman of my acquaintance—even one twice Brielle's age—who would have had the temerity to coerce a man like Gerald Knight into signing such an agreement.

Unfortunately, I thought, brewing a cup of tea on the brazier I keep in the back room of my office, Miss Bouchard's courage and foresight had likely gained her little. Even if the young woman had, as she insisted, been faithful to Knight, there was no way to prove that her child had been sired by him. In the end, it came down to her word against his, and I knew well enough that few people would side with a prostitute, even if they suspected she was telling the truth.

Unless, I reflected, I could devise a plan to force the newsman to take responsibility for Brielle and her child. To be honest, nothing would please me more than to see men like Gerald Knight—who habitually deceived their wives with an endless string of paramours—held accountable for their actions. I experienced a small thrill of excitement at this thought. Given Miss Bouchard's circumstances, it would be a difficult if not impossible task, I told myself. And yet . . . already my mind was busy churning over possibilities.

I was just carrying the tea back to my desk when my outer door was suddenly flung open and Robert Campbell burst into the room like a spring-released jack-in-the-box. My brusque friend, who was, until several months earlier, my colleague at the law firm of Shepard, Shepard, McNaughton, and Hall, had the regrettable habit of showing up unannounced and uninvited whenever the mood came upon him.

Without so much as a word of greeting, he slapped a copy of that morning's *San Francisco Tattler* on my desk. "Now what outrageous mess have you gotten yourself involved in?" he said, sinking his tall, muscular frame into the chair facing my desk.

"And good morning to you, as well, Robert," I said, reaching for the paper to see what all the fuss was about. I did not have to look far. Midway down the front page appeared the headline BAT-TERED BODY FOUND ON RINCON HILL. Of course, I thought, the discovery Saturday night would have been too late to make the Sunday editions, and so had had to wait until this morning. I was not surprised to find that the article had been penned by my brother's nemesis, Ozzie Foldger.

"Hmm," I murmured. "I can't believe Samuel allowed Foldger to scoop him on this story."

With a pleased harrumph, Robert handed over a second news-paper, then leaned back in his seat, his intense turquoise eyes focused unblinkingly on mine. "Scooped, nothing. Your brother's account of the discovery in the *San Francisco Chronicle* is just as thorough, if not as sensational."

"There is tea in the back room," I told him without looking up from the newspapers. "Why don't you pour yourself a cup while I read these?"

I hurriedly scanned Foldger's piece and instantly saw what Robert was referring to. He had described Nigel Logan's unfortu-nate death in far more graphic detail than had Samuel. His article, along with so many lurid details, was sure to appeal to those of our citizens with a taste for the prurient, and thereby sell more copies than its competitors. It would also boost the *Tattler's* well-deserved reputation as a scandal rag.

Glancing down the column, I was dismayed to see that Samuel's rival had gone on to report that Judge Horace Woolson and his son Samuel, along with his daughter Sarah, were inexplicably present at the scene. Taking care not to say anything which might precipitate a lawsuit, Foldger nonetheless managed to convey a tone of vague suspicion, going on to point out "Miss Woolson's penchant for involving herself with the seedier elements of our fair city."

I felt my face grow hot as I dropped the *Tattler* and pushed both newspapers to the side of my desk. Looking up, I found Robert smiling at me with smug satisfaction.

"So, I repeat, what have you gotten yourself involved in this time?"

I regarded him evenly. "I have not become involved in anything which need concern you."

"Please spare me, Sarah," he said, chuckling. "You attract murders like metal to a magnet. I can't imagine another woman in this city leaving the comfort of her bed to go out looking for bodies in the middle of the night."

"I did not go looking for bodies, as you so colorfully phrase it. George Lewis knew that Samuel would want to be the first reporter on the scene, and brought us there." I shuddered, remembering poor Mr. Logan's battered corpse. "Actually, it was quite horrible."

"I'm sure it was." He nodded gravely toward the newspapers. "According to Samuel and that other fellow, the police have no suspects."

"Sadly, that's true. The men who discovered the body claim they saw a figure scrambling up the opposite embankment. Unfortunately, it was too dark for them to describe the villain."

With a rather too theatrical sigh, Robert leaned back in his chair, his body language feigning indifference. "I can see that you're bursting to share all the grisly details, Sarah, so you may as well tell me the story from the beginning. The articles say the dead man carried no identification, yet the police claim to know his name, and that he taught science at the Jesuit university."

I rolled my eyes, but in the end gave him a brief outline of Saturday night's gruesome adventure.

"And the men who found the body can't tell the police anything about the figure they saw running away?" he asked when I was finished.

"No. It mightn't have even been the killer, but merely a beggar or street urchin they inadvertently frightened off."

"That's possible, I suppose. And your father says he'd just met this biologist fellow at a party he and your mother attended a few hours earlier?"

I nodded. "He claimed he particularly remembered Mr. Logan because of an argument he had with the Reverend Erasmus Mayfield, who was the guest of honor."

"Oh? What kind of argument?"

"According to my father, the Reverend Mayfield took exception to Logan extolling Charles Darwin's theories on evolution."

"Oh, that ridiculous nonsense."

I looked at him curiously. "Have you read Darwin's work, then? *Origin of Species,* or *The Descent of Man?*"

He made a dismissive gesture with his hand, very nearly knocking over his teacup. "Yes, yes, I've read them. Or, at least I've skimmed through as many pages as I could stomach. The whole notion that the human race started out as some sort of amoeba crawling out of the sea is pure nonsense." His eyes fixed on me. "Don't tell me you agree with that claptrap?"

I admitted that I had not yet formed an opinion on the matter, then added, "However, I'm well aware that a number of religious institutions strongly disagree with Mr. Darwin's hypotheses, given that it goes against the story of Creation as written in the Book of Genesis."

"And they bring up some valid points. But you can't be seriously suggesting that this Logan fellow was killed because he defended Darwin's wild theories of natural selection?"

"Not at all. I merely offer it as a possibility. Given the timing of the murder, Nigel Logan's public disagreement with the Reverend Mayfield must be taken into account."

"Just a minute, Sarah. You can't suspect that the Reverend Mayfield had anything to do with this? My God, according to these newspaper accounts, Logan was beaten to death with a hefty section of two-by-four!"

"I know how he was killed, Robert, I was there, remember? I simply believe a victim's last few hours of life must always be examined."

"All right, you've examined them. Now, try looking at the

crime logically. You know the number of undesirables who trek under that bridge every night. Logan was very likely set upon by a group of toughs." He regarded me through narrowed eyes. "I don't like that look on your face, Sarah. Surely you don't mean to involve yourself in this business."

"Of course not." I finished drinking my tea, and pushed the cup aside. "May I remind you, Robert, that you were the one who begged me for all the gruesome details of this murder. Well, now you know as much about it as I do. Am I to understand that information gathering was the only purpose for your visit this morning?"

Robert looked at me blankly, then recollected himself. "No, not at all. Actually, I came here for some advice. It's less than three weeks before Christmas, and I must send presents to my niece and nephew in Edinburgh, not to mention my parents. I wondered if you'd be kind enough to—" He hesitated, then with a slightly pink face went on. "Dash it all, I came to ask you to go shopping with me. You have a nephew and niece roughly the same age as my sister's children, and I haven't the first spark of an idea of what to get them."

I could not repress a smile. The idea of Robert choosing suitable gifts for two small children was comical in the extreme. However, a shopping excursion suited me well enough as I, too, had gifts to purchase.

"Unfortunately, you have put off your shopping until it is too late to ship it to Scotland in time for Christmas. However, it is better to have the gifts arrive late than never to arrive at all. I'm sure your family will appreciate them."

His face took on even more color as he added, "I am also in need of a new suit to wear to your parents' Christmas dinner next week. I, ah, that is, I could use your help in selecting something appropriate for the occasion."

"Yes, of course," I agreed, stifling a smile. Robert was a private man, and I knew how difficult it must be for him to ask my help in such a matter. I decided the less fuss I made about the request the better.

Picking up our cups and saucers, I started toward the back room.

"Allow me a moment to tidy up and we can be off."

CHAPTER THREE

I spent that evening in my father's library, ensconced in a comfortable armchair in front of the fire. On the floor by my feet were a dozen law tomes, most of them covering contracts and civil lawsuits initiated in the state of California. The books made for disheartening reading. My initial fears concerning Brielle Bouchard's agreement with Gerald Knight were, if anything, growing more dire with each subsequent text. She had tried so hard to protect herself before becoming Gerald Knight's mistress, it was bound to come as a bitter blow to learn that all her precautions had been in vain.

I was still mulling over possible tactics we might explore when, shortly after nine o'clock, my brother Samuel joined me, bearing a tray containing a pot of coffee and two cups.

"You look as if you could use this," he said, placing the tray on an end table. He angled a second armchair closer to mine, so that we were both facing the hearth. "What are you doing secreted in here, anyway? Do you have a new client? Lord knows you could use the income."

"I wish I could say that I did," I said, closing the last book I'd been perusing. "But not because of the money. This is a case I could really sink my teeth into."

"Hmm, it sounds interesting," he said, filling both cups with coffee. He added sugar and cream to his own, then stirred it with a spoon. "Tell me more."

I considered this for a moment. "You realize I can't give you all the details because of client privilege. To tell the truth, though, I would appreciate your opinion."

I took a sip of coffee, then proceeded to relate the highlights of that morning's visit with Miss Bouchard.

"An uncommonly beautiful young woman came to my office this morning. And by young, I mean *very* young, only nineteen." Without mentioning anything that might compromise Brielle's client-attorney confidentiality, I went on to describe her story in very general terms, ending with an account of the contract she had signed with her lover.

"Good Lord! You're saying this girl is a prostitute?" He laughed. "I must say, you attract some of the most remarkable people. So she was what—only seventeen at the time she became his mistress? She certainly demonstrated a lot of nerve demanding such an agreement. Was it a proper contract? Signed by witnesses?"

"Yes. Apparently it was witnessed by two of her lover's employees. It appears to be in order, but—"

"It would never hold up in court," Samuel finished for me. "Even if a judge were to uphold such a document—which I heartily doubt—it would be impossible to prove if the girl's child was fathered by her lover, or by some other fellow."

"Exactly," I seconded with a sigh. "It just maddens me that a man of money and position can so carelessly toy with a young girl, then discard her like so much rubbish the moment he realizes he has gotten her with child."

Despite my anger, I could not suppress a smile when I thought of little Emma. "You should see her baby, Samuel, she is perfect in every way. I cannot understand any man who would not be honored to claim that child as his daughter."

Samuel regarded me with genuine sympathy. "I know it's not fair, Sarah. Yet it's been the way of the world for eons."

Neither of us spoke for several minutes, but sat in companionable silence in front of the fire. Not for the first time, I felt deeply grateful that I had been blessed with a brother like Samuel. As the youngest two of four children, we had been extremely close all through childhood. In adulthood, that camaraderie had evolved into a bond which often required no words for us to perfectly communicate with one another.

"Is there no one who can help this girl?" he asked at length. "Does she have family in the city?"

"Evidently not."

"Then where are she and her baby living?"

"She wouldn't tell me. In fact, she was purposely vague when it came to supplying me with any personal details."

Samuel watched silently as I finished my coffee and placed my cup and saucer on the mahogany end table. "She really is quite a remarkable young woman," I went on, remembering Brielle's serious violet eyes and the determined tilt of her chin. "Whatever she's experienced in her short life has served to make her resourceful beyond her years."

"Beauty and brains," he said, a smile playing across his handsome face. "A compelling combination. I'd very much like to meet this remarkable young woman of yours."

"She's hardly *my* young woman. Moreover, given the circumstances, she's not likely to be my client, either. Sadly, even beauty and brains were not sufficient to save her from the very fate she sought to avoid."

Samuel displayed the slightly off-center grin that melted so many young women's hearts. "Are you sure you can't tell me her name? Who knows, perhaps together we could do something to help the girl."

I would have sworn that as Samuel's sister I was immune to that smile, but for a moment I was sorely tempted to give in to his cajoling. In the end, however, professionalism triumphed, and I held my ground. If, after our upcoming meeting, she was no longer my client, I would refund her deposit and that would be the end of it.

She would be forced to raise that lovely little girl as best she could, entirely on her own.

Unless, I thought with a surge of what was surely irrational hope, I could come up with a scheme to change Gerald Knight's mind.

"A penny for your thoughts, little sister. What devious plot are you hatching?" He started to say something else, but was forestalled when the library door opened and our father stepped into the room.

"I thought I might find the two of you in here," Papa said. His eyes moved to the nearly empty coffeepot perched on the table between Samuel and myself. "What, no cup for me? I'll just ring Edis for a fresh pot. And perhaps a dollop or two of brandy," he added with a wink.

He rang the bellpull to summon our aging butler, then crossed to the fireplace and added several fresh logs to the fire. As I watched him skillfully manipulate the tongs, I realized with a sinking heart that Papa was setting the stage for more than a casual chat. In spite of his convivial manner, there was obviously something serious on his mind.

This fear was substantiated when he turned his back to the fire and studied us both for several long minutes. He was standing just to the right of his prized bronze bust of Abraham Lincoln, and for an eerie moment their expressions seemed to mirror each other.

I caught Samuel's eye, and he returned my look of foreboding. No words were required to convey our suspicion that the discussion concerning our presence at Nigel Logan's murder scene was, as Papa promised, about to resume where it had left off.

Samuel and I obligingly shifted our chairs so that Papa could position a third seat between us. When we formed a comfortable half circle before the fire, he leaned back and amused us with anecdotes from a trial he was currently presiding over. My brother and I dutifully laughed on cue, but I could sense Samuel's anxiety level rising as he waited for Papa to finally come to the real reason he had joined us in the library.

We were afforded a brief respite when Edis carried in a tray of fresh coffee, along with various cookies and pastries from Cook's kitchen. Sure enough, beside the coffeepot rested a bottle of aged brandy.

Thanking our devoted butler, Papa refilled our cups with the aromatic brew, then added a generous portion of the distilled liquor.

"There we are," he said, stirring thick cream into the dark liquid. "Now we can enjoy a nice little chat."

Out of the corner of my eye I saw Samuel stiffen, as Papa turned shrewd blue eyes on his youngest son. "Your friend Sergeant Lewis paid an unexpected visit to my chambers in the courthouse this afternoon, Samuel."

Samuel's initial reaction to this comment was relief that perhaps he was not to be the primary focus of the conversation after all. Then as he absorbed what Papa had said, he looked puzzled. "What reason did George give for coming to your chambers?"

"That is exactly what I wanted to know," our father replied. "Evidently he's changed his mind about robbery being the motive in young Nigel Logan's death. He now appears to believe that the murder might be connected to the Tremaines' party that night."

"The Tremaines?" repeated Samuel, looking puzzled. Then he remembered. "Oh, yes, that's the family from your church who live in the next block. They hosted the dinner party last Saturday night in honor of your rector."

Papa nodded. "It was the Reverend Mayfield's twenty-fifth ordination anniversary. If you recall, Reginald Tremaine owns the Men's Emporium downtown."

"I remember now," my brother said. "But whatever gave George the idea that someone from the Tremaines' party killed Logan?"

"Humph! Unfortunately, Sergeant Lewis did not see fit to take me into his confidence." Papa reached for his pipe and tobacco pouch. "I, too, was under the impression that—"

"Just a minute, Papa," I broke in. "Didn't you say that Nigel Logan quarreled with the Reverend Mayfield at the party?"

My father did not immediately answer, as he carefully filled his pipe bowl. When it was packed to his satisfaction, he began searching his pockets for a match. Finally locating one, he lit the tip with his thumbnail and lowered the flame to the bowl. He drew several times on the pipe stem, then leaned forward to toss the match into the fireplace.

"That seemed to be what Sergeant Lewis was getting at," he answered at length. "However, I cannot see how Nigel Logan and the Reverend Mayfield's disagreement can be connected to the unfortunate man's death. And that was precisely what I told Lewis." He gestured with his hand, using his pipe for emphasis. "Naturally, he didn't give a dash for my opinion. He actually asked me to list everyone I knew who had been at the Tremaines' house that night."

I have to admit that I was taken aback by George's uncharacteristic boldness. Whenever he was in my father's presence, he tended to become singularly self-conscious.

My brother evidently agreed with me concerning his friend's atypical behavior. "Well, well, it looks as if old George has found some starch for his backbone. So, did this list of yours turn up anyone of interest?"

"No, because I didn't supply him with one," Papa replied shortly. "I have no idea how he came up with such a notion, but he's sure as fiddles barking up the wrong tree."

"You said the Reverend Mayfield and Nigel Logan were quarreling over Charles Darwin's book *Origin of Species,* didn't you?" I asked.

Drawing on his pipe, Papa said, "I suppose you could say that *Origin* provided the kindling that started the fire. However, I'll allow that it was the more distasteful—at least in Mayfield's opinion—conclusions Darwin put forward in his later book, *The Descent of Man,* that gave the good reverend a conniption fit. Still, I hardly think he was suddenly so overwhelmed with outrage that he dashed after the Logan boy and beat him over the head with a two-by-four!"

"All right, I agree that the Reverend Mayfield seems an unlikely suspect," put in Samuel. "But what if the argument provoked one of Mayfield's supporters to chastise Logan for daring to defy the reverend's public declaration on the subject? I can't think why else George would ask you to list the guests at the Tremaines' party."

Papa gestured impatiently with his pipe. "Whatever his motivation, it didn't get him from his kitchen to the back stoop. Don't forget that this so-called *interview* took place in my chambers, and I had no time to be writing out lists for him or anyone else. I told Lewis that if he was so all-fired determined to find out who was at that party, he could jolly well contact Reginald Tremaine and not waste any more of my time with his tomfool questions."

"Hmm," I said thoughtfully. "I wonder if George learned anything of interest from Mr. Tremaine?"

"I'd be curious to know that, too." Samuel agreed. "Grudges can be surprisingly long-lived. If some guest at the party was already hostile toward Logan, his fight with the Reverend Mayfield might have provided the final straw."

Papa did not look as if he bought this argument. "Nigel Logan was a botanist, Samuel. I find it hard to imagine that someone could carry on a long-standing feud with a man who spends the better part of his day studying grass and onion plants."

"Logan must have enjoyed a private life," said Samuel, a bit defensively. "Perhaps he was carrying on an affair with a married woman and her husband had only recently discovered it. Or maybe he had gambling debts and the lender grew tired of waiting to be paid back. Just what do we know about Nigel Logan, anyway?"

"Not very much," replied Papa, rolling his eyes in amusement at Samuel's imaginative speculations. He drew on his pipe and stretched his feet out until they were closer to the fire. "When Reginald Tremaine introduced Logan to me the other night, he indicated that the young man taught natural science at Saint Ignatius College, you know, the school that just moved to Van Ness Avenue. Anyway, he said that Logan's specialty was botany."

"Yes, but all of that is public knowledge," said Samuel. "Surely you must have overheard something about his private life."

"Why in Sam Hill would you suppose that? I had no reason to care one way or the other about the silly young pup." Papa's gaze sharpened as he regarded his youngest son. "Samuel, why this sudden interest in what went on at that party, or about the personal life of a man you saw just once, and then only when the poor soul lay dead at your feet?"

My brother's expression instantly changed to one of profound innocence, a transformation he had smoothly perfected over the past several years, ever since giving birth to the Ian Fearless persona.

"No reason, really," he said, feigning a casual, indifferent tone. "I was just curious. It's not every night someone is killed so close to our house."

"No," Papa agreed. "And we can be grateful for that. I told your sergeant friend to take a look at the Chinese coolies who've been attacked in that area more than once since that absurd Cut began. Gangs of young white scoundrels like nothing better than to stand on the bridge and hurl rocks down upon the poor Johnnies coming and going from Chinatown to the docks. That is, when they aren't actually taking sticks and poles to them. Wouldn't blame the Chinese one jot if they decided it was their turn to take a whack or two at any white man foolish enough to be wandering about at that time of night. As far as I'm concerned, that theory makes a damn sight more sense than trying to place the blame on a respectable church minister."

"What did George have to say about that suggestion?" I asked.

Papa shrugged. "Not much, but then no surprise there. I've noticed that once the police get a bee in their bonnet, it takes more than a flyswatter to shoo it out. After more than twenty years on the bench, I've come to the sad conclusion that the San Francisco police squad is not composed of the sharpest tacks in the toolbox."

Papa drew on his pipe, then once again used it to emphasize his point. "Mark my words, sooner or later even our dull-witted men in blue will be forced to conclude that Logan's death was a tragic but all too common case of a robbery gone awry. Sad to say, even

Rincon Hill is not immune to violence, especially at that godforsaken hour of the night."

I sensed that Samuel was about to argue this point. Fearful that this would only succeed in pushing his foot even further into his too inquisitive mouth, I rushed in to change the subject. I was about to inquire about the upcoming Christmas party my parents were planning the weekend after next, when Papa held up his hand.

"Speaking of the Tremaines, your mother mentioned that Celia has invited the family over on Wednesday night to celebrate Mrs. Tremaine's birthday. Evidently she and Celia have become good friends."

Samuel looked at him in surprise. "That sounds a bit insensitive. What with Nigel Logan dying shortly after he left their house Saturday night."

"That's what your mother thought," Papa replied. "But Celia seems determined that the murder had nothing to do with the Tremaines, and that it shouldn't stand in the way of honoring her friend's thirtieth birthday." He pulled on his pipe, then chuckled. "When you reach my age, birthdays become a trial to be borne, rather than a cause for celebration."

"It sounds like something Celia would do, though," I put in affectionately. "She has such a kind heart."

"Too kind, I sometimes think. I hope one day it doesn't lead her into trouble." Samuel stretched and rose from his chair. "I have an early morning, so I'm off to bed."

"Not so fast, son," Papa said. "There's something I want to discuss with you."

My father's expression reminded me of the look he often assumed when he was presiding over a trial. It did not bode well for my unfortunate brother.

Sure enough, Samuel darted me a worried look as he turned slowly back to face Papa. "Of course, Father. What is it?"

Instead of returning to his seat, Samuel walked with contrived casualness to the hearth and stoked the fire that was crackling along nicely all on its own. His show of virtue did not fool our father for one moment.

"Sit down Samuel," Papa directed in a tone which brooked no insubordination. "Before you come up with a way to sidetrack the issue, I want to know what you and your sister were doing at the Harrison Street Bridge last Saturday night? And this time I would appreciate an honest answer."

I was thankful Papa's attention was on Samuel and not me, for the rush of heat to my cheeks would surely have given me away. I feared that after several successful years dodging the delicate matter of his future, Samuel was about to have his journalistic alter ego exposed to the light of day.

To his credit—or just plain pigheadedness—my brother seemed not yet ready to admit defeat. Instead of returning to his seat, he stood with his back to the hearth, rocking back and forth on his heels as if nothing could be easier than satisfying Papa's curiosity. Unfortunately, this effort was somewhat spoiled by his clenched jaw and the anxious crease line between his eyes.

"Ah, well it seems Sarah was having difficulty sleeping that night, and happened to see George passing by on the street." I had to admit that he was doing a valiant job of keeping his tone casual, even if his face was not cooperating. "She called out to him, and he said they'd found a murder victim beneath the Harrison Street Bridge." He forced a dry chuckle—laying it on a bit too thick, I thought. Be careful, brother dear, I silently told him, before you manage to place your entire foot in your mouth!

"You know Sarah. Once her curiosity is aroused, there's no stopping her. Of course she could hardly accompany George alone at such an hour, so she woke me and, well, you know the rest."

"I see." Papa looked dubious. He turned doubtful eyes on me. "So that's your story, is it? Sergeant Lewis was on his way to the Harrison Bridge on foot. That's a considerable distance from his station downtown, don't you agree, especially at that hour of the night? Interesting that he didn't make use of a police wagon—or even a cab."

I opened my mouth to reply, but could think of nothing to say, at least not without adding yet more lies to an already unlikely story.

"I didn't think to ask George why he chose that way to reach the murder scene," said Samuel, by way of another pitiful explanation.

Of course, it was no less than the truth, I told myself, as far as it went. The fact that George had arrived at the bridge in one of the police wagons—then walked to our house to wake my brother—was, if only by omission, the lie. Really, I thought, guarding Samuel's covert life was becoming far too complicated!

"Perhaps there were no cabs handy at such an early hour," my brother finished lamely.

The firelight reflected in Papa's eyes, streaking them with darting shafts of flame, and making his usual jovial face appear sinister. He studied Samuel for a long, uncomfortable moment, then turned his gaze on me. I shifted in my chair, but said nothing which might thrust us any deeper into this hole we'd dug for ourselves.

When it became clear that neither of us was prepared to add to this woefully weak fabrication, Papa shook his head and sighed.

"Evidently I was mistaken when I assumed the two of you had matured beyond the age of ten. Don't think I'm too old or addled not to recognize when my own children are having me on. And it would be a mistake to assume that I won't eventually get to the bottom of this, because I promise you I will."

He continued to regard us over the rim of his coffee cup as he drained the dark liquid. This time, when he poured fresh brew from the silver pot, he added rather more brandy to his cup than he had previously. Stirring the hot liquid, he once again turned to my brother.

"Although you hardly deserve it, I have good news for you, Samuel. I was speaking this afternoon to Arthur Cunningham, of Cunningham and Brill Attorneys, and he said his firm would be pleased to take you on as an associate when you have passed your state bar examinations." His eyes narrowed. "You *are* planning to take the exams in early February, are you not, son? I believe you indicated as much the last time we had this conversation."

I watched my brother's Adam's apple move up and down as he swallowed hard. "I, ah, actually, I haven't signed up to take them yet." At our father's tightening expression, he quickly added, "But of course I will—first thing tomorrow."

"See that you do," Papa told him sternly. "You have put off taking this last step for entirely too long. You could do a good deal worse than to accept Arthur Cunningham's generous offer. It's all well and good that you've been working part-time as a paralegal for—" He looked at Samuel questioningly. "What's the name of that lawyer friend of yours? I'm always forgetting it."

"Andrew Wayburn," Samuel answered a bit feebly.

My brother and I exchanged a quick glance. I was one of the few people who knew that Samuel's paralegal work for Andy Wayburn was more fiction than fact, a handy way to account for the income he actually brought in as a crime reporter. In truth, Andy had inherited a comfortable nest egg upon his father's death, and had engaged in little real legal work since passing his own bar examinations. As one of my brother's old school friends, he was happy to let Samuel use his name in order to explain his mysterious livelihood.

"You know, it's strange that I've never met Mr. Wayburn," Papa said, giving him a curious look. "You'd think that after all my years on the bench, I would have run into the man at least once."

"Actually, Andrew handles mostly wills and probate," Samuel told him. "He spends little actual time in court."

"I see," said Papa, although I wasn't sure if he truly accepted this explanation. "Nevertheless, it's time you join a more established law firm. At Cunningham and Brill you'll be able to experience all aspects of a distinguished practice from the ground floor up."

I started nervously when a log suddenly dropped in the hearth. At the same moment, I heard the lusty cries of Celia and Charles's three-month-old son, Charles, Jr.—or little Charlie, as he was known to his doting family—coming from the nursery. Almost immediately, his sister—four-year-old Mandy—joined her baby brother in a loud, and stridently off-key, duet.

"Oh, dear," I said, rising from my chair. "I had better help settle Mandy while Celia feeds the baby."

To be honest, I was relieved to have such a timely excuse for leaving the tense scene which had developed between Samuel and our father. I had long since run out of tall tales to excuse my brother's endless delays in taking his bar examinations. It was high time he dealt with the consequences of this deceit on his own.

Samuel darted me a reproachful look as I took my leave of the library. Ah, well, I thought, repressing a small twinge of guilt. As the old saying went, my dear brother had made his bed, and now he would have to sleep in it!

CHAPTER FOUR

The following morning I arrived at my Sutter Street office to find Eddie Cooper's brougham parked at the curb outside the building. I paused to check the gold watch pinned to my shirtwaist; it was some fifteen minutes shy of eight o'clock. While it was true that the boy had agreed to meet with me this morning for his regular reading and writing lesson, he rarely if ever arrived early. I had to smile. His punctuality, I was certain, was not due to any eagerness to commence today's instruction, but to ensure that he would have time to visit my downstairs neighbor. Dear, generous Fanny. My young protégé knew all too well which side of his bread had been spread with butter.

I believe I mentioned earlier that Mrs. Goodman and her late husband had not been blessed with offspring of their own, which had come as a bitter disappointment to them both. Possessed of a warm and munificent nature, Fanny had formed an instant attachment to my young cabbie, and loved nothing better than to ply him with sweets and even a hearty dinner now and again. Her largesse made for somewhat shorter reading lessons, but I could not bring myself to complain.

Obviously, her efforts were bearing fruit. Eddie's mottled complexion appeared to have grown considerably less inflamed. His bone-thin body was filling out, and I could have sworn he'd grown at least one or two inches since I had first met him some ten months earlier during what I have come to refer to as the Russian Hill murders.

As expected, I found the lad happily ensconced in Fanny's cozy kitchen, located behind her ground-floor millinery shop. He was seated at the table, making a good job of dunking home-made doughnuts into a large mug of hot chocolate. At my entrance, he looked up and grinned, and I was amused to see that his mouth sported a chocolate mustache, and was liberally smeared with dough-nut crumbs.

"Mornin', Miss Sarah. I got here earlier, but you wasn't in yet. Mrs. Goodman said I should wait for you in her kitchen where it was warm."

"And while you were waiting, you thought you should sample some of her doughnuts," I commented wryly.

I smiled as Fanny motioned me to a seat at the table. I had hardly made contact with the chair than a plate of freshly baked doughnuts sprinkled with sugar was placed in front of me, along with a cup of coffee. "If you continue feeding me like this, Fanny, I will end up as round and plump as a Christmas goose."

"Which wouldn't do you the least bit of harm," replied Fanny, regarding me with a critical eye. "As it is, you're hardly more than skin and bones."

I took in Fanny's ample, grandmotherly figure and hid a smile. "Now you sound like my mother."

Since meeting my downstairs neighbor six months ago, I'd grown inordinately fond of her. Initially, I'm ashamed to admit, I'd considered her a friendly, if somewhat ordinary, shopkeeper, little different from the dozens of other merchants whose stores lined the streets of downtown San Francisco.

I could not have been more mistaken! As part of an ongoing les-son in humility, I have learned to appreciate Fanny Goodman and her remarkable accomplishments. When faced with early widow-hood, she'd had the foresight and courage to pool every cent she and her husband had saved, and open a small millinery shop. A store, I might add, that has proved to be remarkably successful. She is also a staunch supporter of women's suffrage. Ten years earlier she had helped organize the first annual meeting of the California Women's Suffrage Society in San Francisco, a noble cause that she remains actively involved with to this day. To my chagrin, I've learned that there is nothing the least bit *ordinary* about Fanny Goodman!

"Now, what's this I hear about you and Samuel finding a murdered man Sunday morning?" asked Fanny, moving a third straight-backed chair to the table. "What in heaven's name were you and your brother doing out and about in the middle of the night?"

Since Fanny and Eddie were both aware of my brother's secret life as a crime journalist, I was free to tell them the real story of how we happened to be at the Harrison Street Bridge at two o'clock on Sunday morning. When I finished the tale, Eddie had stopped eating and was listening with rapt attention.

"Who was the bloke?" he asked excitedly. "Was there much blood? Do the coppers know who done it?" His eyes grew suddenly bright. "Are you and Mr. Samuel gonna help the leatherheads bag the burker?"

When I first met Eddie, his street jargon would have made as much sense to me as Egyptian hieroglyphics. Gradually, however, I was learning to follow the boy's more colorful phraseology.

At Fanny's confused expression, I translated, "He wants to know if Samuel and I are going to aid the police in their murder investigation."

"Oh," she said, smiling fondly as she shook her head at the boy.

"Does that mean we're gonna have a go at it?" persisted Eddie.

"I'm sorry, Eddie, but neither my brother nor I have any intention of becoming involved in Mr. Logan's death."

The boy's face dropped as he dolefully lowered his head and took another large bite of doughnut. "But it happened right next to your house, or close enough that it don't matter," he protested, his full mouth slurring the words. "Thought you'd be all het up to pinch the bloke what done it."

"The man who did it," I automatically corrected.

"That's what I just said," Eddie replied, giving me a look which implied that he doubted my hearing ability.

I resisted the urge to explain his grammatical error, having no wish to belabor the more minor issues of the boy's education. All in all, the lad was making excellent progress, even though I took exception to Samuel's habit of supplying him with copies of the lurid *Police Gazette*.

"Do the police know why Mr. Logan was killed?" Fanny asked. "Was he robbed?"

"At first everyone assumed it was a robbery, but now they seem to think his death might be connected to a dinner party that night at the home of the Reginald Tremaines. Actually, my parents were there as guests, as were my brother Charles and his wife, Celia."

"Reginald Tremaine," repeated Fanny thoughtfully. "Isn't he the fellow who owns the Men's Emporium on Market Street?"

"Yes, that's the man," I told her. "I gather his store is quite successful."

She laughed. "It's one of the largest retail stores in San Francisco. I seem to recall that Mr. Tremaine originally came here from Sacramento some ten or twelve years ago."

"Closer to twelve, I believe. Evidently he left shortly after the death of his first wife. My sister-in-law Celia is a good friend of Mr. Tremaine's second wife, Faith. According to her, he arrived in San Francisco with a new wife and two small children, twins, actually, a boy and a girl. They must be sixteen or seventeen by now."

She shook her head sympathetically. "It's a real tragedy to lose your mother at such a tender age. I'm sure it must have been difficult for their father, as well."

"I'm sure it was. I haven't formally met the family, although I've seen them at church. Celia tells me the twins get along well with their stepmother, who has borne two children of her own since marrying Mr. Tremaine."

"What do you suppose gave the police the idea that Mr. Logan's death was connected to their dinner party?"

"To be perfectly frank, I think they're grasping at straws. According to Samuel, City Hall is exerting pressure on the police to solve the case as speedily as possible. Robbery probably would have simplified matters, but since Mr. Logan still had some cash in his pockets, as well as his gold watch and other jewelry, they've decided to focus their investigation on the Tremaines' dinner."

I went on to describe what I had learned about Nigel Logan's argument with the Reverend Erasmus Mayfield that evening, concerning Charles Darwin's controversial books on natural selection.

"Personally, I have a difficult time believing that such a relatively small—and hardly unusual—disagreement could have led to a man's murder."

Eddie looked up after finishing his third doughnut, once again showing an interest in our conversation. "Who's this Darwin feller the coppers think done in the bloke under the bridge?"

As was too often the case, I had a difficult time repressing a smile at the boy's ever-active imagination.

"The police don't suspect Mr. Darwin of being a murderer, Eddie. Charles Darwin is a scientist, a naturalist, actually." At Eddie's confused expression, I explained, "That means he studies plants and animals. He's written several books and articles that have upset a lot of people."

Eddie shook his head. "Can't see why a feller would get offed because of some book."

"No, Eddie, neither can I. However, not everyone is blessed with your common sense."

Fanny and I spent the next quarter hour chatting about our city's new mayor, Maurice Blake, whose inauguration was that very day. After the turbulent reign of his predecessor, Isaac Kalloch—who built the Metropolitan Temple at the corner of Fifth and Jessie streets, only to be shot in front of this same edifice several years later by

San Francisco Chronicle owner Charles de Young—the majority of the city's citizens hoped for a more peaceful administration this time around. In my humble opinion, a calm and honest municipal government was asking for a good deal more than our fair city was capable of delivering!

I was about to pry Eddie out of Fanny's kitchen to start his reading lesson, when the bell that hung above the front door rang. A moment later, a familiar voice rang out, "Mrs. Goodman? Are you here?"

Fanny broke into a broad smile. "We're in the kitchen, Mr. Campbell." She rose and went to the stove to pour another cup of coffee from the pot. "Have a seat at the table. You're just in time for coffee and doughnuts."

Robert inclined his head politely at our hostess. "That sounds very agreeable, Mrs. Goodman. It's uncommonly cold outside."

Settling himself in the chair Fanny had just vacated, he turned to me. "When I found your door locked upstairs, I thought I might find you here." He looked at Eddie's food-smeared face, and shook his head. "I see you have availed yourself of Mrs. Goodman's pastries, Eddie."

"I been eatin' 'em, Mr. Campbell," replied the boy, looking confused and a little guilty. "I don't know nothin' about this availin' business. It weren't like I nicked 'em or nothin'. Mrs. Goodman gave 'em to me on a plate."

This was too much, even for Robert, and I saw him fighting not to laugh. "I'm sure she did, lad. And I can see that you're enjoying your treat."

Reassured, Eddie grinned. "They're the goldurn best doughnuts I ever et, Mr. Campbell. You otta try one."

"Yes, Mr. Campbell," urged Fanny, placing a plate and a cup of coffee in front of him. "Do help yourself while they're still warm."

"Thank you, Mrs. Goodman." Robert reached for one of the pastries, biting into it with obvious appreciation.

"I'm surprised to see you here at this time of morning," I told him.

Robert continued chewing for a moment, then took a sip of coffee. "I'm due at the courthouse in less than an hour. Trevor Lansing is ill with catarrh today, so I am to take his place as Mr. Shepard's second chair this morning. I thought I'd stop by on my way to ask if you might agree to do a bit of work for me." He pulled a sheaf of papers from his briefcase and set them on the table, well away from Eddie's sticky fingers. "I've fallen behind at the office and I'd appreciate your help. If you can manage it, of course."

I was tempted to laugh. Naturally, Robert knew all too well how easily I could "manage it." My professional self-respect was cut to the quick when I calculated just how much idle time I spent upstairs in my lonely two-room office. Although I knew he would never admit it, I was certain he had made off with the files without Joseph Shepard's knowledge. I am ashamed to confess that this afforded me secret pleasure. If Joseph Shepard were aware of Robert's subterfuge, he would surely have suffered one of his infamous bouts of apoplexy. Ah, yes, he certainly would. And glory be, I would no longer be obliged to stand helplessly by and listen to it!

This was not the first time Robert had pressed me to accept paperwork from Shepard's firm since I'd established my own law office. At first, pride had prevented me from availing myself of this extra income—although heaven knows the money was sorely needed. In the six months I had been in business, I had represented but two paying clients. One payment had consisted of an exquisite antique tea service—the kettle filled with cash. The other had been an old gold brooch which supposedly had belonged to Maria Alexandrovna, the wife of Russia's Czar Alexander. It was a lovely piece of jewelry, and despite my ailing finances I could not bring myself to sell it.

It was imperative, however, that I do something to fortify my dwindling savings. And as it says in Proverbs 16:18, "Pride goeth before destruction, and a haughty spirit before a fall." Admonishing myself to count my blessings, I accepted the papers from Robert. "Of course, I shall be more than happy to give these my attention."

"Excellent." Looking relieved, he helped himself to another

doughnut. "You have surpassed yourself this morning, Mrs. Good-man," he told Fanny. "If you were to add a small bakery to your millinery store, your fortune would be made."

Fanny's flushed cheeks revealed her pleasure at this praise. She was fast learning that the Scot's rare accolades were not to be taken lightly.

Tucking Robert's paperwork into my own briefcase, I rose from the table. "It is past time we commenced your lesson, Eddie. Come, *The Adventures of Tom Sawyer* awaits upstairs."

Eddie's eyes went to the few doughnuts remaining on the table, then sighed and rose up from his chair.

"Don't know why we can't use the *Police Gazette*," he com-plained. Noting my disapproving expression, he hastily amended, "Although I guess Tom Sawyer ain't such a bad feller when you get right down to it."

"He *isn't* such a bad fellow, Eddie," I corrected. Then at his puzzled look, I said, "Oh, never mind, I'll explain it to you later. Before we leave—" I nodded my head at Fanny and gave the boy a pointed look.

"Oh, yeah," he said, correctly interpreting my silent prompt. "Thanks for the doughnuts and hot chocolate, Mrs. Goodman."

"You're very welcome, Eddie, dear." My neighbor beamed at the boy. "Why don't you come by after you finish driving your cab this evening? I'm making shepherd's pie."

"Yes, ma'am, I will," he promised, eyes alight as he anticipated one of his favorite dinners.

I doubt that Eddie ever saw meals, much less pastries, like this at his own home. The boy spoke little about his family life, but from the odd comment he occasionally let slip, I gathered he had a num-ber of younger siblings, an alcoholic father, and an overworked mother who was not in the best of health. No wonder he had em-braced Fanny as his surrogate grandmother, as readily as she had adopted him as her grandson.

After bidding Robert a good morning, Eddie and I stepped through Fanny's tidy millinery shop, and out onto the street. Before we could ascend the stairs to my office, however, our progress was impeded by a gentleman, who stepped forward to block the doorway.

I started to address this rude behavior, when the rebuke died in my throat. Moving my eyes upward, I was stunned to realize that the interloper was none other than Pierce Godfrey, the tall, enigmatic shipping mogul I had met several months ago when I'd become involved in the Russian Hill murders.

I had forgotten how handsome he was: his tanned face, ebony hair, and midnight-blue eyes nearly took my breath away. He was wearing a dark gray, fashionably cut suit, a white shirt, and had tied a tasteful dark blue and gray cravat beneath his well-muscled neck. If possible, his broad shoulders seemed even more powerful than I remembered, by contrast making his slender waist appear even more taut.

"Mr. Godfrey, I—that is—you're back in town," I sputtered rather lamely.

My chest seemed bereft of breath, and I wondered why I had suddenly lost the ability to speak coherently. The man who had offered me my first proposal of marriage had left San Francisco some months earlier to open Godfrey Shipping's Hong Kong office.

Naturally, my discomfort did not escape his notice, and his self-satisfied grin did nothing to alleviate my embarrassment.

"Hello, Sarah," he said, his voice as rich and compelling as ever. "Since you instructed me to send all my correspondence to this address, I thought it best to visit you here, rather than at your home."

"Yes, ah, of course. I'm glad you did." Furious with myself, I struggled to get my thoughts in some semblance of order. I'd requested that he direct his letters to my office because my mother, who was increasingly desperate to see me married, tended to become overeager when she spied Pierce's name in the post. Given that I had long since disavowed the married life to pursue a career in the law—and not wishing to cause my mother pointless pain—I did my best to avoid conversing with her on this sensitive subject.

The simple truth was that I could not remain firm in my life's resolve if I permitted a man to gain power over my life. Sad to say, that is exactly the abysmal state I would find myself in if I were to marry. Under our frequently misguided legal system, a modern-day married woman hardly possessed more rights than those allotted to a child. A husband controlled his wife's finances, had the final say on her choice of reading material, the upbringing of their children, and even which church they attended. I could not allow myself to fall into this wretched position.

As Eddie fidgeted restlessly beside me, I realized I had become lost in my thoughts. Recalling myself to the present, I said, "You remember Eddie Cooper, do you not, Mr. Godfrey?"

He stretched out his hand to the lad, taking him by surprise. After a brief hesitation, Eddie wiped his doughnut-sticky fingers on his pant legs and reached out to return the handshake. The boy smiled broadly at this unaccustomed display of adult recognition, especially coming from a person he held in such awe.

"I certainly do remember the lad," replied Pierce. "How are you, Eddie?"

"I'm mighty fine, Mr. Godfrey, sir." The boy stared up at Pierce. "Did you really sail all the way here from Hong Kong?"

"I did, indeed." With twinkling eyes he went on, "Perhaps you'd enjoy going aboard one of our ships sometime over the Christmas holidays, Eddie. I could give you the grand tour."

For a moment I feared the lad might burst with excitement. "Yes, sir, Mr. Godfrey," he gushed. "I'd like that all to pieces!"

With an inward sigh, I realized I could expect no substantive work from the lad after Fanny's doughnuts, and now visions of tall ships sailing the seven seas. Extracting a promise that he would arrive at my office no later than eight o'clock sharp the following morning, I released Eddie from today's lesson.

He was still grinning from ear to ear as he hopped aboard his brougham, and clicked his patient dappled-gray horse toward Market Street to begin his day's work as a cabbie.

"You realize, of course, that he will give me no peace until you've made good on your promise," I told Pierce, as we watched Eddie's departing carriage.

Pierce laughed. "Thank you for the warning, but I meant what I said. I'll be happy to allow the lad onboard. I haven't forgotten my excitement as a boy when my father and uncle allowed my brother and me to board their ships." His look grew serious. "Speaking of Leonard, I have to meet with him shortly. Perhaps you would afford me the pleasure of dining with me tomorrow evening? That way we'll have the leisure to catch up on the events of the past few months."

I experienced a brief panic, then remembered that I had a perfectly valid reason for refusing his invitation. "I'm sorry, but my sister-in-law is holding a dinner party at our house tomorrow night."

"Tonight then," he said, seeming not in the least put off by my refusal. "Don't tell me your sister-in-law is holding a dinner party tonight, as well?"

My panic returned, before common sense exerted itself. Surely a casual dinner between friends was perfectly innocent. It did not mean I had to marry the man! And I could not deny that I was eager to hear of his recent adventures in the Far East.

"All right, Mr. Godfrey," I agreed, trying to ignore my racing heart. "That would be quite pleasant."

"Excellent. But tell me, why have I suddenly become Mr. Godfrey?"

There was that familiar gleam in his dark eyes again, a look I remembered all too well from when we'd first met some six months ago. Just thinking back to that fateful evening still caused me to shudder. In all fairness, however, I could not allow the spate of murders which followed our initial meeting to influence our current friendship.

"Well?" he persisted, in that tone of voice I still found altogether too smooth and self-assured. "If I didn't know better, Sarah, I'd say that you were frightened of me."

I felt blood creep up my neck until it warmed my cheeks.

"Don't be ridiculous," I countered, realizing even as I spoke that my reddened face bespoke the lie. "We are on a public street. It is only decent that we observe proper decorum."

To my consternation, these simple words caused him to laugh aloud.

"What do you find so amusing?" I demanded, irked and embarrassed by this show of disrespect.

"I apologize," he said, making an obvious attempt to rein in his laughter. My anger was further stoked when he could manage nothing better than an amused chuckle. "But really, Sarah, that excuse is akin to the pot calling the kettle black. You pay remarkably little attention to decorum when you're defending a client, or out hunting a murderer. Leonard wrote to me in Hong Kong describing your recent adventures battling ghosts and goblins. I found the entire affair intriguing, if difficult to comprehend."

He referred, of course, to my last case involving a Russian psychic and a series of murders following a séance conducted at San Francisco's Cliff House.

"Your brother was not privy to the particulars of the situation, so he can only report the drivel he read in the newspapers. I assure you, Pierce, those articles fell well short of what actually happened."

"Finally! You're back to using my given name. That's more like the feisty, determined young woman I have come to admire."

"You're impossible!" I declared, my anger turning inward as I belatedly realized how easily I had allowed him to bait my temper.

"Yes, I suppose I am," he admitted good-naturedly. "All right, then. Shall I call for you here this evening? Or am I permitted to come to your home?"

I was momentarily taken aback; I had not considered this dilemma when I had accepted his invitation. If he came to the house, Mama was sure to read far too much into a harmless dinner out with a friend. On the other hand, the severely tailored gray suit I had chosen to wear to the office that morning was hardly suitable attire for dining out. I seemed to be left with little choice.

"You may call for me at my home," I told him, already wondering how I might keep him away from Mama's eager eyes.

As if guessing my thoughts, Pierce said, "Don't worry, I shall assure your mother that we are nothing more than friends." Again, his midnight-blue eyes twinkled. "Unless you've changed your mind and have reconsidered my proposal of marriage?" Before I could protest that indeed I had not reconsidered, he gave a dry little chuckle that sent goose bumps shivering down my arms. "Until tonight, then, shall we say around seven o'clock?" He bent down his handsome face until his dark eyes filled my vision. "My dear Sarah, I look forward to a most pleasurable evening."

All I could do was stare at him speechlessly. With a slight bow and an all too knowing smile, he made his way down Sutter Street to where his driver and carriage were waiting.

"So, he's back," proclaimed a voice from behind me, startling me out of my stupor. "Doesn't he have some ships to waylay in China, or in the West Indies, or wherever he's been for the past few months?"

I turned to find Robert behind me. I wondered how long he had been standing there.

I took in a deep breath of cool morning air, and sought to regain control of my inexplicably wayward emotions.

"Mr. Godfrey has been in Hong Kong opening up a new office for his shipping company, as you well know," I told him, not hiding my annoyance. "Your repeated quips referring to him as a pirate are rude in the extreme, Robert, not to mention childish."

"I might say the same thing about you, Sarah. I cannot understand why you continue to be taken in by that scoundrel. Where he's concerned, you behave like a gullible schoolgirl."

I felt my temper, and embarrassment, rise. This statement fell uncomfortably close to its mark. Even I could not explain why I behaved so irrationally whenever I was in the presence of the dashing shipping mogul.

"Don't be ridiculous," I told Robert, lowering my eyes as I straightened my pleated skirt. "He's a good friend, and that is all there is to it. I will never understand why you have taken such an irrational dislike to the man."

Robert harrumphed. "And I will never understand why your usually acute senses stultify whenever Pierce Godfrey walks into a room."

I fought down a sharp retort, disconcerted to realize that I had just asked myself this same question. Suddenly I wanted nothing so much as to escape to the privacy of my own rooms, where I could put the aggravating Pierce Godfrey out of my mind.

"Good day, Robert," I said, indicating my briefcase. "I have a great deal of work to do."

Without another word, I turned and started up the stairs to my office. I caught a glimpse of Robert's bemused face as he stood below me on the street, watching as I turned the key in the lock and stepped inside.

CHAPTER FIVE

Throughout the day, I found my eyes constantly straying to the timepiece pinned to my shirtwaist, and to thoughts of that evening's dinner engagement with Pierce Godfrey. I should be concentrating on the work Robert had deposited with me that morning. The brief I was attempting to write was tedious in the extreme, but that was no excuse to give it less than my full attention.

It was humbling to admit that my usually rational emotions were in such turmoil. It was even more maddening to realize that Robert had so easily seen through my protestations. Were my feelings so easy to read? I wondered. Was I deluding myself into believing that I was immune to Pierce's considerable charm?

No! I could not credit the notion. Irritably, I pushed up my sleeves and stabbed my pen rather too vigorously into the inkwell, causing a trail of blue spots to dribble across the top of my desk. I blotted them with my handkerchief, then looked over what little I had managed to write over the past hour. Just as I feared, it was complete gibberish. I crumpled up the page and flung it into the wastebasket to join several other failed attempts.

Rising from my desk, I moved to the small back room of my office, where I brewed a cup of strong tea. Carrying it to the armchair I'd situated in front of the window overlooking Sutter Street, I sat down, determined to examine my muddled emotions.

It was no use, I thought. I could not go on lying to myself like this. It was time to admit that I had found Pierce Godfrey intriguing since our first meeting at his brother's charity dinner on Russian Hill earlier that year. I had to smile. It was no mystery why it had happened—the man was handsome and self-assured enough to turn any woman's head. It just shouldn't have been *my* head. I was supposed to be immune to such girlish flights of fancy!

My attention was caught by a black and white dog rushing headlong into Sutter Street, and nearly being hit by a fishmonger's cart. The startled horse reared onto its hind legs and it required all the driver's strength—and a barrage of swear words—to bring him under control. Oblivious to the commotion it had created, the canine culprit completed its sprint across the street and into the alley that cut between the butcher's shop and Millie Thomas's flower store.

From my perch above the fray, I watched as the drivers caught in the gridlock behind the cart grew angry and strident. It struck me that the congestion below my window provided an apt analogy for my disordered thoughts. Just like the carriages and wagons piled one upon the other on the street, my feelings seemed to be caught in a traffic jam of their own: bunched together, making a great deal of racket, and not one of them getting me anywhere.

It was ironic, really, and not a little humbling. I had long prided myself on my ability to control my emotions, and boldly forge ahead on the path I had chosen for my life. Now, it appeared I was caught on the horns of a dilemma I had never expected to encounter. Sarah Woolson, I told myself wearily, it seems that you are a fallible human being after all!

My mind traveled back to the night several months ago, when Pierce arrived at my house to propose that we marry and travel to Hong Kong together. It was embarrassing to admit that I could still remember how he had kissed me. It had been totally unlike any kiss I had experienced before or since.

Once again, I had to smile. In truth, I had kissed less than half a dozen men in my entire twenty-eight years. Before Pierce, only one man had left any lasting impression on my heart: the handsome and entirely too dashing Benjamin Forest.

Just remembering his name caused my cheeks to burn. Benjamin had been my first love, the man I had never thought, nor intended, to meet. By nineteen, I had already vowed to dedicate my life to the law. If spinsterhood was the price I must pay for achieving this goal, so be it.

This obsession with my future left me woefully unprepared to meet a man like Benjamin. He'd been twenty-two, one of Samuel's university friends, who spent considerable time at our house. Like me, he planned a future as an attorney, and to my delight we shared the same vision of how everyone, women as well as men, poor and rich alike, might one day be entitled to equal representation under the law. My error was in imagining that he would want an idealistic female attorney to take her place at his side.

In hindsight, I understood how he had so effortlessly swept a naïve girl off her feet. Benjamin was charm itself, ever ready to praise my mind, my wit, and, to the delight of my youthful vanity, my beauty. The summer before he left for law school, we spent long hours sharing our hopes and aspirations, even planning where he would eventually establish his San Francisco law practice. Blinded by love—or what I thought was love—I envisioned a fairy-tale future where we would toil side by side in our own law firm, joining our talents to make our city, and perhaps all of California, a better place for its citizens to live.

Benjamin gave me my first kiss, a magical experience for a young girl who had grown up sheltered by a doting father and three older brothers. I had been swept away by emotions I hadn't truly known existed.

Thinking back upon it now, I found it humiliating to admit how close I had come to succumbing completely to Benjamin's well-practiced powers of seduction. If it hadn't been for the sound of footsteps on the stairs outside my room, God only knows what folly I might have committed. And with a man who I later discovered had recently become betrothed to a young woman prominent in San Francisco society. Even if Benjamin had returned my feelings—which of course he had not—I was forced to admit that he would never have sanctioned my becoming an attorney, much less welcomed me as an equal partner into his law practice.

With a sigh of irritation, I drained my tea and rose from the chair. Whatever pique had possessed me to travel down that particular memory lane, it had nothing to do with my dinner engagement that evening. My foolish behavior with Benjamin Forest could not in any way be compared to my friendship with Pierce Godfrey. Nine years ago I had been little more than a child; I was now a woman, no longer naïve and fired with unrealistic notions about saving the world. While I could not deny a powerful attraction to the adventurous shipping magnate, my reasons for refusing his proposal of marriage three months ago had not changed.

Sadly, I thought with an unexpected pang of regret, they never could.

Unable to come up with a more imaginative plan, I made certain that I was dressed and ready for Pierce well before he was due to arrive. My idea was to wait for him in the foyer, where I would be on hand to answer the door before our elderly butler Edis could respond to the bell.

Briefly, I thought I might actually pull off the deception, but alas I had underestimated my mother's powers of observation. Having learned from the traitorous Cook, who had given me her word to remain silent, that I would not be home for dinner, she had quizzed our ladies' maid, Hazel, who admitted she had helped me dress and style my hair. She turned next to Edis, who assured her that no one had called for me at the door, whereupon she had commenced a systematic search of the house. I was finally discovered sitting quietly in a dimly lit corner of the library, awaiting an opportunity to slip out of the house unobserved.

"So, here you are," she said, turning up the gas lamp and standing in front of me, hands on her hips. "Why didn't you tell me you were going out this evening? It's embarrassing having to hear of my own daughter's plans from the servants."

I tried to think up a halfway believable excuse, then gave up. "I feared you would make more of the occasion than it warranted, Mama," I finally admitted. "I didn't want a fuss."

Her eyes sparkled with satisfaction. "Then it's true. I heard that Mr. Godfrey was back in San Francisco. Is he the gentleman you're stepping out with?"

"I'd hardly term it 'stepping out,'" I replied, objecting to the phrase which was generally taken to describe a relationship a good deal more serious than mere friendship. "Mr. Godfrey and I are simply dining together. He's been away for several months, and this appeared to be a good opportunity to catch up."

Mama beamed at me. "Of course, darling. If that's the way you choose to portray the situation, far be it from me to contradict you. I do expect you to invite Mr. Godfrey in for an aperitif before you leave, however. It is no more than common courtesy."

Courtesy or no, asking Pierce in with the entire family at home was the last thing I'd had in mind. On the other hand, I trust I am woman enough to admit when I've been outmaneuvered.

"Very well." I gave in with what grace I could muster. Please understand that I am devoted to my mother and love her dearly. Her obsession with seeing me married, however, can, at times, be trying. The delighted glow on her face at that moment, however, went a long way toward making this small sacrifice worthwhile.

"Perhaps Edis could show Mr. Godfrey into the front parlor when he arrives, Mama. He should be here at any moment."

My worst fears were realized when everyone—Mama, Papa, Samuel, Charles, and Celia—was already gathered in the parlor when Pierce arrived. Although he was faultlessly polite, I could see by his slightly strained expression that he had not expected to be presented to the Woolson clan en masse.

"Mr. Godfrey, it is good to see you again," said Charles, handing our guest a glass of whiskey and shaking his hand with genuine pleasure. "I don't know if you remember, but my wife, Celia, and I first made your acquaintance at the charity dinner your brother and his wife held at their lovely home earlier this year."

The words were scarcely out of Charles's mouth than he abruptly seemed to recall the tragedy which had occurred at that very dinner party.

"My dear Mr. Godfrey, I'm so sorry." He looked helplessly toward Celia, as if searching for suitable words to undo the unintentional damage he had caused.

"Please do excuse my husband, Mr. Godfrey," said Celia in her sweet voice. "He did not mean to bring up what must be a painful subject."

"Not at all, Mrs. Woolson," Pierce assured her, smiling graciously at Charles. "Please do not distress yourselves. I prefer to recall the evening for the generous amount of money we were able to raise for the Women and Children's Hospital." His gaze went to me, and his dark blue eyes grew teasing. "Then, too, that was the evening I met your charming sister, an occasion I can only remember in the most favorable light."

For a moment, everyone's eyes rested on me, then the brief, uncomfortable silence was broken when Samuel said, "That is a brave confession, Mr. Godfrey, given that my little sister is prone to find herself in some, shall we say, awkward circumstances when it comes to murder and mayhem?"

I shot my brother a thunderous look, but my irritating sibling merely smiled and raised his wineglass as if in salute. My mother, however, did not appear to find his comments amusing.

"Please, Mr. Godfrey," she nervously gushed. "Pay no attention to Samuel. At the risk of appearing a boastful mother, I am proud to say that Sarah works tirelessly for the poor and disadvantaged of this city, as well as involving herself in good works for our church. We are enormously proud of her."

"Mama," I protested. Uncomfortable with the direction the conversation was heading, I said, "It's getting late. We really must take our leave."

"Before you go, Mr. Godfrey," Papa put in, "perhaps you would give me your thoughts on that new five-masted schooner, the *David Dows*. The one that set sail on the Great Lakes last April? It looks impressive, but does it handle in the water? That's what it all comes down to, doesn't it? I hear that weather on those lakes can become as violent as a storm on the open sea."

Pierce smiled. "It can indeed, Judge Woolson. I agree that the *Dows* is an amazing lady, but as I'm sure you know, her first voyage on Lake Erie proved less than notable."

Papa chuckled. "That's an understatement. I hear she ran aground and was stranded high and dry for two days. Still, her builders continue to call her the grandest cargo schooner ever to sail the Great Lakes."

"They can hardly say anything less after all the time and money they've invested in her," said Pierce. "In my opinion, her very size renders her too ungainly for practical shipping purposes. She may look impressive, but I wouldn't want her in our fleet."

"Wouldn't you, now? Well, despite the shipbuilders' folderol, I bow to your expertise." Papa was obviously enjoying this turn in the conversation. "Tell me, Mr. Godfrey, do you and your brother have plans to expand your business beyond Hong Kong?"

I could see that my mother was bristling with impatience. "Horace, really, leave the poor man alone. You heard Sarah, they must leave for dinner." Turning to Pierce, she asked hopefully, "You will honor us with your presence at a Christmas party we will be hosting a week from this Saturday, will you not, Mr. Godfrey? That is, if you plan to remain in town through the holidays."

"I plan to stay in the city until some time after the first of the year, Mrs. Woolson," he replied, his smile actually causing her to blush. "I would be delighted to accept your invitation."

My heart sank. The knowledge of when Pierce would once again set sail gave Mama nearly three weeks to play matchmaker.

Even worse, I had long since invited Robert to our Christmas dinner. I shuddered to imagine him forced to spend an entire evening with a man he considered to be little better than a buccaneer!

Before the conversation could further complicate my life, I placed my wineglass on the table and reached for my evening cloak and reticule. "Shall we, Mr. Godfrey?" I said, starting toward the drawing room door. "We mustn't keep your carriage waiting."

We dined at one of San Francisco's most noted French restaurants, the Poodle Dog, located on Bush Street. Stories about how the dining establishment came to acquire its name had been rife since it set up business in a wooden shanty in 1849. Some claimed the restaurant's original owner owned a French poodle called "le Poulet d'Or," a name the semiliterate forty-niners who frequented the establishment at that time could not pronounce. Soon it became simply the Poodle Dog. Other stories maintained that the poodle was a stray taken in by the Frenchmen who ran the restaurant, while others insisted that the famous poodle was named Ami, and that he had actually stood at the door and greeted customers.

Whatever the truth regarding its name, the Poodle Dog left its humble beginnings far behind when it moved to Bush Street in 1868. Its new brick building towered six stories high, and featured a lavish dining room on the first floor, ornately decorated in French Louis XIV style. More private dining rooms were situated on the second floor, and decidedly risqué accommodations for private assignations could be found on the third, fourth, and fifth floors. These latter rooms came furnished with elegant beds, imported carpets, and a strict policy of silence, as long as the proper hands were crossed with silver. The sixth floor was reserved for large banquets and parties suitable for the general public.

It goes without saying that Pierce and I were led to a table in the very respectable first-floor dining room, where a number of well-dressed guests were already enjoying the Poodle Dog's excellent

French cuisine. Some of the groups were families with children, who were on their best behavior. If the distinguished gentlemen's wives were aware of the "private" accommodations to be had upstairs, they did not appear to be making an issue of it, at least not openly.

"I apologize for subjecting you to the family's predinner interrogation," I said, after the waiter left with our orders. "I'd hoped to slip out of the house unnoticed."

"No need to apologize. I think you have a delightful family." His dark eyes revealed more insight than I found comfortable. "I'm complimented that your mother considers me an appropriate suitor. I only wish her daughter felt the same."

I gave a soft groan. "You noticed."

He laughed. "I felt rather like a specimen under a microscope." At my pained look, he hurried on, "Sarah, I'm only teasing. I truly do take it as a compliment. Your family obviously cares very deeply about you. They only desire to see you happy."

"Yes, I'm sure you're right."

This was nothing less than the truth. I realized full well that Mama had only my best welfare at heart. At twenty-eight I was aware that Mama's friends considered me a hopeless spinster, an eccentric one at that. Their opinion had not unduly concerned me until this unsettling man sitting opposite me had come into my life. Now, my emotions were in a turmoil; my life's course no longer seemed as logically defined as it once had. How could I make Pierce understand my feelings, when I could scarcely understand them myself?

My expression must have betrayed my confusion, for he reached across the table and took my hand, gently stroking the skin with his thumb. To my dismay, I felt my pulse leap at his touch.

He must have felt the involuntary flutter, for he went on softly, "My dear Sarah, I did not ask you to dine with me tonight in order to cause you discomfort. You made your feelings perfectly clear the night before I departed for Hong Kong."

"The night you—" I gulped, but was unable to utter the words I could not forget.

"The night I asked you to become my wife, yes."

Without releasing my hand, he leaned closer until his face filled my vision. His dark blue eyes captured mine so completely that it would have been impossible for me to turn my head even if I had wanted to, which, to my chagrin, I did not.

"My feelings for you haven't changed, Sarah. I doubt they ever will. You are the most remarkable and intelligent woman I have ever met. And the most beautiful."

I hesitated, not sure what to say. In truth, I was bowled over by these unexpected, and to my mind, undeserved, words of praise. "Pierce, I—"

"No, my dear, please, there is no need for you to say anything. We understand each other perfectly, you and I."

"I'm not sure that you do understand," I said, endeavoring to explain. "It's all rather complicated."

"I'm sure it is. You may find it hard to believe, but I truly do realize the many obstacles blocking the path of a woman trying to compete in a man's world." He gave my hand a little squeeze. "It's important that you understand how much I admire the principles that drive you to dedicate your life to helping others. After all, it's these very ideals which first attracted me to you, that and your refreshing honesty." He paused, and his face grew serious. "I also appreciate your fear that marriage will prevent you from achieving these goals."

If these words were meant to alleviate my misgivings, they had the opposite effect. How much easier it would be, I thought, if he behaved like the great majority of men whose paths I crossed every day. They, along with a deplorable number of individuals of my own gender, sincerely believed that a woman had neither the ability, nor the temperament, to engage in work outside the home. It would be simplicity itself to reject such a man, without in the least troubling my emotions.

Pierce's tolerance and empathy, on the other hand, were undermining the very determination which defined my adult life. His patience and consideration left me conflicted and—to my surprise—angry. How dare he march into my life and upset the equilibrium I had worked so long and hard to achieve!

I drew breath to tell him exactly what I thought of this invasion, when he once again seemed to second-guess my thoughts.

He smiled, and the candlelight danced and flickered in the dark recesses of his eyes. "Let's enjoy a quiet dinner, shall we, Sarah? Just two friends catching up with each other after being apart for too long. There is no need to concern ourselves with the future. It's been my experience that tomorrow has a way of taking care of itself."

Before I could reply—although I had no idea what that reply might have been!—the waiter returned with our soup. Pierce released my hand and refilled my glass with the excellent wine he had ordered.

Raising his glass, he toasted with a smile, "To friendship. And to a lovely Christmas."

Try as I might, I could find no fault with these sentiments. Vaguely wondering why my justifiable anger had suddenly evaporated, I found myself returning his smile. I raised my glass and clicked it against his.

"To friendship," I said. "And to Christmas."

CHAPTER SIX

Wednesday morning found me seated behind my desk in my Sutter Street office, plodding through the mind-numbing legal work Robert had deposited with me the previous day. Although I was grateful for the supplemental income, even this welcome addition to my meager coffers was hardly sufficient to keep the wolves from my door. I expelled a deep breath. How I longed for the day when my modest law firm would provide me with financial independence!

You note that I employ the word "when" and not "if." I am not one to promote false modesty; it is, therefore, no more than the simple truth to admit that I am a competent attorney. Were it not for the happenstance of being born a member of the so-called fairer sex, I am certain I would not be facing this particular adversity. However, since one cannot change one's gender, I had little choice but to play the cards the Almighty had seen fit to deal me.

As I trudged through Robert's work—a tedious and extremely boring responsive brief concerning one of Shepard's lesser clients—I frequently consulted my timepiece. I was ready, nay, eager to put the wearisome documents aside the moment Miss Bouchard arrived for our meeting. To my disappointment, however, there was no knock upon my door at the appointed hour. Nine o'clock came and went, then nine thirty. Where could she be? I asked myself.

This question had hardly taken form in my mind than the door suddenly flew open and Robert Campbell strode purposefully into my office.

"I came to see if you've completed the work I left with you yesterday morning," he said without preamble.

As I am sure I have mentioned ad infinitum, Robert Campbell is sadly lacking in the social graces. Nor, I might add, does he appear to care one jot if he ever acquires them.

"I see you continue to refuse to adopt the civilized habit of announcing your arrival with a knock upon my door," I told him sardonically.

"Knock?" he asked, as if this word were strange to his vocabulary. "This is a law office open to the public, is it not?"

"Yes, but—"

"And I am currently visiting that office as a client, is that not also correct?"

I knew, of course, where this was headed, but was forced to nod my head in reluctant agreement. "I suppose you could technically be termed a client."

"Oh, aye? Have I not brought you business, you ungrateful woman?" he declared, his Scottish burr rolling along nicely. "And have I not paid good money for your legal services? From the dearth of clients queued up at your door, I should think you'd regard me as a very fine client, indeed." Without waiting for an invitation, the irksome man sank into the chair opposite my desk. "Now, have you finished my work or not?"

Once again I consulted my lapel watch. "It is barely nine forty-five, Robert. Even I cannot proceed that quickly. I am barely halfway through the Walton brief, a very wearisome one, too, I might add."

I was taken aback, and not a little irritated, when the big Scot laughed. "Why do you think I brought it to you? For some odd reason, Joseph Shepard has decided that I possess an inexhaustible tolerance for drudgery. Since he is mistaken—and you are in need of income—I have settled on a mutually satisfactory solution to the problem."

I felt my temper rising. "So, you finally admit that you are bringing me this work out of pity?"

He looked affronted. "What are you going on about? I just finished saying that you were doing me a favor by attending to this claptrap. Damn it all, woman! Why must you always read drama and intrigue into even the most straightforward conversations?"

My temper bridled at this. "I am doing nothing of the sort, Robert. I'll have you know that my law firm is doing very well, considering I have been open for less than—"

I broke off as a knock sounded on my door. I straightened in my seat, certain that it must be Brielle Bouchard's tardy arrival. I would have to send Robert quickly on his way so that we might have a private conversation. To my surprise, however, Fanny Goodman poked her head in, giving us a cheery smile.

"I saw Mr. Campbell going upstairs and thought the two of you might enjoy some fresh coffee and a bit of a morning nibble." Balancing a heavily laden tray, she held the door open with her ample hip, then passed inside. Although Robert rose to offer her a helping hand, she cheerfully brushed him aside and made her way to my desk. I was not particularly pleased by the interruption, but the aroma emanating from the tray was tantalizing, especially the large gingerbread cake still warm from the oven.

"Fanny, it smells wonderful, but I'm expecting a client at any moment."

"If you mean that Bouchard girl, I don't think she intends to keep her appointment." She set the tray down on my desk, then poured coffee into several cups she had brought up from her kitchen.

"Excuse me, Fanny," I said. "What makes you think Miss Bouchard will not keep her appointment?"

"Because she's been here and gone," she replied, handing each of us a cup of the steaming brew. "I saw her not thirty minutes ago crossing Sutter Street with the same determined look on her face she wore the first time she came to see you on Monday. I thought

I'd just step out of my shop and take a quick peek at that darling baby of hers, when two men came out of nowhere and stopped her dead in her tracks."

"What sort of men, Fanny?" I asked in growing alarm.

Robert looked from Fanny to me, his blue-green eyes suspicious. "What's this about two men, Mrs. Goodman? And who is Brielle Bouchard?"

"Miss Bouchard is a new client, Robert," I explained. "Well, actually a prospective client. She was to meet with me here at nine o'clock this morning." I turned back to my neighbor. "Can you describe the men, Fanny?"

Fanny hesitated in the act of cutting a generous slice of gingerbread. "Let me see. They were both young, maybe in their late twenties or early thirties. One was tall with a lot of wild-looking black hair. The other man was shorter, but very thin and well on his way to going bald. Both men had mean faces that gave me the willies."

I thought about this disturbing news. Then, as Robert drew in air to speak, I said, "You say Miss Bouchard changed her mind about coming up to my office after she spoke to the men? Could you hear what they told her?"

"I could see them plain as day from my doorway, but I was too far away to hear what they were saying. I can tell you one thing, the poor Bouchard girl didn't look any too happy to see them. I could see she was trying to back away from the bullies, all the while clutching that dear little baby of hers. Then she suddenly turned and bolted back across the street as if the devil himself were after her. The two thugs had a good laugh behind her back, then took themselves off up Sutter Street.

"Good Lord!" Robert jumped out of his chair. "What kind of men would threaten a woman, especially one carrying a baby? You said they went up Sutter Street, Mrs. Goodman? Maybe I can catch them up."

Fanny seemed a bit taken aback by his enthusiasm. "You'll never find them now, Mr. Campbell. They've had too much of a head start. And I was ready enough to call for help if they'd shown any sign of actually harming the girl."

"Frightening the poor young woman was crime enough," he said, his deep voice tight with indignation. "There is only one fit place for men such as that, in jail!"

I started to speak in support of these sentiments, when I heard footsteps on the stairs leading up to my office, and an ever exuberant Eddie Cooper burst into the room. To my dismay, I spied a copy of the *Police Gazette* tucked beneath the boy's arm. If Eddie thought I could be persuaded to use this rag sheet in lieu of Mark Twain's exciting tale *The Adventures of Tom Sawyer* for his reading lesson, he was very much mistaken.

The boy's eyes grew large when he saw Fanny and the tray of gingerbread on my desk. "Mornin', Mrs. Goodman," he said, politely removing his cap as I'd instructed him when in the presence of a lady. "Mornin', Miss Sarah, Mr. Campbell," he added as an afterthought, his eyes never leaving the food-laden tray.

"I see we've come just in time," my brother Samuel remarked, entering the room behind the boy. "Hello, Fanny, Robert. It's good to see you."

"And you," Robert replied, shaking my brother's outstretched hand. Although the two men came from different countries, cultures, and backgrounds, they had formed a genuine friendship over the past year.

"Fetch yourself a cup from the back room, Mr. Samuel," Fanny directed him. "The coffee's hot and fresh."

She nodded toward the spare room that, as I have mentioned, I currently used for reading and brewing tea. Eventually, I intended this second room to serve as my law library, but so far I'd been able to stock it with only a handful of legal tomes, most of them borrowed from my father's home library.

"What brings you here, Samuel?" I asked, reading the barely suppressed excitement on his handsome face. "Why do I have the feeling that this is more than a social call?"

"I come bearing news," he replied. "But first I must assuage my craving for Fanny's excellent coffee and gingerbread." He glanced teasingly at Eddie. "I don't suppose you'd care for a slice, would you, lad?"

The boy grinned from ear to ear. "You know better than that, Mr. Samuel. No one bakes better gingerbread than Mrs. Goodman."

Fanny beamed at this compliment, while at the same time good-naturedly slapping at the boy's fingers, which had begun inching toward the cake plate. "Not so fast, young man. First, go wash those filthy hands."

The boy scooted into the back room where I kept soap, a basin of water, and a towel to freshen up during the day. He was back so quickly, I had to wonder how thorough a job he had made of it. Fanny must have been satisfied, though, for as soon as Eddie returned she began to cut him a very generous piece of the cake.

"Now, eat this quietly and behave yourself," she told him with a playful wink.

"Thanks, Mrs. Goodman," he said, accepting the plate. Grinning broadly, he carried the gingerbread over to his favorite perch on the windowsill. There he sat and, opening the rag sheet I was sure Samuel had just given him, began to devour Fanny's unexpected treat.

"So, Samuel," I said after we had all been served. "What's this news you're bursting to tell us?"

"I should leave," Robert said, once again rising from his chair, "before Joseph Shepard has a fit of dyspepsia. Trevor Lansing is still ill with catarrh, so I must take his place as second chair to Shepard in court again this morning."

"Please, Robert, just another minute," Samuel said, holding up a hand. "I'm sure what I have to say will interest you, as well."

Robert nodded and sank back onto the edge of his seat. Despite his hurry, he looked intrigued, as did Fanny and I. "All right, but I really can't stay long."

We were all staring at Samuel, and as I watched his expression grow somber, I felt a sudden chill trickle down my spine.

"What is it, Samuel? What has happened?"

"There's been another murder," he told us gravely. "And once again it's happened on Rincon Hill."

Fanny drew in her breath. "Another murder?" She executed a hasty sign of the cross, and sank down heavily on the chair Samuel had placed for her beside Robert. "Lord help us, who was it this time?"

"The victim is Dieter Hume," explained my brother. "I'm sure you're acquainted with him, Sarah. He was the deacon at the Reverend Erasmus Mayfield's church."

Fanny, Robert, and I sat regarding him in stunned silence. Eddie abruptly ceased reading the *Police Gazette,* and was staring avidly at Samuel, his thin cheeks bulging with gingerbread.

"Was it a robbery?" I asked.

"Apparently not," my brother said. "His wallet was still in his pocket, and his watch was left undisturbed."

"Deacon Hume was a guest at the Tremaines' party Saturday night," I mused. "And didn't you mention that he was a friend of Mr. Logan's?"

"Nigel Logan," Fanny put in thoughtfully. "You mean the poor fellow who was beaten to death under the Harrison Street Bridge last Saturday night?"

I nodded solemnly, then turned to Samuel. "Surely the two murders must be somehow connected."

I caught Robert giving me a suspicious glance out of the corner of his eye, but he forbore to question—or censure—this very logical statement. Given the link between the two men, as well as the fact that they had died in the same neighborhood a mere four days apart, surely he could not accuse me of manufacturing "drama and intrigue," as he was wont to phrase it.

"My thoughts exactly, Sarah," Samuel said. "Hume's body was found this morning only a hundred yards or so from where they discovered Nigel Logan."

"Again, only two blocks from our own home," I muttered.

Robert was beginning to look concerned. "Isn't that unusual for Rincon Hill? I thought that area was relatively free of violent crime."

"It is," I answered quietly.

"How was—that is, what was used to kill the poor man?" Fanny asked in a small voice.

Samuel hesitated, fearing, I was sure, that the details might upset my matronly neighbor.

Fanny must have guessed what lay behind his uncomfortable silence, for she said, "Don't think that whatever you have to say is going to cause me to faint dead away, Samuel Woolson, because I'm made of stronger stuff than that. Now, give us the truth of the matter."

"Yeah, Mr. Samuel," Eddie said, staring wide-eyed at my brother from his window seat. "What done in the bloke?"

"I'm afraid he was bludgeoned to death, just like Nigel Logan," Samuel reluctantly explained, regarding Fanny, despite her assurances, with a wary eye.

"Oh, my dear Lord," she gasped, sitting back in her chair and growing a bit pale. "How horrible!"

Robert eyed her apprehensively. Reaching out, he placed a hesitant hand on her shoulder, obviously unsure how to go about comforting the poor woman.

Fanny gave him a wan smile. "Thank you, Mr. Campbell, but I'm all right. It is a terrible shock, though. It isn't every day two young men are brutally murdered in such a fine neighborhood."

"Do the police have any idea who was responsible for Deacon Hume's murder?" I asked Samuel.

"Was it the same knuck what done in the other feller?" Eddie asked, the question coming out somewhat garbled due to the large amount of gingerbread stuffed inside his mouth. He had left his perch on the window ledge and was standing expectantly behind Samuel. "Lordy, was there a lot of blood, then?"

"Eddie, please!" I admonished. "Sit down and eat your cake with some semblance of good manners. I'm sure Mr. Samuel will tell us what he knows about this tragedy, if you will but give him an opportunity."

The boy reluctantly retreated to the window. His large eyes

never left my brother, however, as he once again lowered himself onto the edge of the sill.

"There's not much more to tell," said my brother. "According to George—my friend on the police force—" he explained for Fanny's benefit, "Dieter Hume's death has only increased the police's interest in the Reverend Mayfield and the other guests who were present at the Tremaines' party. Evidently, they questioned the minister again this morning. I'm sure they'll be paying the Tremaines another visit, as well."

"The Reverend Mayfield?" exclaimed Robert, looking shocked. "You mean the police actually think a clergyman could have committed two such abominations?"

"I doubt that the police have singled out Reverend Mayfield as their prime suspect," Samuel replied. "But he's one of the people they're investigating. Frankly, Robert, they don't have much to go on."

"So they're revisiting all the guests who were present at Saturday night's party," I said.

"What else can they do?" my brother answered. "As you pointed out, it's a bit much to suppose the two murders can be mere coincidence."

"No," I agreed quietly, with a growing sense of unease. This was not because San Francisco lacked its share of crime, including a fair number of murders committed every year, but rather because few victims were actually killed so close to our own home. While it was true that the Second Street Cut had attracted a few unsavory individuals to our neighborhood, nothing like this had occurred as far back as I could remember.

"I wonder if Dieter Hume shared Nigel Logan's enthusiasm for Darwin's revolutionary theories?" I went on, speculating aloud.

Robert gave a little snort. "Even if he did, that would hardly provide a motive for murder. These crimes are far too violent for any decent man to commit. Surely the killer is a vagabond, or some kind of madman."

"That would assume that the two deaths were random," I argued, "which is a theory I cannot entertain. Hume and Logan were friends, and their bodies were found in the same vicinity, just yards apart, although not on the same day. They were both present at the Tremaines' party, and the same method was used to kill them both. Common sense demands that there be a connection."

Robert shook his head, causing his unruly red hair to fly helter-skelter about his expressive face. "If you're right, Sarah, then those two men shared a very dangerous enemy."

He rose from his chair. "I must go now. It will mean my job if I arrive late at the courthouse." He pointed to the paperwork he had brought me, which was still spread out on my desk. "Since I may be in court again tomorrow, I'll pick these up on Friday. Surely you'll have finished with them by then."

I gave him a level look, not pleased with his tone. "I will complete them this afternoon, Robert. You may, of course, collect them at your convenience."

Ignoring me, he again expressed his thanks to Fanny Good-man, nodded politely to Samuel, and took his leave.

"He's right, you know," Samuel said after he was gone. "If, as we believe, the two murders were linked, then Logan and Hume managed to acquire an extremely determined and vicious enemy."

"I agree," I said, draining the last of my coffee. Such was my distress regarding Samuel's news, I had barely touched my ginger-bread. Judging by Eddie's hungry glances at my plate, however, I was confident it would not go to waste. "What we must do is find that connection."

My brother gave me one of his ironic grins. "*We,* little sister? Does that mean that you intend to help me follow up on the story?"

This brought me up short, and I realized I was not quite sure *what* I had meant. "If I can be of any assistance to you, Samuel, I'll be happy to help. Other than that, I have no reason, or intention, of becoming involved in this dreadful matter."

My brother continued to grin at me, which I found annoying. I knew what he was thinking, and was not well pleased.

"You're becoming as bad as Robert," I told him. "I grow weary of being accused of poking my nose where it is not appreciated. These murders are appalling, and it frightens me that they occurred so close to our home. But I agree that this is a story you must pursue, and I'm willing to lend you a helping hand."

In truth, I had not realized until this moment how deeply I'd been affected by Nigel Logan's and Dieter Hume's deaths, or how I had taken the security of my Rincon Hill home for granted. In less than a week that feeling of complacency had been shattered, and I found myself asking who might be next.

It was not uncommon for gentlemen, including my own father, to enjoy late-evening constitutionals in our neighborhood. My brother Charles, who was a physician, frequently came and went at all hours of the night while attending his patients, and of course Samuel regularly kept late hours. The thought that a member of my own family might fall victim to this unnamed monster was truly alarming.

"It's high time I was on my way, too," Fanny said, stacking the empty gingerbread plate and coffee cups onto the tray. "I am already late opening my shop. I'll let you know if I catch sight of the Brielle girl, Sarah, or those hooligans I saw talking to her earlier."

When I failed to respond—or even to look up from my gruesome reverie—she quickly guessed my concern.

"The deaths of those two young men are tragic, Sarah. But if their murders are truly related, as you and Samuel suspect, the motive must stem from something to do with their personal lives. Rincon Hill is still one of the safest areas in San Francisco. I'm certain these deplorable events will not affect your family or friends."

And with this pitifully erroneous prediction, Fanny picked up her tray and coffeepot and headed downstairs to her shop.

CHAPTER SEVEN

As soon as Fanny left, Eddie hopped down from the windowsill and appropriated the woman's vacated chair across from my desk. "I was wonderin', Miss Sarah. Are you, ah, gonna eat that gingerbread?"

Samuel chuckled as I wordlessly passed the boy my plate. "Hurry up with that cake, Eddie," he said. "I need the services of your cab."

"Oh?" I asked curiously. "Is your errand by any chance connected to this latest murder?"

"As a matter of fact, it is," he replied. "I'd like to have a chat with the Reverend Mayfield about his deacon."

"Samuel, you never go to church. He hardly knows you. What makes you think he'll agree to an interview?"

"Oh, I think he'll agree, all right," he said with a smile. "If you're with me. Nothing like a pretty female companion to loosen a man's tongue, even a minister's."

"Samuel!" I protested.

"Don't look so surprised, Sarah. You're the one who offered to help, remember? Besides, you're as interested in this case as I am, you just don't care to admit it."

He pushed his chair away from my desk and stood. "Actually, the timing is perfect. You don't have to finish Robert's brief until

Friday. That gives you more than enough time to assist your brother in his effort to scoop Ozzie Foldger and the *Tattler*."

In far less time than it ought to have taken at a more civilized pace, Eddie reined the dappled gray to a stop in front of a wood and stucco church, located on Howard Street between Second and Third. It boasted a modest bell tower, a tall steeple, and a Roman structure with several unexpected Greek and even Moorish features. It was my considered opinion that whoever designed the Church of Our Savior had been confused about just what style he intended to emulate.

As we pulled up, we spied a short, portly man in his fifties descending the church steps. I recognized him as the Reverend Erasmus Mayfield, the church's rector for the past fifteen years. The man's balding head was down, and he held his hands behind his back as he walked in the direction of the rectory, a small wooden house located to the left of the church. He seemed distressed, shaking his head and muttering to himself.

"Reverend Mayfield," I called out, as Samuel assisted me out of the carriage.

When he seemed not to hear, I started after him, calling his name out louder this time. He finally stopped, but looked at us blankly, as if having visitors appear unexpectedly at the church was an extraordinary occurrence.

"Yes?" he said a bit sharply, appearing annoyed to have his musings interrupted. Belatedly realizing how harsh this must have sounded, he managed a weak smile. "I am sorry. Is there something I can do for you?"

"Excuse us for dropping by unannounced, Reverend Mayfield," I said. "I'm Sarah Woolson, and this is my brother Samuel. Judge and Mrs. Elizabeth Woolson are our parents."

His face suddenly cleared, as recognition slowly dawned. "Yes, yes, of course, how remiss of me not to know you at once. It has been a rather arduous day, and I fear my mind has been sadly preoccupied.

Please allow me to apologize. I have frequently observed you accompanying your parents to services, Miss Woolson, although I don't seem to recall your face, Mr. Woolson."

My brother looked embarrassed, and I experienced a pang of guilt. In all honesty, I found the Reverend Mayfield a good deal less than inspiring. Sunday services tended to be tedious, sadly repetitive, and devoid of passion. The primary reason I continued to attend with my parents was to please my mother, who held the firm belief that any path to heaven must include weekly church attendance.

I came out of my thoughts as Samuel cleared his throat. I realized he was searching for a way to answer the rector without jeopardizing the interview. "It's not always possible for me to attend church, Reverend Mayfield. My, um, work, you know."

Apparently, Mayfield did not know, or he was accomplished enough at judging character to recognize a spurious excuse when he heard one. "I'm sure that must be very trying for you," he said, a glint of disapproval darkening his pale gray eyes.

"We have come to extend our sympathies on the loss of your deacon, Mr. Hume," I said, steering the conversation out of dangerous waters and back to the real reason for our visit. "It is a shocking tragedy."

The Reverend Mayfield nodded. "Oh my, yes. Terrible, terrible. Very difficult to grasp. Just yesterday, Mr. Hume and I were discussing possible plans to replace the church roof. It is old and badly in need of repair. I doubt it will survive another winter."

He gave a little shiver and looked about, as if suddenly aware of the damp fog that was rolling in from the ocean. Rubbing his plump hands together briskly, he said, "It has become quite chilled. Come inside, please. My housekeeper will brew a pot of coffee."

Without waiting for a reply, the portly little man turned and led us inside the two-story dwelling which served as his residence.

"Mrs. Brown?" he called out as we entered the foyer. "We have visitors." He took our wraps and hung them on a coat tree standing by the front door. He had just added his own long coat to the rack when a small, gray-haired woman of about sixty came bustling toward us. "Ah, yes, there you are, Mrs. Brown. Would you be so good as to put on a fresh pot of coffee for our guests? You may serve it in my study."

As we followed the rector into a small room off the hallway, I was delighted to see a fire crackling in the hearth. It truly had grown chilly outside, and I felt a pang of remorse that we had left poor Eddie to wait outside with the carriage. I hoped that our interview with the Reverend Mayfield would not be overlong.

After Mrs. Brown brought us coffee and a plate of cookies, Samuel took charge of the conversation. I was pleased to see that he was trying to broach the subject tactfully.

"I understand Mr. Hume came to this parish directly from seminary school," he began.

"That is correct," Mayfield replied, choosing one of the housekeeper's cookies from the platter. "It has been nearly a year now. You should try these. Mrs. Brown is an excellent cook. I don't know what I would do without her."

Samuel dutifully reached for a cookie and took a bite. "You're right, these are delicious." When he finished chewing, he went on. "Mr. Hume was a bit older than the usual seminarian, though, wasn't he, Reverend Mayfield?"

"Yes, he was in his late twenties, but that is not altogether remarkable," the rector explained. "A fair number of young men do not immediately receive, or do not accept, their spiritual calling until they have experienced something of the world. On the whole, I do not consider it a bad thing to wait a year or two to make such an important decision. The ministry is, after all, a lifelong commitment."

"No doubt you're right," Samuel agreed. "I imagine commencing one's church service at a more mature age would tend to make a man more responsible in fulfilling his duties. Particularly a man who had attended university."

The Reverend Mayfield hesitated a moment, then nodded, albeit without overmuch enthusiasm. "Yes, that is true. Given, of course, that the man in question possesses the necessary qualities to join the ministry. Unfortunately, higher education does not guarantee those qualities. In fact, university life has been known to instill just the opposite behavioral tendencies. In the end, character and commitment must always be the primary considerations when dedicating one's life to the church."

My brother raised an eyebrow. "Are you implying that Mr. Hume might have been mistaken in his vocation?"

"No, no, not at all," Mayfield replied, wincing a bit at Samuel's bluntness. He sipped his coffee, then added, "Naturally, no one can see into another man's soul, but Dieter performed his responsibilities well enough. In time, I'm confident he would have smoothed out the odd rough spot here and there and made an excellent career in the church."

"I understand Mr. Hume attended university with Nigel Logan," Samuel said.

Mayfield looked startled at the mention of the biologist. "Nigel Logan. Yes, I believe that is correct. Dieter and Mr. Logan had been friends for some time."

He drained his coffee, then sat forward in his seat, regarding Samuel with grave eyes. "I am loath to speak ill of the dead, Mr. Woolson, but I feel obliged to admit that I did not consider Mr. Logan a suitable friend for Dieter. As a man of science, Mr. Logan held some rather unsettling, dare I say misguided, beliefs. Hardly the sort of ideas appropriate for a young church deacon to espouse. I attempted several times to explain this to Dieter, but he was loyal to his friend, and would allow no ill to be spoken against him."

"By that I gather you mean that Mr. Hume shared Mr. Logan's enthusiasm for Charles Darwin's evolutionary theories?" I asked, entering the conversation.

The Reverend Mayfield darted a surprised look in my direction, as if he had forgotten I was in the room. "Whatever leads you to think that, Miss Woolson?"

I attempted to mimic my brother's well-rehearsed expression of innocence. I daresay, I was not as successful.

"My father happened to mention that you and Mr. Logan exchanged words last Saturday night—at the gathering Mr. and Mrs. Tremaine arranged in your honor. I assumed that must be what you were referring to when you mentioned Mr. Logan's inappropriate influence on Deacon Hume."

The Reverend Mayfield's face flushed, and for a moment I feared he would deny the argument, or simply refuse to discuss the matter with us. After all, we had already overstepped social civility by bringing up what surely must be a sensitive subject. He took several moments to mull over his response, then sighed and sat back in his armchair.

"Yes, Miss Woolson, you are correct, I fear I did allow Mr. Logan to arouse my temper. More than some other of the man's . . . heterodox beliefs, his views concerning Darwin's misguided theory on the origin of species troubled me. I must agree with Adam Sedgwick who wisely maintained that "the Author of Nature will not permit His work to be spoiled by the wanton curiosity of Man.""

"Adam Sedgwick." This name rang a distant bell in my memory. "Wasn't he a professor of geology at Cambridge some years ago?"

"Precisely the man, Miss Woolson," Mayfield replied, appearing agreeably amazed that I was familiar with his source. "He was also president of the Geological Society and of the British Association of Geologists. A learned man, Professor Sedgwick, possessed of a keen mind which, I am pleased to say, saw right through Darwin's ungodly notions of evolution."

"Am I to assume that, despite your efforts to dissuade Deacon Hume from this heresy, he persisted in supporting Mr. Darwin's theories?" Samuel asked.

Reverend Mayfield did not immediately answer, and once again I feared we were guilty of abusing his hospitality. However, he merely reached into a pocket for a large white handkerchief and gently mopped his brow.

"I am sorry to say that he remained entrenched in this profanation. Most unfortunate, especially as the angel of death was even then setting out to reclaim his immortal soul. But as it reads in the Book of Common Prayer, 'In the midst of life we are in death.' We never know when, or from whence, it may come. It behooves us all to maintain constant vigilance."

Samuel cleared his throat, then assumed the innocent expression I had tried, but failed, to imitate. "I understand that most of the guests present at the Tremaines' party Saturday night have been questioned about Mr. Logan's death. I know the police have visited our father. Have they, er, interviewed you, Reverend Mayfield?"

Again, the minister's face colored slightly, but after a moment he slowly nodded his head. "Yes, the police have been here to see me, although I fail to understand how they can suspect one of us of such a heinous crime. Obviously, those unfortunate young men were victims of robberies gone terribly awry. It is my understanding that gangs of Chinese highbinders have been known to roam the area surrounding the Cut. That is where the police should concentrate their search, instead of wasting their time on decent, law-abiding citizens. Particularly members of the clergy," he added, looking affronted.

"Yes," Samuel solemnly agreed, "I can understand your feelings. It is a great tragedy. Deacon Hume's death must have caused his fiancée great pain."

"His fiancée?" Mayfield regarded my brother in surprise. "I know of no fiancée, Mr. Woolson. Indeed, I had long encouraged Dieter to find a nice young woman and settle down—it is by far the best situation for a young man entering the church. I myself was married for nearly thirty years when my poor wife, Ada, passed on. Unfortunately, Dieter did not appear interested." He paused. "Although of late—"

"Yes, Reverend Mayfield?" Samuel prompted. "You felt he was revising his views on matrimony?"

"It was no more than a vague feeling," the rector replied, looking uncomfortable. It was clear he felt that he had spoken out of turn. "I simply received the impression that Dieter was softening in his views concerning the married state. I wondered if perhaps he had found some woman in particular."

He placed his cup and saucer on the table and got to his feet. Judging by his weary expression, I was certain we had at last exhausted the man's patience. "I do not wish to appear rude, Mr. Woolson, Miss Woolson, but there are pressing matters which require my attention."

Samuel and I immediately put down our own coffee cups and stood.

"Of course, Reverend Mayfield," I said. "We have taken up entirely too much of your time as it is."

"Yes, I apologize," Samuel added, smiling a bit sheepishly. "I fear that we have presumed on your kind hospitality. It's just that Mr. Hume's tragic death—and Mr. Logan's, of course—have profoundly affected us all, especially those of us who reside on Rincon Hill."

"They have, they have," Mayfield said, nodding somberly. "It has been most distressing. I fear it will be difficult to calm my congregation. Mr. Logan's death was unfortunate, but their own deacon! That strikes all too close to home. Yes, the ladies will be most distraught. And fearful, of course. I will have to address the tragedy in Sunday's sermon, although what I can say to reassure my flock . . ." His voice trailed off and he once again used the handkerchief to mop his brow. "But then it is all in God's hands, we must remember that. Somehow we shall overcome."

He led us to the rectory door. "Thank you for taking the time to visit this morning, Miss Woolson, Mr. Woolson. Let us pray that the police will quickly apprehend the villain who has committed these monstrous crimes."

What do you make of the Reverend Mayfield?" Samuel asked, as we headed back to the carriage.

"I can't imagine him as a murderer, if that's what you're thinking," I replied. "Clearly he wasn't particularly fond of his deacon, but I hardly think that would induce him to beat the young man over the head with a two-by-four."

Samuel chuckled. "No, I have a hard time envisioning that as well. To be honest, George didn't seem overly taken with the idea, either. I suspect that police interest in the good rector indicates how desperate they are to make an arrest."

"Very probably. But why suspect the Reverend Mayfield more than the other guests at the Tremaines' party? Any one of them could have killed Nigel Logan, and conceivably Deacon Hume."

We had reached the brougham, only to find no sign of Eddie, either on the driver's seat or inside the carriage. As I looked up and down the block to see where he might have run off to, I spied a short, pudgy-looking man with a brown cap pulled low over his forehead, watching us from across the street.

"Samuel," I said, keeping my voice quiet. "Don't look now, but isn't that Ozzie Foldger of the *Tattler* over there, half hidden by that tree?"

Making a show of searching for Eddie, Samuel darted a discreet peek at the man across the way. "That looks like him, all right. What do you suppose he's doing here?"

"More than likely, he's trying to scoop you on the Deacon Hume story." I gave a low laugh. "He can't be happy to see that you beat him to it."

"I doubt it will bother him one iota. When he can't get access to the facts, Ozzie has the habit of making his stories up out of whole cloth."

Hearing the sound of running feet behind us, we turned to see Eddie all but flying across the lawn that divided the church from the rectory. He held his left hand behind his back, his eyes alight with excitement.

"I've been doin' some investigatin' on my own," he announced proudly, if a bit out of breath.

Screwing his eyes into a suspicious squint, he melodramatically peered up one side of the street and down the other. My eyes immediately flew to where Ozzie Foldger had been standing only a moment before, but to my surprise he was no longer there. Several carriages were passing by on Howard Street, but both sides of the block were devoid of foot traffic.

"Look what I found," Eddie continued in an exaggerated whisper. Moving closer, he brought his left hand out from behind his back. Tightly clutched inside it were several dog-eared magazines, all of them bearing extremely lurid covers. "Don't this beat all?" He looked up at my brother as if he had discovered a secret treasure. "They're even better than the *Police Gazette*!"

"Eddie, where did you get these?" I demanded, averting my eyes from the sight of the scantily clad, and crudely posed, women.

The boy flushed, as he suddenly realized the inappropriateness of his plunder. "Oh, ah, sorry, Miss Sarah," he stammered. "I didn't mean to—that is, I—"

"Never mind that, Eddie," Samuel put in. "Where did you find these magazines?"

"That's just it," the boy answered eagerly. "I found them in that feller's room what got himself bashed in. You know, the dealer bloke."

"Do you mean Deacon Hume?" I asked, regarding the boy in disbelief. "How do you know it was his room? And what were you doing there?"

The lad had the good grace to look ashamed. "I seen his name in the newspaper, and there was some mail addressed to him lyin' on a table." He shifted from one foot to another. "I didn't do nothin' wrong, at least I didn't mean to. I was waitin' with the carriage like you said, when I seen this dog chasin' a cat hell to split behind them trees over there. I thought I'd just take a look to see if the dog got the cat or not, when I heard this really pitiful cryin' comin' from inside a little house behind the church." He paused in his narrative to give me a guilty look.

"Well?" Samuel prompted. "What did you do then?"

"I, ah, well, the door weren't locked, so I peeked inside, you know, just to see if someone was hurt and needed help. The noise was comin' from a box under the bed." His face brightened. "It was full of kittens, tiny little things all crawlin' over each other, and cryin' for their ma. I went to pick one up, and it was then I saw the magazines. I just took a few to show you, Mr. Samuel. There's a lot more under the bed if you want me to get 'em."

"No, Eddie," I said, before he could run off. I caught my brother's eye and knew we were both thinking the same thing. Pornography constituted strange reading material for a young man soon to be ordained a church minister.

"I should probably give these to George," Samuel said, taking the magazines from Eddie, who reluctantly turned over his booty. "They may have nothing to do with the case, but he should be told."

"Can I have 'em back when the copper is finished with them?" the boy asked hopefully.

"Certainly not!" I was so nonplussed by the lad's discovery that I forgot to remind Eddie to hand me properly into the brougham. Stepping in unaided, I directed the boy to drive us back to my office.

As we rode, Samuel and I discussed what we had learned about the late Dieter Hume.

"Considering his controversial beliefs and disgusting reading material, Hume appears to have been an unlikely candidate for the ministry," I said, grasping hold of the seat as Eddie took a corner so fast that I was sure only two wheels were making contact with the ground. Samuel shouted for the boy to slow down, but if Eddie heard my brother, he paid him no mind. Perhaps, I thought, he was still disgruntled because Samuel had appropriated his pilfered reading material.

"I wonder if the Reverend Mayfield was aware of his deacon's interest in pornography?" Samuel asked.

After racing through the streets, our carriage had now come to a virtual standstill due to heavy lunch-hour traffic. Frankly, I did not mind. It was a relief to be able to catch our breaths, before Eddie once again gave vent to his passion for speed.

"I doubt it," I said, trying not to look at the magazines my brother was holding on his lap. "The Reverend Mayfield does not strike me as the sort of man who would ignore such a weakness in a young man under his supervision. If he did somehow find out, surely he would have confronted Hume and put an immediate stop to it, or else reported his findings to the bishop."

Samuel nodded in silent agreement. We were once again moving, albeit slowly, and I very nearly slid into his lap as a coal-box buggy came precariously close to broadsiding us. The driver shook his fist and shouted out an obscenity, but was forced to take his place behind us when Eddie refused to give way.

"Traffic in this city is becoming downright hazardous," my brother exclaimed. "Most of the streets are too narrow, and we could go swimming in some of these potholes. Yet City Hall refuses to allot any real money to rectify the situation."

"I understand a citizens' committee has been formed to address the problem," I said.

"That may be, but I give it little chance of success. Ah, well, I suppose we should look on the bright side. Eddie may drive like a speed demon, but he seems miraculously adept at avoiding pedestrians or colliding with other vehicles."

"You say that because your own driving is almost as harrowing as his," I said with a smile.

I fell silent as I spied a young woman pushing a baby in a pram. It immediately reminded me of Brielle Bouchard.

"What's wrong, Sarah? You look worried."

"I'm concerned about the young woman who visited my office a couple of days ago," I told him. "Although since she failed to keep her appointment with me this morning, I'm not sure I can honestly count her as a client."

His eyebrows rose with interest. "If that's the case, then you're no longer bound to keep the details of that visit confidential."

"That's painting the situation in rather broad strokes," I told him, still reluctant to break client confidentiality, but even more reluctant to let the matter go without seeking his advice. "Frankly, Samuel, I'd be grateful for your help."

Briefly, I told him the details concerning Brielle's visit to my office that I had originally left out. When I identified the girl's lover, Samuel whistled softly between his teeth.

"Well, well. So Mr. Righteous Morality himself is that young girl's lover."

"*Was* her lover," I corrected.

"All right, was. The fact remains that the man is a complete hypocrite. I've sold articles to that bounder, and he's actually forced me to rewrite portions to suit his newspaper's rigid rules of respectability. 'We must not offend our readers' is one of his favorite justifications for chopping up a story. And all the while he was seducing a seventeen-year-old girl. What a charlatan!"

I nodded in agreement. "The problem now is, what should I do? If she had failed to keep this morning's appointment of her own volition, I would let the matter go. But after hearing about the men who waylaid her outside my office, I can't help but be anxious for her safety."

"I gather you'd like me to look into the situation?"

I smiled. "I would appreciate it, Samuel. I know so little about her: where she comes from, if she has family, or even where she went after Gerald Knight threw her out onto the street. I won't rest comfortably until I can be certain that she and her baby are all right."

He squeezed my hand reassuringly. "Don't worry, Sarah. I will see what I can find out tomorrow. No promises, mind you, but I'll do my best."

"Thank you, Samuel," I said, squeezing his hand in return. "I knew I could count on you."

He had Eddie drop me off in front of my office, then instructed the boy to take him to an appointment across town. After I alighted from the brougham, I was unnerved to see newsboys hawking their papers to shouts of: *"Second Death on Rincon Hill,"* and *"Chinese Devils Loose on Rincon Hill!"*

This last cry stopped me in my tracks. Hurrying to the corner, I purchased a paper from one of the boys and stared at the headline: POLICE SEARCH CHINATOWN FOR RINCON HILL KILLER!

I hastily scanned the front-page article, anxious to see whether the police were seriously considering this theory, or if the newspapers had once again singled out the Chinese as handy scapegoats. It was true, as Papa pointed out, that the Chinese often used the Second Street Cut as an early-morning shortcut to waterfront warehouses which lay just beyond Rincon Hill. This had occasionally precipitated violence, but it was always directed at the Chinese, who were resented by other immigrants for their hard work and willingness to accept lower wages. Could Papa be right in suggesting that members of the Chinese community had finally decided it was time to retaliate?

I wondered if Li Ying had seen today's newspapers. If so, how would he react to this latest accusation levied against members of his community? True, he was one of the district's most powerful tong lords, but I also knew him to be a man of integrity who genuinely cared about the welfare of his people.

And if he did know, what could he do? Would he be powerful enough to protect his countrymen from what might very well develop into a lynch mob?

CHAPTER EIGHT

For once I was relieved when it was time to leave my office for the day. I was so troubled by what the newspapers were saying about Nigel Logan's and Deacon Hume's deaths, I found it all but impossible to concentrate on Robert's paperwork. Moreover, Celia had invited the Reginald Tremaines to dine at our house that evening. Although I was not in a party mood I had promised her that I would attend, as had Samuel, which was a testament to our sister-in-law's gentle powers of persuasion.

To be honest, I admit that I was curious to learn more about the Tremaines, whom I was acquainted with only casually through the Church of Our Savior. I was especially interested in the family since their dinner in the Reverend Mayfield's honor, the previous Saturday night, seemed to feature so prominently in the violent deaths of two men.

According to my sister-in-law, who had grown to know the Tremaines well, the entire family would be present tonight, apart from the two youngest children from Mr. Tremaine's second marriage. This included Reginald Tremaine, his wife, Faith, his elderly father, Major Zachariah Tremaine—who made his home with the couple—as well as Mr. Tremaine's older children from his first marriage, seventeen-year-old twins, Melody and David.

I enjoyed watching Celia act the role of hostess that evening. As I have often mentioned, she is one of the most loving and thoughtful women I know. I could well understand how she and Faith Tremaine had become such fast friends, given that they both had small children and served together on several church committees.

Although Mrs. Tremaine was but two years older than me, it was not surprising that we remained but casual acquaintances. Our lives were simply too dissimilar to encourage a more intimate friendship. She was a married woman with four children—if one counted the twins by her husband's first marriage—while I had chosen to remain a spinster and seek my livelihood in a man's profession. I sensed that she regarded me in silent disapproval which, as I say, was not altogether unexpected.

Actually, I reflected, as our little Irish maid Ina Corks served the soup course, most of my girlhood companions had drifted away since marriage, and our friendships had suffered by consequence. Not only did we share little in common, but San Francisco society strongly censured any woman improvident enough to choose a career over so-called domestic bliss. Few women were crass enough to say it to my face, but I knew well enough what was tittle-tattled behind my back. My mother was generally pitied because her only daughter seemed so determined to remain single. The fact that I had become—horror of horrors!—a *lawyer* merely added grist to the ever-flourishing gossip mill.

As I sipped Cook's excellent clam chowder, I allowed myself to study our guests. Reginald Tremaine was a handsome man who looked to be in his late forties. He was a great deal taller than his wife, and his slender physique was only beginning to take on a slight paunch. I admired the thick head of curly brown hair which he wore parted down the center. A neatly trimmed brown mustache, which showed only a light sprinkling of gray, lay beneath a long Roman nose. His eyes were hazel, and twinkled good-naturedly.

Faith Tremaine was a small woman, barely five feet tall, and possessed the fragile beauty which, I've noticed, most men can't resist pampering. That evening, her pale, strawberry-blond hair was gathered into a neat chignon atop her head, and her light green dress very nearly matched the color of her eyes. I thought her to be a pleasant, if sometimes opinionated, woman who appeared to be a devoted mother and generous volunteer at her church.

Reginald's father, Zachariah Tremaine, was a former army major who had served in the Mexican-American War, and later in the American Civil War. He was a distinguished-looking gentleman, tall and slender and somewhere in his mid-seventies. Although he was many years retired, he still carried himself with military erectness. He had a thick white mustache, bushy white eyebrows, and a full head of longish gray hair. Despite his military demeanor, however, he was a cheerful man who laughed easily and treated everyone with polite respect.

I deduced from the affectionate way he interacted with his seventeen-year-old grandchildren that he was particularly fond of the twins. Judging from the way they remained close to him throughout the evening—one twin sitting to either side of the elderly gentleman at the dinner table—it was obvious that they fully reciprocated this affection.

My eyes drifted to Melody and her brother David. The boy was tall and quite handsome, but his sister was nothing short of stunning. She had a slightly upturned nose and the fair, milk-and-honey skin which was currently much sought after by women of all ages. Her lips were full and tinted a deep natural pink, her cheeks had a rosy glow, and the delicate bones of her face were gracefully sculpted. To say that her hair was brown would do it an injustice; highlights in the thick, lustrous strands more closely resembled the tawny rays of a setting sun. Tonight it was pulled back from her oval face and gathered at the crown with a ribbon, from there to cascade down her back in a flurry of curls. Her very feminine gown of shaded blue lampas brought out the sky-blue color of her eyes, which were framed by long fans of dark lashes. The simple lines of the bodice emphasized the gentle swell of the girl's bosom, and displayed her tiny waist to good advantage.

Her twin brother David shared his sister's lovely blue eyes and fair coloring. His amber-brown hair was also thick, and had a tendency to curl. He was nearly his father's height, quite slender, and shared the older man's classically handsome bone structure. Where Reginald was animated and outgoing, however, his son was reticent and not inclined to join in the dinner conversation, although he seemed to be following it with quiet attention.

I, too, said little as I ate my food, allowing the others to carry on with their more or less mundane discussion concerning the rapidly approaching Christmas holidays, the party we would be hosting the following week, and the unusual amount of rain we had been experiencing of late. Papa—who loved nothing better than a lively dialogue involving politics or other controversial subjects at mealtimes—was obviously on his best behavior, no doubt thanks to Mama's strict admonitions. I noticed that she kept darting furtive looks in his direction, as if fearing this uncommonly polite behavior might evaporate at any moment.

Actually, I wished Papa would ignore whatever promise he had made Mama, and bring up the Tremaines' party, and the part, if any, it played in the subsequent murders. When I saw from his pained expression that this was not going to happen, I decided it was up to me to ask the questions in his stead. Before I could decide how to broach the topic, however, Samuel jumped in ahead of me.

"Mr. Logan's death last Saturday night was certainly tragic," he said, directing the question primarily to Reginald Tremaine. "I was wondering if you knew whether the police are any closer to apprehending the culprit?"

My brother had once again composed his features into an expression of admirable innocence. Since I knew that George Lewis had been put in charge of the investigation, and kept him updated on how the police were progressing, Samuel's question—along with his blameless air—made it difficult for me not to laugh.

Talk at the table suddenly ceased. Everyone regarded him as if he had suddenly released a basket of snakes onto the dinner table.

Everyone, that is, except Papa. My father was practically rubbing his hands together in glee at this unexpected upturn in the conversation, especially since he had not been the one to initiate it.

"Samuel, please," protested Mama, looking mortified. "This is hardly the proper time or place to bring up such a distressing subject."

Reginald Tremaine raised his hand as if to dismiss Mama's objections. "Please do not distress yourself, Mrs. Woolson. Your son's question is understandable. The city's newspapers have talked of little else since poor Mr. Logan was attacked. Unfortunately, I cannot think who might have committed such a vile act. I can only surmise that it was a robbery gone wrong. It is impossible for me to imagine that the young man had any enemies, at least none who might wish to do him bodily harm."

"You knew Mr. Logan well, then, Mr. Tremaine?" Samuel persisted, ignoring Mama's disapproving expression.

"I would not describe our friendship as close," the clothier answered. "Mrs. Tremaine and I became acquainted with the gentleman through our church, which he occasionally attended. Although why he did so, I am at a loss to understand, since he was something of a rogue in his religious beliefs."

Samuel looked surprised. "Given Logan's unorthodox opinions, I'm surprised you invited him to a party in honor of the Reverend Mayfield who, I understand, adheres strictly to church doctrine."

Reginald Tremaine appeared momentarily confused, as if even he was unsure why Nigel Logan had been invited. He turned questioningly to his wife.

"Mr. Logan was a good friend of Dieter Hume's, our church deacon," Faith explained. "Naturally, before extending the invitation, I brought the subject up with the Reverend Mayfield, but he expressed no objections to the young man attending."

"Was the Reverend Mayfield acquainted with Logan's views on Charles Darwin's *Origin of Species*?" Samuel inquired.

Before Mrs. Tremaine could answer, Mama broke in, darting

furious glances at her youngest son. "Samuel, please. You are annoying our guests with all these unsuitable questions."

Once again Reginald Tremaine appeared to brush off my mother's objections. Chuckling, he said, "Yes, the Reverend Mayfield certainly was aware of Mr. Logan's views on the subject. The two were always going on about those silly books. Actually, I think they rather enjoyed the bickering. Nigel was very serious about his work in the field of biology, and of course we all know the dim view the church has taken of Darwin's controversial theories." He gave a deprecating smile. "I fear I find all the sciences incomprehensible, so I am unable to describe Logan's studies in more detail."

"His work was in the field of biogenesis," his son David put in. Since this was the first time the boy had ventured into the dinner conversation, we all regarded him in surprise. He flushed self-consciously, then clarified, "Mr. Logan was particularly studying the microbic origin of infectious disease."

Although Major Tremaine beamed at his grandson with undisguised pride, the only one present who seemed to comprehend this explanation was my brother Charles, who is a physician.

"That's correct," he confirmed. "Nigel was studying the protozoal parasites of animals. Malaria, as I'm sure some of you know, is of protozoal origin, as are certain forms of dysentery and syphilis. Nigel and I enjoyed a number of interesting conversations on the subject."

My mother, Celia, and Mrs. Tremaine had blanched at the mention of this last disease. Realizing too late the inappropriate nature of his remarks, Charles mumbled an apology and lowered his head to concentrate on his braised beef and steamed clams.

"Of course," David added, seemingly oblivious to the ladies' discomfort, "one must ask how an infectious disease originates in the first place. The parasite lives in or on its host. In that limited habitat, its organs are lost and it becomes degenerate. That was one of the mysteries Mr. Logan was attempting to solve, or at least to observe in a clearer and more impartial light."

Once again there was utter silence at the table. Papa and Major

Tremaine were smiling broadly, while the women stared at the boy with a mixture of confusion and consternation. Samuel gave me a sly wink and Charles cleared his throat. Was he trying to warn the lad? I wondered.

Reginald Tremaine eyed David unhappily. "I must apologize for my son. He has a passion for studying any plant, insect, bird, or rodent that crosses his path. He has made up his mind to be a scientist. I have tried to make him listen to reason and come to work at my Men's Emporium, but sadly, he would prefer to sit in his room dissecting bugs."

He sighed, then gave a dry chuckle. "Children today—they have no concept of what is required to earn a living for one's family. Fortunately, my younger son, Reginald, Junior, has indicated his desire to take over the Emporium one day."

"Come now, Reginald," Major Tremaine told his son. "You are being too hard on David. He has a fine brain and an active curiosity. Most importantly, he has the determination to study and learn. He may not be suited for managing your store, but I believe he will make a fine life for himself in the field of science, which is the coming thing, you know."

Faith Tremaine was eyeing her father-in-law with displeasure. "Nonsense, Father Tremaine, what Reginald says is nothing less than the truth. David has his head in the clouds. I fear he will come to regret that he did not listen to his father. Fortunately, young Reggie has a practical head on his shoulders. He will make a splendid manager."

A wounded look flitted across David's handsome face, but was quickly gone. The major eyed his grandson sympathetically, while the boy's father and stepmother seemed oblivious to his feelings.

Faith smiled at her stepdaughter. "And this dear girl loves nothing better than to sing the day away." She gave a high little laugh. "Can you imagine, she has gone so far as to indicate that she would like a career on the stage! Quite out of the question, of course."

"The child has a lovely voice," her father-in-law put in, smiling fondly at Melody. "Surely it is only natural for a young girl to dream. She has been blessed with beauty and genuine talent, a formidable recipe for success."

"Dreams do not settle a girl with a good husband, Father Tremaine," Faith protested. "She and David will be eighteen next June. It is high time she accepted the reality of her future. Unfortunately, she insists on having nothing to do with gentlemen callers, and takes to her room if I dare suggest she attend a ball. I have done my best to introduce her to society, but it has been disastrously unsuccessful."

She smiled tightly at Melody, who was staring fixedly at her plate, her full lips pulled into a thin line of silent mortification. "She possesses a great many admirers, but she will have none of it. I swan, I simply cannot understand the girl."

"I can remember how frightened I was when I first came out," Celia said, bestowing a kind smile upon the young woman. "I'm sure my mother despaired of me. But I eventually came around. Melody is only seventeen; this must be a bit overwhelming for her. I'm certain that given a little time, she'll become more at ease in strange company."

Melody gave my sister-in-law a grateful smile. Celia possessed such compassion and empathy; I constantly admire her easy ability to mother her own three children. And I, too, sympathized with the girl. I had resisted my own mother's efforts to establish me in San Francisco society. The gatherings Mama insisted I attend meant endless hours of boredom, the conversations invariably revolving around the latest fashions, or which gentleman was currently paying court to which young lady. My goals in life had been established early, and even at that age I had refused to wander off my chosen path.

I wondered if this could be the case with Melody. Although she had hardly spoken all evening, I suspected there were multiple layers of emotion hidden beneath that lovely exterior. At present, she appeared to be working extremely hard to keep them all in check. How sad that the girl had lost her mother at such a tender age. Faith Tremaine might mean well, but it was evident that she possessed no genuine understanding of her beautiful stepdaughter's true temperament and aspirations.

"I fear that your sympathies are misplaced, Mrs. Woolson," the woman told Celia. "I have ensured that Melody is trained in all aspects of housewifely duties. She has proven to be an apt, if unenthusiastic, student. As I said, she is very nearly eighteen, and I have quite made up my mind that it is time for her to marry and establish a home of her own. I assure you that I have only her best interests at heart."

I caught my mother's quick intake of breath, and her hasty glance in my direction. It was not difficult to deduce her thoughts. I had passed this courting milestone ten years ago, yet to her chagrin I appeared no closer to entering the married state than when I'd been Melody's age. As always when this sensitive subject reared its painful head, I felt a wave of guilt and regret that I continued to cause my dear mother so much anguish.

Mrs. Tremaine smiled at her husband, as if seeking his approval that she had performed her duty with his eldest daughter. He did not disappoint, but returned her smile and gave her hand a gentle pat.

"Melody could not do better than to follow my dear wife's example," he said fondly. "She is devoted to my two elder children. Indeed, she has raised them as if they were her own. They could not have been blessed with a more dutiful stepmother."

Major Tremaine coughed gently into his napkin, but held his tongue. Faith beamed at her husband's praise. David seemed about to open his mouth to speak, but in the end remained silent. Only his clear blue eyes—bright with the dissent he evidently did not feel free to express—betrayed his true feelings. It was impossible to read Melody's reaction, since she kept her head lowered, as if preoccupied with her dinner, although it was clear she was merely playing with her food.

Since neither Samuel nor I felt inclined to pursue our inquiries into Mr. Logan's death, subsequent conversation continued at a rather desultory pace, boring everyone, I was sure, but at least not causing Mama further concern.

Once the interminable meal finally came to a welcome conclusion, the women excused themselves from the table, and the men enjoyed their after-dinner brandy and cigars. However, even in the front parlor, Mama's polite attempts to make casual conversation held little interest for me.

In fact, I was mulling over possible excuses for retreating to my room, when the men rejoined us and Melody was coaxed by Mama and Major Tremaine into taking a seat at our piano and entertaining us with a song or two. Blushing attractively, the girl nonetheless did as she was bidden, selecting several songs from Gilbert and Sullivan's popular opera *H.M.S. Pinafore,* which had enjoyed its first major San Francisco production at the Tivoli Opera House two years before.

Although after-dinner recitals were virtually de rigueur, I must admit that I've not always been an eager spectator. I have sat through more of these impromptu recitals than I care to remember, some of which have required the patience of Job to endure.

Which was why it came as such a delightful surprise to realize that Melody Tremaine's musical talents were far and away above average. Major Tremaine had not exaggerated when he claimed she possessed a gifted singing voice—amazingly rich and melodious. Moreover, she accompanied herself on the piano with a sensitive, deft touch, her attention rarely focusing on her slender fingers as they danced lightly over the keys.

She seemed, in fact, to have entered a world of her own; the expression on her face was one of angelic delight. Her lovely blue eyes shone with an inner bliss, as if now that she had been given the opportunity to display her talents, she could truly come alive. I stole a surreptitious glance at her grandfather and found him glowing with approval, his foot tapping out the beat of the music.

My gaze moved to Faith Tremaine, to find that she was not even watching the stepdaughter. Rather, her head was bent as she played with the folds of her gown, smoothing the pale green silk with short, slender fingers.

At the conclusion of Melody's first piece, Faith looked up,

smiled, and added her applause to that of the rest of the party. Still, I thought her attitude toward the girl was a bit perfunctory, as if she had little interest in her stepdaughter's undeniable musical abilities.

Looking toward the girl's brother, I was touched to see David regarding his sister with unselfconscious pride and love. Their profiles were very similar, I thought, admiring the boy's straight nose which, like Melody's, turned up just a bit at the tip, and the full, sensitive mouth which was presently curved into an admiring smile. Along David's still boyish jawline, I could detect the barest shadow of a beard. The lad would soon be a man, I thought. And a very handsome one at that.

It was apparent that brother and sister were very close, which was hardly surprising considering how much they'd been through together during their short lives. How fortunate they were to have each other, I mused. My own childhood had been loving and nurturing, yet there was so much I might have missed if it had not been for Samuel. According to our parents, we had frequently behaved like little terrors, yet what wonderful adventures we had shared! Even today, the best part of our relationship was the ability to be totally honest with one another. This must be the sort of bond that Melody and David shared.

These thoughts of my brother caused me to glance in his direction. He had been watching Melody as avidly as everyone else in the room. However, sensing my gaze, he turned and mouthed, "She is gorgeous!"

I nodded my agreement. I knew my brother well enough to guess that he was regretting the fact that she was so young. In truth, a man would have to be blind not to take notice of Melody Tremaine's striking beauty. I could well believe Faith Tremaine when she spoke of Melody's many gentlemen admirers!

When the girl concluded her performance, everyone broke into enthusiastic applause. Melody seemed not to hear. She sat very still for several minutes, her lovely eyes fixed upon the keyboard, almost as if she were in some kind of trance. When she finally returned to the present, she smiled happily, her face flushed, her clear skin glowing. Rising with a little bow from the piano bench, she hurried to take a seat beside her brother on the settee. His look said far better than words how much he had enjoyed her performance.

"My dear, that was marvelous," Mama gushed, rising from her own chair to take the girl's hands. "You are remarkable, absolutely remarkable!"

"That is how she came by her name, you know," the girl's father announced. "She was born Irene, but as soon as the first glorious notes issued from her throat, her mother began calling her Melody. My first wife, Mary, God rest her soul, had a lovely singing voice. And the most beautiful clear blue eyes. That is where the twins get their unusual eye color, not from me, I'm afraid."

He laughed, then went on as if picturing the scene in his mind's eye. "Ah, yes, I well remember the way Melody and her mother filled our home with laughter and song, just like two beautiful songbirds." I was surprised to see tears glistening in the man's eyes. "We are very proud of our girl, aren't we, Faith?"

His wife returned his smile with a rather stiff one of her own, and I guessed she did not appreciate this reference to her husband's late wife. However, she dutifully nodded her approval to the girl, then leaned over to give her a light peck on the cheek. "Yes, of course. We were delighted by your performance, my dear."

"I am the most fortunate of men," Reginald declared with pride. "Four lovely children and the most devoted wife any man could wish for. Yes, I am very lucky indeed."

He stood and raised the snifter of brandy he had brought in from the dining room. "A toast, everyone. To my dear Faith's thirtieth birthday. May she enjoy many more."

CHAPTER NINE

Arriving at my office the next morning, I completed what remained of Robert's work, even though I was aware he might not collect it until the following day. It would depend, of course, on how long he would be forced to act as Joseph Shepard's second chair at court. It is not, however, my custom to put off until tomorrow what I could do today. As Edward Young wrote in *Night Thoughts,* "Procrastination is the thief of time."

When my desk was clear, I spent a restless hour pacing the back room of my office, or my library, as I preferred to call it. I believe I have mentioned that I'd been able to add only a dozen or so volumes to the shelves my brother Charles had constructed for me, but I had promised myself that I would purchase one new book for every case I was able to bring to a successful conclusion. This vow never failed to lift my spirits.

In truth, I believe my restiveness was caused by the secret hope that Brielle Bouchard might yet keep her appointment with me. As I'd told Samuel, I could not help but worry about the girl and her small baby. How was she to manage, so young and so alone, in this hectic and self-absorbed city? What had those two men said to her the previous morning to cause her to run off like a frightened rabbit? Was she in physical danger? And where was she staying now that her lover had cruelly ejected her from his house?

From Brielle, my thoughts went to the two violent deaths that had occurred so frighteningly close to our home. Because I could not shake the fear that the killer might strike yet a third time, I tried to settle my thoughts and focus on what little was known about the cases. Assuming we were correct that the two crimes were connected, the most obvious link between them had to be Nigel Logan and Dieter Hume's friendship, a relationship which continued despite the divergent paths the men had followed after their university days. Surely this suggested that the motive was of a personal rather than a professional nature. But what might that motive be?

To answer this, I attempted to list the interests and beliefs the men held in common. Did their mutual acceptance of Charles Darwin's theories on natural selection, for instance, play a role in their deaths? Could someone feel so threatened by this hypothesis, that he would brutally take the lives of two men?

What other similarities might they have shared? Because of Eddie's recent adventure playing detective, we were aware that the deacon had a secret interest in pornography, but there was nothing to suggest that Logan was also taken by this fetish. The men had attended university together, and neither was married. Were either of these commonalities significant? According to the Reverend Mayfield, Deacon Hume had shown a recent interest in taking a wife. I couldn't recall anyone mentioning if Nigel Logan was seeing a woman, or if he had plans to marry.

This exercise was futile. I simply did not know enough about the victims' private lives to hazard a guess as to why they had been murdered. I wondered how thoroughly the police were looking into Logan's and Hume's pasts. Surely that was of primary importance in finding the killer.

When noon arrived I gave up on fruitless speculation and decided I would take my lunch in a small Italian restaurant located in the next block. To my surprise, as I was locking my office door Samuel came darting up the stairs.

"Good," he said a bit out of breath. "I'm glad I caught you. I'm leaving this afternoon to spend the weekend with the Talbots in Menlo Park. But first I wanted to deliver my report concerning your new client. Do you have time for a quick lunch?"

"As a matter of fact, that's exactly where I was going," I told him. "I'm delighted you'll be able to join me."

We settled upon the restaurant I'd had in mind, and were lucky to find a table, since the eatery was very popular at this time of day.

"I can't believe you have news of Miss Bouchard so soon," I said while we awaited our orders.

"Never underestimate the power of a newsman's nose, my dear sister," he said, tapping this appendage with a forefinger.

"So, what can you tell me?"

"Not as much as I would like, although I think I've made a good start. I spoke to a maid who works at the Pacific Avenue house Gerald Knight reserves for his paramours. It seems that the girl was fond of Brielle, and felt sorry for her when Knight ended their relationship and sent her packing."

I experienced a flicker of hope. "Does the maid know where Brielle went after she was forced to leave?"

"She claims she doesn't." At my expression of disappointment, he hurried on. "However, she thinks it's possible she may have gone to live with a Madam Valentine, who operates a parlor house for the upper crust on Montgomery Street, near Pacific Avenue."

"Whatever makes her think that?"

"According to the maid, Madam Valentine came to see Brielle several times while the girl was living with Knight, and was recognized by one of the servants."

I frowned, remembering something Brielle said when she came to my office on Monday morning. "That's strange. Miss Bouchard assured me that she was an innocent when she commenced her relationship with Gerald Knight. Indeed, she was only seventeen."

Samuel gave a grim little laugh. "That isn't so young when it comes to prostitution, Sarah. Some girls are barely fourteen or fifteen when circumstances force them into that trade."

"I'm painfully aware of the tender age at which some girls are forced into white slavery," I said grimly.

"Yes, of course," said Samuel, looking a bit abashed. "I'd forgotten your wild midnight raid with Miss Culbertson of the Presbyterian Rescue Mission last year. But what makes you think Brielle Bouchard was telling you the truth? She might well claim she was an innocent to present herself in a more sympathetic light."

"It's possible, of course, but somehow I believe her. In fact, I was astonished by how frankly she discussed her situation. She is obviously well bred, yet she made no excuses for her present predicament. She claimed that her sole reason for consulting me was to seek justice for her child." I hesitated, not sure how to explain the impression I had formed of Miss Bouchard. "I don't know, Samuel. It's one thing to imagine her as the mistress of a prominent businessman. It's quite another matter to think of her living in a brothel!"

I was interrupted by the waiter delivering our entrees. When he left, Samuel said, "Don't look so stricken, Sarah. As these places go, Madam Valentine's is one of the more fashionable establishments."

"Being fashionable does not alter the nature of its business. I just find it difficult to understand why she would agree to live in such a place—even the kind of parlor house you have described. And with her baby!"

"Has it occurred to you that she might have nowhere else to go?" Samuel said, his tone challenging. "If, as you say, she was evicted from Gerald Knight's home when he discovered she was pregnant, the poor girl might well have considered a high-class brothel a great deal more attractive than living on the street. Where, I might add, many of these women end up when their beauty fades and they've outlived their usefulness."

"But Brielle is only nineteen," I protested. "And she's extremely lovely."

Naturally, I was aware that places such as Madam Valentine's parlor house existed in San Francisco. Nay, I knew that they thrived in our city and had since the forty-niners first landed on its shores. I did not advertise the fact, but I had even visited one during the Nob Hill murders, although admittedly I did not actually enter the establishment. I could not, however, keep from wondering what this said about our society when, in order to avoid the poorhouse, innocent young girls were often forced into such a life.

"If what you suspect is true, it's no wonder Brielle refused to tell me where she was living," I said, toying with my plate of lasagna. It smelled delicious, but I seemed to have lost my appetite. "From a grand house, jewels, fine clothes, and a seemingly devoted lover, to a—"

"Life of a common prostitute," Samuel finished for me. "I understand what you're saying, Sarah. However, you must understand that not all girls who end up in such places have been forced into the business, nor are they there simply to ensure a roof over their heads. Some choose the life because it pays a good deal better than being a domestic servant or a seamstress—especially in quality houses like Madam Valentine's."

"You paint a pretty picture, Samuel," I commented, not bothering to hide my skepticism. "But I still have a hard time imagining why any woman would willingly choose such a life for herself."

"Of course it isn't all pretty," he said, swallowing a bite of his spaghetti. "I didn't mean to imply that it was. Many, perhaps most, of the houses in town are unclean, often violent, and treat their girls little better than slaves. I'm merely pointing out that a few of them, like Madam Valentine's residence, are held to higher standards. . Take my word for it, Sarah, you will not be welcomed with open arms if, for the women's sakes, you attempt to close them down."

"I understand what you're trying to tell me, even if I don't like it. The important thing now is to establish if Brielle has actually gone to stay with this Madam Valentine."

"Of course it is. Unfortunately, I didn't have time this morning, but I promise to look into it when I return to town on Monday."

"Not until Monday?" My heart sank. "Is there no way you can postpone your trip until tonight? Or even tomorrow morning?"

"I'm to ride in the Talbots' carriage, Sarah, and there is to be a dinner party tonight that I really can't miss. One or two members of the jury who overturned Laura Fair's conviction will be there, as well as several reporters who covered both trials."

"And you hope they'll be able to provide you with valuable information for your book," I said with a sigh of acceptance.

Samuel was referring to the book he had recently commenced writing, revisiting famous murders, robberies, and mayhem committed in and around San Francisco since the days of the Gold Rush. He planned to include Laura Fair's case, which captured headlines some ten years earlier when she fatally shot her married lover, Alexander P. Crittenden, a member of the California bar and recording secretary of the State Supreme Court. Laura Fair's first trial concluded with her being found guilty and sentenced to death by hanging. Her second trial, held shortly thereafter, ended in her acquittal, a reversal which caused a torrent of outrage and disgust throughout the city.

He had stopped eating his pasta and was watching me with a worried expression. "I know what you're thinking, Sarah, and it is a very bad idea. You can't possibly visit a brothel on your own, not even one as upper-crust as Madam Valentine's. If Mama found out, there would be hell to pay—probably for me! There's no reason you can't wait until Monday, when I can go with you."

"I understand your concern, Samuel," I said calmly. "But I assure you there is no need to worry."

I considered his answering laugh to be rude in the extreme. "Don't you believe me?" I demanded hotly.

"Not for one minute." He stared at me for a moment, then said, "All right, little sister, I know well and good that you're going to do whatever you please no matter what I say. Just promise me that you won't visit Madam Valentine's parlor house alone."

I hated it when Samuel pressed me into making a promise I had absolutely no desire to keep.

"Well?" he prompted, and I knew he had no intention of letting the matter rest.

"Oh, all right," I gave in ungraciously. "I don't know why you insist on making such a fuss about this. It's not as though I'm planning to spend the night roaming about the streets of the Barbary Coast. You said Madam Valentine's parlor house is on Montgomery Street. That isn't such a bad neighborhood."

He didn't answer. Given my brother's streak of stubborn German tenacity, I decided it was time to change the subject.

"Were you able to learn the identities of the two men who confronted Brielle outside my office yesterday morning?"

"It seems probable that they were Gerald Knight's men. Unlike the Bouchard girl, it wasn't difficult to uncover information about him. I don't know if you're aware of this, but Knight is married to the former Lily Randolph."

"Randolph? You mean of the Randolph steel family in Pittsburgh?"

"The very one. She's several years older than her husband, and it's her family money that keeps that awful broadsheet of his up and running."

"I thought you sold several stories to that 'awful broadsheet,'" I put in with a wry smile.

"One or two of my articles have appeared there," he admitted, "but very early on in my career, when I was all too pleased to see any of my scribblings in print."

"Didn't I hear his name mentioned in connection with Millie Javers, the singer who took San Francisco by storm two or three years ago?"

"You have a good memory. According to my sources, Knight did his best to hush up that particular scandal. He fancies himself to be a patron of the arts, though, at least of the Tivoli Opera House, and any other theaters in town that employ lovely young singers and actresses."

"You mean he's actually involved in the productions?"

Samuel smiled. "No, although I'm sure he'd love nothing better. He contributes financially, which probably affords him some say on minor cast members. As I mentioned, he's well known for his roving eye when it comes to beautiful young women, *very* young women, I might add."

"If he's contributing to the arts, then his paper must be doing better than I thought. I could have sworn I read somewhere that the *Daily Journal* was closing its doors a year or so back."

"It did. Circulation dropped nearly in half after the paper printed dangerously libelous gossip about some prominent members of city government. Evidently, it was only his wife's influence, and a great deal of money, that kept him out of court. Still, bad publicity nearly cost Knight his newspaper."

"How long have they been married?"

"Close to twenty years, I'd guess. About fifteen years ago, Knight bought the newspaper using her money. They have three children and a large home on Nob Hill. Mrs. Knight is a prominent member of San Francisco society. I'm sure Mama must know her."

"I believe I've heard her name. I just didn't connect it to Gerald Knight." My mind was racing, trying to digest this information. "What makes you think it was Knight's men who convinced Brielle not to keep her appointment with me yesterday morning?"

"Apparently this isn't the first time he's pulled a heavy-handed tactic in order to shape a story to his liking—or to squelch an unfavorable rumor. My guess is that he's been keeping an eye on the girl since she left his house. They parted under less than harmonious circumstances, and you know the old saying about a woman scorned. He can't afford to let this get back to his wife, particularly since she controls the purse strings."

I sat quietly pondering my brother's words. "I wonder if there's some way we might use this information to our advantage?"

Samuel stared at me. "Sarah, you can't be serious. Brielle Bouchard's case is hopeless. Gerald Knight would never risk his wife's fury by publicly honoring that contract. The foolish girl should have known that from the start of their liaison."

"A much older woman might have been misled," I said, coming to Brielle's defense. "She was a girl of barely seventeen."

Samuel dabbed his mouth with a napkin. "It's not that I don't sympathize, but there is simply no way to prove that he fathered Brielle's child."

"I know you're right, but— At the very least, we have to do what we can to ensure that she's protected from Gerald Knight's thugs."

"All right, I agree that providing for her safety would be an admirable idea," Samuel said with feeling. "And while we're about it, why don't we protect the thousands of other homeless women and children living from hand to mouth in this city?"

"Samuel, Brielle Bouchard is more than just a faceless statistic to me. I've met her. I've seen her beautiful little daughter. I cannot bring myself to abandon them without doing everything possible to help."

Samuel sat back in his seat and gave a long sigh. "Of course you can't. It simply isn't in your nature to give up without a fight. I suppose I just wanted to state the realities of the situation, on the off chance you might actually listen to your big brother for a change."

Pulling out his fob watch, he looked at the time. "I have to be on my way. I'm supposed to be at the Talbots' home by three o'clock, and I have to make a quick stop at the newspaper before going home to pack."

He rose from the table and reached for the check, then looked down at me until I raised my face and met his eyes.

"I know what you mean to do, Sarah," he said, his voice sober. "But I insist that you keep your promise. Do not pay a visit to Madam Valentine's parlor house, or any other brothel for that matter, alone. Do you agree?"

Realizing he would worry all weekend if I did not accede to this demand, I grudgingly nodded.

"Good," he declared. "I'll see you on Monday, then."

After Samuel walked me back to my office, I spent an hour or two reading through several of the law books I kept in my library, then found myself at sixes and sevens. Without something tangible to occupy my mind, I was unable to concentrate on anything besides Brielle Bouchard and her impossible situation.

I still had a difficult time accepting that she would take refuge in a bordello, even the fashionable one Samuel described. It was sad enough to contemplate a woman trading her body for a comfortable home and a generous weekly allowance.

To my mind, it was infinitely worse to take a different man to your bed every night—perhaps more than just one! For a woman as beautiful and refined as Brielle it seemed little less than a tragedy. And the baby! What kind of life would it be for a child growing up in a brothel?

By half past four, I was on tenterhooks and decided to leave the office for the day. I told myself that anything was better than pacing the floor until I wore a groove in it.

I was just gathering up my things to leave, when there was a knock on the door. Pulling it open, I found a street urchin standing on the landing, his face smudged with dirt, hair so mussed it resembled a mop, and with a worn burlap bag slung over his bony shoulder.

"You Miss Woolson?" he asked. At my nod, he said, "Got a message for ya, miss."

He dug into the bag and presented me with a sealed white envelope. It was fine quality paper, and my name was neatly written upon its face. I recognized the script at once. The missive was from Pierce Godfrey.

"The feller what gave this to me said he'd be obliged if you'd send him back an answer," the boy added. "He said I was to run yer message back to him full chisel."

Requesting the boy to wait, I slit open the envelope and read:

My dear Sarah,
I have obtained two tickets for tomorrow night's opening of
The Merry Wives of Windsor, *being performed at the Baldwin*

Theater. I would be honored if you would accompany me as my guest.

The boy has been instructed to wait for your reply.

Yours respectfully,
Pierce Godfrey, Esq.

For a moment I was not certain how to respond to this unexpected invitation. On the one hand, I am a great admirer of the theater, and particularly of the works of Shakespeare. On the other hand, I had no wish to lead Pierce to believe I had changed my mind concerning our relationship.

"Miss, I got a lot more letters to deliver," the boy complained impatiently, as I stood pondering what to do.

"Yes, of course." Realizing I must come to a decision, I impulsively reached for a pen and paper and accepted Pierce's invitation with my thanks. I went on to request that he pick me up here at the office, rather than at my home.

Sealing the envelope, I handed it to the boy along with a coin for his services. He regarded the money, then grinned up at me, displaying several cracked teeth.

"Thanks, miss," he said, already turning back to the stairs. "I'll get this right back to the gent."

At least, I thought, as I stood in a queue on the corner waiting for the public horsecar line, Mama need not know that I would be seeing Pierce again so soon. Of course, it meant that I would have to bring a suitable change of costume to my office the following morning, and engage Eddie's services.

Thinking of the lad gave me a sudden idea. I had promised Samuel that I would not pay a call on Madam Valentine's parlor house alone, *not* that I would entirely refrain from visiting the establishment. I felt immediately uplifted by this plan. All might yet work out to my satisfaction.

Instead of going directly home, I transferred to a cable car on Franklin Street which would take me to Laine Carriages, where Eddie was employed as a driver. Now that I had formulated a plan,

I hardly noticed the dreary weather as I departed the cable car and briskly walked the last two blocks to the cab company.

As it turned out, Eddie wasn't at the terminus. Undeterred, I penciled a quick message, making sure to print in neat characters—although the boy's reading skills had greatly improved over the past few months, he still experienced difficulty reading cursive—instructing him to pick me up at my home tomorrow morning at eight o'clock. He was not to come to the door, I told him, but to wait for me discreetly down the street, hopefully away from my mother's observant eyes. From there we would drop my evening clothes off at my office, pick up the paperwork I had completed for Robert, then proceed directly to Joseph Shepard's law firm. Sealing this missive inside an envelope, I handed it over to the care of the office clerk to deliver to Eddie when he came in from his day's work.

As I exited the omnibus and walked the short block to my home, I suddenly wondered what I would do if Robert were not available to accompany me to Madam Valentine's brothel the following morning. I had to smile as the answer came to me immediately. It would be a good deal less than ideal, but at least I would not have to break the silly promise I had given Samuel at lunch. If all else failed, Eddie would go with me, of course.

Satisfied that I had duly considered all aspects of my little plan, I opened the front door and entered my home.

CHAPTER TEN

I n the end, I was forced to enlist Celia's assistance in slipping out of the house unnoticed the following morning. Naturally, my mother was accustomed to seeing me depart for my office before eight o'clock, however, I had never done so carrying an evening gown—wrapped in a garment sheet—a hat suitable for the opera house, as well as a change of shoes, jewelry, and some personal items which would be required to dress my hair.

Dear Celia carried out her part of the subterfuge to perfection, asking Mama to care for baby Charlie while she saw that Tom and Mandy were fed and dressed for the day. Charles and Celia employed a most capable nanny, Mary Douglas, to care for the children, but Celia delighted in attending to many of her offsprings' daily routines herself. Consequently, Mama sensed nothing suspicious when asked to rock and soothe her precious new grandson, a charge she was more than happy to fulfill.

It was lightly raining when I exited the house, but as I had instructed, I found Eddie waiting with the brougham halfway down the block. He grinned broadly as he jumped down, took my belongings, and laid them out neatly on one of the two carriage seats which comprised the double brougham.

"Are we workin' on a new case, then, Miss Sarah?" he eagerly inquired, eyeing the items he'd just arranged with intense curiosity. "I knew somethin' was up when yer note said I was to wait fer you down the street and not in front of yer house like usual."

I was at a momentary loss as to how to explain the situation to the boy, without explaining my mother's keen interest in my social life.

"I'm going to the theater tonight, Eddie," I explained, as he assisted me into the carriage. "Since I won't have time to come home after work, I thought it would be easier to change my garments at the office."

Eddie's face fell. "Dang it all, anyway. I thought maybe we was investigatin' them murders you and Mister Samuel was talkin' about the other day. You know, them two fellers what got their heads bashed in."

"No, Eddie," I told him, cringing at the all too vivid picture this brought to mind. "However, we do have several errands to run after we drop these things off at my office." I refrained from explaining that if Robert were in court, he would be playing a much more prominent role in the morning events than I found comfortable. "Please take me there first."

"Righto," he called out, closing the carriage door and bolting up onto the driver's seat.

"Oh, and Eddie," I called out to him. "I would appreciate it if you would deliver us there in one piece, if you please!"

As usual, the lad mostly ignored my admonition to drive in a safe and sane manner, and we arrived at my Sutter Street office far quicker than I would have liked. After we had taken the clothes upstairs and hung them in my back room library, I gathered up the papers I had completed for Robert, and instructed Eddie to take us to Joseph Shepard's offices, which were located on Clay and Kearny streets.

The rain was coming down in sheets as Eddie reined in his dappled-gray horse in front of the familiar building where I had toiled as associate attorney for the first nine months of my legal career. Instructing the boy to stay with the carriage, I made my way quickly through the downpour and entered the lobby.

Utilizing Elisha Otis's hydraulic lift, or "rising room" as they were generally called, I exited at the sixth floor and walked to the imposing oak door engraved with the name Shepard, Shepard, McNaughton, and Hall. I paused for a moment to straighten my suit, then opened the door and marched boldly inside.

Hubert Perkins, the annoying little clerk who guarded the door like a fire-spewing dragon, looked up to frown as I dared to invade his hallowed territory. Mr. Perkins and I had never seen eye to eye on a variety of subjects, including his disdain for any woman presumptuous enough to consider herself an attorney. The few times I had encountered him since terminating my employment at Shepard's firm had done nothing to improve our relationship. If anything, he invariably greeted me as if I were carrying the Black Plague with me.

"Good morning, Mr. Perkins," I said, not bothering to summon up a smile. "Is Mr. Campbell in this morning, or is he still in court?"

"He is in, Miss Woolson, but unless you have an appointment I fear it is impossible for you to—"

Paying no heed to the man's sputtering protests, I sailed past his desk without further comment. Head held high, I marched down the hall toward the closet-sized room that had once been my office, and which now belonged to my friend and colleague.

"Good heavens," Robert exclaimed, as I knocked once then entered the room. "Sarah, what are you doing here?"

"I'm delighted to find that you are not in court this morning, Robert," I said, handing him the paperwork I had recently completed. "I assume that Mr. Lansing has sufficiently recovered to rejoin Mr. Shepard as second chair?"

"Yes, but why—"

"I have come to request a favor," I interrupted, not wishing to remain in this claustrophobic room one minute longer than necessary. I removed Robert's long coat from a hook behind his desk and handed it to him. "Since Mr. Shepard is out of the office, he cannot object if you accompany me on a brief errand."

He stared at me in openmouthed astonishment. "What are you going on about? I have been out of the office for two days. I have work to do."

"I appreciate that, Robert, which is why I'm prepared to help you to complete it, at no charge, of course." I crossed to his desk and began thumbing through the array of papers spread out untidily in every direction. "In return, I would appreciate it if you would give me an hour of your time, perhaps two at the outside."

"To do what?" he demanded. "Dash it all, woman, I can't just up and leave the office because you've gotten some crazy bee in your bonnet. And for God's sake, stop rummaging through my papers!"

It took me only a few minutes to pack some of the work into a folder and tie the clasp.

"The Tanner file must be finished by the close of business today," Robert protested. "Shepard expects it on his desk when he returns from court."

"Don't worry, Robert," I promised. "It will be ready by four this afternoon. Now please put on your coat. Eddie is downstairs waiting in the brougham."

As was his habit, Eddie drove with his usual breakneck abandon, but for once I was actually grateful. It served to take Robert's mind off where we were headed. In fact, we were within three blocks of our destination before he relaxed his grip on the seat, and finally seemed to take notice of the neighborhood.

"Where are we going, anyway?" he asked, looking out the carriage window.

"You'll see in a moment," I answered evasively. "We're almost there."

He stared at me suspiciously. "I don't like that look in your eye."

I pretended to gaze at the shops we were passing, and with a soft harrumph, he fell silent. When Eddie reined up in front of the address Samuel had given me for Madam Valentine's parlor house, I was relieved to see that it looked little different from other houses lining the street. Like its neighbors, it had probably been built sometime in the late sixties or early seventies. It took up much of the narrow lot, and was constructed mainly of wood, with a goodly number of slat-sided bay windows and, in my opinion, far too much exterior ornamentation. It appeared, however—at least from the outside—to be a perfectly respectable residence, and I wondered if Samuel could have inadvertently given me an incorrect address.

Looking up and down the street, Robert said, "Who lives in this house? I hope you haven't dragged me along on another of your wild-goose chases!"

Again without answering, I allowed Eddie to assist me down from the carriage. It was apparent from the eager expression on his narrow face that he had taken other fares to this house. He certainly looked as if he were well aware of its line of business.

"I know Annie Watkins, one of the maids what works here, Miss Sarah," he told me, his thin voice rising in excitement. "Want me to go round back and fetch her? She's sure to let us in, even if it is so early in the mornin'."

This comment took me aback, and I consulted my timepiece. It was just going on ten o'clock. For the first time since hatching my little plan, I realized that given the hours required when running a business of this sort, the, er, ladies in residence undoubtedly slept in late of a morning. Ten o'clock—which was, after all, past midmorning—hardly seemed early by my standards. Madam Valentine's establishment, however, most likely did not follow a conventional time schedule. For a moment I considered postponing my errand until later that afternoon, but one glance at Robert's wary face made me realize the unlikelihood of prying him out of his office for a second time that day, especially if he learned I required his company to visit a brothel!

"Yes, Eddie," I told the boy at length. "I would appreciate it if you could persuade your friend to allow us inside."

He was off and running before the words left my mouth, and I saw Robert's expression grow ever more suspicious.

"What's going on, Sarah? You have purposely evaded answering my questions. Who lives in this house, and why are we calling on them at this ungodly hour of the morning?"

"It's nearly ten o'clock, Robert. I would hardly characterize that as an ungodly hour." I attempted an innocent smile, hoping it would put him off until Eddie reappeared with someone who might open the front door.

"Oh, you think not?" His tone was derisive. "Since when has San Francisco society started paying social calls before lunch? Even I know that is hardly the done thing."

No, it's not, I silently agreed, and felt a cold shiver run down my spine. Unfortunately, the delay in getting inside the house was causing me to entertain second thoughts about this mission. What in heaven's name was I doing here? Proper women took care to avoid being seen anywhere near establishments of this sort. Much less maneuver their way inside! What would my mother say if she knew her only daughter was visiting a brothel, with or without an escort? For that matter, what would my father say? Once again I'd allowed my fervor to help a client ride roughshod over my good judgment.

Thankfully the front door to the house was flung open before I completely lost my nerve. With a self-satisfied grin, Eddie beckoned us inside. Behind him stood a pretty, plump, and obviously apprehensive young parlor maid, wearing a spotlessly clean and stiffly starched apron and cap.

"This is most irregular, ma'am," she said, nervously twisting the corner of her apron until it became hopelessly wrinkled. Her dark eyes regarded me as if I were a creature from another planet, who had suddenly materialized outside her door and was seeking permission to launch an invasion. "I don't know what Madam Valentine will say if I let you in."

"Bet she ain't used to ladies like you showin' up at her door," Eddie put in with a suggestive smirk.

"What do you mean 'ladies like you'?" Robert asked, guardedly eyeing the boy's expression.

Eddie gave Robert a sly wink. "You know, Mr. Campbell, the kinda place where a bloke has to pay a mighty grist of Vs and Xs to, ah . . ." He glanced uncomfortably at me, then finished cautiously, "To, ah, spend time with a gal."

Robert raised his rusty-colored eyebrows until they very nearly met his unruly hairline. "For the love of all that's holy, Sarah, what in tarnation is this boy going on about? I thought you and Samuel were teaching him to speak proper English."

It was clearly time to tell the truth and shame the devil, as Papa was wont put it. "This is a parlor house, Robert," I explained. Doing my best to appear confident, I quickly stepped inside before either the maid or my beleaguered friend could stop me. "It is also known as a brothel, or a bawdy house, albeit one of the higher-quality establishments of its kind," I added to appease the maid, who appeared affronted by my explanation.

Robert opened his mouth, but seemed too dazed to speak.

"Ain'tcha gonna come in, Mr. Campbell?" Eddie asked, holding the door open wider.

"Yes, do come in, Robert," I told him, wondering if I would have to forcibly pull him in by the coat sleeve. "You are making a spectacle of yourself standing out there huffing like a beached blowfish." Turning to the little maid, I said, "Please be so kind as to inform Madam Valentine that she has visitors. Where would you care for us to wait?"

Appearing as taken aback by this perfectly normal request as by my colleague's peculiar behavior, the young woman reached out with a slender arm, and somewhat reluctantly pointed in the direction of a parlor leading off the entrance hall.

"Thank you," I said, then turned to our young cabbie. "Please wait for us in the carriage, Eddie. You might want to make profitable use of your time by reading chapters eight and nine of *The Adventures of Tom Sawyer*."

The pleased-as-pudding smile on Eddie's face vanished, replaced by an expression of profound consternation. "But Miss Sarah, I got us in. I kin help you—"

"Yes, I'm sure you could, Eddie," I said, calmly but firmly nudging him out the door. "However, Mr. Campbell and I have a delicate matter to discuss with Madam Valentine, and we require privacy. We should not be long."

Before the boy could conjure up any further excuses to protest his abrupt dismissal, I closed the door firmly behind him.

"Stop gawking and come along, Robert," I said, swallowing down my own nerves and walking determinedly across the large foyer toward the room indicated by the maid. "I believe I see a fire in the grate. We should be able to wait comfortably in there."

I could well understand Robert's discomfort. To be honest, I felt as if I were entering a strange world, completely outside of my experience, or indeed any frame of reference I could call to mind. If I were landing on the moon itself, I doubt I could have experienced any more trepidation than I was currently suffering.

As we made our way through the foyer, my fears gradually lessened as I took notice of our surroundings. This was hardly what I had expected. The dark wood of the vestibule floor was polished until it gleamed like a mirror, and was partially covered with an elegant, and obviously expensive, Persian carpet. Overhead was an exquisitely painted ceiling which, judging by its ornate and colorful design, might have been imported from Italy. One of the walls featured a collection of antique pistols, artfully arranged inside a glass cabinet. Directly opposite the guns hung an oil painting of a beautiful nude, wearing nothing but a single gold bracelet, her lovely eyes gazing out over a peaceful lake, as if lost in dreamy contemplation. The brush strokes and skillful use of color suggested the artist might be the gifted young Impressionist Pierre-Auguste Renoir. Good Lord, I thought. Could that be possible?

To the left of the painting was an enormous, gracefully curved wooden staircase. The intricately carved balustrade led up to the second floor and, I assumed, the rooms where the resident "ladies" took their gentlemen. The door the maid indicated led off the vestibule to the left, and turned out to be a large, luxuriously furnished parlor. And indeed, as I had glimpsed from the foyer, there was a welcoming fire crackling inside an intricately carved, white marble hearth.

Following behind me as I slowly made my way past a Flemish tapestry, and a larger-than-life reproduction of the *Venus de Milo*, I could hear Robert muttering beneath his breath as we passed one treasure after another. Obviously, he was as surprised as I was to find a bordello this splendidly—and expensively—furnished. In fact, were it not for one too many gilded mirrors on the walls, and a preponderance of red velvet chairs and sofas, Madam Valentine's parlor house would have made any Nob Hill millionaire proud.

"This place is like a museum, or a bloody palace," he said, standing in front of a particularly erotic painting of a generously endowed nude woman, who appeared about to be ravished by a muscular warrior. "Do you suppose any of this art is genuine?"

"I have no idea," I answered, tracing a finger along the base of an enameled silver kerosene lamp. "They appear to be authentic, but I'm hardly an art expert."

We were still admiring the room's numerous and unique objets d'art, when an attractive, if slightly disheveled, young woman peered in at us from the foyer, tittering like a silly schoolgirl when she spied Robert. She was wearing a flimsy—indeed, almost transparent!—nightdress, which did nothing whatsoever to hide the curvaceous body which lay beneath. A moment later, another giggling girl appeared, then another. Soon half a dozen young women, in various degrees of undress, had gathered in the foyer to stare at us, their droll expressions making me feel as if Robert and I were freaks of nature who had inadvertently ventured inside their lair.

"Hello, handsome," the first girl chirped, licking her lips and posing seductively for Robert's benefit. "Why don't you come up-stairs and I'll show you my own art collection."

"Shut yer trap, Sally," one of the other girls told the first one with a low laugh. "Mr. Handsome has set his cap for me, haven't you, darlin'?"

"Look at all that red hair," teased another. "Do you have as much fire in your furnace as you do on your head, Mr. Handsome?"

The other girls seemed to find this hilariously funny. As if by silent command, they all began thrusting out their bosoms and wriggling their derrieres playfully, as if putting on a private perfor-mance for my embarrassed companion. Robert's face had turned beet red, but he appeared strangely incapable of tearing his eyes off the tittering women.

"Robert!" I exclaimed, not in the least amused by this crude display nor, I must admit, by Robert's reaction to it.

He jumped at least two inches off the floor at the sound of my voice; it was as if hearing his name spoken aloud had awakened him from some kind of trance. He looked so panic-stricken that for a moment I feared he might be about to bolt from the room. Only the fact that he would have to pass through the gaggle of women in the doorway—who were now making wagers as to the size of various body parts, based on his height and muscular structure—prevented him from fleeing.

"Ladies! Remember yourselves," came a commanding voice from behind the young women. There was instant silence as every girl turned as one to watch a tall, regal-looking woman approach from the back of the house. "Where is your dignity? I have trained you better than this."

There were murmurs of, "Yes, Madam Valentine." "We didn't mean no harm, Madam Valentine." "It was all in fun, Madam Val-entine." Then, without being told, the girls turned and scampered up the stairs.

The tall woman cast her dark, penetrating eyes onto Robert and me, her outwardly calm demeanor betraying more than a hint of suspicion. She was on the heavy side, but was so splendidly girdled that one received the impression of a narrow waist and slender hips. She was wearing a beautiful crimson-colored satin kimono, embroidered with dragons and exotic birds.

Despite the early hour, her flaming red hair, which, judging by its unnatural shade, had undoubtedly come from a henna bottle, was stylishly coiffed and arranged atop her stately head. Her robe fell open at the bosom to reveal deep cleavage and a small black beauty mark strategically placed above her right breast. In a somewhat flashy, overstated way, she was a very attractive woman. Moreover, she possessed such self-confidence and poise, I had no doubt she would immediately take command of any room she entered.

"I am Madam Valentine," she said in a low, deeply resonant voice. "And you are?"

I tried to smile, but feared it fell well short of the sangfroid I was attempting to achieve. Clearing my throat, I said, "My name is Sarah Woolson. This gentleman is Robert Campbell. We are both attorneys at law."

For the first time since entering the room, Madam Valentine seemed taken aback. By now I'd become so accustomed to this reaction when people first learned of my profession, that I hardly gave it a second thought. Robert, on the other hand, was shifting nervously behind me.

"Sarah, we should, ah, that is, we have made a mistake coming here." Taking hold of my arm, he attempted to lead me toward the door. I refused to budge.

"We have done no such thing," I protested, pulling free of his grasp. I turned to face Madam Valentine, determined not to leave this house until I had obtained the information I had come for. "Actually, we are seeking a Miss Brielle Bouchard. Is she by any chance staying on these premises?"

This seemed to startle the woman even more than learning I was an attorney. "Brielle Bouchard? Whatever gave you that idea?"

I decided that honesty was the best, perhaps the only, recourse. This woman appeared far too astute to be taken in by fabrication.

Moreover, the purpose of this visit was to locate Brielle; any attempt to deceive the woman who might well be the girl's benefactress would hardly benefit my cause.

"Miss Bouchard called at my office earlier this week," I told the woman. "She asked me to initiate a lawsuit against a certain gentleman who had, according to her, reneged on a contract they had signed. However, she left no address where I might—"

"Wait a minute, Sarah," Robert said, breaking in. "Are you referring to that young woman with the baby? The one who was waylaid outside your office the other morning by those thugs?"

Madam Valentine's neatly plucked eyebrows rose at this, but she held her tongue.

"Yes, that is the girl I'm seeking," I told him.

"But I had no idea—" he sputtered. "Good heavens! You didn't mention that she is a—a painted lady."

The "lady of the house" laughed at this, the sound coming from deep inside her ample bosom, and echoing through the room. Still, she said nothing as she regarded my companion with genuine amusement.

"I'm not sure I would label Brielle a 'painted lady,' Robert," I said, keeping my eyes on the woman. "The gentleman Miss Bouchard would like to sue for breach of contract, Madam Valentine, is evidently little Emma's father."

The woman remained silent, not to be rushed. She stood tall and straight-backed before us, very much in charge of the situation. Her dark eyes continued to regard us with silent amusement as they traveled from the top of my hat, over the neat knot of hair pinned to the nape of my neck, and down the length of my business suit until they reached my polished boots.

After she had thoroughly studied my companion in the same bold manner—to his considerable discomfort—she nodded toward a red velvet sofa, indicating that we should take a seat. It was only after she had lowered herself, back still erect, onto one of the red velvet armchairs, that she finally spoke.

"I apologize for not recognizing you sooner, Miss Woolson.

You are the attorney who represented that Gypsy psychic who was accused of murder several months ago, are you not?"

"I am," I answered, attempting to hide my surprise that she was familiar with the case. I tended to forget that my picture had been featured on the front page of every newspaper in town after the murderous affair at the Cliff House.

"I read about you in the newspaper," she explained. confirming my suspicions. "As I recall, I showed the article to Brielle. That must be why she consulted you."

"She didn't tell you that she planned to seek my advice?"

"No, but then Brielle is not a girl who easily shares her thoughts," the woman replied. "For one so young, she is remarkably independent."

"Yes, that was my impression exactly," I said. "She is also strikingly beautiful. I can well understand why Mr. Knight found her so captivating. Are you acquainted with the gentleman, Madam Valentine?"

Again, the woman hesitated before replying. "If Brielle did not confide the circumstances of her relationship with the gentleman, I must respect her wishes and let her decide if she cares to go into more detail."

She rose to her feet, once more demonstrating considerable grace for a woman of such generous proportions. "I'll have one of the maids inform her that you are here, Miss Woolson. It will, of course, be up to her to decide whether or not she chooses to speak to you."

With that she swept out of the room and I heard her footsteps as she ascended the stairs to the second floor. The minute she was out of earshot, Robert stood as well, reaching out a hand to me.

"Get up, Sarah," he said urgently. "We must leave this house before she returns. I can't believe you tricked me into coming to such a place. You have finally gone too far. Even for you!"

"Don't be absurd, Robert, of course we're not leaving. I came here to find Brielle Bouchard. Now that I have, I must make certain that she is all right."

"This house is no place for a lady, Sarah. What would your parents think if they knew you were in a—in an establishment of this sort? Good God! What would your father say if he knew I'd actually accompanied you here?"

"He would be extremely angry with you, of course," I answered calmly. "The point is that he doesn't have to know. I certainly have no plans to tell him. And if you care whether or not you ever win a case in his courtroom, I'd advise you not to speak of it, either. Now be reasonable and sit down. I hear someone coming."

Robert looked nervously toward the foyer, as if fearful the gaggle of girls might have returned to continue their teasing. He must have seen someone approaching, for he fairly darted back to the sofa, sinking as deeply into the cushions as his tall, muscular frame would allow.

I turned in my seat and was rewarded to see Brielle Bouchard enter the parlor, closely followed by Madam Valentine. The young woman was wearing a simple blue cotton day dress. Her soft blond hair appeared to have been hastily arranged, and she wore no jewelry. Despite the casualness of her attire, her beauty nearly took my breath away.

From beside me I heard Robert gasp, and knew that he, too, was struck by her perfection. In fact, he had risen to his feet so abruptly at her entrance, you would have thought the queen of England herself had just walked into the room.

"Good morning, Miss Woolson," the angel in blue said, coming to stand before me and holding out her hand. "I did not expect to see you here. You have the entire house in an uproar."

Her striking blue eyes moved to Robert's tall figure, causing him to flush slightly. He quickly forced an artificial cough to mask his embarrassment, but I noticed that he continued to eye the girl from over the broad hand he had placed over his mouth.

I introduced Brielle to my flustered companion, hiding a smile as the gruff Scot practically melted like warm butter as she took his proffered hand.

Appraising him with frank interest, she laughed. "The girls are right, Mr. Campbell, you are completely charming. I rather think it is your friend who has set the house aflutter, Miss Woolson. He is quite as handsome as they described. And see how prettily he blushes. It is irresistible, quite a change from the gentlemen who normally visit this house.

Now," she continued, sinking into the chair recently vacated by Madam Valentine. "What business has brought you here, Miss Woolson? And how on earth did you find me?"

CHAPTER ELEVEN

Madam Valentine sank gracefully into a second red velvet armchair. Reaching into a pocket hidden within the folds of her robe, she pulled out a long, intricately carved ivory cigarette holder. She casually selected a cigarette from a gold case lying on one of the polished wood end tables, fixed it into the holder and lit it with a match, inhaling deeply with obvious satisfaction.

Robert dropped back down beside me on the sofa. I noted with some interest that he no longer seemed intent on fleeing the house while we still could. In fact, he had not taken his eyes off Brielle since she'd stepped inside the parlor.

"It is good to see you again, Miss Bouchard," I said with a smile. "I trust little Emma is well?"

"She is, indeed," replied the girl in her sweet, cultured voice. "She has become quite the darling of the house. It won't be long, I fear, before she is thoroughly spoiled."

Again, I received the impression that Brielle had been gently raised and well educated. I longed to learn more about her, but realized I could not rush the matter. It was best to take my time and first gain her trust.

"I am delighted to hear that," I said. "When you failed to keep your appointment Wednesday morning, I worried what might have happened to keep you away."

Her face clouded, and she glanced nervously at Madam Valentine. Before she could invent an excuse, I hurried on, "I should tell you that I know about the two men who accosted you outside my office. My downstairs neighbor, Mrs. Goodman, saw what happened and was concerned for your safety."

A startled expression crossed the girl's face, before she quickly regained her composure. "Mrs. Goodman seems quite an agreeable woman, but I fear she misinterpreted the incident. It's true that I was on my way to see you, Miss Woolson, but I simply changed my mind."

"Or had it changed for you," Robert put in, his voice edged with anger. "Why are you protecting those hooligans, Miss Bouchard? If you know their names you must tell us. I would like to personally throttle them both for frightening you in such a manner."

Brielle's smile was forced. "I'm sure you could make a good job of it, too, Mr. Campbell. However, I fear I don't know their names. I never saw those men before."

She was not a good liar and her frightened eyes betrayed her. I felt certain that she did know the men who had confronted her. At the very least, she knew the identity of the individual who had hired the two ruffians.

"Come now, Miss Bouchard," I said, "you must be forthright with us, if we are to help you. Are those men associates of Mr. Knight? Perhaps when he discovered you were seeing an attorney he feared you might find a legal way to redress his deplorable conduct, and sent the men to frighten you."

"Miss Woolson is right, Brielle," Madam Valentine put in. "Gerald Knight is a brute, and you know it. Visiting Miss Woolson on your own was rash and dangerous. You should have told me of your plan to consult an attorney, and allowed me to go with you. I might have been of some help."

Brielle slowly shook her head, setting her blond curls bouncing about her lovely face. "How could you help me, Madam Valentine? I know you mean well, and I am deeply indebted to you for all your help, but how can any woman stand up to a man like Gerald Knight? I considered myself so clever when I coerced him into signing a contract before I agreed to become his mistress." She gave a self-deprecating laugh. "Now I realize how foolish I was to believe I could ever protect myself from any man, much less one who wields so much power and influence in the city. After nearly two years, all I am left with is a worthless piece of paper."

"But you lived up to that contract in every respect," protested Madam Valentine, angrily snubbing out her cigarette in a cut-glass ashtray. "We both know that Gerald Knight had that house watched day and night. He probably has the name of every person who ever visited you on Pacific Avenue."

Brielle's face lit with sudden hope. "Yes, that's true, he did—I had forgotten. Miss Woolson, can we not use that information to prove that I was faithful to Mr. Knight, and to our contract?"

"I can vouch for the fact that Brielle was an innocent when she went to live with that man," Madam Valentine declared. "I had her examined by my personal physician. All my girls must undergo this inspection before they are allowed to join my house."

While this precaution appeared to me to be perfectly reasonable, even essential given the nature of the business, I felt Robert stiffen beside me on the sofa. Sensing that he was about to speak, I nodded for Madam Valentine to continue before he said something we might both regret.

"Before my young ladies are permitted to entertain a gentleman," the older woman went on, "it is necessary that I first ensure that they are healthy and free from disease. Next, they must be fitted for a new wardrobe, including undergarments and gowns. They are then schooled in how to deport themselves befitting the standards of this house, how to dress their hair, enhance their faces, and, most importantly, become skilled in the art of seduction."

"I see." Although I could not approve the purpose of this training, it was impossible not to admire her thoroughness. "If Brielle was being prepared to work in your parlor house, Madam Valentine, how did she happen to forge a personal relationship with Mr. Knight?"

Madam Valentine sniffed, as if in disapproval. "I personally do not approve of Mr. Knight. He is arrogant, demanding, and the worst kind of hypocrite. I have read a number of his articles extolling family values, only to witness him blatantly carousing with my girls that same evening."

She paused to insert another cigarette into her ivory holder, lit it, then continued. "However, Gerald Knight is one of our best clients, so naturally no effort is spared to please him. As it happens, he caught sight of Brielle one evening when we were shorthanded, and she was carrying a bottle of champagne to one of the bedrooms. He was immediately smitten, and demanded that I introduce him to her straightaway. When I explained that Miss Bouchard was but newly arrived, and had not yet commenced her duties, he was delighted, declaring that if she was as innocent as I claimed, he would take her as his new mistress."

"He took your word for her, er, innocence?" I asked.

Once again, Madam Valentine sniffed. "He did not. I told him she had already been examined by a doctor, but nothing would do but that she be seen by his own physician."

"And this satisfied him?" I asked.

"It did," she replied. "The following day he sent men to fetch Brielle and bring her to the house on Pacific Avenue."

"From that day onward, my every move was watched," put in Brielle. "I was aware that the maids were providing Gerald with regular reports on how I spent my days and who visited. When I left the house, I was always accompanied by a servant, or one of his men."

"There, you see it is just as I said," said Madam Valentine, a note of triumph in her voice. "Is there no way we can use his own precautions to prove that this unfortunate girl did not break the contract?"

"We might, if the men who kept her under surveillance were

impartial witnesses," I replied, wishing I could be more hopeful. "But as you pointed out, they were in Mr. Knight's employ. They would undoubtedly swear to anything he asked them to say."

"That is exactly what they would do," Brielle agreed, her voice taking on a note of bitterness. "I came to realize the hopelessness of my situation even before Gerald's men stopped me outside Miss Woolson's office. Their threats of violence toward me—and even toward you, Miss Woolson—convinced me of how futile it would be to go forward with the lawsuit."

"They threatened Miss Woolson?" exclaimed Robert, once again jumping up from his seat. "That settles it. If you know the identities of these scoundrels, Miss Bouchard, you have an obligation to tell us. Their threats must be reported to the police. Immediately!"

"Please, Robert," I said, reaching up to take hold of his sleeve. "Sit down. Brielle is correct, we're dealing with a shrewd and unscrupulous man. We must tread with care."

"Care be damned!" Agitated, he stepped away from the sofa and out of my grasp. "This Knight fellow has sent his hoodlums to frighten a helpless girl. He even has the gall to threaten you, Sarah. He cannot be allowed to get away with such villainy."

Madam Valentine gave a deep sigh. "Please, Mr. Campbell, do sit down. Miss Woolson is correct in advising caution. Even if Brielle did report the matter to the police, it would be her word against those two men. And Knight has powerful connections within the police department. It would be an exercise in futility."

"Sarah's neighbor, Mrs. Goodman, saw them accost the girl," persisted Robert. "Surely she could act as a witness."

"Did this Mrs. Goodman hear what the men said to Brielle?" inquired Madam Valentine.

Robert looked at me questioningly.

I shook my head. "No, she was too far away to make out their words."

It was Brielle's turn to sigh. "As I say, it is hopeless. I have no choice but to accede to your wishes, Madam Valentine."

The older woman reached out a hand to the distraught girl, and I detected true compassion in her dark eyes. "My dear, I have no desire to force you into a life which repulses you."

"I know you don't," Brielle said, forcing a smile she obviously didn't feel. "But I cannot impose on your hospitality any longer. I am taking up a bed which should be occupied by a girl who is earning her keep. I am no longer an inexperienced child. The past two years have taught me a great deal about the art of love. I am determined to repay you for all the kindness you have shown me."

Robert, who was still standing, had been following this dialogue closely. "Do you mean to say, Miss Bouchard, that you intend to join those other girls as a—as a—"

"Painted lady?" Brielle said with an ironic smile. "Madam Valentine told me you'd used that epithet to describe me earlier. I am well aware I will be called that and a good deal worse, Mr. Campbell. While I would not have chosen this life if another had been open to me, neither do I disparage it. As you can see for yourself, our lady of the house is more like a mother hen than a tyrant, and we are all treated with respect, provided with the latest fashions, clean linen, and access to a most capable and respected doctor. It may surprise you to learn that although many girls desire to work in this parlor house, few are accepted. Madam Valentine's standards are considerably higher than most."

"I don't care how much you try to beautify this business, it is still prostitution!" Robert protested. "Surely there must be something else you can do to support yourself and your child, Miss Bouchard."

"Don't you think I have tried, Mr. Campbell?" Brielle's blue eyes flashed. Frustration and a sense of helplessness were clearly causing her to lose her temper. "Ever since my parents died when I was fourteen, I have attempted to live up to the standards they set for me throughout my childhood."

"What happened to your parents, Brielle?" I asked.

A look of pain crossed her lovely face. "They—" She glanced helplessly at Madam Valentine.

"Go on, Brielle," the madam told her. "Miss Woolson and Mr. Campbell are here to help you. I believe they have a right to know about your past."

That this was a distressing subject could be clearly read on the girl's pale face. With a force of will, she explained, "My parents migrated to the East Coast from Sweden several years before my birth. Father worked for a prominent accounting firm who, unbeknownst to him, was embezzling from their clients. When the crime was discovered, the major partners responsible for the fraud fled the country, leaving my father as one of the primary suspects. Shortly before his trial, my mother and father were—" She swallowed hard, attempting, I was sure, to keep from crying. "They were killed in a carriage accident. My father's name was never cleared."

"What did you do?" asked Robert, regarding the girl with genuine sympathy.

She sighed. "The authorities took our home and all the money my parents had saved to repay those who had been swindled. I was left with nothing." She paused as if gathering her thoughts, as well as her emotions. "For two years after my parents' deaths, I worked as a governess. When my pupils' father became rather too friendly toward me, I was forced to leave that employment. After that, I attempted to work as a seamstress, a laundress, a cook, and even a shopgirl. Unhappily, I lacked the skills necessary to succeed in those occupations. While providing me with an excellent education for a girl, my poor parents did not foresee a time when I might be in need of such training."

Brielle paused. I spied the glimmer of repressed tears in her eyes. "It was only when I was no longer able to buy food, and had been evicted from my modest lodging, that a friend suggested I visit Madam Valentine." She smiled at her benefactor. "This dear lady was good enough to take me in that very day."

Robert harrumphed. "You are a beautiful young woman, Miss Bouchard. I don't imagine it posed any great hardship for Madam Valentine to accept you into her, ah, establishment."

Before the lady in question could voice the retort I saw forming on her lips, I asked Brielle, "Have you no other family then? No aunts, or cousins, perhaps, who might take you and little Emma in?"

"Except for my daughter, I have no living relations, Miss Woolson," the girl replied, once again in command of her emotions. "I am quite alone in the world. I regret if I have offended your sensibilities, Mr. Campbell, but my first responsibility is to support my little girl, and see that she receives the best upbringing I can manage."

Beside me on the sofa, I felt Robert bristle, but thankfully he managed to keep his thoughts to himself, perhaps realizing for the first time the difficulty women face if there is no one else to provide for them.

Although Brielle appeared resigned to her fate, and was doing her utmost to depict her circumstances in the most advantageous light, her sensitive face could not mask the hopelessness she was obviously feeling inside.

"You have been through a great deal in your young life, my dear," I told Brielle. "And I understand that this is one of the better houses of its kind in the city. I mean no offense, Madam Valentine, but once a girl has chosen this life, she carries the stigma with her for the rest of her days. And you must agree that a brothel, even one of this quality, is no place to raise a child."

Madam Valentine, who continued to dart angry looks at Robert, had puffed out her ample chest and seemed about ready to take umbrage with this comment, when Brielle broke in, her angelic face set in resolute lines of determination.

"Your concern is understandable, Miss Woolson. However, needs must. Unless you can find a way to persuade Mr. Knight to honor our contract and support his daughter then, as I say, I am left with no choice but to accept Madam Valentine's generous offer. If I am frugal, it may be possible for me to eventually set off on my own and settle my daughter in more traditional surroundings. There are a great many young women in this city who would be delighted to face such a hopeful future."

Before I could respond to this, Madam Valentine cleared her throat and said, "I appreciate your kind words, Brielle, but it wouldn't do for Miss Woolson and Mr. Campbell to leave here with the wrong impression. All this talk about mothering my girls is all well and good, but I am first and foremost a businesswoman."

She gazed from one of us to the other, obviously determined that we should take her meaning. "My sole reason for running this house is to provide my clients with a pleasurable and discreet experience. In return, I expect to turn a good profit, for myself as well as my young ladies. They're treated well because it's in my best interest to keep them healthy and content. This is a transient business, and as you can see I put a great deal of time and effort into training my girls. If I can keep them happy, I find that they tend to stay here longer before moving on.

"Moreover, I run a respectable house. Drunkenness, profanity, and violence are not permitted inside these premises, either from my gentlemen or from my girls. Other than these few rules, however, my clients are free to do pretty much as they please. I'm a long way from being a puritan, and I know what men like. And what they like, they get. I'm proud to boast that Madam Valentine's Parlor House enjoys the finest reputation in the city of San Francisco."

Robert shifted in his seat and said, "Yes, but surely that sort of reputation is not—"

"I have not yet finished," she interrupted, darting my befuddled colleague a look which could have halted a herd of stampeding elephants. "It is because of this reputation that my girls may, if they're careful with their earnings and guard their looks, retire after six or seven years. Very few continue in the business beyond the age of thirty. You'd be surprised how many of them marry, often with respectable gentlemen, and go on to raise families." She looked steadily at Robert. "As Brielle pointed out, Mr. Campbell, there are far worse situations a girl might find herself in than my parlor house."

As Madam Valentine spoke, Robert had sunk back onto the sofa beside me. His earlier anger was turning into unease as she presented

141

arguments in favor of a house of pleasure, her own house in particular. From the dazed expression on his craggy face, I was beginning to think that he was as much a neophyte when it came to these establishments as was I.

"That may be, Madam Valentine," he said when she seemed to have come to the end of her discourse. "But not all your ladies enjoy such a happy ending, do they? Once their youth and beauty is gone, some of the lasses end up in—" His face reddened and his voice trailed off as he searched for an inoffensive way to describe the fate of girls reduced to these tragic circumstances.

"They end up in the cribs or cowyards of the Barbary Coast?" Madam Valentine smiled as Robert could manage only a brief nod of his head. "Yes, Mr. Campbell, I am all too aware that some girls are reduced to that unhappy state. My young ladies, however, are advised to set aside a portion of their earnings each week. In fact, several of them request that I perform this service for them. By exercising a bit of frugality, they often find a tidy nest egg awaiting them when they make the decision to move on with their lives."

"Even so," Robert said, unwilling to give up the argument, "they're still engaging in, er, that is, you can hardly describe their activities as, well, respectable."

The older woman met his eyes without flinching. "That depends on your definition of 'respectable,' Mr. Campbell. If longevity is any measure, then we have the edge on most occupations. After all, many would agree that we are engaged in one of the world's oldest professions."

Robert sputtered, but seemed unable to find words to dispute this statement. I was growing weary of this discussion; no matter how long they argued, neither Robert nor Madam Valentine were likely to change the other's opinion on the matter. Moreover, I had come here to find Brielle Bouchard and ascertain that she was unharmed. Now that I had successfully completed that duty, it was time to discuss her lawsuit.

"Miss Bouchard," I said matter-of-factly. "Let us proceed to the matter at hand. Have you any further interest in pursuing your lawsuit against Mr. Knight?"

Brielle hesitated, then said, "I would like nothing better than to compel Gerald to honor his responsibility toward our daughter. But as you said yourself, it is impossible to prove that he is Emma's father."

"That's true," I admitted. "However, I still have one or two ideas I'd like to try before we give up on the matter entirely."

The sudden blaze of hope that lit her eyes nearly prompted me to take back these words. What right did I have, I thought, to suggest there was the smallest chance Gerald Knight might change his mind and accept Emma as his child? Still, I could not bring myself to allow the man to win so easily.

I was well aware of the time constraints faced by my client. If we were to succeed in helping her, we must do it soon, before Brielle committed both herself and her tiny daughter to years of life inside a brothel—even one as grand as Madam Valentine's!

When we exited the house some few minutes later, we could find no sign of Eddie. The brougham remained standing in front of the parlor house where we had left it, and the dappled-gray horse stood contentedly munching a bag of oats.

"I thought you told the boy to stay with the carriage?" muttered Robert, opening the brougham door to peer inside. "He's not in here. Where do you suppose he's run off to?"

Just then, Eddie came scampering around the house and onto the street. "Sorry, miss," he said, slightly out of breath, and stuffing the piece of bread he was carrying into his mouth.

Endeavoring to chew with his mouth closed as I had taught him, he opened the carriage door and reached out a hand to assist me onto the step. I paused to instruct him to drop Robert off first at Joseph Shepard's law firm, then gathered up my skirts and stepped inside.

"So where did you take yourself off to?" Robert asked the lad before ascending into the cab behind me.

The lad swallowed his bread, then explained, "Annie Watkins—you know, my friend what's a maid here?—she gave me some fresh bread Cook just took outta the oven. And a cuppa hot coffee. It's almighty cold out today, ain't it?"

"Eddie, I swear you could find three square meals a day if you were stranded on a cement island in the middle of the Pacific Ocean," Robert said, not bothering to correct the boy's grammar. Stepping into the extended brougham, he settled himself in the seat across from me. "Judging by the amount of food that boy puts away every day, he should be as round as a pork barrel. Instead, he's thin as a matchstick."

"He works hard, Robert, and rarely sits still longer than five minutes at any given time. I'm convinced that he no sooner ingests food, than it transforms into the energy required to keep him going all day. Food acts as a fuel to run his internal engine."

As Eddie clicked the dappled-gray forward, I happened to glimpse a man crossing Montgomery Street, heading in the direction of Madam Valentine's parlor house. My heart skipped a beat as I noted that he was short, overweight, and wore a brown cap pulled low over his eyes. Good Lord, I thought. The man looked for all the world like Samuel's nemesis, Ozzie Foldger. Had he seen us coming out of the brothel? Was I to be tomorrow's lead story in some disgusting gossip tabloid?

We were jostled in our seats when Eddie pulled in front of a carriage as he joined afternoon traffic. Looking back, I strained to see where the man was going, but he was no longer in sight. Had he entered the brothel? I wondered, heart pounding in my throat. If he had, would Brielle and Madam Valentine keep my secret? I silently prayed that the discretion the madam afforded her customers would extend equally to a female attorney whose reputation might well be ruined if it were known she was visiting brothels!

"Sarah, you're not listening."

I came back to the present to find Robert staring at me as if I had suddenly gone hard of hearing.

"I'm sorry, Robert, what did you say?"

Before he could answer, the brougham swerved to avoid a pedestrian, causing one of the wheels to fall into a deep pothole, and we were very nearly jolted out of our seats. Never wholly at ease when riding in Eddie's cab, Robert leaned tentatively back onto the leather-upholstered bench, hands clutching his seat, ready, if it became necessary, to hold on for dear life. When he was finally settled, he favored me with an annoyed look.

"I asked if you would please enlighten me about this so-called brainstorm of yours. How do you propose to coerce Gerald Knight into admitting that he fathered Brielle Bouchard's child?"

"I'm not sure," I admitted, still unsettled that the man crossing the street might have been Ozzie Foldger. "I need to discuss the matter with my father over the weekend. And I may have a word or two with Samuel when he gets back in town on Monday," I added, not mentioning that I would also inform my brother that I might have seen Foldger outside the brothel.

"I'm not sure about your brother, but your father is a sensible man," said Robert, seeming relieved to find that I wasn't planning any sort of drastic action. "No doubt he'll agree that this is a hopeless case. It's understandable that you want to help Miss Bouchard, but you would better serve her by calling a spade a spade. You must make her understand that she hasn't a snowball's chance in hell of proving that Gerald Knight fathered her child."

"I know only that I must give the matter further thought," I replied a bit sharply. "I do not plan to give up until I have exhausted all of our options."

"All of what options, Sarah? You know there is no way you can uphold that ridiculous contract. I can't think of a single judge in this city who wouldn't laugh you out of his courtroom, if you were foolish enough to try to file this lawsuit."

"I didn't say I planned to file suit, at least not yet. There may be other ways to protect Brielle and her baby without taking the case to court." Even to my ears I sounded a good deal more confident than I felt.

"Oh, aye? Well, I wish you luck if that's the route you plan to follow. Believe me, you're going to need it!"

CHAPTER TWELVE

It was nearly noon when Eddie's carriage reined up in front of my Sutter Street office, and I ascended the stairs to my rooms above Fannie's shop. I took a seat at my desk, opened my briefcase, and removed the papers I had taken from Robert's office earlier that morning. Sorting them into neat piles, I searched for the documents I had, perhaps foolhardily, promised to finish by the end of the day. When I finally located them, my heart sank. I had indeed bitten off a great deal more than I could chew—at least in four short hours!

Unfortunately, the case in question was a good deal more tedious than the one I had completed for Robert the day before. I honestly couldn't understand why he put up with it. One of the main reasons Robert had left Edinburgh was to distance himself from his father's position as one of Scotland's foremost defense attorneys.

By coming to America, he had hoped to establish his own reputation as a trial lawyer. He had now been with Shepard's law firm for over five years, yet he had rarely been accorded the opportunity to sit second chair, much less been entrusted with the responsibility of trying a case on his own. More often than not, he was required to research and write briefs concerning the most dreary litigations that crossed Shepard's desk. As far as I was concerned, it was a terrible waste of a first-rate mind. It would have given me immense pleasure to say this directly to Joseph Shepard's face!

I had invited Robert countless times to join me in my practice. He invariably refused, stating sarcastically that he had become accustomed to eating three meals a day and living with a roof over his head. It was his decision, of course. For myself, I think I would have chosen starvation, rather than continue on as Joseph Shepard's overworked and unappreciated lackey!

Rising, I went into my back room library to brew a fresh pot of tea, then returned to my desk and settled down to work in earnest. So intent was I on completing the documents before Robert called for them at four o'clock, that I lost track of time. When they were finally finished, I was surprised to see that it was well past that hour. And there was no sign of Robert.

Gathering his papers into a neat pile, I crossed to the window and looked out over Sutter Street, which was already growing dark. Christmas was just over two weeks away and the shops along the street were brightly decorated, while the sidewalks were crowded with holiday shoppers. As it was a Friday, vehicular traffic was also heavier than usual. I fervently hoped that Robert wouldn't be too late, as Pierce would be calling for me at seven o'clock. If I were to be ready when he arrived, I would soon have to change my clothes and see to my toilette.

Hearing the newsboys at the corner hawking the evening's newspapers, I threw on my cloak and dashed downstairs. Making my way through the throng of people purchasing papers, I bought not only a copy of the *Tattler,* but of every evening edition.

Back in my office, I quickly scanned each newspaper, holding my breath for fear I might find my name in bold print, along with the story of my visit to the brothel that morning. When I could find no mention of either myself or Madam Valentine's parlor house, I settled in with a fresh cup of tea, and read through the papers more leisurely.

To my intense relief, it appeared that I had dodged the bullet, at least for the time being. It was always possible that I had simply imagined the man outside the brothel to be the reporter. Or, if it truly had been Foldger, perhaps his presence on Montgomery Street had been just a coincidence. Of course I wouldn't be able to truly breathe freely until I saw tomorrow's papers.

For the next hour I busied myself going through the remaining work I had appropriated from Robert's desk that morning, sorting it by case into separate stacks. Fortunately, what was left did not seem particularly urgent, and could wait until Monday. Nevertheless I could not help but think that he had received the better part of our bargain. In my eagerness to induce him to accompany me to Madam Valentine's parlor house, I had saddled myself with a full two days' work. Moreover, I had rashly promised to complete the research and write the briefs at no charge!

With a sigh, I put down my pen. Despite the extra work, and my shock at spying a man who looked very much like Ozzie Foldger, I considered our visit to the brothel a success. I had located Brielle Bouchard and satisfied myself as to her well-being. Whether or not I would be able to help her, of course, remained a question I could not as yet answer.

Hopefully, after I'd had an opportunity to speak to my father and Samuel, I would finally be able to lay the matter to rest. One way or the other.

When Robert still had not put in an appearance by six o'clock, I could no longer put off getting ready for the theater. The gown I had chosen for the evening was a deep shade of mauve, and was constructed of soft cashmere and satin merveilleux. Although the back skirt was gathered at the waist, the bodice was tailored and, other than a delicate ruffle of cream lace at the neckline, contained a minimum of flounces. My mother had persuaded me to choose this gown for a dinner party we had attended at Thanksgiving, insisting that the shade contrasted nicely with my raven hair and ivory complexion. Since Mama possesses a keen sense of style which I shall never be able to emulate, I inevitably yielded to her counsel.

After I had pinned my thick mane into a reasonably fashionable arrangement atop my head—finally giving up on the stray curls to either side of my face which stubbornly refused to be tamed—I added a small black felt hat, with the brim raised on the right side, and decorated with several feathers stuck into a band of dark rose velvet encircling the crown. Examining myself in a small looking glass I kept to hand, I decided it was the best I could be expected to achieve under the circumstances, and returned to the front office.

Spying the files of legal documents still stacked on my desk ready to be picked up, I wondered once again what could be keeping Robert. According to my lapel watch, it was after six thirty. What would I do, I worried, if he was still here when Pierce appeared to collect me for the theater? Given Robert's unreasonable dislike for Pierce, compounded by his unfortunate lack of tact when expressing his opinions, there was a very real possibility that he would precipitate an unpleasant scene.

My worst fears were realized, when Robert came bursting into my office—as usual without so much as a knock—barely fifteen minutes before the hour of seven. I had the files ready to turn over to him, but naturally the infuriating man ignored me, sinking instead onto the chair facing my desk and expelling a deep sigh.

"Ah, you've got them ready, then," he said, finally accepting the papers from my outstretched hand. "I know I'm late, but Shepard hauled the lot of us into his office to discuss a new case the firm has accepted. The old bugger is too miserly to assemble us during normal work hours, but he'd be perfectly content to keep us there until the wee hours of the morning, if the whim struck him."

"I thought you said he required these briefs by four o'clock?" I asked, annoyed that I had worked so diligently to meet this deadline.

"Oh, aye, but he changed his mind. Says he and his wife have been invited to spend the weekend out of town, and that he won't have a chance to go over them after all." He looked at me hopefully. "I don't suppose you could manage a nice hot cup of tea? It's close to freezing out there tonight, and in words of the vernacular, I'm completely exfluncticated."

I eyed him in sharp surprise. "Good heavens, Robert, you've been spending too much time around Eddie."

"Oh, I don't know. In his own inimitable fashion, the boy occasionally has the knack of hitting the nail precisely on the head." He stretched out his long legs in obvious relief. "So, do you think you could manage a cup of tea before I'm forced to go back out there and brave the elements?"

"I'm sorry, Robert," I told him, rising to my feet. "I wish I could, but I simply don't have the time. As it is, I'm late for an appointment. In fact, I was just about to leave."

He gave me a very direct look, seeming to notice for the first time what I was wearing. After he made a careful examination of my gown and hat, I was startled to see his ruddy face turn a slightly deeper shade of red. "Sarah, you, ah, look beauti—" He stopped and cleared his throat. "That is to say, you look quite presentable. Where are you off to, then?"

"Thank you for the compliment," I said dryly, not sure whether to laugh or lecture him on the proper social graces when admiring a lady. "At least I assume that's what it was meant to be. As a matter of fact, I'm attending the theater with a friend. So, if you will just—"

His reddish-brown eyebrows rose as he regarded me suspiciously. "A friend? And what friend would that be?"

"Really, Robert." I felt my temper rising. "What possible concern can that be to you?"

Naturally, he ignored my question, studying me instead through considerably narrowed blue-green eyes. "That friend wouldn't happen to be Pierce Godfrey, would it? He's only been back in town for a few days and already he's making a nuisance of himself. First dinner, and now the theater."

"Oh, fiddlesticks. What a terrible fuss you make out of nothing. Pierce Godfrey and I are good friends and that is all there is to it."

"Nothing? You call this nothing? The man is no better than a buccaneer, Sarah. He's dangerous, and frankly, I don't trust him. Especially with you." The minute these words were out of his mouth, Robert's lips clamped together, as if wishing he could take them back.

"Now you're being absurd!" I attempted to control my temper, but the man was irksome beyond endurance. "Pierce Godfrey is invariably polite and agreeable toward you, Robert, yet I have yet to hear you utter one civil word about him."

His face flushed an even darker red, but he did not reply.

"Not only that," I went on, "but you will insist on referring to him as a *pirate,* an appellation which infers that he is dishonest in his business dealings, and for which you possess not a modicum of proof. I simply cannot comprehend such unwarranted behavior, or why you have developed this unreasonable dislike for the man."

With this, I folded my arms across my chest, sat back down in my chair, and waited for him to respond to these justifiable charges.

"Are you quite finished?" he asked.

I started to make a sardonic reply, then decided I had said enough and held my tongue, contenting myself with giving him a brisk nod of my head.

"All right, then, I'll tell you why I mistrust the man." He fixed me with steely eyes, all the while moving forward until he was perched on the edge of his seat which, considering his muscular build, caused the chair to creak in protest.

"I understand that, as a woman, your knowledge of the world is limited. If it were not, you would realize that men of the sea are notoriously capricious, especially when it comes to the ladies. Even as a wee lad growing up in Edinburgh I knew that a sailor had as many women as the ports he visited. Believe me, Sarah, Godfrey is no exception. In fact, I'd be willing to wager that his reputation as a lothario is well known throughout the Orient. You are too naïve by half to recognize his true intentions, but I assure you they are anything but honorable."

I was so taken aback by this froth of utter nonsense, I could scarcely draw breath to speak. As I fumbled to find words severe enough to express my outrage, he was off again, rising from his chair and punctuating each ludicrous accusation by slapping a hand down on my desk.

"He has besotted you, Sarah. It's not your fault, of course, but it's your very innocence that's placing you in such peril. I wish you could see your face when that man—"

His tirade was brought to an abrupt halt by a knock on the door. I was so caught up in anger and exasperation that I did not immediately answer, and the knock was repeated.

"Come in," I finally managed, giving Robert a warning look as I rose from my chair.

The door opened, and Pierce strode into the room. He did not appear surprised to find Robert standing in front of my desk, his broad face glaring at him like a thundercloud. Pierce's composed and doggedly fixed expression led me to believe that he had overheard some of Robert's angry harangue from outside the door.

"Sarah," Pierce said, smiling as his eyes ran appreciatively over my gown and hat. "You look exquisite, as always." His smile faded as he turned to Robert, acknowledging his presence with a terse, "Good evening, Campbell."

"Good evening," Robert responded with equal curtness.

I could tell by the pained look on Robert's broad face that he was trying to smile at Pierce, but the effort fell far short of its mark; if anything, it had the unfortunate effect of making the Scot appear as if he were suffering a painful toothache. Neither man proffered his hand to the other, as common courtesy dictated.

"Are you ready, Sarah?" Pierce inquired, his dark eyes in no way mirroring his pleasant demeanor.

"Yes, I am." I left my desk and started for the back room. "Just let me get my wrap."

It took me but a moment to fetch my cape and rabbit hair muff. Returning to my office, I allowed Pierce to help me on with my cloak. Standing, arms folded, in front of my desk, Robert silently glowered at us both.

I had reached the end of my patience with this rude, and entirely uncalled-for, behavior; it did not deserve to be acknowledged. Turning my back on my exasperating colleague, I swept through the door Pierce held open for me. As I left, I threw over my shoulder, "Please ensure that the door is properly latched when you leave, Robert."

Closing the door firmly behind us, Pierce followed me down the stairs and assisted me into his waiting carriage.

The Baldwin Theater was filled to near capacity for the opening night of Shakespeare's comedy, *The Merry Wives of Windsor*. Comfortably seated in Pierce's proscenium box, we had a clear view of the nearly two thousand patrons seated below us in plush red upholstered seats—which, paradoxically, reminded me of the sofas and chairs featured in Madam Valentine's brothel. The theater boasted velvet hangings, filigree decorations on pillars and walls, as well as rich tapestries and paintings on display in the lobby and adjoining saloons, where theatergoers could refresh themselves during intermissions.

I had borrowed Pierce's opera glasses to examine the theater's furnishings, when I spied a familiar group of people taking their seats in a box across the theater from our own. There was no mistaking the tall, erect figure of Major Zachariah Tremaine, as well as that of his son Reginald and daughter-in-law Faith. The twins, Melody and David, followed behind their parents and grandfather. The last gentleman to enter the box and take a seat was the Reverend Erasmus Mayfield, rector of the Church of Our Savior. He seemed in high spirits, chatting animatedly with the younger Mr. Tremaine as the two men, along with the elder Tremaine, took their places behind the women and young David.

My eyes were immediately drawn to Melody, who was wearing a lovely dusky gold gown, overlaid with cream-colored, open-mesh silk netting at the neckline and around the wrists. Her glorious tawny-brown hair had been pulled back from her face, and was decorated with a few simple combs and matching gold ribbons.

Even at a distance, I was once again struck by the girl's innocent beauty and grace, as she allowed her brother to seat her in the center of the box, next to their stepmother on her right.

Faith Tremaine was attired in a dark blue gown, with delicate pale blue lace lining the bodice and the wrists. The cut of her neckline was considerably lower than her stepdaughter's, and the long, slender design of the dress was cleverly cut to make her appear taller than her barely five feet. She was wearing a small evening hat decorated with contrasting feathers, several artificial flowers, and an assortment of brilliant stones, and she was carrying a small reticule which sparkled when it caught the light of the huge crystal chandelier hanging from the ceiling.

"Look, Pierce," I said in a whisper, lightly touching his arm and handing him the opera glasses. "Do you see the girl in the gold gown? The one who has just taken her seat in that box across the way?"

Training the glasses in the direction I had indicated, he nodded. "Yes, I see her. She's very lovely."

"That's Melody Tremaine. Her twin brother, David, is sitting to her left, and that's her stepmother, Faith Tremaine, on her right."

I went on to explain the three men sitting behind them, including the Reverend Mayfield.

"It was the Reverend Mayfield's deacon, Dieter Hume, who was found murdered two nights ago near the Harrison Street Bridge."

Pierce appeared interested. "Wasn't another man killed near that same bridge earlier in the week?"

"Yes," I replied softly. "That was Hume's friend Nigel Logan. The two men attended a party in the Reverend Mayfield's honor at the Tremaine house the night of Logan's death."

He gave a soft whistle. "That seems a bit of a coincidence. The newspapers have made little of that connection. Instead, they make it sound as if a madman is on the loose."

"I know, and those stories are frightening a great many people, especially those who live in the Rincon Hill neighborhood. It has crossed my mind to wonder if Reginald Tremaine has exerted some influence to keep the Tremaine name out of this awful business, although at the time the police seemed to consider the Reverend Mayfield a possible suspect."

Pierce looked surprised. "A church rector? Why would he do such a thing? And to his own deacon?"

"Why, indeed? It's food for thought, isn't it?"

"How do you know the Tremaines?" asked Pierce, once again training the glasses at the box across from us.

"They live less than two blocks from our house," I explained. "Although I'm not well acquainted with the family, I occasionally see them at church—the Reverend Mayfield's church, actually."

I went on to describe the birthday party my sister-in-law Celia held for Faith Tremaine at our house, adding that the surprise of the evening came when young Melody sang for us after dinner.

"She's remarkably gifted," I told him. "The girl is so shy she hardly uttered a word throughout dinner. It was only when she sat down at the piano and began singing that she truly came to life. You should have seen the glow on her face, Pierce. It was as if she had escaped into a world of her own. The rest of us no longer appeared to exist."

"If she is as gifted as you say, she should consider a career on the stage," he said, continuing to study the girl through the glasses.

"I agree. Unfortunately, her father and stepmother seem set against it."

"She's still very young," Pierce said, laying aside his opera glasses. "Perhaps when she turns eighteen she can decide for herself what she wants to do with her life."

"I doubt that her stepmother will allow that to happen. Faith Tremaine seems determined to marry her off as quickly as possible."

"What about her brother?" he asked. "Does he also express an interest in the theater?"

I laughed. "Hardly. That boy has the mind of a true scientist. I gather he has his heart set on becoming a biologist, or perhaps a botanist. He already shows a remarkable understanding of the natural sciences."

"Surely his father and stepmother can find no fault with his choice of a career."

"On the contrary, Reginald Tremaine seems disappointed that his eldest son shows no desire to follow him into the men's retail business." I took a moment to describe the Men's Emporium, then went on to tell him about the two children he'd fathered with his second wife, Faith. "Fortunately, his younger son, Reggie, seems happy to take over the store when his father retires."

Before Pierce could comment on this, the houselights dimmed and I, too, fell silent. A tremor of excitement ran through the audience as the curtain rose to reveal an imaginatively designed stage, set off to good advantage by clever lighting. Then Justice Shallow, his cousin Slender, and Sir Hugh Evans stepped onto the stage and the play began. The three were colorfully costumed, as befitted their roles, and as soon as the three began to speak their opening lines, all thoughts of the Tremaines were swept from my mind.

The play ran a full three hours, and it was nearing midnight when Pierce and I ordered a late dinner at a nearby restaurant. I admit that I was weary after such a long day, and ordered a light supper of soup and sole, baked in a delicate white sauce. The first part of our meal was taken up with lively talk of the play, then the conversation returned to our earlier discussion of the Tremaine family.

"How does the Tremaine girl feel about marrying so young?" Pierce asked.

I paused in taking a sip of wine to consider his question. "It's hard to say. As I told you, she barely spoke more than a dozen words all evening. However, based on her stepmother's laments about how Melody balks at entertaining young men, or attending social events, I'd say she would far prefer to pursue her music than settle down with a husband and children. At least for now. I'll never forget the expression of pure joy on her face when she began to sing."

"Is she really as good as you say?" he asked.

"Absolutely," I said with enthusiasm. "I don't claim to be a music critic, of course, but I have heard voices far less splendid than hers on the stage. It's more than just her voice, though, it's her innocence and beauty, the mood she somehow manages to create. I hardly know how to describe it. All I can say is that it's truly magical. That's why I find it so unfair that her parents refuse to share her with the rest of San Francisco, or the world, for that matter."

Pierce thought about this. "If she's half as gifted as you claim, Sarah, perhaps I can help. Joseph Kreling happens to be a friend of mine. A few years ago, he and his brother John built the Tivoli Opera House on Eddy Street. I'm sure you've been there."

"Yes, several times."

"Perhaps I'll have a talk with Joe and see if he'll allow your Melody to sing for him."

I experienced a rush of excitement. "Oh, Pierce, that would be wonderful! I'm sure Mr. Kreling will love her." Then I remembered Reginald and Faith, and my enthusiasm waned. "The difficulty will be in convincing her parents to let her audition."

"Let's not cross that bridge just yet, Sarah. First I must speak to Joseph about the girl. If he's interested, then we'll see about persuading her parents to allow her this opportunity."

"It won't be easy," I said. "But we must at least try."

He took a sip of wine. "I have never understood the pressure society exerts on a young woman to marry before she's ready. It seems that girls barely make it out of childhood when they're expected to establish a home for their husband, then set about filling it with children. I realize that most women aspire to motherhood, but so many of them live their entire lives without once venturing more than a few miles beyond the place where they were born. I love San Francisco, yet a large and exciting world exists beyond its boundaries. Never to explore its cities and customs seems a terrible waste."

"Spoken like a true adventurer," I said, smiling at him over the flickering candles. "I daresay a good many women would agree with you. I certainly do. As you pointed out, though, society wields tremendous pressure on a young girl. As does her family. It reflects badly on them if their daughter flaunts contemporary mores, and instead chooses to carve out her own path in life."

"You mean as you have?" His eyes stared into mine with dark intensity, but they were gentle and sympathetic.

I paused, then nodded. "Yes, exactly as I have."

"Which is why you asked me to pick you up at your office this evening. I gather your mother made rather too much of our dinner engagement the other night."

I nodded. "My poor, long-suffering mother. I can't blame her, you know. As her only daughter I must be a terrible disappointment."

"You could never be a disappointment," he objected. "To anyone. Least of all your family."

I gave him a wry smile. "Oh, but I'm afraid I could. Much as I love my mother, I simply cannot imagine myself as anything but a lawyer. That's been my dream since I was a child."

"I understand dreams."

I looked into his handsome face, and I saw the passion reflected in his dark eyes. "Yes, I believe you do."

"I often dream of you, Sarah," he said softly. "At the risk of sounding melodramatic, I imagine sailing around the world with you at my side." He reached across the table and took my hand. "It would be a wonderful adventure."

"I'm sure it would," I told him, and I meant it. Part of me longed to set off and see the world, especially with a man I cared for deeply. I had been independent enough to go against society's dictates and become an attorney, but in other ways I was very much like the women Pierce had just described. Except for a trip I had taken with my parents to England several years ago, I had not traveled far from San Francisco, the city of my birth.

"But you won't change your mind?" He already knew my answer, still his look was hopeful.

I shook my head. "No." At his downcast look I hurried on. "Pierce, I'm sorry. I—"

"Please, Sarah," he interrupted, giving my hand a gentle

squeeze. "Don't say anything else. Not now. Let's continue on the way we agreed at the start."

He raised his wineglass and repeated the toast we had made the other night. "To friendship, my dear Sarah. And to Christmas."

He sat close beside me in the carriage as we drove home. Perhaps it was my imagination, but he seemed to take advantage of every bump and pothole in the road to steady me with his hands, going so far as to place his arm around my shoulder. The last time this happened he used his arm to pull me even closer to his side. Then, before I had time to fully register what was happening, his lips were suddenly on mine.

We had kissed but one time before, but the startling sensations I'd felt then came back to me in a bewildering rush. It was as if I had caught on fire, and was melting beneath an unrelenting heat. This disturbing feeling traveled from my lips all the way down my body, leaving me confused and breathless.

A faint voice from somewhere deep inside my head told me I should protest, but the simple truth was that I didn't want to break away from him. I cannot say how long we remained in this embrace. In truth, time no longer seemed relevant. It shames me to admit it, but I suspect that had he not at last released me, I might never have broken free of my own volition.

As if from a distance, I felt the motion of the carriage stop. I expected the coach door to open, but the driver did not move from his raised seat behind the vehicle.

After the noisy rumble of the wheels on the uneven streets, it was suddenly very quiet. I heard the horse snort once, then we were cocooned in silence. Unable to speak, I could only watch helplessly while Pierce studied my face in the glimmer of moonlight filtering in through the carriage windows.

"You are even more beautiful than I remembered," he said softly. "I haven't been able to get you out of my mind."

"Pierce, we shouldn't—I cannot—"

160

"I know you can't, my dear. And I don't want to do anything to frighten you away."

Slowly, and very gently, he traced his forefinger down my cheek, and again I felt my breath catch in my throat. As if I'd been rendered strangely paralyzed, I found it impossible to move away as his lips once again pressed against mine.

This kiss was shorter and less intense than the first, as if he really did fear I might become frightened enough to bolt. Then, as if some unseen signal had passed between them, the driver abandoned his perch and opened the carriage door. Pierce stepped out before me, extending a hand to assist me down to the street.

"I'll let you know if I'm able to reach Joe Kreling," he said, walking me to my door. He rang the bell, then bent down and placed a chaste kiss upon my cheek. "Sleep well, Sarah."

The door was opened by Edis, but I hardly took notice of him. I stood quite still on the front stoop as Pierce's carriage drove out of sight. In my muddled state, I could not for the life of me remember who Joe Kreling was.

CHAPTER THIRTEEN

I did not sleep well that night. However hard I tried to settle my thoughts and drift off into peaceful slumber, images of Pierce kept tumbling about in my head. The few times I did doze off, my dreams were filled with his face and disturbing memories of our embrace.

I blamed myself for what had happened, even more than I blamed him. The mistakes I'd made with Benjamin Forest when I was nineteen could be excused because of my youth and inexperience. Such justifications were no longer valid. I was now a mature woman, aware of my vulnerabilities as well as my strengths.

After hours of fretful tossing and turning, I gave up thoughts of sleep and rose from my bed shortly after dawn. Although Cook tried to tempt my appetite with boiled eggs, bacon, and freshly baked bread, I could only pick at my breakfast. Leaving the poor woman to lament that I no longer appreciated her cooking, I wandered about the house searching for something to do, anything that might take my mind off Pierce.

The moment the morning newspapers arrived, I escaped into the library and nervously scanned them for any mention of my visit to Madam Valentine's parlor house the previous day. Thankfully, my name did not appear in any of the morning editions. Of course, we did not subscribe to the *Tattler,* I reminded myself, so I might not yet be entirely out of the woods.

When I finished with the newspapers, I went searching for my father, eager to seek his advice about Brielle Bouchard. Unable to locate him anywhere in the house, I sought out Edis, who informed me that he had left early to take care of some pressing business at his office.

By quarter to ten, I had grown so restless that I finally gave up trying to manufacture busywork, and decided to steal a page from Papa's book and go downtown to my own office. On the way, I would pick up a copy of Ozzie Foldger's paper, and make sure that he had not chosen me as Saturday's headline story.

It was a cool, dark morning, and as I walked to the horsecar line I was grateful I'd decided to wear a warm woolen wrap and carry an umbrella. Overhead clouds threatened rain, but so far it was only coming down as a light drizzle. Reaching Sutter Street, I purchased a copy of the *Tattler,* and quickly examined it. When I could find no mention of myself, nor my visit to Madam Valentine's brothel, I felt a tremendous sense of relief. Perhaps seeing Ozzie Foldger outside her parlor house truly had been a figment of my imagination.

When I reached my office, I thought I might find Fanny in her shop downstairs, but her door was locked and the CLOSED sign was visible. Peering through the window, I could detect no sign of activity in her small apartment located behind the store.

Disappointed, I realized how much I had been looking forward to sharing a cup of coffee and a nice chat with my neighbor. Instead, I trudged up the stairs and unlocked my office door. Once inside, I removed my wrap and hat, then sat down at my desk to face the remainder of the work I had removed from Robert's desk the previous morning. I hoped that being busy would help take my mind off Pierce, as well as my worry over Brielle Bouchard.

Unfortunately, this was a hopeless endeavor. I spent the next hour dutifully applying myself to Robert's paperwork, but it was not nearly interesting enough to distract my mind from more pressing matters. When I could bear it no longer, I decided that I might as well attend to some last-minute Christmas shopping I had been putting off. This was hardly my favorite activity, but at least I would be out and about, and completing a task too long procrastinated. Moreover, anything was better than writing a brief for a man suing his neighbor for refusing to pay his half of a shared fence!

As I set off at a brisk pace down Sutter Street, I looked up to see that the dark clouds overhead had grown heavier since I'd left my house. They now appeared to hang over the city like a giant black umbrella. We'd had more than the normal amount of rain this fall, and we could probably expect to receive a good deal more throughout the winter months—which typically constitute our rainiest season. I hoped it would hold off until I had completed my errands.

Pulling my wrap more tightly around my shoulders, I hastened my step. My destination was Gabel's Fine Shirts on Market Street, where I would collect the dress shirts I had ordered to be made for Samuel and Charles. After that, I planned to walk farther down Market Street to Sanborn and Vail's Picture Shop, where I hoped to find a suitable picture frame for my sister-in-law Celia.

Emerging from Gabel's some twenty minutes later, and carrying two very satisfactory dress shirts neatly folded into a parcel, I was surprised to happen upon Melody and David Tremaine. The boy was juggling several awkward-sized boxes, while the girl carried two large brown parcels tied with string.

David inclined his head politely, while his sister exclaimed, "Miss Woolson, how delightful to see you. Are you Christmas shopping?"

I smiled and nodded. "As are you by the look of all your packages. How are you, Miss Tremaine, Mr. Tremaine?"

"Melody, please," the girl protested. "And I'm sure my brother would prefer to be called 'David.' I am well, thank you, although I fear that David may be developing one of his sick headaches. He suffers from them periodically, and they are quite painful." She smiled at her brother, who did not look well pleased that she had revealed his ailment. Realizing she had spoken out of turn, the girl hurried on, "And you are correct, Miss Woolson. We made an early start of it this morning, and have just written paid to our holiday shopping. Thank heavens!"

She smiled, and I was once again struck by her delicate beauty. Even a rather large hat could not disguise those glorious auburn-brown curls, and her lovely blue eyes.

"And none too soon," she added, looking up at the ominous sky. "It looks as if it is about to rain at any moment."

No sooner had she spoken these words, than the first drops of rain fell onto our faces. A moment later, it was pouring.

"Here," I said, guiding them into a nearby restaurant I sometimes frequented. "This seems a good place to get out of the storm."

Melody nodded an enthusiastic agreement. "That's an excellent idea. Food sometimes helps David's headaches, especially if he eats before they become too severe."

We took seats at a table by a front window, and lowered our parcels onto the floor at our feet. There was a fire crackling in the restaurant's hearth, and the café was warm and filled with delicious aromas. Altogether, I thought it provided a cozy refuge from the rain, which beat down upon the window in heavy rivulets, making it difficult to see the street, or anything else outside.

A waiter took our orders, and soon we grew comfortable enough to remove our outer wraps and hang them on a coat tree standing to the side of the door.

Melody smiled and gave a little shiver of pleasure. "This really is delightful. I love rainy days, as long as I am snug and dry inside. I am truly glad we met you, Miss Woolson."

"As am I," I said, returning her smile.

"It's been just terrible since Mr. Logan and Deacon Hume were killed." Melody gave a little shudder. "Our father fusses so about locking the windows and doors, even during the day, and he forbids anyone in the house to go out after dark."

"You can hardly blame him," I said. "My mother is so nervous, she's taken to examining visitors' calling cards as thoroughly as if they were all potential assassins."

"It is particularly frightening when you know the victims,"

agreed Melody solemnly. "I have never before been acquainted with anyone who was murdered. And now, suddenly, I know two."

"Was Mr. Logan a frequent visitor to your home?" I inquired, curious to learn more about the young botanist.

"Only for the past year or so," she answered. "We were introduced to him by Deacon Hume." She smiled at her brother. "David was always after Father to invite Mr. Logan to dinner, so that they might discuss disgusting bugs and snakes and such. They could talk by the hour."

"As your church deacon, Mr. Hume's death must have come as a dreadful shock," I said.

"Yes, it was horrible." She hesitated, then went on, "It shames me to admit it, but I was not particularly fond of Deacon Hume. Mr. Logan was quite another story. He was a delightfully pleasant gentleman."

"I understand Mr. Logan was well regarded at the university," I said.

"He was brilliant," David declared, speaking for the first time. Then, as if self-conscious that both his sister and I had turned to look at him, he lowered his head and went on more quietly, "I learned a great deal from him."

Melody's eyes suddenly flooded with tears. "I still can't believe they're both gone. So suddenly—and so violently. It's a ghastly nightmare!"

Dismayed to see our luncheon taking such a disturbing turn, I endeavored to change the subject. "Did you enjoy the play last night, Melody? I happened to see you and your family as you took your seats."

"Oh, were you at the Baldwin Theater?" she asked in surprise.

"I was. Unfortunately, my escort and I were seated some distance from your box, so I couldn't greet you personally. I thought it was quite a good production of *The Merry Wives of Windsor*."

Melody's lovely eyes sparkled. "I thought it was excellent! And wasn't Miss Nelson wonderful? I do so love attending the theater."

She hesitated, and her face lost some of its glow. "I just wish

Father and Mother Faith would allow us to go more often. They seem determined that we should be exposed to nothing but the classics. Just once, I long to see a Gilbert and Sullivan light opera at the Tivoli, or watch Emelie Melville and the great Fanny Davenport."

I hardly knew how to respond to this. In my opinion, Melody Tremaine's tastes in the theater were beyond reproach. I could think of no reason why her parents would deny her these simple pleasures. Yet I was reluctant to provoke additional tension between the girl and her family, especially her stepmother, by voicing my agreement. I compromised by turning my attention to her brother. "I trust you, too, enjoyed last night's performance, David?"

"Yes, it was quite entertaining, Miss Woolson," the boy answered, his voice so soft that I had to strain to hear him above the sounds of the storm, as well as the conversations going on around us.

"David is a bit shy," explained Melody, looking at her brother with fond exasperation. "Unless, of course, the topic involves the most dreadful creatures of nature."

"I believe you said you hoped one day to become a scientist," I inquired. "A biologist, is that correct?"

The boy nodded. "I would like nothing better than to attend university and obtain my degree in biology. Unfortunately . . ." His handsome face grew somber and his voice trailed off. Turning his head, he stared out the window at the pounding rain.

"Father is against it," explained Melody. "It's no secret that he had his heart set on David's taking over the business one day."

"You mean the Men's Emporium?"

"Yes, the store he started when we moved here from Sacramento. Father's been better about it of late, ever since our younger brother Reggie expressed an interest in following in his footsteps."

"He's ten, is he not?" I asked.

"Eleven," corrected Melody. "And our little sister, Carolyn, is nine. I've been around enough children to know that they can be little terrors at that age, but Reggie and Carrie are quite sweet."

"I've let my father down," put in David unexpectedly.

I looked at him, a bit taken aback by this abrupt statement. "You mean because you lack interest in his store?"

"He cannot understand why I wish to become a scientist. He claims that is no way for a gentleman to earn his livelihood."

I regarded him sympathetically. "Yes, I remember him saying as much the night your family dined with us."

"Father feels the same way about my singing," lamented Melody. "He claims that if he ever saw me performing on a public stage, he would die of mortification."

"That's unfortunate," I said with true regret. "You have a marvelous voice, a rare gift."

"Yes, she does," David agreed. He regarded his sister fondly. "All Father and his wife can think about is seeing Melody settled down with a husband. But surely she's too young for that, not yet eighteen! And she has too much talent to be trapped in a loveless marriage."

"It needn't be loveless," I pointed out, again a little surprised by this comment. "When she's older she may find someone she cares enough about to marry."

"Yes, if she's allowed to wait until she's ready. And if she's permitted to choose her own husband." David's voice was startlingly bitter, although I thought his irritability might be due to the onset of a headache. I noticed that he had been rubbing his right temple since we had sat down, and his eyes had taken on a somewhat glassy look.

"I can't even imagine getting married for years yet," Melody proclaimed. "Before I settle down I want to sing—on a stage, in a real theater." Her lovely blue eyes shone with passion. "I know that isn't the life my father envisions for me, but it's what I dream of doing above all else."

I thought of Pierce's promise to speak to his friend who owned the Tivoli Theater, but felt it would be premature to mention this until we knew if she would be invited to audition. And, of course, whether her parents would allow their daughter to sing for Mr. Kreling.

"When we were very young," Melody went on, "I remember

our mother—our *real* mother—taking David and me to a theater in Sacramento. I can still picture the singers and dancers, all the bright colors, and especially the wonderful music. I think that's when I first made up my mind to go on the stage."

"It doesn't seem fair that Melody is to be deprived of doing what she wants with her life," proclaimed her brother. "Why does society insist that girls marry so young, while men can wait until they're thirty, or even older, before settling down?"

"When we were children, David and I used to say that when we grew up we would travel all over the world," Melody said with a little laugh. "I would be a famous singer, and he would be a brilliant scientist and make great discoveries." Her lovely eyes grew somber. "Truly, Miss Woolson, I have no desire to marry before I have experienced life."

I didn't know how to respond to either of them. Since I had suffered the same pressure to get married from my parents, particularly my mother, when I was Melody's age, I could well understand her frustration. On the other hand, I knew better than most the alienation and scorn a woman was all too likely to receive if she followed her dream to pursue a career outside the home. It was a steep price to pay for one's freedom.

As if reading my mind, Melody said, "You don't know how much I admire you, Miss Woolson. You had the courage to stand up to your family, and even society, in order to become an attorney. It can't have been easy for you."

"At times it has been difficult," I admitted, "and it isn't a path I would suggest a woman follow unless she is very determined." My thoughts went to Pierce and the feelings he aroused in me. "It necessitates making a great many sacrifices, Melody. Some of which can be painful."

She looked at me for a long moment, then asked with blunt curiosity, "Is that why you've never married?" Belatedly realizing she had overstepped the boundaries of good manners, she flushed and hastened to apologize. "Do forgive me, Miss Woolson. That was unpardonably rude. What must you think of me?"

"I think you are splendidly forthright in speaking your mind, Melody," I told her. "It is an admirable quality, if it is judiciously utilized. I have often been accused of the same offense."

I sighed and sat for several moments watching the rain hit the windowpane. "You're correct, you know," I went on at length. "My desire to become an attorney is the reason I have not married. It wouldn't be fair to my husband, nor to any children we might have, if I attempted to divide my time between a career and my family. It's not always been an easy route to follow, my dear. You should give it careful thought before you decide upon your own course in life."

Just then the waiter arrived with our lunches. When we had all been served, Melody gave a sad smile and continued. "I understand what you're saying, Miss Woolson, especially about the time and dedication that is required to raise children. I have often helped our stepmother care for Reggie and little Carrie. It is a great responsibility."

"You were very young when your own mother passed away, were you not?" I asked.

"Yes, barely five years old. I still remember the series of nannies and housekeepers our father hired to care for us while he was at work. They were good women, but they could never take the place of our dear mother."

She paused as David touched her hand. His eyes, too, were wistful, as if he were reliving those unfortunate days along with his twin sister.

Sighing, she went on, "I would not willingly permit my own children to suffer such a loss. That is why I want to live out my dream before I settle down to raise a family. I know that David and I could manage quite nicely on our own, he with his bugs, while I establish a name for myself in the theater. A few years on the stage, that is all I ask."

All she asked, indeed, I thought. Melody claimed she understood the sacrifices she would face if she chose a life in the theater, but looking at her innocent face I had to wonder if she had any true notion of how difficult this fantasy would be to achieve. I had been fortunate to have a judge as a father, one, moreover, who was willing to school me along with my three older brothers. Melody, on the other hand, had no one to support her aspirations, other than perhaps her grandfather, Zachariah. But did he wield enough influence over his son and daughter-in-law to sway their objections to Melody's performing on stage?

By the time we had finished our lunch, the rain had let up enough for Melody and David to make their way to the nearest cable car line, and for me to dash the several blocks back to my office. Only when I was inside my two small rooms did I belatedly realize that, other than picking up the shirts I had ordered, I'd completed no Christmas shopping at all.

Using the storm as an excuse not to attempt any more errands that afternoon—and loath to continue with Robert's tedious paperwork—I soon departed my office to return home. When I arrived in the mid-afternoon, it was to find the entire household busily preparing for the Christmas party we were hosting the following Saturday.

Promising to join them as soon as I had changed out of my damp clothes, I hurried to my bedroom. I had no sooner come back downstairs, however, than Edis announced that George Lewis was at the door asking to see Samuel. Curious, I invited him in out of the rain, and informed him that my brother was spending the weekend in the country.

He declined my offer, continuing to stand outside the front door. Something in his expression caused the muscles in my stomach to tighten.

"What is it, George?" I asked. "What has happened? Don't tell me there's been another murder!"

"No, no, Miss Sarah, nothing like that. Fact is, we've arrested a couple of Chinamen for the killings."

I regarded him in surprise. "You've arrested two Chinese men? I thought you were questioning the guests at the Tremaines' party the night Mr. Logan was killed."

"We were, but we've come up with some witnesses willing to swear they saw two Johnnies skulking around the Harrison Street Bridge when Deacon Hume was beaten to death Wednesday morning. They've identified the men."

I could hardly believe my ears. "But I thought you agreed that the same man who killed the deacon also murdered Nigel Logan. Now you're telling me that two Chinese men have been arrested for killing one of the victims, but not the other?"

George looked uneasy. "I'm afraid so, Miss Sarah. At least for now."

"What does that mean—'for now'?" I asked suspiciously.

He looked around cautiously, as if fearing someone might be eavesdropping on our conversation.

"I shouldn't be telling you this, Miss Sarah. But there's talk at the station that they're going to try to pin Logan's murder onto the two Chinese fellows, as well."

"But the men who witnessed Mr. Logan's death claim they saw only one man running from the scene of the crime," I protested. "I heard them say that myself. And neither of them mentioned anything about the man being Chinese."

"I know, Miss Sarah. But the captain says they might not have seen the man all that clearly, seeing as how it was such a dark night. He claims it would have been easy enough to miss a second man, say, if he was hiding behind a bridge stanchion, or maybe was faster than his partner, and had already run out of sight."

"This is ridiculous!" I exclaimed. "It was just as dark the night Deacon Hume was murdered. Why should the police believe one set of witnesses and not the other?"

I put up a staying hand before he could answer. "No, don't bother telling me, George, I understand what's going on here. It's much easier to credit witnesses who claim to have seen Chinese men commit the murder than to suspect a white man of the crime."

To his credit, George did not attempt to defend his captain's dubious reasoning.

I gave a frustrated sigh. "Oh, for heaven's sake, George. All right, then, when did this arrest take place?"

"About an hour ago. We haven't made a formal announcement about the arrest yet. Since I just got off duty, I thought I'd drop by and tell Samuel."

"I see." I wondered if I should send word to Samuel, or simply wait until he returned home on Monday.

George made my decision for me when he went on, "It's nothing that can't wait until he gets back, Miss Sarah. We've locked up the Johnnies and they aren't going anywhere, at least for the time being. And the captain didn't seem too eager to tell the reporters before he had to. They're going to swarm the station soon enough when they find out."

"You say these witnesses positively identified the two Chinese men?" I asked skeptically. "But we both know it was a cloudy night. How can they be certain these are the same men they claim to have seen? Most white men have a difficult time telling one Oriental face from another under ideal conditions. Much less in the dark." I regarded him thoughtfully. "Or, if they were drinking."

Reluctantly, he nodded. "They admit that they'd had a few drinks before they started home."

"Oh, for heaven's sake! I don't see how anyone could possibly pick out any particular Chinese under those circumstances."

He hesitated, as if weighing his words, then admitted, "To be honest, I don't think they can be sure. But our department's been under a lot of pressure to catch whoever's responsible for the killings."

"So the police jumped at the chance to accuse the Chinese of Hume's murder."

He nodded unhappily. "The two Chinamen are very young, and neither of them can speak a word of English. I don't think they have the least idea why they've been thrown into city jail."

"They must be terribly frightened," I said, incensed that any individual, no matter his race, should be treated so shamefully. "Hasn't anyone provided them with an interpreter?"

"No. I suggested it to the captain, but he said it could wait until Monday, or, more like it, when he had a chance to get around to it." He appeared embarrassed.

"That's inexcusable! When will they be charged?"

He gave a helpless shrug. "I don't know. I shouldn't be saying this, but I think the captain's holding off as long as he can, hoping we'll uncover more concrete proof linking them to the murders."

"I see." I watched in thoughtful silence as he placed his hat back on his head. As usual, a tuft of sandy-brown hair swept untidily across his forehead, making him appear younger than his thirty-one years.

"You'll tell Samuel I was here, then?" he asked.

"Of course. As soon as he returns on Monday. I'd appreciate it if you'd keep me informed on the case, George. Especially any news about the two Chinese men you've arrested."

"Of course, Miss Sarah, if that's what you wish."

He started to say something else, then seemed to change his mind. Silently, he tipped his hat and departed the house.

CHAPTER FOURTEEN

I spent the next quarter hour thinking about the unfortunate Chinese men who had been arrested for Deacon Hume's murder. The sad fact was that the Chinese had become so hated for "stealing" (Dennis Kearney and his Workingmen's Party's constant accusation!) jobs from other immigrant groups, that they were regarded as easy scapegoats for any number of crimes committed in San Francisco, even those for which they had no possible motive.

The way these hardworking people had been mistreated by virtually every other race in the city was appalling. Over the past few years a number of Chinese had been attacked by unruly mobs and their meager dwellings had been burned to the ground. Discrimination against them was so acute that they were largely restricted to Tangrenbu, the dense ten-block area more commonly known as Chinatown.

Having once defended a Chinese chef arrested for murdering a white man, I knew better than most how vicious prejudice against the "celestials" had become. My client had been depicted as a "yellow-skinned devil" by nearly every newspaper in town. To make matters worse, the epitaph was often accompanied by a drawing of a demon, complete with a pitchfork and forked tail. At the start of his trial, I doubt I could have found even a handful of individuals willing to concede the possibility of his being innocent.

This train of thought inevitably led me to Li Ying, the tong leader who had asked me to represent the accused cook. I wondered if he had any idea that two of his countrymen had been imprisoned. Li was always extremely well informed, but if, as George said, the police hadn't publicly announced the arrest, there was a possibility he did not know.

It took me only a moment to make up my mind. Reaching for my cloak and reticule, I slipped out of the house and, for the second time that day, walked to the horsecar line. My destination this time was the Yoot Hong Low restaurant on Waverly Place, the address I'd been given in the event I needed to reach Li Ying. Although I had visited Li's home on several occasions, I had no idea where it was located, other than it certainly must be somewhere in Chinatown. Each time we'd met, I had been kept blindfolded until I was inside his house. Upon leaving, I had once again had my eyes covered until his carriage left Tangrenbu. This subterfuge, he had explained, was as much for my protection as it was for his own. If his many enemies suspected I knew where he lived, he explained, my life would be in danger.

Arriving half an hour later at Yoot Hong Low's restaurant, I asked to see Kin Lee, the man I had been instructed to contact. The waiter, who was wearing the customary loose white cotton tunic and black trousers, listened respectfully to my request, then escorted me to a table where he indicated that I should wait. Bowing low, he disappeared behind a painted screen at the back of the dining room. A moment later, a second waiter arrived, carrying a tray which he silently deposited before me on the table. Pouring steaming hot tea from a China pot into a cup, he, too, bowed low and departed.

I had taken but a single sip of the light green brew, when an older man, whom I recognized as Kin Lee, emerged from behind the screen. He bowed, then stood as still as a statue waiting for me to speak. When I explained that I would like to see Li Ying, he bowed yet again, and without asking any questions, slipped back behind the screen.

It was not an unpleasant wait. I enjoyed my pot of excellent tea, as well as a dish of some sort of Chinese dumplings which I found to be quite delicious. Most interesting, however, was watching the human beehive of people hurrying up and down the street. Every available inch of Chinatown seemed to be taken up with small shops and restaurants announcing themselves with gold, red, and black signs, and displaying crates of vegetables, hanging chickens, ducks, fish, hams, and vast numbers of vibrant lanterns of various shapes and sizes. The unusual aromas, strange customs, and rapid patter of an unintelligible language always made me feel as if I had left San Francisco and entered an exotic foreign land.

Perhaps fifteen or twenty minutes after Kin Lee's departure, he returned and beckoned me to follow him through the bustling kitchen, a crowded storeroom, and out into a back alley. There, pulled up behind the restaurant—and taking up very nearly all the width of the narrow alley—was a hansom cab. The driver, who was dressed entirely in black, sprang lightly down from his elevated seat in the rear of the vehicle, and politely opened the carriage door.

Before I could step up, however, he bowed and said, "Missy, please forgive. Must wear this."

Since I was no stranger to this procedure, I was not surprised or offended when the man produced a brightly printed silk scarf from a pocket, and handed it to me. With a polite nod I accepted the blindfold and placed it over my eyes, tying it into a knot at the back of my head. When the scarf was securely in place, the driver carefully assisted me into the cab and closed the door.

The cab moved and, as always, I experienced a surge of excitement. My visits with the tong leader always triggered a feeling of exhilaration, as if I were embarking on an exotic and possibly dangerous adventure. Which in the truest sense of the word, I was. For all his brilliance and flawless manners, Li Ying was undeniably one of the most ruthless leaders of Chinatown's underworld.

As was invariably the case, we drove about for some little

time—executing a good many twists and turns—before the driver finally reined his horse to a stop. Since we had commenced our journey on Waverly Place, which was situated in the heart of the ten-square-block area known as Tangrenbu, so-named after the Chinese goddess of heaven, I knew the cab driver had deliberately prolonged the journey, undoubtedly to further impede me from pinpointing the exact location of Li Ying's residence.

The blindfold was not removed until I had been escorted inside the house, guided up the carpeted stairs, and led to a comfortable armchair. When I once again regained the use of my vision, I saw that I had been placed in the room Li always used for my visits. I was delighted to see that a lovely porcelain tea service had been laid out on a black-lacquered table next to my chair, including a plate containing Western-looking cakes and cookies. Each time I called upon Li Ying, I was served refreshments from a different tea set, each more exquisite than the one which had preceded it. At the conclusion of the Russian Hill murders, he had presented me with an exquisite hand-painted tea set which had been in his family for centuries. Much to my mother's delight, it was now proudly featured on the buffet table in our Rincon Hill dining room.

As I gazed around the lovely, and eclectically decorated, room, I was once again struck by the deep peace and sense of well-being I always experienced here. Actually, it was this unexpected tranquility which had most impressed, and surprised, me on the occasion of my first visit to Li's home. Li Ying wielded more power within Tangrenbu's ten square blocks than any other single individual, Chinese or white. Given his fearful and well-deserved reputation, I had been shocked to discover that he was also a Mandarin scholar, a connoisseur of fine art, and, most significant as far as I was concerned, a gracious and sensitive gentleman.

This private and gentler Li had managed to furnish his inner sanctuary with fine examples of American and European objets d'art, sculpture, and paintings, some by the old masters while others were decidedly avant-garde. Despite the contrasting styles, they strangely blended together in harmonious coexistence.

I was examining several new additions to his collection, when there was a small noise to my right. Turning, I saw that my host, Li Ying, had quietly glided into the room.

The distinguished-looking man sat, as was his custom, on a square-backed *kuan moa* chair which had been placed on a small raised dais. Li possessed a regal bearing, sitting with a straight back, head held high, hands resting on each arm of the chair of state, yet his smile was so genuine and welcoming it quickly dispelled any fear or anxiety I might have otherwise experienced. This afternoon he was wearing an intricately embroidered green satin tunic, with an equally impressive black satin hat which was also decorated with elaborate silk embroidery.

Li was tall for a Chinese, and very slender, with coal-black hair shaved and oiled into a long queue falling down his back. It was difficult to judge his age: his hair betrayed almost no gray, his face was unlined, and he moved with youthful grace and flexibility. His dark eyes, however, betrayed a wisdom and insightfulness that takes many years to acquire, leading me to guess that he might be a great deal older than he appeared.

"Miss Woolson," he said, bowing his head. "You grace my humble home with your presence." His English was very nearly perfect, his tone pleasant and well modulated. "Again, I must apologize for requiring you to wear a blindfold."

"I appreciate the need for such a precaution, Mr. Li." I suppressed a little shiver. "Frankly, I prefer this minor inconvenience to what might happen if your enemies decided I could lead them to your home."

"I am relieved that you understand," he said with a smile. "I only wish that other visitors could accept this regrettable necessity with such intelligent forbearance."

"It is good of you to see me at such short notice, Mr. Li," I said, pleased by the compliment. "You are a busy man."

"I am never too busy for you, Miss Woolson." He nodded his head ever so slightly, and a manservant appeared out of nowhere to pour tea into the two delicate cups which sat on the tray. "Let us enjoy our tea, shall we? Then you can tell me what has brought you to my home."

Aware that this was Li's custom, I relaxed and savored the excellent tea and cakes. We spoke of my last case at San Francisco's famous Cliff House, then went on to discuss the current political climate in the city. Inevitably, our talk moved to the pending Chinese Exclusion Act, which, if passed, would provide a ten-year moratorium on Chinese labor immigration, as well as impose additional restrictions on the Chinese who had already entered the country.

"Such legislation was inevitable," he said in a tone of matter-of-fact resignation. "One limitation has built upon another over the years, emboldening anti-Chinese factions to grow ever more bold." He reached out and took a small piece of cake. "I find I have developed a taste for American sweets. You see, Miss Woolson, even I am becoming Westernized."

I regarded his long queue and very *un*-Western clothing, but said nothing. My mind boggled at the thought of Li outfitted in Western attire. It would be akin to an elephant trying to masquerade as a rabbit.

When we had finished our tea, and the ever silent servant had dutifully borne away the tray, Li settled back in his chair and finally inquired what business had prompted my unexpected visit.

"I wondered if you were aware that two of your countrymen were arrested this morning and placed in city jail?"

Li's eyebrows rose nearly to his shaved scalp. It shames me to admit it, but I was secretly pleased to have finally informed the tong lord of something he did not already know.

"You have taken me quite by surprise, Miss Woolson," he said, eyeing me with intense curiosity. "I know nothing of this matter. Of what crime have they been accused?"

"They've been charged with killing Dieter Hume last Wednesday night. He was the deacon at the Church of Our Savior on Howard Street."

"I am aware of the young man's death." His long, sculpted face was grave. "However, I do not understand why the police should suspect two of my countrymen of committing such an assault."

"Some men have come forward and identified them as being in the vicinity of the Harrison Street Bridge the night Dieter Hume was murdered." I did not add that I found the so-called eyewitness accounts a great deal less than convincing.

His mouth tightened. "That is all? They were simply seen in the area?"

I was embarrassed to admit that our all-white police force had acted upon such flimsy evidence. "Yes, I'm afraid so. It's very little to go on, and if they had not been—"

"Chinese?" he finished for me. "Indeed, Miss Woolson, you are correct. If the two men had not been Chinese, they would simply have been questioned and released."

Since I could think of no response to this all too fair indictment, I remained silent.

"Do you know their names?" he went on when I didn't respond.

"No, and I rather doubt the police know, either. I've been told that they are quite young and that neither speaks any English. Unfortunately, the authorities have not provided them with an interpreter. They must find their predicament very frightening."

Li's face remained outwardly composed. His black eyes alone betrayed his disquiet. "It was most kind of you to notify me of this unfortunate situation, Miss Woolson. I am in your debt. The two men of whom you speak must have only recently arrived in San Francisco. Otherwise, I would have received a report of their disappearance."

He sat very still for several minutes as he contemplated the situation. "I assume there is little hope of obtaining their release on bail?"

I shook my head. "It would be virtually impossible, Mr. Li. The fact that they're foreign nationals, along with the ease with which they could disappear within the boundaries of Chinatown, makes them an extreme escape risk."

I thought of the disturbing newspaper reports of the two murders. "Actually, their safety might be better served if they remain in jail, at least until the real killer is apprehended."

"You fear a lynch mob."

"Yes, I do," I told him truthfully. "People are afraid. And Deacon Hume's murder was particularly brutal."

"As was Mr. Logan's. I presume that at some juncture the authorities will attempt to connect my young countrymen to this prior killing?"

"They haven't done so as yet. But, yes, at some point I'm afraid that's exactly what they will do. The newspapers have been stirring up people's fears until they're afraid to venture out after dark. It's bound to come as a relief to learn that two suspects have been incarcerated. I fear their reaction if the two men were freed on bail."

"Especially when those two men are Chinese," Li added, his face inscrutable. Neither his expression nor his tone of voice revealed his private feelings on the matter.

"Exactly," I quietly agreed.

He nodded. "As is your custom, you speak no less than the truth, Miss Woolson. I have missed our little chats."

Subtly shifting his position in the thronelike chair, Li gave the impression of suddenly growing taller and, although I wouldn't have thought it possible, even more regal. He made a tower with the long fingers of both slender hands, and eyed me with unsettling directness.

"Tell me, Miss Woolson, what can we do to help these men?"

Thankfully, I was ready for this question, having thought it through on the ride over in the hansom cab.

"First, we must ensure that the young men receive a speedy arraignment," I told him. "The police are holding them on the flimsiest of evidence. It's my guess that they'll attempt to put off officially charging them for as long as possible, hoping, of course, that they'll uncover more definitive proof of their guilt."

"You would be willing to represent these unfortunate young men, Miss Woolson?"

I had also anticipated this request, and although this was certain to become yet another unpopular and high-profile case, I could not turn my back on two young men who might otherwise not receive justice.

"Yes, Mr. Li," I replied, after a brief hesitation. "I will do whatever I can for them. It will be necessary, of course, to provide me with the services of an interpreter."

"You shall have one," he immediately agreed. As if guessing the reason behind my brief hesitation, he went on, "I am not unaware of the difficulties you will face by accepting this case, Miss Woolson, both personally as well as professionally. Once again, I am amazed by your courage and dedication to justice. I seriously doubt that I could find another attorney in this city willing to risk his career, and certainly incur private disdain, for the sake of two young 'coolies.' "

I nodded, but could think of nothing to say. It would be fruitless, as well as naïve, to deny that these words were no more than the simple truth.

We spent the next quarter hour discussing the details of my visit to city jail on Monday morning, including the time and location where I would meet the translator.

When we had concluded our business, the man who had served us tea once again slid silently into the room and handed Li Ying an envelope. With a low bow, he turned and just as quietly exited. Without examining the contents of the envelope, Li Ying handed it to me.

"Please consider this a retainer, Miss Woolson."

Gravely, he shook his head. "As in the case of the early Christians, I feel as though I am throwing you to the lions. I can only pray that you will escape from the arena unscathed."

During the ride home, I had time to reflect upon my decision to represent Li Ying's countrymen. As I had told the tong lord, there was virtually no possibility that I could obtain their release on bail. The most I could reasonably hope to achieve was to get their arraignment hearings scheduled as quickly as possible. Other than that, I could only ensure that they were being treated fairly at the jail which, given their nationality, was hardly an assured thing.

Of course I had yet to meet my clients, but it required no great leap of faith on my part to believe in their innocence. As Samuel and I both agreed, it stretched coincidence beyond reason to presume that Nigel Logan and Dieter Hume had been murdered by two different villains. I remained convinced that there was only one killer, and that that person had chosen his victims with care, and then carried out the murders with deadly forethought. To my mind, the only crime those unfortunate young Celestials were guilty of was being in the wrong place at the wrong time!

What concerned me most at this particular moment, however, was that now that the police had two suspects in custody, they would give up looking for the real murderer. The citizens of San Francisco were in an uproar. When the city's newspapers discovered that two Chinese men had been arrested for the crimes the situation was bound to become even more volatile.

As soon as I was allowed to remove my blindfold, I took Li's envelope from my reticule. Inside, I discovered a thick wad of bills amounting to an extremely generous retainer. Closing my eyes, I felt almost light-headed with fear. Unless I could somehow manage a miracle—which almost certainly would require me to find Nigel Logan and Dieter Hume's murderer myself—how was I possibly going to prove my new clients' innocence? I continued to believe wholeheartedly in our Constitution's promise of justice for all, but at this particular moment I simply had no idea how to achieve it.

I would have preferred nothing more, when I returned home, than to spend what remained of Saturday afternoon contemplating this latest dilemma, as well as the challenging matter of Brielle Bouchard and her baby. Not for the first time in my brief legal career, I felt out of my depth. I wished that Samuel were not spending the weekend in the country. If he were here, I would at least have someone to discuss the cases with. Samuel was adept at playing devil's advocate; between the two of us we often came up with ideas neither of us would have considered on our own.

Much as I might have desired time for much needed contemplation before dinner, however, it was not to be. I had no sooner stepped inside the house than Mama swept me up to help with the preparations for next Saturday's Christmas party.

My sister-in-law Celia, along with her two eldest children, Tom and little Mandy, were already seated at a table in the kitchen stringing popcorn and cranberries to be used as decorations for the Christmas tree (although it seemed that as much popcorn was going into their mouths as was making it onto the string). The newest addition to the Woolson family, three-month-old Charlie, was sleeping peacefully in his cradle at his doting mother's feet.

Hazel Bentley, our ladies' maid, and the children's nanny, Mary Douglas, were seated well out of range of the children's sticky fingers, busily tatting white snowflakes and other delicate patterns which would also be hung on the tree. Cook was busy at the stove baking gingerbread men and other hard cookies, while Ina Corks, our Irish maid, bent over a tray, her small tongue protruding slightly from between set lips as she carefully decorated the cooled pastries with colored icing squeezed from an assortment of piping bags.

Brooding over my legal quandaries was all but fruitless, when surrounded by so much joyful family activity. If I had been lacking Christmas spirit before this afternoon, it was present now all around me. Our warm, cozy kitchen was filled with happy chatter, childish giggles, and mouthwatering smells, all of which I found impossible to resist. Taking off my suit jacket, I slipped on the apron Mama handed me, and set to work.

Since I was hopeless at tatting, as well as embroidery, knitting, crocheting, and other womanly skills, I was set to work twisting sprigs of mistletoe, holly, and other greenery into arrangements to be hung about the house. Time permitting, Mama had instructed me to commence work on the paper streamers which would also be used for tree and room decorations. The following week, of course, would find the entire household staff turning our home upside down in a frenzy of last-minute housecleaning.

Several hours later, after a simple dinner of cold meat, bread, cheese, and apples, I sought out my father, hoping to discuss Brielle Bouchard's case with him. *Only* Brielle's case. I knew he would not be happy to learn that I had once again ventured into Chinatown alone, or that I'd had a private audience with Li Ying. He certainly would be upset if he knew that I'd agreed to represent the two Chinese men arrested for Dieter Hume's murder. As I had other fish to fry this weekend, I preferred to leave that particular confession until later.

I was disappointed, although not surprised, to learn that he was spending the evening at his club. It did not require a mind reader to guess that he had probably slipped out immediately after dinner before Mama could involve him in the flurry of Christmas preparations which resumed immediately after our evening meal. Unfortunately, I had no club to escape to, and was once again recruited to paste together the paper streamers.

This busywork with my mother and Celia had one undeniable benefit: It once again kept me too occupied to worry about Brielle Bouchard, and the two young Chinese men I had rather rashly agreed to represent. Time for that would come later, when I retired for the night. Then I would have entirely too much time to consider my two all but impossible cases.

I feared I was destined to pass another long night.

CHAPTER FIFTEEN

As it turned out, I had no opportunity to speak to my father about Brielle Bouchard until the following afternoon. My hope that he would be able to conjure up some scheme to help the girl, however, had faded with each passing hour. Papa might be a brilliant if slightly unorthodox judge, I told myself, but he was not a miracle worker. His job was to enforce the law, not invent new ways to circumvent it. On the other hand, he had an uncanny ability to pull a rabbit out of his hat when one least expected it, and in the end I couldn't bring myself to give up on the young mother until I had at least run the problem by him.

I found Papa supervising Marco Ciatti, an affable part-time gardener and general handyman who was much sought after to do odd jobs in the neighborhood. They were clearing out several overgrown rhododendron bushes that were encroaching on the back fence.

"*Buon giorno*, Miss Woolson," Marco said with a broad grin. He jauntily tipped his cap as I joined the two men.

I was about to address my father when, for a startled moment, I actually thought I caught the little Italian winking at me. When I turned back for a second look, however, he was whistling cheerfully and taking up a large pair of clipping shears to attack the overgrown bushes. I remembered odd bits of gossip I'd overheard from several women in the neighborhood, implying none too subtly that the good-looking handyman had a well-developed eye for the ladies. Since Marco's behavior toward me had always been pleasant and well mannered, I chided myself for possessing an overactive imagination.

"How are you, Marco?" I asked, returning his smile.

"*Bene,* Miss Woolson," he replied, beaming. "*Grazie.*"

"Hello, Sarah," my father's voice greeted me. A moment later, he appeared from around the side of a large rhododendron bush. "Did you finally grow tired of pasting strips of paper together? I swear, your mother has become obsessed with this Christmas party of hers. In the end, she'll have our house looking like one of those ridiculous scenes inside a snow globe."

"Actually, Mama is helping Celia with little Charlie. Mary Douglas has the afternoon off to visit her family," I said, referring to the children's nanny.

"Good. Then maybe it'll be safe to go back inside the house. I don't understand why women have to make such a fuss over the Christmas holidays. If she didn't want everything to look so perfect for that dad-burn party of hers, she'd have had a conniption fit to see me working out here on a Sunday afternoon." He chuckled. "Never mind that the back fence is about to be bowled over by these bushes."

He took a few steps to the right and studied the rhododendron bush from another angle, then pulled back a thick branch and nodded to our handyman.

"Cut it here, Marco. With this bit gone, we should be able to reach around back and trim the branches that are invading the fence."

Whistling cheerfully, Marco did as he was instructed, then tossed the cuttings onto a pile of debris in front of some shrubs. Making his way farther around the overgrown rhododendron, he was momentarily lost to sight, although his merry whistle continued unabated.

"I planned on speaking to you after we were through here,"

Papa said, turning back to me. "I was wondering if you knew when Samuel would be returning from his weekend in the country?"

I gave Papa a suspicious look, then immediately tried to disguise it by idly using my foot to nudge some stray leaves onto the pile of cuttings.

"I believe he said he would be back sometime tomorrow morning. Why do you ask?"

"I've made an appointment for him to see Arthur Cunningham Tuesday morning. I planned to tell him about it Friday night, but he'd already taken off for the weekend—without saying anything to me, as usual."

His normally cheerful face grew serious. "I've gone to an almighty amount of trouble arranging this interview, Sarah, and I don't intend to let Samuel wriggle out of it. He's thirty years old, high time he stopped cavorting around and took his bar exam. He can't spend the rest of his life as a part-time paralegal. Arthur Cunningham and John Brill run a respectable law firm. Samuel could do a good deal worse than start off his career with them."

I gave a little shudder to think of how Samuel would react to this news. Misunderstanding my shiver, Papa started to remove his jacket. "Here, Sarah, it's grown cold and you'll catch a chill."

"Thank you, Papa, but I'm fine."

Nervously, I cleared my throat, then I hurried on before my face inadvertently gave away my brother's secret.

"Actually there's something I'd like to discuss with you, too, Papa," I said, as another large branch came flying out from behind the bush.

"Is that so?" my father replied, wiping his hands on a handkerchief and starting toward a wooden bench that stood beside an acacia tree. "Well, there's no time like the present. I think Marcus has the rhododendrons well in hand."

Settling onto the bench, Papa gave a tired sigh, and I suspected he was only too happy to be afforded a break from the pruning. Although he was fond of telling his family and friends how much he enjoyed gardening, I've often thought it would be more accurate to say that he enjoyed a supervisory role in the garden, rather than actually tilling the soil himself.

"So, what's on your mind, my girl?" he asked, brushing small clumps of dirt off his coat sleeves. "If you're looking for Christmas gift ideas for your mother you're out of luck. In fact, I was going to ask you for suggestions. I swear, that woman gets harder to shop for every year."

I smiled at this. "She is, isn't she? But that's not why I wanted to talk to you. I need your advice about a young woman who visited my office last week."

"A new client?" he said, pleased. "Excellent! I always knew it was only a matter of time until your law firm took off."

"A *possible* client," I amended, and went on to describe Brielle Bouchard's visit to my office the previous Monday morning. His eyes widened when I mentioned that she had spent more than a year and a half as a "kept woman." They became absolutely huge when I told him the name of Brielle's lover.

"Gerald Knight!" He slapped his knee and exploded with laughter. "The oh so virtuous preacher of righteous living. My, my, how the mighty have fallen."

"You're familiar with his newspaper, then?"

"I've glanced over the *Daily Journal* a time or two," he admitted a bit shamefacedly. Considering Papa's oft-spoken views—all negative—on the daily press in general, I was surprised at this confession. "More to keep up with who he's currently lambasting than to read his pitiful prose. As far as I'm concerned, Gerald Knight is a perfect example of plug-ugly journalism."

"I'm not familiar with Mr. Knight, other than to recognize his name and that of his newspaper. From what I've heard, though, he strikes me as being rather pompous and narrow-minded."

"You're right there, my girl," pronounced Papa. "That paper of his is always going on about one cause or another, especially the sanctity of the family. Which is all-fired ironic, don't you think?"

I nodded my head in agreement. "According to Brielle, he kept two previous mistresses in the Pacific Avenue house before she moved in."

"All the while posing as the champion of all that is good and moral," Papa spat in disgust.

He looked up to see Marco moving on to the next rhododendron bush. "Just a minute, Sarah."

He rose a bit stiffly from the bench and went to speak to the handyman, returning several minutes later after issuing a fresh set of instructions.

"Of course, listing Gerald Knight's faults does nothing to help this young girl of yours," he said, sitting back down beside me. He shook his head in obvious appreciation. "She sounds like a right little fireball. Imagine the nerve it took for her to visit you, waving that contract and insisting on suing the bounder. By God, I'd like to try the case myself. I'd throw the book at that womanizer. He deserves to pay through the teeth for being such a two-faced good-for-nothing. It's a shame the poor girl doesn't have a leg to stand on."

"I know, that's the problem. There's no getting around the issue of paternity."

"What do you propose to do?"

I sighed. "I have no idea. I've examined the problem from every angle, and I can't come up with a single strategy to help the poor girl. I realize I'm grasping at straws, but I hoped you might have some suggestions."

He chuckled. "I'm touched by your faith in me, my girl. But I haven't yet mastered the art of performing miracles."

"If we fail, Brielle will be compelled to work at Madam Valentine's parlor house."

"Which is hardly a desirable place to raise a child." He sat quietly for several minutes, presumably mulling over the situation. Finally, he shook his head. "I wish I could help, Sarah. But you know as well as I do that there is simply no way to prove that Knight is the child's father." He paused. "Not legally, anyway. Unless—"

"Unless what, Papa?" I asked, unable to repress a flicker of hope.

"Has Knight seen the baby?"

"No, I don't think so. According to Brielle, he made her leave the Pacific Avenue house when she refused to consider an abortion. By then I believe she was about four or five months into the pregnancy, and the baby is now three months old." I did some rapid mental calculations. "That means he most likely hasn't seen her for seven or eight months." I studied my father. "Why? What do you have in mind?"

"Don't get your hopes up, Sarah. It's a very remote chance at best. But since there's no possibility of taking the case to court, it's worth a try. If you can arrange it, Gerald Knight should see his child. Right now, the baby is a nonentity, merely a name, if he even knows that much about her. It's much easier for him to ignore a daughter he's never met."

"You think that if he sees Emma, he might change his mind about providing financial support?"

Papa shrugged. "Probably not. But at least he'll no longer be able to deny the child's existence. And if she's half as sweet as you claim, there's always a chance—an outside one, mind you—that he might relent."

"He and his wife have three children of their own. No matter how adorable little Emma is . . ." My voice trailed off, my initial excitement quickly evaporating.

Papa gave my hand a reassuring pat, then rose to his feet. "We won't know until you've tried, will we, my girl?"

I was surprised to see Samuel enter the house shortly after dinner that evening. He looked tired, but smiled when I greeted him in the foyer.

"I thought you weren't planning to return until tomorrow?" I said. "Was it a terrible weekend?"

"Not completely," he said, handing me one of his smaller bags to carry upstairs. "On the other hand, it was not what I would call lively."

Entering his room, we placed the bags on his bed. "The important thing was that I was able to obtain the information I need for my book, which is the primary reason I agreed to go there in the first place." He chuckled. "It was amusing to see how eager those two jurors were to reprise their roles in the famous Laura Fair murder case. They've been milking that trial for over ten years now, and receiving God only knows how many invitations to partake of a weekend in the country."

"But other than that?" I asked, sitting down on the bed.

"Unutterably dull." He unsnapped the largest bag and flung it open. "Of course, the almost constant rain did nothing to help. The Talbots had planned some outdoor activities which had to be canceled. That meant we were all trapped together inside the house for most of the weekend." His look grew teasing. "Are you certain I haven't been gone for an entire week instead of only two days?"

I laughed. "At times it's seemed that long to me, too. I've been dying to talk to you."

He rather carelessly emptied the contents of the case into some bureau drawers, snapped the bag shut, then dropped down beside me on the bed.

"Did you now. Tell all, little sister. Lord knows I could do with some interesting news after enduring two days of dreary weather and even drearier company."

"Well, to begin with George came here looking for you yesterday afternoon," I began. "It seems the police arrested two Chinese men for Dieter Hume's murder."

Samuel looked genuinely surprised. "Good Lord! On what grounds?"

"Some people claimed to have seen the men loitering about near the Harrison Street Bridge the night Hume was killed. They maintain it's the same two men the police arrested. Mind you, it was after midnight and evidently they observed the men from some little distance away."

"Not to mention that most white people rarely make the effort to distinguish one Chinese from another." He eyed me questioningly. "Did George say that the police actually believe these witnesses?"

"I don't think it's a matter of whether they believe their stories or not," I answered grimly. "People in the city are growing increasingly frightened. According to George, City Hall is exerting a great deal of pressure on the police to solve the murders."

"When did the police arrest these men?"

"I think they had just taken them into custody when George came looking for you yesterday afternoon. According to him, the men are very young and speak next to no English."

"Surely they've assigned them an interpreter."

"No, impossible as it seems, they haven't. Those poor boys probably have no idea why they've been arrested. And heaven alone knows how they're being treated at the jail."

My brother was eyeing me warily, and I attempted to smooth my face into a more neutral expression. Clearly, my effort was not entirely successful.

"You haven't gone and done anything foolish, have you, Sarah?"

"That rather depends upon what you consider foolish," I answered evasively.

"Good Lord!" he exploded. "You really can't be left alone for five minutes without involving yourself in some trouble or other. What have you done?" His face suddenly cleared as he guessed at what I had been unwilling to tell him. "Oh, no, Sarah. You went to see Li Ying, didn't you?"

"As it so happens, I did," I admitted a bit defensively. "Which was just as well, since Mr. Li hadn't been informed of his countrymen's arrest."

"Those boys must be very new to San Francisco, if Li didn't know they'd been taken into custody," Samuel stated dryly. "He usually knows everything that goes on in San Francisco, not to mention Chinatown." He gazed at me with weary resignation. "Don't tell me, Sarah. Li has asked you to represent the men. And naturally, you've accepted."

I nodded, but did not elaborate.

"You realize, of course, that defending two Chinese men of committing such a brutal murder will do nothing to help your practice, which, I might add, is hardly flourishing as it is."

I did not appreciate being reminded of my precarious financial situation. "I can hardly stand by and do nothing while two frightened young men are accused of crimes they didn't commit."

"Oh? And how do you know they're not guilty? Have you suddenly acquired a crystal ball? What if the witnesses actually *can* place those two at the scene of the crime?"

"Given the circumstances, that's most improbable."

"But not impossible," insisted my brother. "Listen, Sarah, even if you're right and those men really are innocent, how can you possibly prove it? As a female attorney, you'll be going up against white eyewitnesses, *male* eyewitnesses. Whose side do you think the jury will take?"

"I'll have to cross that bridge when I come to it." I was determined not to allow my brother to sense my own doubts concerning the case. "Mr. Li is sending an interpreter to meet me at the jail tomorrow morning. I'll have a better idea of what I'm up against after I've spoken to my clients."

He sighed. "I know better than to try to change your mind once you've got it set on something. Still, considering the public furor surrounding these murders, you may be biting off more than you can chew. And you could be placing your own life in danger. Have you thought of how much public animosity you'll be facing, especially from Dennis Kearney and his party of bigots?"

I stiffened my chin. If I was being subjected to this much resistance from my staunchest ally in the family, I dreaded to think what my father would say when he found out about my new clients.

"I'm well aware of what I'm up against, Samuel. Nevertheless, I have given Mr. Li my word."

"Oh, yes, I forgot." His tone was rich with sarcasm. "You've given your word to one of Chinatown's most notorious tong lords. Of course you're duty bound to honor such an admirable agreement."

He rose from the bed and unlatched the smaller of his two cases. "So be it, then. Just don't expect me to take your side when Papa finds out what you've done."

"Don't worry, I wouldn't dream of it."

He must have caught my injured tone, and regretted his harsh words. After all, I had kept Ian Fearless a secret for over five years. He could hardly do less than support me when it was my turn to undergo one of Papa's cross-examinations.

Perhaps in an effort to smooth things between us, he said, "I haven't forgotten my promise to visit Madam Valentine's brothel with you, by the way. Tomorrow is going to be pretty busy for me, but I could take you on Tuesday morning."

Something in my face must have given me away, for he closed the bag and once again sat down on the bed. "You did stick to our bargain, didn't you, Sarah? You promised you would stay away from any brothels or parlor houses until I returned from my trip."

At my sheepish look, he threw up both hands in obvious disgust and not a little anger. "Sarah Louise Woolson. You gave me your word!"

"Calm yourself, Samuel. I promised that I wouldn't go to a brothel alone. And I didn't. Robert accompanied me, and Eddie, too, as it happens. In fact, it was Eddie who managed to gain us entry into the house. We arrived a bit earlier than was civil, I'm afraid, given the late hours that sort of business must keep."

"You say Robert went with you?" His bad temper abruptly deserted him at the mention of my erstwhile colleague. "Good Lord, that must have completely beat the Dutch. How in God's name did you get him to agree to go there with you?" His eyes widened as he suddenly figured it out. "Wait a minute, you didn't tell him where you were going until you'd arrived, did you?"

"Of course I didn't. If he'd known he would have become as immovable as a mountain. As it was, it was all I could do to prevent him from bolting out of there like a greased pig when the first girl came at him dressed in nothing but a flimsy, see-through nightgown."

The image of this scene caused my brother to erupt with laughter. "This gets better and better! I just wish I could have been a fly on the wall to see poor Robert's reaction when he discovered you'd lured him inside a brothel."

Remembering the look on the Scot's face, I could not repress a smile of my own. "I must admit the visit had its humorous moments. For some reason, Madam Valentine's ladies found him wholly irresistible."

I went on to describe the details of our visit to the parlor house, including the new information about how Brielle had come to be Gerald Knight's mistress. Samuel raised one sandy-brown eyebrow, when I mentioned the constant watch Knight kept on the girl.

"Madam Valentine was right. What a shame you can't use Knight's own suspicious nature against him. That would certainly qualify as poetic justice, wouldn't it?"

"Yes," I agreed with a sigh. "If the men doing the watching didn't work for Knight."

"That's true. So, what are you going to do about the lovely Miss Bouchard?"

I related Papa's suggestion that I arrange for Gerald Knight to see his child and ex-mistress. Unfortunately, my brother appeared no more hopeful about the plan than did I.

"I suppose you can try," he said doubtfully, "but it strikes me as being pretty futile. Knight doesn't strike me as the sort of man to be swayed by sentiment."

"Considering his behavior toward Brielle, I'm sure he isn't. But it's our only option and I have to try. It infuriates me that he should so easily get away with shirking his responsibilities toward his own child. Brielle will be forced into a life of prostitution, while he continues to enjoy a comfortable, even luxurious, life. It's patently unfair!"

"Sadly, life isn't always fair, Sarah, you should know that by now. And from what you said the girl went into this with her eyes open. She and Knight went so far as to draw up a contract."

"Which he broke when he cast her into the street."

"That's true. But allow me to point out the obvious—that contract never had a chance from the beginning."

"I know. That's why I'm determined that Knight at least see his baby."

"You must do what you think best. But I guarantee that Gerald Knight will not endanger the future of his marriage, and his newspaper, by admitting to having an affair behind his wife's back. The same wife who controls the family's purse strings."

There was no sense arguing the matter. Samuel was probably right anyway. However, I had one chance and one chance only to help Brielle. As soon as possible I planned to put my plan into action.

Before I left Samuel's room, however, I suddenly remembered the interview our father had arranged for my brother. "I think you should know that Papa has set up an appointment for you at Cunningham and Brill's law firm on Tuesday morning."

"What?" Once again, Samuel stopped unpacking and sank down onto the bed. "Good Lord!"

"I thought that would be your reaction. What are you going to tell him?"

He threw up his hands in a gesture of helplessness. "I always knew it would eventually come to this. It all boils down to two choices: either I take the bar exam and go to work for Arthur Cunningham, or I admit to Father that for the past five years I've been masquerading as Ian Fearless, the infamous crime reporter he holds in such disdain.

"Either way, one of us is going to end up very unhappy."

CHAPTER SIXTEEN

As planned, the following morning I met Li Ying's interpreter outside the city jail. He was a short, wiry man, with jet-black hair carefully shaved above the temple and worn in a long queue, or braid, down his back. He was dressed in the dark, high-necked tunic and baggy trousers which were the predominant mode of costume among the Chinese. On his shorn head he wore a black cap, and his feet were encased in simple black slippers. With a deep bow, and speaking broken, if carefully precise, English, he politely introduced himself to me as Sun Kin Lu.

"I am honored to meet you, Mr. Sun," I said with equal courtesy. "I am pleased that you have offered to assist me in speaking to the prisoners."

"Li Ying say give you much assistance," he replied, once again executing a deep bow. "We go inside, missy?" Nodding his head, Sun Kin Lu indicated that I should lead the way into the jail.

Unfortunately, I was not familiar with the uniformed police officer stationed inside the jail's anteroom. This meant, of course, that I would have to undergo the usual battery of questions before I would be allowed to visit my new clients. On this occasion, the procedure was further complicated by the fact that the men I wished to visit were Chinese and, moreover, could not speak a word of English.

Because of this, there was no way the jailer could verify that I had, indeed, been hired to represent them. Furthermore, he refused to believe that I was an attorney, and declared that under no circumstances would he allow a well-bred lady in to visit such godless and sadistic criminals.

It was not until I insisted that the officer call upon his superior for guidance, that Sun Kin Lu—whom the jailers regarded with anxious contempt—and I were finally allowed inside the block of cells.

The guard who led us in was a man I had seen once or twice on previous visits to the jail, but to whom I had never spoken. It was a relief to see that he at least recognized me, and that he restrained himself from making any caustic comments about my companion, or my validity as an attorney, as he led us down the row of barred doors.

Halfway down the corridor, we stopped in front of a cell inhabited by two wretched-looking Chinese men, each stiffly perched upon the edge of a cot. They were very young, no more than eighteen or nineteen, I guessed, and their tunics and trousers were torn and disheveled, indicating that they had been roughly treated by the police. As the jailer opened the door and allowed us to step inside, the two young Chinese regarded us with dark, fearful eyes.

As we passed into the cell, I was instantly overcome by a foul stench. Placing my handkerchief over my mouth and nose, I searched the small space for the cause of this odor. It did not take me long to locate the source; in one corner of the room, covered by a ragged and very dirty cloth, was a rusty bucket which appeared to be full of waste matter. The presence of the bucket itself was not unusual, but customarily these were emptied and rinsed out twice a day. Obviously, this pail had not been attended to since the men were incarcerated two days ago!

Attempting to breathe as much from my mouth as possible, I studied the inhabitants of the cell. They were very pale, and had shrunk back from me as far as possible on their cots. They were regarding me in such obvious terror that Sun Kin Lu stepped around me and addressed them in rapid Chinese. While he spoke, the prisoners stared at me in confusion, as if they had never before set eyes upon a Western woman, much less one who claimed to be a lawyer!

Then Sun mentioned Li Ying's name, and the men instantly became very still, their attention now riveted on the interpreter. I would have thought it impossible, but their frightened, already white faces grew even more drawn. I thought it said a great deal about the tong lord, that even men who had so recently arrived in Chinatown already recognized his name and respected his formidable reputation.

In response to Sun's questions, the taller of the two men spoke briefly. As he did, I noticed that his hands were trembling rather badly. In his turn, the smaller man mumbled something to the interpreter, then dropped his face and stared at his mud-caked slippers.

Sun nodded toward the first man, explaining, "This one Lee Yup." Pointing to the other man he continued, "Him say name Fan Gow. They come *Gum San* three, maybe four week ago."

Loosely translated, *Gum San* meant "The land of the Golden Mountain," and was a name the Chinese frequently employed when referring to San Francisco. If it was true that Fan Gow and Lee Yup had so recently arrived in our city, then they must indeed find their present situation terrifying.

I was considering how best to commence the interview, when Sun Kin Lu again spoke to the men in rapid Chinese. From his tone and body language, I guessed that he was rebuking the men for not offering me a seat. That I was correct in this assumption, was borne out when the two young Chinese sprang to their feet and bowed low, pointing meaningfully at their vacated beds.

Warily, I eyed the grimy condition of the cots. The threadbare bedding was torn and a filthy gray color. I doubted that it had seen soap and water for months, if ever. Heaven alone knew how many bugs infested its grubby folds. If given a choice, I would happily have remained standing. Realizing, however, that by doing so I would embarrass Mr. Sun and cause him to lose face, I politely inclined my head in thanks, and went to sit gingerly on the bed which had formerly been occupied by Lee Yup.

Addressing Sun Kin Lu, I said, "Would you please ask Mr. Lee and Mr. Fan how they came to be arrested for Deacon Hume's murder?"

Mr. Sun did as I requested, then listened as Lee Yup—who seemed to be the older, or at least the more outspoken, of the two Celestials—answered. Turning to me, he translated, "They say not know why they here. Say they mind own business when police grab them, throw onto ground, hit with clubs, drag here. They not understand why."

"I see," I replied, feeling profound sympathy for the two young men. "Would you please ask them where they were when they were arrested by the police?"

Dutifully, Sun spoke to the men, then said, "They not sure, say they lost. Only know somewhere outside Tangrenbu." He clucked disapprovingly. "Big mistake, leave Chinatown. Many troubles outside."

That was true enough. As long as the Chinese stayed within the ten-block radius of Chinatown, they remained relatively free of interference from the white man. Even the police were leery of entering this area, especially at night. It was mainly left to the Chinese, usually in the form of the Six Companies—organizations representing the six districts of China—to take care of crimes committed within their boundaries. It had been foolish indeed for two young men, who spoke not one word of English between them, to venture beyond the security afforded them by their own people.

"Have they been questioned since arriving here in jail?" I asked.

"When first come here," Sun translated, "man in uniform talk to them, but they not understand what he say. Food come—awful white man cooking—but no see anyone since."

"Would you please ask them what they were doing in the Harrison Street Bridge area the night Deacon Hume was murdered?" I asked.

Again, there was a rapid exchange of Chinese, then the interpreter turned to me. "They say not know where bridge is, never heard name. They smoke pipes, maybe gamble, not remember much that night."

"By pipes, I assume you mean they were smoking opium?" I asked. Some months ago I had witnessed firsthand the devastating effects of the addictive opium poppy.

"Yes, yes, opium," Sun confirmed, bobbing his head up and down like a yo-yo, all the while grinning like the Cheshire cat. "Cloud mind, so not remember."

"I see." I attempted several more questions, but it was clear that the young men had no idea why they had been set upon by the police, or why they were currently languishing in city jail. I had no difficulty believing that they were telling the truth when they claimed they had been wandering lost in the city, undoubtedly under the influence of opium, the night they'd been arrested. There seemed no logical reason why they would deliberately seek out the Rincon Hill district, especially at that hour of the night. Moreover, I consider myself a reasonably shrewd judge of character, and I could not for one minute imagine these frightened, bewildered boys to be cold-blooded killers.

There were a good deal more inquiries I wished to make concerning their case, but clearly these unfortunate young Celestials were incapable of supplying the answers.

"All right, Mr. Sun," I said, rising from my unhappy perch upon the cot. "Please tell Mr. Lee and Mr. Fan that I will do everything possible to secure their release from this place. At the very least, I intend to ensure that their treatment is more humane."

Wrinkling my nose, I glanced at the disgusting bucket. Having that emptied, I determined, would be the first order of business. After that had been taken care of, I would see what I could do about the filthy cots, and then make certain that they were fed decent food. I fervently wished that Mr. Sun could explain to them some of the legal hurdles we would have to overcome, as well as the reasons why bail would very likely be refused.

Unfortunately, I could think of no way to communicate this to the interpreter, much less expect him to successfully pass the information on to the prisoners. For now, it seemed more important that Lee and Fan understand that they were not alone, that someone from the white community was on their side, and would be there to help guide them through this nightmare.

After we left the cell, I made arrangements to meet with Sun Kin Lu at my office the following afternoon, after which I sent him back to Chinatown with my thanks. Before I left the jail to visit the courthouse, I confronted various guards, along with as many of their superiors as I could lay my hands on, concerning the deplorable sanitary conditions present in Lee Yup and Fan Gow's jail cell. Despite an initial display of resistance, I was finally able to bully two of the younger jailers into cleaning the cell, changing the linen, and emptying the revolting waste bucket.

My visit to the courthouse was not as successful. Just as I feared, there was nothing I could do about obtaining Fan's and Lee's release on bail. Not only were they considered major flight risks, but the authorities feared—not without reason—that an angry mob might overrun the courthouse if the two men were allowed to leave the jail. I was, however, able to move up their suspiciously vague arraignment date to Wednesday morning, the day after tomorrow. With that small victory, I was forced to be content.

As I made my way from the public horsecar to my office, I passed a newsboy hawking the morning editions of several San Francisco newspapers. I stopped in my tracks when I saw the bold, black headlines announcing the arrest of two Chinamen for the murder of Deacon Dieter Hume: CHINAMEN CAUGHT RED-HANDED IN KILLING! CHINESE DEVILS ON A RAMPAGE! TWO JOHNNIES ACCUSED OF CHURCHMAN'S MURDER!

Purchasing copies of each paper, I tucked them beneath my arm and, thoughts reeling, completed the short walk up Sutter Street. My plan was to read the articles in the privacy of my office, but I was intercepted by Fanny as I started up the stairs. She was holding a copy of that morning's *Examiner*.

"So, you've already seen the story," she said, indicating the newspapers under my arm. "I'll warrant you haven't eaten since breakfast, if then. Why don't you come inside for a bite of lunch? I'd like to hear what you think of the article."

"I haven't had time to read any of them yet, Fanny," I told her. "But I'd be happy to join you for a cup of coffee."

Naturally, Fanny insisted that I partake of more than just coffee, and I must admit I put up little resistance. As I scanned the front-page stories—the worst of which carried the name of Samuel's nemesis, Ozzie Foldger—she placed a thickly sliced ham sandwich before me, the bread fresh from that morning. Laying out a similar plate of her own, she took a seat opposite me at the table.

"So, what do you think about those two Chinese fellows the police brought in over the weekend?" she asked. "Why do you suppose they suspect them of murdering that church deacon? Seems to me the police arrested them on precious little evidence."

"I agree, Fanny. I think that's exactly what they did. The truth is that they're hardly more than frightened boys. They haven't the least idea between them about what's going on."

I went on to relate my interview with the two young men at city jail that morning. As it was my habit not to discuss my association with Li Ying unless it became necessary, I left out my meeting with the tong lord, and neither did I tell her that he had requested me to represent Lee Yup and Fan Gow. Very little gets by my downstairs neighbor, however, and she quickly guessed the more pertinent facts that I had omitted from the story.

"So that tong leader friend of yours has asked you to take their case, has he? Well, somebody has to defend them, and I can't see any other lawyer in town caring two figs for what happens to those poor Johnnies."

"I'm not sure how much I can do for them," I admitted gloomily. "So far, all I've managed to accomplish is to get their cell cleaned, and coerce the powers that be into setting their arraignment for the day after tomorrow, instead of some indeterminate date in the future."

"Well, that's something, isn't it?" She smiled and patted my hand. "If anyone can help those poor boys, it's you, Sarah. Mr. Li knows that or he wouldn't have trusted you to do the job. Give it some time to percolate in your mind. I have faith that you'll come up with a way to save them."

"I sincerely hope you're right," I said, wishing I shared her confidence in my abilities.

She stood and went to the stove, returning with fresh coffee. "Now, tell me all about that Bouchard girl and her baby. Have you had any luck finding them?"

"Yes," I answered, then paused, reluctant to tell my neighbor where Brielle was staying. Naturally, Fanny was having none of it.

"So, where is she?" she asked, regarding me with direct gray eyes. Her straightforward manner clearly indicated that she expected an equally straightforward reply.

I sighed. "She and little Emma are currently living at Madam Valentine's parlor house on Montgomery Street. Madam Valentine took her in when—"

"Matilda Abernathy!" interrupted Fanny with a much amused laugh. "My swan! Where did you meet her, Sarah? Don't tell me you actually went to the brothel?"

"Matilda Abernathy?" I asked in confusion.

"Madam Valentine, dear. Matilda Abernathy is the name she was born with, although she hasn't used it for so long I'm not sure she even remembers it. She told me she made her way west from a little town in upstate New York—Waterburgh or Waterville, I think it was."

I regarded her in amazement. "How do you know so much about her?"

"Why, we met ten years ago when we were both involved with organizing the first California Women's Suffrage Society meeting here in the city." She was smiling at what must be pleasant memories. "I seem to remember that she managed a small brothel on Commercial Street at the time, smack-dab in the middle of the Barbary Coast."

I could not hide my surprise. "She ran a brothel on the Barbary Coast—*and* was an active suffragette?"

"Was and still is, as far as I know. Now that she's so busy with that fancy house of hers on Montgomery Street, I don't see her at as many meetings as I used to. But I have no reason to believe she's changed her opinion on women being given the vote. Or making a decent living for themselves."

I was still trying to grasp the fact that my grandmotherly, down-to-earth neighbor was friends with one of the most notorious madams in all of San Francisco, when Fanny laughed and went on.

"Never met another woman like Matilda when it came to twisting a man right around her little finger. Had a real way of getting them to come around to seeing things her way, without them being any the wiser."

"Did the other women of the Suffrage Society know that Matilda Abernathy worked as a madam?"

"I doubt it," said Fanny, fetching more cream from the ice box, pouring some into her cup, then placing the pitcher on the table. "The only reason I found out was because we worked together on the same committee."

"And she freely shared this with you?" I found it amazing that the woman would voluntarily confide such personal, and potentially damaging, information. What if Fanny had betrayed her secret to other women involved in the local suffrage movement? Surely Matilda Abernathy would have been instantly ostracized.

Fanny seemed embarrassed by my question. "Not exactly. Actually, I found out when Matilda sent several of her girls to purchase some millinery goods from my shop. One of them was very talkative, and I fear not terribly bright. I think she assumed I knew what Matilda did to earn her living."

She sipped her coffee. "I'm ashamed to say that I found the girl's rather risqué stories about life in a brothel fascinating. I said nothing to correct her misunderstanding concerning the degree to which Matilda did or did not confide in me."

I started to comment on this deception, then realized it was hardly any of my business. What's more, I was interested to hear the young prostitute's gossip. At this point, I welcomed any information which might help me better understand the life Brielle meant to adopt.

"What else did the girl tell you? That is, if you don't mind repeating it."

Fanny appeared relieved that I did not plan to pass judgment on her harmless ruse. Settling her plump body more comfortably in her chair, she leaned forward and dropped her voice conspiratorially, although we were the only ones in the room, or in the front shop for that matter.

"Well, I gathered from what the girl said that the place didn't amount to much. As I say, it was located on the Barbary Coast, as bad a neighborhood then as it is now. Matilda's place wasn't the only house of ill fame on the block, either. The girl said there was heavy competition among the brothels and gambling houses, and drunkenness and rowdy customers were a constant nuisance. And of course the Society for the Suppression of Vice was forever campaigning against all the brothels in the district, which made it even more difficult to make a decent living."

"How in the world did she manage to move from the Barbary Coast to the house on Montgomery Street?"

"Oh, I think even then Matilda was determined to make something of herself. According to the chatty prostitute, she did her best to dress up the place, make it more high-class, which, given the area of town she was operating from, must have been a pretty frustrating task."

"Did Matilda own the house herself?"

"No, it was rented, which was something else that stuck in her craw. For all that the place was a dump, the landlord—whom she never even met, by the way—kept raising her rent so that there was little enough cash left over to make the improvements she had in mind."

"Still, she must have done well enough to set up her current house," I said, finding it impossible not to admire the woman's ingenuity and business acumen. "Which, if you haven't seen it, is very modish."

"Yes, she finally made good, if that's the way you want to phrase it, although it didn't happen overnight. And she didn't move directly from the Barbary Coast to where she is now, I assure you. About two or three years after I met her, she opened a second brothel in a classier area of town. She must have done a lot better there, because after a couple more years, she was able to move to Montgomery Street in '77."

"Do you still keep in touch with her?"

"Not much anymore. As I said, I've seen little of her at our suffragette meetings over the past few years." She paused to chew a bite of her sandwich. "I can't believe you actually went to the parlor house, Sarah. You do beat all. Now I want you to tell me all about it. From the beginning."

She laughed as I related how I had persuaded Robert to accompany me to the parlor house, then listened in amazement as I described Madam Valentine's lavish accommodations.

"She must be very pleased with what she's achieved," Fanny commented. Then realizing that this praise was directed toward a house of ill repute, no matter how well appointed, she once again laughed. "That doesn't sound quite right, does it? I wonder what my friends would say if they heard me admiring the accomplishments of a madam?"

Our conversation was cut short as the bell over the street door jingled, announcing that a customer had entered the shop. As Fanny bustled out to serve the woman, I quickly cleaned up our dishes, then departed the store and ascended the steps to my office.

There, spread out across my desk, were the papers I had taken from Robert's office the previous Friday. While it was true that I had completed his most pressing case—the one he'd claimed Joseph

Shepard expected on his desk Friday afternoon, but which turned out not to be needed after all!—I had accomplished next to nothing Saturday afternoon, when all I'd been able to think about was Pierce. Considerable work remained to be finished. And I had no idea when Robert might charge into my office, demanding to know if his case files were ready.

Before starting, though, I finished reading the newspaper stories describing my clients' arrests. Every one of them assumed that the two young Chinese were guilty, despite an almost total lack of evidence. As I noted earlier, Ozzie Foldger's article was the most virulent, and I feared that his words would only further incite the citizens of our city to attempt violence against Lee Yup and Fan Gow. It was at times like this that I was inclined to agree with my father's overall indictment against the journalistic community. Although my own brother was a member of the "club," so to speak, I still could not excuse this blatant racism.

Forcing myself to concentrate on the business at hand, I set the disturbing newspapers aside and set to work on Robert's cases. As usual, the ones he'd been given were dull and uninspiring, work that any law student could complete with his eyes closed. However, I dutifully plowed through the pile of papers, and was nearly finished when Eddie burst into the room, waving his copy of *The Adventures of Tom Sawyer* at me. Glancing at my timepiece, I was surprised to note that it was nearly six o'clock. Despite the dreary nature of Robert's files, time had passed surprisingly fast.

"I finished it, Miss Sarah," he said jubilantly, plopping down in the chair across from my desk. "Wasn't half bad, neither. That Tom Sawyer is a real cracker, ain't he?"

"*Isn't* he, Eddie," I automatically corrected.

"Ain't that what I just said?"

"Your meaning was clear, Eddie, but you used an improper contraction," I explained. "You should have said, 'isn't,' not 'ain't.' "

He tilted his thin, angular face and regarded me with suspicion. "Are you tryin' to hornswoggle me, Miss Sarah? I dunno nothin' about no contract, but I swear I ain't cussin' or nothin', if that's what yer gettin' at."

"I know you aren't. It's just that—" I ran my thumb and forefinger over the bridge of my nose, where I felt a headache coming on. As I say, although Samuel, Robert, and I had been amazingly successful in teaching Eddie to read, trying to correct his woefully poor grammar was a different story. Striving for patience, I reminded myself that the lad had spent most of his sixteen years on the street, doing whatever it took to ensure his family's survival. When there is no food to put on the table, syntax cannot be a high priority.

"Never mind, Eddie, it's not important." Giving the boy a smile, I opened a desk drawer and pulled out a narrow volume that Samuel and I had much enjoyed as children. "Here," I said, handing him the book. "This is a perfect story for this time of year. It's called *A Christmas Carol,* and it was written by a wonderful author by the name of Charles Dickens. It's quite short, and I think you'll find it very interesting."

"*A Christmas Carol,*" he said, turning the slim book over in his hands. "You mean like them songs people sing at Christmas?"

"Yes, only Dickens wrote his Christmas carol as a story, instead of a song. It's about a very rich and greedy man who has forgotten how to love, and a very poor family who struggles to get by, but who knows how to appreciate and care for one another."

He looked at the book skeptically. "Sounds pretty grum. I don't figure I need to read no book about bein' poor, seein' as how my family ain't never had no money worth mentionin'."

I realized at once that I had chosen a poor way to describe Dicken's classic story. "It also has ghosts in it, Eddie, rattling chains and all. And the ghosts come at night to haunt Ebenezer Scrooge, that's the selfish rich man."

His eyes lit with immediate interest. "Ghosts, huh? Now that's more like it. Kin I start it right now?"

"Now might not be a good time, Eddie. But you can take it

home with you to read. Actually, I have need of your brougham, if you're free for the next hour or two. There's an errand I wish to run." The lad wouldn't be the ideal companion, but having him along would be better than paying a return visit to Madam Valentine's parlor house on my own.

"Sure thing, Miss Sarah. Where do you wanna go?"

Before I could draw breath to answer, the door opened and Robert strode into the room.

"Have you finished the rest of my work yet, Sarah?" he asked, as usual without bothering with so much as a polite "hello."

Giving an inward sigh, I nodded toward the neat pile of papers stacked to the side of my desk. "I have finished all but the Ernesto case. I can probably complete that in the next half hour, if you'd care to wait."

He consulted his timepiece, then nodded. "I can wait. When you're finished, perhaps we could, ah . . ." He hesitated, stealing a glance at Eddie, who had taken his favorite perch on the windowsill to read. He seemed relieved to see that the boy was paying us no attention. "I thought we might have dinner."

I smiled, thinking how well this fit in with my own plans. "That sounds delightful, Robert. If you're amenable, however, perhaps you could accompany me on a short errand before we dine."

"An errand where?" he asked, his blue-green eyes regarding me suspiciously from beneath raised eyebrows.

"I must pay a visit to Madam Valentine's parlor house." His mouth opened in disbelief, but before he could explode I hurried on. "Only long enough to give Brielle Bouchard a message. I'll explain in the carriage."

I handed him the copy of that morning's *Examiner*. "Here, you can read this while you wait."

CHAPTER SEVENTEEN

Robert was still grumbling about our return visit to Madam Valentine's brothel as we turned onto Montgomery Street. Even after I had explained the reason for tonight's call, he had come up with a myriad of reasons why my planned confrontation with Gerald Knight was a terrible idea. Bringing Brielle and her baby along, moreover, was sheer folly!

"Please, Robert, stop complaining," I told him wearily, as Eddie brought the brougham to a halt. "This should not take more than a few minutes. You needn't go inside if you'd rather not."

"That's not the point, Sarah. You're leading that poor girl on. This whole idea is doomed to failure, and you know it. Miss Bouchard's life has been difficult without your making matters worse."

"I understand your concern, Robert, but this is our only hope to change Gerald Knight's mind about his daughter. You said yourself that a brothel is no place to raise a child."

He threw up his arms in a gesture of defeat. "Why do I even try? You never listen to me. I just hope Miss Bouchard has the good sense to say no to this whole crazy scheme."

"Fine. We'll let Brielle make the decision for herself then, shall we?" I gave him a pointed look. "Without attempting to assert our own views upon her, one way or the other."

Allowing Eddie to assist me out of the carriage, I let my gaze sweep up and down the street. By now it was eight o'clock and quite dark. Street lamps had been lit, but they were set far enough apart that they did little to penetrate the deep shadows which were present to either side of the block. I admit that I was filled with a sense of quiet expectancy. Turning my attention back to Madam Valentine's brothel, I noted that lights were visible in nearly every window, and dark silhouettes bustled about behind the drawn shades.

As Robert was exiting the brougham, a cabriolet reined up behind Eddie's cab, and a well-dressed man stepped down onto the street. He started to walk toward Madam Valentine's parlor house, then caught sight of me and abruptly stopped. A look of mixed astonishment and dismay crossed his face, and for a moment I thought he might be about to address me. Then, as if having second thoughts, he turned abruptly on his heel and bolted back inside the cabriolet. I could hear the sound of his voice yelling for the cabbie to drive on.

"You're not good for business," Robert commented, chuckling at the man's abrupt departure. He looked at Madam Valentine's house with misgivings. "I'm not sure what sort of welcome we're likely to receive, especially at this time of the evening."

"I can go around back and see if Annie's there," offered Eddie hopefully, popping up from behind us.

"Thank you, but we'll ring at the front door," I told him, determined not to sneak around the house like some beggar or thief in the night. "Please wait here with the carriage, Eddie. We shouldn't be long."

With a disappointed look, the lad kicked at some loose pebbles in the street, then made his way dejectedly back to the brougham. As he walked, I heard him bemoan the many injustices he was forced to endure, and that his Annie would surely have seen to it that we got inside the barrelhouse without a fuss, and probably come up with a piece of cake for him to eat in the bargain.

Ignoring the boy's self-pitying laments, I ascended the stairs and rang the bell. A moment later a Negro maid, wearing a neat black dress, a starched white uniform, and lacy cap, opened the door. She started to welcome us inside, then stopped when she caught sight of me.

"I'm sorry, missus, but y'all got the wrong house," she said with a Southern drawl. Without waiting for an answer, she began to close the door in my face.

"Wait, please," I cried, pushing against the door to hold it open. Behind the maid, I saw a great bustle of activity: Servants hurried about carrying drink trays, bottles of champagne, and even furniture, while men dressed in formal evening clothes carried musical instruments down the hall and into the room where we had spoken to Madam Valentine and Brielle several days earlier. Since that visit, the house had been colorfully bedecked for the holidays, and bright, glittering candles set a scene of Yuletide revelry.

"We are here to see Miss Brielle Bouchard," I told the maid, as she once again exerted pressure to close the door.

"Ain't no girl here by that name," she insisted, looking confused and increasingly alarmed by my insistence. "I told y'all, you've got the wrong house."

Belatedly, I remembered that the "ladies" of Miss Valentine's house did not go by their real names, but by more exotic sobriquets better suited to their line of work. Since I had no idea what pseudonym Brielle might be using, if indeed she had yet chosen one, I asked to see Madam Valentine herself.

The maid stared at me as if I had requested an audience with President Arthur himself, then reluctantly stood aside and allowed Robert and me to enter the foyer.

"I'll get her. Y'all wait here," the girl said, and with one last doubtful look at me, set off up the stairs.

"We've come at a bad time," Robert said from behind me. "They're getting ready for tonight's business. I don't see why this can't wait until . . ."

His voice trailed off when two beautiful young women came

down the stairs dressed in stunning evening gowns. As the women passed by us in the front hall, they slowed their pace and stared openly at my companion.

"Hello there, big boy," purred one of the girls, allowing her ring-bedecked hand to sweep seductively over his chest. "My name is Honey, 'cause I'm extra sweet. You and me could have a real good time together."

"And I'm Rose Petal," the second young woman breathed, letting her hand rest lightly on Robert's flushed cheek. Giving him a little wink, she added, "Me and Honey are real good at sharing, sweetie—if you know what I mean."

If my associate's face turned any redder, I feared it might actually burst into flames. He stood there staring at the two girls in genuine alarm, as if afraid they might actually attack him on the spot.

Giggling merrily—and well aware of the effect they were having on my bedazzled companion—the young women gave him one last pat on either cheek, then continued down the hallway. Robert's blue-green eyes seemed glued to the girls' derrieres, as they gracefully swished their way into the parlor behind the musicians.

"My knowledge about these establishments is admittedly limited," I said to him, after the ladies had disappeared from view. "But is it usual for the, er, young women who work in these places to dress so elaborately, or for there to be musicians present every evening?"

He started to answer me, when three more girls, each of them wearing tight and extremely low-cut gowns, made their way down the stairs, swaying seductively past his wide, awestruck eyes.

"Robert," I said a bit sharply, nudging him with my elbow. "Close your mouth and stop gawking. You look as if your eyes are about to pop out of your face." When he still did not move, I poked him again, this time not so gently.

"Ouch!" he exclaimed, rubbing his ribs. "What did you do that for?"

"I'm attempting to bring you down to earth," I told him crisply.

"I asked if you knew whether all this folderol is normal for places of this nature. This seems more like a soiree on Nob Hill than a typical night at a brothel."

"That's because it is not a typical night at a brothel, Miss Woolson," came a voice from behind me.

Turning, I found Madam Valentine standing on the lower landing of the stairs. Again I was amazed that a woman of her bountiful proportions could move so gracefully. She was beautifully attired in a black velvet gown cut low at the neck to display a generous amount of cleavage, and with a waist cinched so tightly that it spoke well of her corseting, although how she could breathe was a mystery. Her thick dyed hair had been arranged in intricate curls atop her head, and was decorated with ebony combs, inlaid with what appeared to be real diamonds, rubies, and other precious gems.

"Every month, we hold a reception to introduce girls who are newly arrived in San Francisco," she explained. Nodding her head in the direction of a statuesque, sloe-eyed brunette with glowing ebony skin, she said, "That is Cleopatra. She has come to us from Kate Townsend's house in New Orleans. That blonde coming out of the front parlor is Evangeline. She has just arrived from New York."

"You say that you hold these receptions every month?" I asked, marveling at the organization and expense required to arrange such an evening. "Do these young women really move so easily about the country?"

She nodded. "Most don't stay in any one place for more than a month or two. That's why I work so hard to entice my girls to stay longer. After all, I have invested a great deal of time and money in their training and wardrobes."

I remembered what Fanny had told me about Matilda Abernathy's determination to make something of her life. If one cared to credit a very active and luxurious parlor house as an indicator of success, then Matilda had indeed caught her golden ring.

We were jostled by servants making their way up and down the stairs, causing Madam Valentine to suggest that we adjourn to her office. Robert and I followed her down the hall and into a room which was considerably smaller, but every bit as expensively furnished as the parlor where tonight's soiree was being held. She indicated that we should be seated on a settee, while she took her place opposite us in a comfortable-looking armchair, once again upholstered in a vibrant shade of red.

"Now Miss Woolson, Mr. Campbell, what has brought you to my house this evening?"

"I wish to have a word with Brielle Bouchard," I told her. "I can see that you're very busy tonight, so it needn't take long."

She looked at me guardedly. "What has happened? Do you have news for her?"

Before I could answer Robert broke in, his tone disparaging. "Sarah has some bizarre plan to introduce Gerald Knight to his daughter. She hopes that he'll be instantly taken with the tyke, leave his wife, and he, Brielle, and the baby will live happily ever after."

"Don't be absurd, Robert," I said, annoyed. "Pay no attention to him, Madam Valentine. While it's true that I—"

There was a knock on the door, and Brielle's lovely face peered into the room. "Nancy said you wished to see me, Madam Valentine. Oh," she said, noticing Robert and me on the settee. "I didn't realize you and Mr. Campbell were here, Miss Woolson."

"Sit down, Brielle," the older woman told her. "Miss Woolson has something she would like to discuss with you." She rose and indicated that Brielle should take her seat in the red upholstered armchair. "If you will excuse me, Miss Woolson, Mr. Campbell, I have a great number of things to attend to before our first guests arrive." With that, the woman swept out of the room, closing the door behind her.

"What is it you wish to tell me?" Brielle asked, after she had seated herself on the edge of Madam Valentine's chair. "Does it have to do with the lawsuit?"

I felt Robert draw in breath and spoke quickly, before he could blurt out the purpose of our visit, along with his negative view of the plan.

"I'm sorry to bear discouraging news, Brielle, but there is simply no way we can take your case to trial."

"Because we cannot prove that Gerald is Emma's father," she said with a sigh of resignation.

I nodded. "Even if we could somehow convince Mr. Knight's men to testify that you entertained no male visitors except their employer, we would still have a difficult time proving that you did not once slip out of the house unobserved during the entire time you lived in the home. And realistically, I doubt we could ever persuade those roughs to take our side against the man who pays their salaries."

She smiled wanly, trying without notable success to disguise her disappointment. "Please, Miss Woolson, do not distress yourself. You have been wholly honest with me since my first visit to your office. I see now how naïve I was to believe I could protect myself from a man like Gerald Knight. He must have had a good laugh over that silly contract I insisted he sign, knowing full well that it would never hold up in a court of law."

"You were only trying to protect yourself," Robert told her gallantly. "That man is the worst sort of cad."

"Yes," she agreed in a small voice. "I know that now. In the beginning, he appeared to genuinely care for me. He bought me beautiful clothes, settled me in a lovely home, saw to my every need. In a way, I think I gradually grew to return his love, or what I imagined to be his love. Now, of course, I know better, and I shall have to accept the consequences of my foolish choices."

I leaned forward in my seat. "I don't want to unduly raise your hopes, my dear, but there is one thing more we might try."

"Really, Miss Woolson, what do you have in mind?"

Robert harrumphed, but surprised me by managing to keep his misgivings to himself.

"I wonder, Brielle, has Mr. Knight ever seen his daughter?"

"No, he hasn't." She looked at me questioningly. "Why? Have you been in touch with Gerald? Has he asked about Emma?"

"I haven't contacted Mr. Knight," I told her. "But it occurs to me that he has gotten off far too easily in this affair. If, as you say, he has never seen Emma, then it has been simplicity itself for him to pretend that she doesn't exist."

Unable to contain himself any longer, although in milder tones than I might have expected, Robert put in, "Sarah has some absurd idea that you should confront Knight with his daughter."

Brielle looked at him in surprise. "You mean introduce Emma to her father?" She sat quietly for a moment pondering the idea, then turned to me in obvious enthusiasm. "But that does not strike me as the least bit absurd. It's true that he has never set eyes upon her. Once he has, perhaps he will no longer be so eager to abandon her."

I was taken aback by the renewed hope I saw shining in the girl's eyes. So, apparently, was Robert, for he said, "My dear, you mustn't get your hopes up. Given Mr. Knight's reputation, this meeting is not likely to alter his behavior toward the child."

"I understand what you're trying to say, Mr. Campbell," Brielle said, her excitement seemingly unaffected by his warning. "But Miss Woolson is correct, it is something we must try. I feel that if Gerald can but see Emma, there is a good chance that his heart will melt."

Robert gave me a pointed look, but with effort managed to keep his views on Gerald Knight's alleged ownership of a heart—much less one capable of melting—to himself. I, too, was concerned that he was right, and that I had fostered false hope in the girl.

"I know just how I will dress her," Brielle chattered on. "She has a little blue dress that will bring out the color of her eyes. Emma looks a great deal like her father, you know, even Madam Valentine agrees. Surely he will see the resemblance and be forced to admit that she is his daughter!"

Despite our efforts to make the girl view tomorrow's meeting with Knight more realistically, Brielle fairly danced out of Madam Valentine's office, still planning how she might present the baby to her father in the most favorable light.

Robert and I followed in her wake, to find the first guests of the evening already being shown into the parlor. Inside the room, musicians were playing a lively tune, and the sound of men and women's laughter was accompanied by a strong odor of tobacco and expensive whiskey. It seemed that Miss Valentine's monthly reception was off to a good start.

Robert appeared so subdued when we left the parlor house that I suggested we partake of a quiet dinner at a small restaurant I had noticed upon our first visit to Madam Valentine's establishment.

"I'm sorry for dragging you into this, Robert," I apologized, feeling responsible for his dour mood. After we were seated at a table and presented with menus, I went on, "I insist on paying for dinner. It's the least I can do."

"You'll do no such thing!" he declared. "That law firm of yours is barely keeping its head above water. At least I'm bringing in a steady salary." He picked up his menu, then placed it back down on the table. "And while I may not approve of this business with Miss Bouchard and that Valentine woman, I would never allow you to visit a place like that on your own. Of all the ridiculous ideas."

His expression was so earnest I felt a sudden surge of gratitude. "Robert, despite all your grousing and hovering over me like a mother hen, I am truly thankful to have you as a friend. No matter how much you disapprove of some of the cases I accept, or the way I manage them, I know I can count on you to be at my side when I most need you."

His startled expression gave way to one I couldn't fathom. The way he was looking at me, his blue-green eyes staring into mine as if he were trying to burrow his way inside my mind, was disconcerting.

"Oh, aye. I hope that I am a good friend to you, Sarah," he said, his voice soft yet strangely intense. He started to say something else, then seemed to think better of it. Muttering unintelligibly, he broke off his scrutiny and once again raised the menu.

When we had ordered, Robert sat back in his chair, seemingly more relaxed than when we had entered the restaurant. I knew him well enough, however, to recognize the line of tension between his eyes, and the way he had pulled his mouth into a taut line. Guessing, incorrectly, as it turned out, that his unrest stemmed from our return visit to Madam Valentine's parlor house, I decided to let sleeping dogs lie, and made no comment. Instead, I quietly sipped my wine and examined our surroundings, along with our fellow diners.

The restaurant, which called itself the "Black Bull," was of moderate size, and decorated in an overstated Wild West motif. Every wall contained paintings of mountains, valleys, and deserts, all of them depicting animals in their natural habitat. Above a large brick fireplace—its flames providing a welcome warmth from the cold outside air—had been hung the head of a massive black bull, its huge horns towering halfway to the ceiling. Most of the tables around us were occupied, and at the far end of the room, a raised, circular stage held a piano and sufficient space for a small musical group. Although the stage was currently unoccupied, I wondered if we would be treated to some sort of entertainment.

"Did you enjoy the theater?"

Robert's question took me by surprise. "Excuse me?" I said, turning in my seat to find him once again regarding me with those curiously probing eyes.

"I asked if you and Pierce Godfrey enjoyed the theater last Friday night?"

"Yes, very much," I replied. "It was a splendid production of *The Merry Wives of Windsor.*"

"How long will Godfrey be in town?"

"He didn't say, although I'm sure he'll stay through the holidays, at least." I studied his face, trying to make sense of his odd expression. I had expected him to go on about tonight's business at the brothel. Instead, he was asking me questions about the theater. "Why do you ask?"

He shrugged his broad shoulders, then said evasively, "No particular reason. I was just wondering."

As I have stated on more than one occasion, I cannot abide ridiculous verbal sparring. "Robert, why don't you simply tell me what's bothering you?"

He started to speak, but was interrupted by the waiter bringing our food. I waited until the man had left, but when Robert showed no signs of returning to my question, I prompted, "Come now, Robert, what is it? Why are you behaving so peculiarly?"

He shifted in his chair, but still seemed reluctant to speak. Then, visibly gaining courage, he blurted, "Just how important is that man to you, Sarah?"

I regarded him quizzically. "What man?"

"Pierce Godfrey, of course." He was looking at me in exasperation. "Who else would I mean?"

"I don't understand. Why would you ask me a question like that? Pierce is a good friend, of course. I'm certain he would like to be your friend, as well, if you treated him more civilly."

He kept his eyes fixed on mine. "Are you sure he doesn't mean a good deal more to you than just a friend?"

"More than a friend—? Robert, what in the world are you getting at?"

"Oh, for God's sake, woman, open your eyes. The man is in love with you. You can't be that blind to his feelings. He may be a rogue, and for all I know a thief on the high seas, but when it comes to you he wears his heart on his sleeve."

I felt my face flush. This was the last thing I'd expected Robert to say. I had been careful never to mention Pierce's marriage proposal to anyone, not even Samuel, and above all, not to my parents. Nor had I divulged his plans for our future, the future I could not imagine us ever sharing.

I was fumbling about trying to think of some way to respond to this startling statement, when Robert cleared his throat and went on, "I see that I have upset you, and I'm sorry. It was not my intention."

"Was it not?" I replied, anger beginning to replace my shock at his temerity. "It's my turn to wonder at your own naïveté, Robert, if you truly did not expect such a personal, and uncalled-for, remark to cause me distress. Moreover, I do not see how my friendship with Pierce Godfrey can be any of your concern."

"I have apologized for irritating you, Sarah, but I stand by my words." His own temper was rising, and his voice had grown so loud that a couple at the next table turned to stare at us in disapproval. "Of course Pierce Godfrey is in love with you, any idiot can see that. Furthermore, however much you try to deny it, it's clear from your face that you're every bit as aware of his feelings as am I. And I consider it to be very much my business, if you must know."

"Please," I hissed, "lower your voice. You're making a spectacle of yourself. What has gotten into you anyway?"

Instead of answering my question, he went on with his diatribe, this unusual show of emotion causing his craggy face to mottle with color. "I may not always agree with your tactics, but I have long considered you to be an intelligent and practical woman, not vulnerable to a handsome face and a flattering tongue. You should see yourself when you're in the presence of that blackguard. It's—it's disgusting! It is almost as if the man has cast some kind of spell over you."

"That is entirely enough, Robert," I warned him, discomfited to note that even more diners had turned in their chairs and were looking in our direction. Lowering my voice, I went on, "You're allowing your imagination to run away with you, and it is most unbecoming. I assure you that Mr. Godfrey has not cast a spell over me. The very idea is ludicrous."

I stared at him over the candlelight. "I realize that you do not approve of Pierce, but why are you making such a fuss simply because he and I attended the theater together? And what do you mean by saying that it is very much your business?"

His angry expression changed to one of chagrin, as if he had stuck his foot in his mouth, and was without a clue how best to pull it out again.

"I, ah—As you just admitted, I'm your friend," he answered, rather lamely in my estimation.

"Robert, you're making no sense whatsoever. Tell me what is really on your mind."

He made a move as if to stand up, then, remembering where he was, sank back down in his seat. Robert is a restless man, especially when he is under duress. I knew by the tight set of his jaw that he was longing to be on his feet, pacing the room, perhaps, if that were possible. Then, as if set free by the opening of a floodgate, the words came tumbling out.

"You should know by now how much I care for—That is, you surely must realize the nature of my feelings for, for—" He ran a large hand through his coarse red hair, causing it to stand up in little clumps like a field of sun-ripened cornstalks. "You're a stubborn, opinionated, often reckless woman, but I find myself hopelessly in—" He gulped uncomfortably, and came to an abrupt halt. "Blast it all, Sarah, I just—well, I just don't want to see you make a fool of yourself over that scoundrel."

I found myself incapable of uttering a single word; all I could do was sit there and stare at him. What in the world was he going on about? Why was he behaving so strangely?

Before I was forced to reply to this astonishing speech, the room was suddenly filled with the sound of piano music. I looked toward the small stage, to see a man seated at the piano, his fingers lightly tripping over the keys. An attractive young woman with a bright head of red hair stepped out from behind the piano, and after a spate of polite applause from our fellow diners, began to sing.

I was so bowled over by Robert's words, and the need to say something, anything, to break the awkward silence that hung between us, that I foolishly blurted out the first thing that came into my head.

"That singer could be your sister, Robert. Her hair is the same color as yours."

He regarded me as if I had suddenly lost the use of my faculties. "That singer cannot be an inch over five feet tall, if that. I am six feet four inches. My two sisters are at least five feet nine or ten in their stocking feet. And as to that woman's hair color, if it didn't come straight out of a henna bottle, I'll eat my hat."

His eyes went again to the tiny singer, then came back to me. Once again, it was impossible to read his expression. "Oh, and it's nice to know that my hair reminds you of an overripe pumpkin patch."

The remainder of dinner was strained; the cab ride home seemed interminable. When we finally reached my house, Robert silently assisted me out of the cab, then walked me to the door. Even in the dim spill of light from the gas lamp, I could tell that he was still disgruntled over what had happened at dinner. Unfortunately, I had no idea what I could possibly say that would make everything all right between us again.

"Good night, Sarah," he said a little stiffly. He paused a moment, as if he might be about to say something else, then turned to go.

Without thinking, I took hold of his arm. "Robert, wait." I still didn't know what to say, I just knew I couldn't let him leave with this awful tension still between us.

Prompted by instinct more than reason, I stood on my tiptoes and kissed his cheek. "Thank you, Robert," I told him softly. "For everything. Your friendship means more to me than I can say."

"Oh, aye," he replied, that strange tone back in his voice. "We're good friends, Sarah. I just wish—"

Again, he hesitated, then mumbled something beneath his breath that I could not make out.

"Oh, damn it all anyway," he suddenly blurted and, placing his strong arms around my waist, pulled me against him and kissed me full upon the lips.

It was no ordinary kiss. Certainly, it was a far cry from the sort of kiss one might share with a friend. In fact, I was completely shocked by the passion of the embrace. Unable at first to move, I felt him increase the pressure of his lips on mine, and his arms tightened as he roughly pulled me even closer to his chest.

When one of his hands circled the back of my head to lift my face closer to his mouth, I was astonished to realize that my fingers, entirely of their own volition, had slid into the thick hair at the nape of his neck. What was I doing? a small, distant voice demanded. This was nothing like the Robert Campbell I knew. Dear Lord! This was totally unlike sensible, controlled, no-nonsense Sarah Woolson!

Feeling as if the world had suddenly gone insane, I could only stand there dazed when he finally broke off the kiss. My head felt slightly woozy and I stood rooted to the spot, afraid that if I moved so much as an inch I might fall flat on my face. I was still trying to catch my breath when he abruptly turned and, without a word, hurried back into the waiting carriage.

I stared after his departing cab, waiting until my body had regained some semblance of normalcy, before I attempted to move. With none too steady hands, I used my key to open the front door, and stepped inside.

To my relief, I saw no one inside the foyer. I could hear the sound of voices coming from the parlor, but the last thing I wished to do was to talk to anyone.

Quietly, I hurried up the stairs, went to my room, and closed the door.

CHAPTER EIGHTEEN

I awoke early the next morning, still weary from yet another restless night's sleep. My natural inclination was to escape someplace where I could be alone and sort through the events of the past ten days—especially the recent episodes with Pierce, and with Robert the night before.

By the light of day, last night had an illusory quality about it, as if it hadn't really happened. Robert's behavior had been so utterly unexpected, that it would have been simple enough to think back upon it as a dream. But, of course, it hadn't been a dream. It was a reality I would have to seriously attempt to unravel. But not this morning.

Entering the brougham Eddie had waiting for me outside my house, I did my best to concentrate on the morning's undertaking. In a few minutes we would pick up Brielle and little Emma at Madam Valentine's parlor house. I would require all my wits to see us through the upcoming encounter with Gerald Knight.

That morning I had donned a woolen cape and small velvet hat against the December chill, adding a colorful scarf to my costume in order to soften the effect of my rather severely cut suit. When I had first opened my law practice, I had commissioned several of these suits to be made for me—in gray, midnight blue, and brown.

Each gown was designed with concealed pockets, a tapered waist, and as little bustle as fashion would permit. All three were at once functional and professional, yet not entirely lacking in femininity. Such was the delicate balance I strove constantly to achieve in order to foster client confidence, while not appearing in any degree masculine to my male colleagues. I could not afford to forget that I was one of only three female attorneys currently practicing law in the entire state of California!

I will not deny that I was nervous. After all, this might be our only chance to sway Mr. Knight's feelings toward his daughter. It was impossible not to worry about the outcome, especially given Brielle's sudden surge of hope that once he saw the child his "heart would melt." Not for the first time, I wondered if Robert hadn't been right after all. The last thing I wanted to do was add yet one more disappointment to the poor girl's life.

As planned, Brielle was waiting for us when Eddie and I arrived. I was pleased to see that she had dressed little Emma in a soft blue baby gown, complete with a matching bonnet trimmed in white lace that truly did bring out the clear blue of her eyes. The little girl was snugly wrapped in a lovely cream-colored blanket which, Brielle informed me, had been crocheted by one of Madam Valentine's "girls." Hiding my surprise that a lady of the evening could be so accomplished in housewifely duties—when I could not knit four stitches in a row without dropping two of them—I limited my comments to praising the fine, intricate craftsmanship of the piece.

Because we were transporting a small baby, I instructed Eddie to drive at a more sedate speed than was his wont. Much to my surprise, he actually did make an effort to take most of the corners on all four wheels, and managed to subdue his natural inclination to pass any traffic which stood in the way of his forward progress. Even at this modest (at least for Eddie) pace, we managed to pull up in front of the large, modern-looking building that housed the *Daily Journal* shortly after ten o'clock, the time I had deemed optimum for finding the newspaper owner ensconced in his office.

He was indeed present, as I had hoped. Unfortunately, he was not disposed to see us, and I felt my heart sink to think that our mission was to end before it truly began.

Brielle and I stood in the anteroom of Gerald Knight's office—she cradling little Emma in her arms—while a young man with greasy brown hair, and a rather sparse beard framing a narrow, sadly pimpled face, curtly informed us that Mr. Knight was out and not expected back anytime that day. This, despite the fact that Knight's door was wide open behind the clerk and we could easily spy the owner, shirtsleeves rolled up to his elbows, seated behind a cluttered desk in a disorderly room, most of his face hidden as he bent over his work. One item of his clothing very much in evidence was a ghastly bright yellow cravat tied carelessly about his neck. Glancing at Brielle, I was rewarded with a quick nod, informing me that this was indeed her ex-lover.

Pointing out Knight's obvious presence to the unpleasant young man was fruitless. He seemed incapable of any original thought, merely parroting back to me that Mr. Knight was out and not expected back for the remainder of the day.

Realizing the hopelessness of our undertaking, Brielle and I turned to leave, when the man who wasn't there looked up, his dark eyes fastening on my lovely young companion as if drawn there by a magnet.

Now that I could clearly see his face, I was startled to realize that he was quite handsome. Somewhere in his early forties, he had sandy-brown hair which curled about his head in attractive disorder, deep blue eyes, and a long, aristocratic nose. He was clean-shaven except for a short, military-style mustache grown atop thin, disapproving lips. Despite that bit of facial hair, and a mouth which looked as if it rarely smiled, I was startled to see how closely the man resembled the small child held in my companion's arms. Brielle had told me nothing less than the truth: Gerald Knight was indeed little Emma's father!

My heart caught in my throat to see his face soften as he appeared to drink in my companion's beauty. Perhaps, I thought, the past seven or eight months had caused him to forget how stunning his ex-mistress truly was. If anything, I imagined that motherhood had only served to enhance her exquisiteness. I wondered if he could see, as could I, her delicate Madonna-like quality as she stood there holding his child to her bosom?

Apparently he could not. Almost immediately his face tightened into an expression of unyielding reserve, his already narrow lips forming one tight, downturned line of distaste. Muttering something beneath his breath, he broke off his gaze and once again bent to his work.

Brielle and I did not speak until we had reached the street, and turning to her I was dismayed to see tears welling in her lovely eyes. I was at once saddened by this show of emotion, and chagrined that, as Robert feared, my desperate act of last resort had resulted in yet one more dashed hope she must endure.

"I heartily apologize, my dear," I told her, feeling like a complete cad. "I should never have brought you here this morning. Gerald Knight is obviously a heartless, irresponsible rogue, who deserves neither you nor your sweet baby. The last thing I wanted to do was put you through yet more pain."

"Please, Miss Woolson, you mustn't take all the blame onto yourself." She forced a weak smile. "Believe me, I well understood the unlikelihood of changing Gerald's mind, but I—I'm afraid I allowed myself to pray for a miracle. I should have known better."

"I understand what you're saying," I agreed. "I knew it was probably a hopeless cause, yet I kept praying that if he saw little Emma, even his callous heart might soften." I felt my anger grow as I replayed in my mind the recent scene upstairs in Knight's office. "I cannot imagine any man not feeling proud to have fathered such a beautiful baby."

She sighed. "I'm the one who feels foolish. You do not know the man as I do. After all, I was his mistress for nearly two years. Now that I look back upon those months, I realize that Gerald Knight possesses neither the heart, nor the capacity, to love."

She looked up and down the street. "I don't see the carriage. Didn't you tell the boy to wait for us here?"

"Yes, I did." The space where Eddie had parked the brougham was now occupied by a heavily loaded dray, the draft horse harnessed in front contentedly chewing on a bag of oats. "Where did that boy take himself off to?"

Thinking Eddie might have found it necessary to move the carriage, I walked around the corner, and was just in time to see a tall man exit the rear of the *Daily Journal* building. He was pulling on his coat as he walked hastily toward a four-wheeled spider phaeton parked on the side street. My eye was instantly caught by the appalling yellow tie. The man was none other than Gerald Knight.

Calling out most indecorously to Brielle, and causing several well turned-out ladies to eye me with displeasure, I motioned that she should follow me, then turned and hurried after Knight. I caught him up just as he was about to enter the vehicle. Without stopping to consider the consequences of my actions, I recklessly took hold of him by the sleeve of the coat he had just donned.

"Mr. Knight, please wait." Glancing over my shoulder, I spied Brielle holding tight to the baby as she made her way toward us with as much haste as she could safely manage. "There is someone you really must meet."

Uttering several unrepeatable expletives, he started to pull his arm out of my grasp when he, too, caught sight of Brielle. He grew suddenly as still as a statue, his eyes fixed on the girl as if she were some sort of heavenly apparition. Watching her approach, I could well understand his reaction. Cheeks delightfully flushed from her exertions, violet eyes bright with renewed hope, golden ringlets flying about her face in becoming disarray, Brielle resembled nothing so much as a figure come alive from a Gainsborough painting. Her loveliness was breathtaking. Apparently, it had the same effect on Knight, for he said nothing, but continued to stare at her as if transfixed.

"Gerald," said Brielle, her voice soft and girlishly breathless. She stopped a few feet away from where we stood by the phaeton, as if hesitant to come any closer to her ex-lover. "I . . . I have brought our daughter for you to see."

Gently, she pulled back the blanket, revealing little Emma's sleeping face. If Brielle had stepped out of a Gainsborough painting, then the baby was unquestionably one of Raphael's cherubs.

Knight did no more than glance at the child, before his eyes went once again to Brielle. Emma seemed to hold little interest for him; all his attention was fixed on the baby's mother.

"Would you like to hold her?" asked Brielle, a bit tentatively. She held the baby out to him. "Her name is Emma, after your mother."

He stared at the child, long nose wrinkled in distaste, as if she were some sort of offensive creature not to be touched.

"No, of course I don't want to hold her," he declared, taking a step back, and appearing fearful lest he come into contact with the baby. "Why should I want anything to do with her? She's not my child."

I watched Brielle's lovely face deflate like a party balloon that has been punctured with a pin. The light went out of her eyes, and the pink drained from her rosy cheeks. She stopped walking toward him, and once again pulled the baby close to her bosom, murmuring soft, crooning sounds to her small daughter, as if to make up for her father's cruel rejection.

"I know neither you, nor your child, madam," he said, his tone imperious. "And I warn you that if you do not cease this unwarranted harassment, I shall be forced to seek legal action."

"Or sic your thugs on her again?" I said, my temper growing with every word that issued from the despicable man's mouth. "We have not been introduced, Mr. Knight, but I am Sarah Woolson, Miss Bouchard's attorney. I am serving you with fair warning that if my client is ever again accosted by your hoodlums, it is you who will be facing a day in court, and very likely time spent in jail."

I stepped closer to the odious man, until I could feel his hot, slightly acrid breath on my face. In for a penny, in for a pound, I told myself, as I prepared to play the last card in my piteously weak hand.

"You may deny your relationship with this young lady, Mr. Knight, but the child in her arms is your spitting image. Shame on you for so heartlessly rebuffing her. You are a cad and a coward of the—"

"Gerald?" came a female voice from inside the carriage. "Gerald! Who are you speaking to?"

There was a movement inside the phaeton, and a woman's head appeared in the open door. Although I had never met the lady, I was certain from Samuel's description that this was Gerald's wife, Lily Randolph Knight. According to my brother, it was she who had brought her family's money into the marriage, and it was she who continued to safeguard the family's purse strings.

As Knight reluctantly helped his wife down from the carriage, I saw that Lily Knight was a rather ordinary-looking woman, somewhere in her early fifties, I judged—at least ten years older than her husband. She was short and stout of girth, with graying, nondescript brown hair tucked into a tight bun beneath a brown velvet hat. Her cheeks were plump and her lips as full as her husband's were thin.

Upon reaching the ground, she arranged her skirts neatly about her ample waist, then studied Brielle and me with intelligent brown eyes. She afforded me but a brief appraisal, seeming far more interested in my young companion and the baby in her arms.

"You must be my husband's latest paramour," she said with surprising frankness. She removed a pair of spectacles from her reticule, settled them upon her nose, then moved closer to Brielle, taking in the girl's face and manner of dress with myopic eyes.

"Yes," she said at length, nodding her head. "I can understand his attraction to you—Miss Bouchard, isn't it? You are undeniably beautiful. Of course you are young enough to be his daughter, but that has never prevented Mr. Knight from having his way with any girl who takes his fancy."

"Lily, really!" sputtered her husband, his stricken face looking up and down the street for fear passersby should overhear his wife. "You're quite mistaken, my dear. I give you my word that I have never seen this girl before in my life."

Lily gave him a deprecating look. "Your word, indeed, Gerald.

Since when has your word been worth the breath required to speak it?" Once again she donned her spectacles, and turned back to Brielle. "Would you be so kind as to remove the baby's wrap so that I may see its face, Miss Bouchard?"

The girl hesitated, then slowly drew back the soft wool blanket to reveal little Emma's angelic face. Just as Mrs. Knight leaned closer for a better look, the baby opened her eyes and looked directly back at the woman.

"Oh, my," said Lily with a start. "Just see how alert she is for such a tiny thing. How old is she, three, four months?"

"She is three months old, Mrs. Knight," Brielle answered, clutching her child tightly, as if not sure what to make of the unexpected attention issuing from her ex-lover's wife.

Paying no heed to this reaction, Lily reached out a finger and lightly tickled the child under her chubby chin, then smiled when the baby chortled happily. "She appears healthy enough. What did you say her name was? I couldn't quite make it out from inside the phaeton."

"Emma, Mrs. Knight. I called her Emma after—"

"Yes, yes, after Gerald's mother," the older woman broke in with a chuckle. "I'm sure Mrs. Knight would find it gratifying to know that her son's illegitimate daughter has been named in her honor. I doubt that Gerald will be sharing this news with his elderly mama, however, will you, dear?"

Her husband did his best to speak, but she ignored him as if he were as invisible as his office clerk had insisted. Her sharp brown eyes had moved to me.

"I believe you said your name was Sarah Woolson, did you not?" she asked. "Could I have heard correctly that you are actually an attorney?"

After I had confirmed this to be true, she clucked, "My, my, that is remarkable. What will women think to do next?"

"Lily, this is quite enough," objected Gerald. "Do not waste any more time on these two and their pack of lies. If we do not hurry we'll be late for—"

"Gerald, be quiet!" Lily ordered. Her attention had gone back to the baby, and she was gently tilting little Emma's face first one way, then the other. All the while, the little girl's eyes never left the woman's face, which the tyke seemed to find inordinately interesting.

"Miss Woolson is quite correct, Gerald," she said, pulling back from Brielle. "This baby looks exactly like you. In fact, she quite resembles our Millicent when she was this age. Millicent is the eldest of our three children," she explained for our benefit. "She is now eighteen, our son Jonathan is sixteen, and our youngest daughter, Deirdre, is nearly fifteen."

Straightening, she looked her husband full in the face. "You may deny your role in this child's parentage until hell freezes over, my dear, unfaithful husband, but the proof of your infidelity lies peacefully cradled in this young woman's arms."

"Lily, please," protested Gerald, taking his wife's arm and attempting to nudge her back to the phaeton. Despite the chill December morning, I saw that he was perspiring heavily. "These women are nothing but cheap burners, out to extort whatever money they can from us. You mustn't believe their outrageous lies. Think of our reputation."

Lily gave a dry, sad little laugh. "That's very good, Gerald. I imagine you refer to the reputation you've taken such pains to create through that crusading newspaper of yours. Created out of whole cloth, of course, since not a word of it is true." At his startled look, she said, "Yes, my dear, I know all about your little peccadilloes. I have my sources, just as you have yours. Ironic, don't you agree?"

She gave a great sigh, and the energy seemed to suddenly drain out of her. For the first time I noticed the pain etched in the fine lines around her eyes, and the grooves set to either side of her generous mouth. How much grief has she endured because of this man? I wondered. And why has she put up with it for so long?

The answer to this question, of course, was easy enough to guess. For all his faults, Gerald Knight was a handsome man, fit and strong for his age, with good skin and a fine head of hair. Many woman would undoubtedly be happy to call him husband. Lily Randolph must have been a spinster in her mid-thirties when Knight came along, I calculated. She probably viewed him as a blessed last chance to marry and produce a family.

He, of course, would have been attracted by her money. According to Samuel, she was the only child of wealthy parents, the Pennsylvania Randolphs, who had made a substantial fortune in steel. A doting mother and father willing to buy their daughter's happiness at any price, I thought.

How long had it taken, I wondered, before Lily discovered the true nature of the man she had married? Not long, I guessed, given his eye for beautiful young women. She had set men to follow her errant husband, but she had stayed with him. I found this last notion impossible to fathom.

"Come, Gerald," said Lily, at last moving away from Brielle and the baby. "We are going to be late for lunch."

Without another word to either Brielle or myself, Knight assisted his wife into the phaeton, gave instructions to their driver, and joined the late-morning traffic.

Moments after the Knights' carriage made its way down the street, Eddie came barreling up in the brougham, his overworked dappled-gray snorting in protest. Muttering abject apologies for leaving us stranded without any notion where he had gone, the boy explained that one of his regular customers had spied him parked in front of the *Daily Journal*, and had begged him to convey him to his office for an urgent meeting. Sheepishly, the lad admitted that the man always tipped generously, and his office was a distance of a mere mile or two at the most. Adopting his most cherubic expression, Eddie shrugged his thin shoulders as if to say, how could a hardworking cabbie resist?

How could he, indeed? Cutting off further apologies, Brielle and I entered the carriage, and I instructed the boy to take us back to Madam Valentine's brothel.

It was a cheerless journey, seeming to take a great deal longer returning to our destination than it had driving to the newspaper office earlier that morning. Even little Emma seemed to sense our melancholy mood, for she soon started to fuss in Brielle's arms. The young mother jiggled the baby gently in her lap, then when that failed to soothe, propped the little one over her shoulder and was promptly rewarded with a loud burp.

"Well, that is that," said the girl resignedly, as Eddie lent her a helping hand down from the carriage. "Please do not feel you have failed me, Miss Woolson. I could not have asked for a braver or more steadfast champion. As Madam Valentine pointed out, my future at her parlor house is not the worst fate to befall a woman."

Before I could respond, she turned and hurried up the steps and into the house on Montgomery Street. She was not quick enough, however, to prevent me from seeing the tears rolling down her cheeks.

In spite of Brielle's kind words, I had seldom in my life felt more disheartened as when I trudged up the stairs to my office on Sutter Street. Eddie expressed surprising willingness to endure his weekly mathematics lesson—his least favorite subject—but for the first time since I began tutoring the boy, I could not muster the energy to teach.

After he left to continue his day's work, I sat a long time at my desk, going over our visit to the *Daily Journal*, and wondering what I might have done, if anything, to ensure a happier outcome. My only consolation was that since we had confronted Gerald Knight in the presence of his wife, the unfortunate woman could no longer be in denial about her husband's infidelities. I prayed that she would somehow find the courage to pack his bags and order the bounder out of her house!

I am ashamed to admit that I had completely forgotten the appointment I had arranged with the Chinese interpreter, Sun Kin Lu, to visit my office this afternoon. Because of my preoccupation with Brielle and the abhorrent Gerald Knight, I was taken aback when I heard a timid knock on my door shortly after one o'clock. Wondering who it could be, I was surprised when the diminutive man entered my office, executing his usual low bow of respect.

"You ask see me, missy," he began, declining my offer of a seat on the other side of my desk.

"Yes, Mr. Sun," I replied with equal formality.

I explained Fan Gow and Lee Yup's arraignment at the courthouse the following morning, and we established a time and a place to meet which suited us both. I went on to inquire if there was anything we could bring the men from Chinatown, which might add to their comfort and well-being during their incarceration.

Sun thought for a moment, then suggested that an assortment of dried delicacies would certainly be welcomed, given that the white man's food at the jail was unpalatable. He went on to list dried duck, dried pig livers, and perhaps even dried frogs and oysters as possible offerings, followed by lychee nuts, lily seeds, and pickled almonds.

Sun was quiet for several moments, and I thought he had come to the end of a mostly futile list of food the jailers would almost certainly not allow their inmates to enjoy. However, he had one more suggestion.

"They likee if we bring joss sticks. Burn sandalwood with cedar or fir—make bad smell go way. It be nice, missy. No more stink in cell. Bring good luck."

I was considering how best to inform the well-intentioned Mr. Sun how difficult it would be to bring in most of these items, particularly the joss sticks, when Samuel burst into the room, his usually immaculate appearance spoiled by a wrinkled shirt and a crooked cravat. His blond hair was uncharacteristically sticking up in clumps, as if he'd been running his fingers through it.

"Samuel, what's wrong?" I asked in alarm, my thoughts immediately going to our mother and father, who were getting on in years. "Is it Mama? Or Papa? Don't tell me it's little Charlie?"

I was referring, of course, to Charles and Celia's four-month-old son, Charles, Jr. Sadly, it was not uncommon for babies to succumb to a variety of childhood illness during their first year of life.

"No, everyone's all right," he assured me, not bothering to take a seat.

"Well, actually not everyone," he hurried on. "I'm afraid there's been another murder."

CHAPTER NINETEEN

After sending Sun Kin Lu on his way, I followed Samuel out of my office. I was more than a little surprised to see Eddie waiting atop his brougham in front of the building. Samuel explained that he and the boy had arrived there at the same time, which was fortunate since my brother wouldn't have had time to contact him otherwise.

"I was worried about you, Miss Sarah," explained Eddie, looking a bit sheepish to admit to such a weakness. "You looked pretty peaked, so after my last fare I thought I'd come by and see if you was okay."

In spite of the horrible news my brother had just delivered, I couldn't help but smile at the boy. One would have to look long and hard to find a friend as loyal and dedicated as this young waif off the street. Once again I was observing firsthand the truth of the old adage that you cannot judge a book by its cover!

"That was most thoughtful of you, Eddie," I told him, resisting the urge to give him a hug, a gesture he would undoubtedly consider beneath his dignity. Instead, I reached out and casually ruffled his already messy hair. "And it seems you are just in time. Where is it we're going, Samuel? You've yet to tell me the name of the victim."

A look of real regret passed over my brother's handsome face. "It was Patrick O'Hara, Sarah. The young man who works at Murphy's Ice Cream Parlor, between Second Street and Folsom. Damn it all, he was only twenty and well liked by everyone."

"Did you say Murphy's Ice Cream Parlor?" Eddie asked, hopping lithely down from his perch. "Is that where we're goin' then?"

"Something terrible has happened there, and it won't be open today," Samuel told him. "We're just going to have a look around, so you can stop salivating."

"Sali—what?" the boy asked in confusion. "What's that you say I'm doin'?"

"You're drooling, my lad," explained Samuel. "Just the mention of ice cream and you get that silly grin on your face. I'll thank you to remember this is serious business we're about this afternoon."

Properly chastened, Eddie saw us seated inside the brougham, then jumped easily back up onto the driver's seat at the front of the carriage. As he took off with his usual abandon, I was once again forced to put my faith in whatever god had taken on the considerable task of guarding over reckless boys, especially those who drove a cab for a living.

"How was poor Patrick killed?" I asked, picturing the good-natured lad with the curly head of strawberry-blond hair and flashing Irish eyes.

"He was stabbed with an ice pick they kept in the shop." He gave a little grimace, then went on tightly, "After O'Hara was killed, he was evidently dragged to the back of the shop, where he wasn't found until this morning. The only reason I know about it is that I stopped by the station to see George on my way back from Cunningham's law firm."

"Oh, Samuel, I'm so sorry," I said, belatedly remembering the appointment Papa had arranged with his old friend Arthur Cunningham. "I forgot all about your meeting this morning. How did it go?"

He waved his hand dismissively. "Never mind about that now. I'll tell you all the gruesome details later."

I started to press him about it, then realized he was far more interested in the tragedy that had taken place at the ice cream parlor than an interview to fill the position of associate attorney, a job I knew all too well that he had no interest in pursuing.

"All right, then. Tell me what else you know about the boy's murder?"

"Not much, I'm afraid. It isn't George's case, and no one connected with it would give me much information. I came here as quickly as I could to get you."

I looked at him in surprise. "To get me? Why?"

"There's got to be a damn good story behind Patrick O'Hara's death," he explained, then looked shamefaced. "I know that sounds callous, but every reporter in town will be running hell-for-leather to Murphy's to get a scoop. I want to be the first one there to have a closer look at where the poor fellow was killed." He gave me an ironic smile. "Since a good number of courting couples frequent the parlor, I thought you would provide excellent cover."

"Surely it will be closed today," I protested. "After what happened."

"I don't expect it to be open, Sarah. Still, I'd like to nose about the place on my own if I can."

"Did George say it was a robbery?" I asked. "You don't think O'Hara was deliberately singled out, do you? He was such a sweet boy. Who would want to harm him?"

"That's just it, Sarah, apparently it wasn't a robbery. And that, taken with Nigel Logan's and Deacon Hume's murders—"

"You think Patrick was murdered by the same person?" I was about to say more, when the brougham's right front wheel hit a pothole and we were nearly bounced out of our seats. I resettled myself and secured my hat, then took the precaution of holding tight to the seat in the event we hit another bump in the road. "I don't see how it could be the same killer, Samuel. I doubt that Patrick O'Hara even knew Logan and Hume. They had absolutely nothing in common."

"No," he said reflectively, "still, it seems an extraordinary coincidence, don't you think? Three murders in just over a week?"

We fell into an uncomfortable silence for the remainder of the ride, lost in our own desultory thoughts. Afternoon traffic was uncommonly light, and we arrived at Murphy's Ice Cream Parlor in good time. Despite being told that the shop would be closed, Eddie had added to our speedy arrival by zigzagging his horse in, out, and around any vehicles unfortunate enough to stand in his way. Despite all our protests, once he had ascended to the driver's box Eddie seemed capable of only one speed—and that was fast!

As far back as I could remember, Murphy's Ice Cream Parlor had been one of Rincon Hill's happiest landmarks. Located on the southeast corner of Second and Folsom streets, Mr. Murphy's homemade ice cream had been one of our favorite treats when Samuel and I were growing up. Every Saturday afternoon, rain or shine, Papa had taken his two youngest children by the hand to walk the several blocks to Lachlan Murphy's bright orange and yellow shop for our weekly treat. Mr. Murphy had passed away some twelve years earlier, but his eldest son, Kerry, had taken over the parlor.

The only changes Kerry made to the shop were to hang a new, but equally colorful, sign above the door, and to add ice cream sodas to the menu. This new innovation—which was created by adding ice cream to one of half a dozen soda water flavors—quickly became a sensation with his customers, especially courting couples out for a summer evening stroll.

Most customers in the neighborhood were aware that Patrick O'Hara was Kerry Murphy's cousin, his mother's sister's youngest son. He was a large, happy, handsome lad, extremely popular with the young ladies who frequented the family-run parlor. It was difficult to believe that this pleasant boy had been the victim of such a vicious attack. If Samuel was right, and it hadn't been a robbery gone awry, who could have disliked the simple, good-natured young man enough to take his life?

When Eddie reined up on the corner of Second and Folsom streets, he parked the brougham across from a police van, which was drawn up directly in front of the parlor. As we expected, the door to the shop was closed, but a number of curious bystanders were milling about the entrance. I noticed that the majority of these onlookers were young women in their late teens or early twenties. Some of them were actually in tears.

Glancing warily at the group clustered about the doorway, some peering inquisitively through the windows, Samuel touched my arm.

Speaking softly, he said, "I'm going around to the rear entrance to the shop. I'd like a word or two with whoever has been assigned to the case."

Instructing Eddie to stay with the carriage, he nodded to me and we unobtrusively made our way around the corner and into the narrow alley backing the shops that fronted on Folsom Street. I knew without being told that the last thing we needed was for the host of gawking girls to follow upon our heels.

We were pleased to find the back door to the ice cream parlor partially open, and we could hear the sound of male voices coming from inside. Giving the door a barely audible knock and, without waiting for an answer, Samuel pushed it open and we entered what was obviously the shop's storage area. The room was in deep shadow. The only light spilling inside—and that dim enough—came from the front of the parlor. Still, after our eyes adjusted to the dark, it was possible to make out a number of crates lined up two or three boxes high against one of the walls, a sink and half a dozen empty soda bottles piled in more crates to the opposite side of the room.

Samuel motioned for me to tread softly, and we made our way toward the voices. Once we reached the parlor's back entrance, we crouched behind yet more piles of crates stacked to either side of the door, my brother on one side, I on the other.

From this position, we could see a visibly distraught Kerry Murphy speaking to a tall, heavily built uniformed policeman, whose back was turned toward us. His ample body and broad neck was topped by a thick head of black hair, but we could see nothing of his face. Samuel gave a little shake of his head, indicating that he couldn't place the officer, and for us to remain where we were for the moment.

As I studied the two men, my gaze went to the floor and I stiffened to spy a large dark discoloration staining the worn wood planks. That must be where poor Patrick had been stabbed, I realized, and the crime was sharply brought home to me in all its gory details. I blinked back hot tears; how heartbreaking to think that such a happy young life had been cut so tragically short.

From where we were standing, it was also possible to make out the trail of blood where the boy's body had been dragged into the storage room behind us. I was aghast to realize that there were one or two stains beneath my boots. God help us! I thought, willing myself not to move from my hiding place behind the crates. Repositioning my feet ever so slightly, I fervently prayed that poor Patrick had died quickly, and with as little pain and panic as possible.

"It must have been a mistake!"

Kerry Murphy's words cut into these macabre thoughts. I looked back up to find that he had moved closer to the policeman, his face jutting out from a thick neck until it was mere inches from the other man's nose. The Irishman's feet were planted apart, and his normally pleasant voice—ever ready to compliment young ladies' hats and ply small children with sugary treats—cracked with emotion.

"I'm tellin' ya, Patrick didn't have an enemy in the world, nary a one," he insisted. "Ask anyone. You couldn't find a better, more decent lad, and that's God's gospel truth."

"Calm down there, b'hoy," said the officer, stepping back a pace or two. "You said yourself nothing was taken from the cash box. Now if it weren't a robbery, then whoever did in your cousin meant to do just that. So, for the last time, who had it in for O'Hara?"

Kerry Murphy's full face flushed red with anger. "I'm tellin' you no one had it in for Patrick! Yer wastin' yer time with all these damn-fool questions. You outta be out there findin' whoever did this to the boy."

"And who would ya have me arrest?" the officer asked, his voice heavy with sarcasm. "How about you, Murphy? Maybe you had it in for your cousin—him bein' such a pretty lady's man and all? What happened? Did O'Hara steal your girl, so you poked holes in him with an ice pick? Crime of rage, was it?"

Murphy's face was now beet red, and I saw his fingers ball up into fists at his sides. Before the Irishman could act on his rage, the back storage door slammed open and I heard the sound of feet scuttling through the dim room.

"Did you find the body?" Eddie's voice inquired in a loud whisper. "Is there a lot of blood?"

With a grunt of dismay, Samuel reached out to grab the boy before he could go any further. "I thought I told you to wait with the carriage," he hissed. "Now you've gone and fixed the flint."

Both men in the parlor had stopped talking at the sudden disturbance. Samuel cleared his throat and walked boldly into the room.

"The back door was open, so I let myself in," he announced, adopting his most amicable smile. "I was sorry to hear about your cousin, Kerry." He turned toward the second man. "I don't believe we've met, Officer—"

"Never mind who I am," snapped the policeman. "Who the hell do you think you are, marching in here bold as brass?" He eyed my brother's blond hair. "Another Murphy, I suppose."

Kerry Murphy scowled at the policeman. "This is Officer Dubbs, Mr. Woolson. And if he's an example of the city's finest, then we're in a bloody lot of trouble."

"I see," said Samuel. "Thanks, Kerry."

Ignoring the policeman's belligerent expression, Samuel calmly held out his hand. "I'm not a Murphy, Officer Dubbs. My name is Samuel Woolson. I'm a friend of Sergeant Lewis's. He spoke to me this morning about Mr. O'Hara's tragic murder."

"So you thought you'd waltz on over here and have a look-see for yourself, is that it?" The officer studied Samuel critically for several seconds, then raised bushy black eyebrows. "Just a minute,

I know who you are. You're that nosy newspaper reporter, the one who writes them stories that make coppers look stupid."

The man's heavy face darkened as he gave Samuel a sour look of dislike. "Well, you won't get anything nosing around here, so get yourself out before I throw you in the paddy wagon for interferin' in a police investigation." He grabbed Eddie by the collar and gave him a push toward my brother. "Here, and take this young hooligan with you."

Looking beyond the boy, he seemed to notice my presence in the doorway for the first time. "And who is this? What did you do, bring half the street in with you?" He took a menacing step toward Samuel, prompting my brother to grab Eddie's arm and beat a prudent retreat.

W hat's that ole leatherhead so riled up about?" asked Eddie, when we were safely back in the alley. He looked at me reproachfully, as if I'd reneged on a promised treat. "And I never saw no body. I thought you said the mark was cut up with an ice pick. Didn't see no sign of that."

I was too upset to correct the boy's use of the double negative. And by now I understood that referring to the officer we had just encountered as "leatherhead" was but one of the seemingly endless sobriquets by which the police were known on the streets of San Francisco.

"The victim's body had already been removed, Eddie," I explained, hastening my step to catch up with Samuel, who had reached the end of the alley. "When you came bounding in with all the subtlety of a stick of dynamite, the—"

"Yeah, I know, the jig was up," the boy said, hanging his head. "I should 'ave known better."

"Well, it's too late now. No sense crying over spilt milk."

The boy's head bobbed up, but before he could ask the inevitable question, I explained, "It's just an expression, Eddie. It means

248

there's no use worrying about something once it's over and done with."

Despite his chagrin at having interrupted Samuel's investigation, a small impish grin crossed the lad's face. "I like that one, Miss Sarah. That pretty much sops the gravy, don't it?"

I had only a vague idea of what "sopping the gravy" entailed, but I had caught up with Samuel and had more important matters on my mind.

"That wasn't very helpful, was it?" I said as we neared the end of the alley.

"I admit I was hoping for a good deal more," he replied, his voice heavy with frustration. "If only that policeman hadn't been there, I might have engaged Kerry Murphy in some meaningful conversation."

"It's almighty hot today, don't you think?" interjected Eddie out of the blue.

I shot the boy a curious glance, then looked up at the gray sky. As a matter of fact, it was an uncommonly dreary day, seasonably cool, with the promise of rain hanging heavily in the afternoon air.

Samuel shook his head, guessing what had motivated the lad into making such a strange utterance. "The shop is closed today, Eddy, remember? There's been a death in the family."

"What's that got to do with them dishin' up some ice cream?" argued the boy. "The body's not even in there anymore."

"That's true, but when people lose someone they care about, they need time to mourn and work through their pain," Samuel told him patiently.

Eddie did not appear completely satisfied by this explanation, but seemed to accept the fact that he would not be allowed to partake of one of Murphy's excellent ice cream dishes this afternoon.

The boy and I had followed my brother out of the alley and onto Folsom Street, when I noticed a familiar, and decidedly unwelcome, face in the crowd gathered outside the parlor.

"Samuel, look," I said, nodding my head toward the man. "It's Ozzie Foldger. And this time I know I'm not mistaken."

"So it is," said Samuel, regarding the rival reporter with ill-disguised distaste. "I'm not surprised he's here. Word spreads fast in this city, especially when it concerns a murder."

Just then Foldger caught sight of us. At first he looked dismayed that we had beat him to the story, then quickly recovering his air of self-confidence, he gave me a strangely ironic smile. Then, with a jaunty tip of his cap, he turned and made his way into the alley from which we had just emerged.

"Do you think he'll get inside like we did?" Eddie asked, following our gaze.

"Maybe," Samuel told him. "But he'll get pretty short shrift if he does. Officer Dubbs will be on the lookout for more reporters. Most likely he's already locked the back door."

We had begun to cross the street toward the brougham, when I spied Major Zachariah Tremaine's tall head above the crowd. As he came closer, I saw that he was accompanied by the twins, David and Melody, as well as a young boy of about eleven, and a small girl who appeared to be two or three years his junior. I recognized the children as David and Melody's half brother and sister from their father's second marriage to Faith Tremaine. Although I had never been formally introduced to the youngsters, I had glimpsed them at church on a Sunday morning.

"Look, Samuel," I said, taking his arm and motioning toward the new arrivals. I needn't have bothered; my brother had already spotted the foursome—or at least he had certainly noticed the lovely Melody Tremaine.

"Good afternoon, Major Tremaine," he said, politely doffing his brown bowler hat to the elderly gentleman. Turning to the twins, he smiled a friendly greeting. "It's good to see you again Miss Tremaine, Mr. Tremaine."

"Good afternoon, Mr. Woolson, Miss Woolson," replied the older man. "You know my grandchildren David and Melody, I believe. And these two are my son's children by his second marriage.

This is Reggie," he said, nodding to the boy, "and this is Carolyn." He gazed curiously about at the crowd of mostly young people gathered in front of the ice cream parlor. "What's going on, do you know? Why are all these people milling about outside the shop?"

"Something dreadful happened here last night," I replied. "I'm afraid that Patrick O'Hara has been kill—" I stopped before actually speaking the dreaded word. In deference to the two young children who were, even as I spoke, darting eager glances toward the shop, I was forced to rethink how best to explain the poor Irishman's death. "There has been an unfortunate accident," I said, rephrasing my words. "The parlor is closed, at least for the remainder of the day."

Melody Tremaine stared at me, her beautiful face puzzled. "Whatever has happened, Miss Woolson? I trust it is nothing serious."

I caught Samuel's eye, and with an almost imperceptible nod of understanding, he turned to Eddie. "Why don't we show Reggie and Carolyn your horse? Perhaps you have some oats they could feed him."

It took Eddie—who had been gaping in open admiration at the beautiful Melody—several seconds to comprehend that my brother was speaking to him. Shrugging reluctantly, he gave the girl a last, adoring look, then turned and led Samuel and the children across the street to where he had parked the brougham.

When they were out of hearing, I set out to explain to David, Melody, and their grandfather what had happened to poor Patrick O'Hara. I made my description as brief and delicate as possible, making no mention of the manner of the boy's death, or the trail of blood which had been left behind. As I spoke, David drew in a sharp breath and his sister's face drained of color.

Holding tightly to her brother's arm, she protested in a stricken voice, "Surely, Miss Woolson, you are mistaken. It cannot have been Mr. O'Hara."

"Melody is right," put in David, looking a bit pale himself. "I can't imagine anyone wishing to harm Patrick. He was pleasant and cheerful to everyone. He even remembered the children's birthdays with a free dish of ice cream. They are—were—quite fond of him. He was an altogether agreeable man."

"Yes, he certainly was," I said, experiencing a pang of regret for causing these two young people such obvious distress. Given their tender years, they undoubtedly lived a quiet, sheltered life, protected by their parents against the violence and other sordid elements which sadly existed in a metropolitan city such as San Francisco.

Major Tremaine was eyeing me intently, as if not quite sure how to phrase his words. "Who—That is, do the police know who committed this dreadful act?"

"Not yet, I'm afraid. They're making inquiries, of course, but as yet they don't appear to have any particular suspect in mind."

I was alarmed to see Melody's face blanch even more dramatically than before. She swayed slightly, and David reached out an arm to steady her.

"Mel, are you all right?" The boy's handsome face was pinched in concern. He had taken hold of one of his sister's arms, while Mr. Tremaine grabbed the other. The major's eyes darted around, as if searching for a place where she might sit until she had recovered.

I hastened forward, having plucked a small vial of smelling salts from an inner pocket of my suit. I had, on more occasions than I care to recall, found it a handy resource in restoring ladies to their senses. Opening the cap, I placed the foul-smelling substance beneath the girl's delicate nose.

"Breathe deeply, my dear," I instructed.

Obediently, she did as she was told. Almost instantly she fell into a violent fit of coughing, and her small hands fought to push away the tiny beaker. To be sure, the mixture of carbonate of ammonium and some sickening, too-sweet fragrance was intolerable. It was, however, an excellent—and speedy—method with which to revive those women who appear prone to light-headedness, or indeed spells of fainting. Once again, I said a private prayer of gratitude that I had never personally been obliged to resort to the nasty stuff.

In a matter of moments, Melody's delicate face had regained its usual healthy color, and she appeared to be quite restored. Throughout this brief but tense ordeal, however, David had been regarding his sister with an expression bordering on panic. For a frightened minute, I feared he, too, might be in danger of fainting away at my feet. As I started to move the vial of smelling salts to his face, however, he shook his head and gently pushed it away.

"I have no need for that, Miss Woolson," he said with a wan smile. "My sister has a fragile constitution, and it worries me to see her fall into such a state." He bent his head and looked into her face. "What happened to Mr. O'Hara was tragic, Melody, but we hardly knew the man. I wish you would not take it so to heart. It is not good for your health."

"David is right, my dear," agreed their grandfather. "You must not allow Mr. O'Hara's death, however unfortunate, to affect your well-being."

"I know, Grandpapa," she said, darting him an embarrassed look. "And I'm sorry to have made such a bother of myself. But it is just so dreadful to think that Mr. O'Hara's killer is still out here—somewhere in our own neighborhood. We live barely three blocks away!"

"Please believe me, my dear, you and your family are perfectly safe," I assured her, aware that I was grossly minimizing the severity of the situation. "I'm certain that the villain responsible for poor Patrick's death is many miles from Rincon Hill by now. You need not be afraid."

"Miss Woolson is right, Melody," concurred the major, sending me a grateful smile. "I'm sure the police will soon catch the blackguard who committed this terrible crime."

I nodded my agreement, although privately I feared the solution to O'Hara's murder might not be anywhere near that simple. If, as the police assumed, his death had not been the result of a failed robbery, then the killer must be someone who knew the young Irishman—or worse, somebody in the boy's own family.

A third possibility, I thought as a chill of dread rippled down my spine, was that the same person who murdered Nigel Logan and Deacon Hume had struck yet again. Whatever the answer, as Melody feared, the villain might still be right here, beneath our very noses.

A most disconcerting thought!

CHAPTER TWENTY

As Samuel and I drove in Eddie's carriage the few blocks from the ice cream parlor to our home, we passed several newsboys hawking evening newspapers with the disturbing headlines: LADY LAWYER REPRESENTS CHINKS! JUDGE'S DAUGHTER DOES IT AGAIN! ANGEL DEFENDS CELESTIAL DEVILS!

Samuel instructed Eddie to stop, then hopped out of the brougham to purchase a copy of each edition. As the carriage once again continued on its way, he scanned the papers.

"Good Lord!" he exclaimed. "I can't believe even Ozzie Foldger would stoop this low."

"What is it, Samuel?" I asked. "What has he written now?"

"You're not going to like this, Sarah."

Without replying, I took this evening's *Tattler* out of my brother's hands and scanned Foldger's article. With a cry of alarm, I clapped a hand to my mouth.

"Oh, dear God!" I gasped. I remembered how relieved I'd been that Ozzie Foldger hadn't seen me at Madam Valentine's parlor house the previous Friday morning. Now the miserable gossipmonger had caught me out after all. He must have been hiding in the shadows along Montgomery Street the night before, when Robert and I entered the brothel.

The first half of his article dealt with my defending the two "foreign monkeys" who had been arrested for Deacon Dieter Hume's murder. The last paragraph read:

> Not only is the above-mentioned lady lawyer championing two heathen Chinamen, but she was seen just last night brazenly entering one of Montgomery Street's most infamous cathouses. It seems the very proper Miss Sarah Woolson—daughter of noted San Francisco Judge Horace Woolson—is intimately acquainted with a celebrated courtesan and her stable of naughty nymphs.

Allowing the newspaper to fall to the floor of the carriage, I closed my eyes and slumped back in my seat.

"Dear Lord, Samuel. What am I going to do?"

"Right now you're not going to do anything, Sarah," he replied, grinding his teeth in suppressed fury. "Not until we come up with some sort of strategy for dealing with this."

"Can you imagine Papa's reaction when he sees this?"

"Yes, but remember that he doesn't read the *Tattler*. With any kind of luck he may not find out about the article, at least for the next day or two."

I shook my head; I was too old to believe in fairy tales. "One of his friends will see the article, Samuel, and someone is bound to tell him about it. By tomorrow, my visit to Madam Valentine's parlor house will be carried in other newspapers as well. The fact that I'm representing Fan Gow and Lee Yup is already a headline story. Just wait until the city reads this!"

Samuel looked solemn and his brows were knitted into a tense line. "That rotten little bast—" He darted me a sheepish look, then went on, "At least now we know why that good-for-nothing scoundrel has been following you around for the past week."

Samuel spent the remainder of the brief ride trying to calm my shattered nerves, but without much success. My mind was too busy imagining my parents' reaction to the story, not to mention the effect it would have on my fledgling law firm. It served me right for letting down my guard. Truth be told, I'd been so intent on my plan to confront Gerald Knight when we'd gone to see Brielle, I'd forgotten all about Ozzie Foldger. I wished now that I'd let Eddie lead Robert and me around to the back entrance of the parlor house, instead of stubbornly insisting on entering by the front door.

When Eddie reined up in front of our house, Samuel assisted me down from the coach, then followed after me.

"I'm going to have Eddie take me to see George. Hopefully, he has more information about O'Hara's murder. I also want to talk to him about that police officer who was grilling Kerry Murphy at the ice cream parlor. I don't for one minute believe Kerry had anything to do with his cousin's murder, and I hate to see him harassed like that."

With a reassuring smile, he gave me a fierce brotherly hug. "We'll find a way to deal with this, Sarah. We spent our childhood going from one scrape to another. We managed to live through them and we'll live through this one, too. I promise."

With that, he hopped back into the carriage. Giving me a broad smile and a jaunty tip of his cap, Eddie pulled back into traffic.

We had two unexpected visitors to our home that evening. Samuel had returned after dinner, accompanied by George Lewis. The three of us had just settled ourselves in Papá's library, when Robert appeared at the door, claiming he was worried about the "madman" who, according to the news spreading like wildfire throughout the city, was running amuck on Rincon Hill.

My heart did a kind of leap when Robert walked into the house. I had not seen him since the night before, and in view of our unexpected kiss I had no idea how to behave toward him.

The moment he saw me, Robert's ruddy face seemed to grow several shades lighter, and I thought I saw his Adam's apple move rapidly up and down. He must be suffering the same discomfiture as I was. Thankfully, before either of us could think of something to say, Samuel showed our unexpected guest into the library.

After we had reestablished ourselves around the fireplace, which now included my self-conscious colleague, Edis carried in a large pot of coffee, four cups, and, naturally, a plate overflowing with cookies and cakes from Cook's kitchen. I noticed that Robert was doing his best to avoid looking at me, and I sighed inwardly. Obviously, we could not go on like this. Sooner or later we would have to discuss this new development in our relationship. But it most definitely would not be in front of my brother and a police sergeant!

I watched George and Robert for signs that they had read Ozzie Foldger's article in this evening's *Tattler*. To my relief, I could see they obviously had not. Nor had anyone in my family, so for one night at least I could breathe easy. Tomorrow, of course, would be a very different story!

When we had filled our cups with Cook's excellent brew, we turned our attention to George, hoping he could provide further enlightenment concerning this latest tragic death. Our expectations were quickly dashed, when George informed us that he knew little more about Patrick O'Hara's murder than we did.

"The department is treating the boy's death as an isolated incident," he told us, stirring sugar and cream into his coffee. "By that I mean they've decided that his murder is in no way connected to that of Mr. Logan or Deacon Hume."

"So they believe that my clients killed Dieter Hume, and someone else murdered Logan and O'Hara?" I asked, not bothering to mask my incredulity. "That's absurd!"

"So it's true that you're representing the two Chinamen we arrested over the weekend," George said, looking dismayed. "I was hoping the newspapers had gotten hold of the wrong end of the stick."

"Those 'Chinamen' have names, George," I informed him a bit sharply. "They are Fan Gow and Lee Yup. Neither of whom can be older than eighteen or nineteen. They speak virtually no

English, and have been in San Francisco for less than a month. What possible reason can either of those poor boys have for killing Deacon Hume? Keep in mind that he wasn't robbed, which suggests a more personal motive, *and* therefore eliminates my clients."

"Not necessarily," argued George. "Our eyewitnesses might have interrupted the two Johnnies before they could empty Hume's pockets."

"Oh? And what about Nigel Logan and Patrick O'Hara?" I asked. "If you recall, neither of them were robbed, either."

Before George could formulate a good argument, Samuel picked up several newspapers lying on a side table—none of them the *Tattler,* thank goodness, since Papa would not allow the rag sheet in our house—and waved them at us. "Have any of you read these? The public is clamoring for Fan and Lee to be strung up from the nearest trees, never mind a trial."

"I've seen them," said Robert, who had thus far been listening in silence. He glanced once in my direction, turned a bit red, then cleared his voice and continued. "While I have no truck with lynchings, we would do well to remember that those 'poor boys' were identified by eyewitnesses."

"Who had been out on a toot, and were so liquored up they probably wouldn't have recognized their own mothers at that time of night, much less two Chinamen," put in Samuel, before I could express much the same opinion.

"I admit that it was dark," Robert persisted, a bit defensively. "Still, those Chinese lads appear to have no legitimate alibis for the time Deacon Hume was murdered. Put together with the witnesses' account and you have—"

"Balderdash!" I was so incensed by this ludicrous statement that all thoughts of the night before flew from my mind. "Fan and Lee told me through the interpreter that they didn't even know where the Harrison Street Bridge was, much less deliberately walk there in the middle of the night."

"Of course that's what they'd say," said Robert heatedly. Obviously, memories of our intimate embrace had vanished from his thoughts, as well. "They'd hardly admit to being there at the same time a murder was being committed."

"I don't know, Robert," put in my brother. "I find it unlikely that two young Chinese boys would wander so far from Chinatown at night, especially when they're ignorant of the language and the city. I find it even more difficult to believe that they could be positively identified by a couple of intoxicated white men."

I turned to face Sergeant Lewis. "Answer me truthfully, George. Do the police honestly suppose that my clients, for no apparent reason, battered to death a church deacon they just happened to pass on a dark bridge?"

George flinched, as if I had just come at him with a baseball bat. "I, ah, actually I think that's what they believe, yes, Miss Sarah."

"Incredible!" I pronounced, throwing up my hands in disgust. I turned to Robert and Samuel. "Mind you, these are the very imbeciles whom we have entrusted to safeguard our city."

"There is no need to take out your frustration on George," said Samuel, coming to his friend's defense. "In all fairness, you asked him what the police thought, not for his own personal opinion."

"You're right, of course, Samuel. I stand corrected." I turned back to George who had begun fidgeting in his chair. "All right, then, George, what do you make of this farce?"

The poor man looked at me, stricken, then glanced at Samuel and Robert as if hoping to be rescued.

"I don't know, Miss Sarah, and that's the truth. At first the department thought maybe the rector of that church, you know, the Reverend Mayfield, might be involved. Because of all that nonsense Mr. Logan spouted about us having come from bugs, or fish, or something."

"Charles Darwin's *Origin of Species*," I put in.

George nodded. "Yes, that's it. Then we got an order to stop questioning the minister, and look amongst the Johnnies for the killer."

Samuel and I exchanged a quick glance, both of us wondering, I was sure, where this sudden order had originated.

"Not long after that, we pulled in those two Chinese fellows."
George nodded to Robert. "And they were properly identified by
eyewitnesses, just like Mr. Campbell said."

I shook my head, not bothering to hide my disdain for the police department's so-called eyewitnesses.

Perhaps in an effort to play peacemaker, Robert broke the uncomfortable silence following George's unconvincing elucidation.

"No matter how you look at it," he said reasonably, "these
murders have the city in an uproar."

"That's one thing on which we can all agree," said Samuel quietly.
"Illogical as it seems, I actually heard rumors this evening that your
clients killed Nigel Logan and Patrick O'Hara, as well as Hume,
Sarah."

"Good Lord!" This was becoming more bizarre by the moment. "This despite the fact that Fan and Lee were in jail when
O'Hara was murdered," I said, throwing George a censuring look.

"Again, Sarah, it's not George's fault," pointed out my brother.
"People are frightened. As they have every right to be. Three men
have been killed in ten days—practically in our own backyard! As
if the Second Street Cut weren't bad enough, San Franciscans are
now declaring Rincon Hill to be the murder capital of the state."

I could only nod unhappy agreement. "I realize people are in a
panic. Have you noticed how empty the streets are after dark? And
not just on Rincon Hill."

"That's how it is where I live, as well," commented Robert.
"Oh, you can still see some men coming and going, but precious
few women or families."

I sighed. "Our mother is so afraid, she's begged Papa not to go
out alone at night."

"She's asked me to stay at home, too, as well as Charles," put in
Samuel. "Which, in Charles's case, is a waste of breath. Can you
imagine our dedicated healer not responding to a sick call? The
Rincon Hill murderer would have to be waiting outside our front
stoop, to keep our noble brother from ministering to the ill, no
matter the time of night."

I felt a bit sick at the thought of our gentle and compassionate brother walking the streets of Rincon Hill at night, his only concern the welfare of his patients. Who was going to protect him? The police? I almost laughed aloud. Now that they had two Chinese scapegoats in jail, I feared they would no longer bother to search for the real killer.

Without pausing to consider the wisdom of my words, I blurted out, "Oh, for heaven's sake! It seems there is nothing for it but to find the killer myself. That is the only way to free my clients, and to render Rincon Hill once again safe for its residents."

George looked startled, while Robert gave a rude snort. "And just how do you plan to do that?" my colleague asked sarcastically. "Especially if the police already have the killer, or should I say *killers,* in custody."

"Robert, please," I said in frustration. "Enough of these ridiculous assumptions. Let's examine the facts as we know them, logically and in order. Fact number one," I began, using my fingers to count off each point. "Three men have been murdered. Fact number two: Nigel Logan and Dieter Hume were good friends. The third victim, Patrick O'Hara, probably never even met Logan and Hume. Fact number four: None of the three victims was robbed."

I looked around, but none of the men seemed eager to interrupt this treatise. "All right," I said, and went on, "fact number five: Although two different weapons were used to commit the murders—in Logan's and Hume's cases, a section of two-by-four, in O'Hara's case, an ice pick—they have one thing in common, they were to hand at the scene of all three crimes. In other words, they were chosen opportunistically, not brought to the scenes by the killer."

The three men remained mute, apparently waiting for me to continue. "Although Patrick O'Hara most likely was not acquainted with Logan and Hume, I refuse to believe that more than one person committed these murders. As I pointed out in fact number four, none of the three men were robbed. So, what then was the motive? Are we to believe that two or more separate killers, acting independently and within ten days of each other, chose three arbitrary victims to kill for no obvious reason? The likelihood of that happening defies the laws of probability."

"Yes, but—" George began.

"I have done some research, George, a simple study I would have expected the police to perform, had they but taken the time. There have been exactly four murders committed in the Rincon Hill area over the past five years. *Five* years, gentlemen! Now we suddenly have three men killed in our neighborhood in ten days."

Samuel appeared impressed. George's round face was screwed up in concentration, as if he were trying to come up with arguments to challenge my theory. Robert was regarding me with quiet speculation.

"Well?" I said, looking at each of them in turn. "Don't you have anything to say?"

"Your arguments are sound, Sarah," Robert commented. "As far as they go. However, there is not one grain of proof in the lot of it. Even more important, it leaves no room for the unpredictable, and life is full of events we can't anticipate. Or always understand."

My eyes flew to his face. Did those words hold another, more private, meaning? I wondered. Was it a veiled reference to what happened between us last night?

"Robert's right, Sarah," Samuel put in, before I could respond. "You and I may discount those eyewitnesses, but unless you can break their story you know as well as I do who the jury is going to believe."

I sighed. He was right. Logic would get me nowhere as long as two white men swore they had seen Fan and Lee by that bridge. It was so unfair. Even if they had seen my clients in the vicinity of the crime scene—which I didn't believe for one minute—they had said nothing about actually witnessing the attack. Guilty by being in the general area of a murder was what it boiled down to. No, it was worse than that: guilty by reason of being Chinese!

263

When Robert and George left, Samuel and I sat in front of the dying fire, each of us lost in our own bleak thoughts. The reality of Patrick O'Hara's death was finally sinking in, and I found myself disconsolate. As was not the case with Nigel Logan and Dieter Hume, I had been personally acquainted with the cheerful young Irishman. In the five or six years I had known Patrick, who had gone to work in his cousin's ice cream parlor when he was fourteen, I had rarely observed him without a grin on his broad, jovial face. He called everyone by name, teased and flattered the girls, and played games of chuck-a-luck and checkers with the boys when business was slow. He was as much a fixture at the ice cream parlor as was the bright orange, yellow, and blue sign that hung above the door. Compared to the loss of poor Patrick, even my problems with Ozzie Foldger seemed to pale by comparison.

After I had endured several minutes of these sad remembrances, I looked up to find my brother watching me, his blue eyes sympathetic.

"You're thinking of Patrick, aren't you?"

I nodded, taken aback to find my eyes filling with tears. "It's such a loss. I simply cannot imagine why anyone would want to harm that boy."

"Nor do I." He gave a long sigh, then looked at me seriously. "Sarah, please tell me that you don't really mean to look for this madman yourself. I understand that you want to clear your clients, but it's not worth putting your own life in danger."

"Don't worry. I promise not to do anything foolish."

"I've heard that promise before, so you'll forgive me for not finding it much of a consolation."

As he rose from his chair and went to the hearth to poke apart the final remains of the fire, I suddenly remembered his meeting that morning at Cunningham and Brill's law firm.

"Samuel, you promised to tell me how your appointment with Arthur Cunningham went this morning."

He placed the fireplace poker back in its iron stand, and turned his back to the hearth. Resting his hand casually on Papa's bronze bust of Abraham Lincoln that stood on the mantel, he gave me a rueful smile.

"It was worse than I expected. Despite my best efforts, it turns out they like me. Depending upon the results of my bar examination in February, it seems that I am to be Cunningham and Brill's newest associate attorney."

I wasn't sure whether to congratulate him or offer my condolences. "So what are you going to do?"

"I don't know, I haven't had time to give it much thought." He stood silently for a moment, looking down at Lincoln's bust. "Good old honest Abe would know what to do, Sarah, but I admit that I'm stymied.

"I've spent so long trying to avoid a career in the law, I can't seem to wrap my mind around the fact that someone actually wants to hire me as an attorney. I knew it would come to this sooner or later, but I became so adept at pushing the day of judgment to the back of my mind, I somehow forgot it was still there."

"And now the day of judgment has arrived," I said, deciding that commiseration was the proper response after all. "It takes courage to follow your heart, Samuel. That was what I decided to do, and in many ways it's cost me dearly. Still, I admit I wouldn't have it any other way."

He smiled. "I know I tease you, Sarah, but the truth is I admire your courage in defying society and blazing your own path through life. I realize how much you've had to give up. But at least Father approves of your choice. He's going to be extremely disappointed to learn what I've been doing since law school. He loathes popular journalism."

"I know. But this is your life, and you have to follow your heart." I smiled with genuine sympathy. "In the end I know you'll make the right decision, Samuel. Just don't allow anyone, including Papa or me, to influence you one way or the other."

He bent over and kissed me on the cheek. "What would I do without you, little sister?" Taking my hand, he pulled me to my feet. "It's getting late, and you have an important day in court tomorrow."

"Oh, Lord, don't remind me, Samuel." During our discussion I had briefly forgotten Fan and Lee's arraignment proceeding the following morning. Now, all my earlier apprehension came flooding back, nearly drowning me in a tide of frustration. "I feel so powerless to help those poor boys. No matter what I say, the authorities have already made up their minds about their guilt. As matters stand, they're being railroaded to the gallows."

"All you can do is your best, Sarah," he said, walking with me toward the door. "That's all any of us can do."

I had hoped that Fan Gow and Lee Yup's arraignment the next morning might be held without attracting undue attention. Unfortunately, the date of the hearing had leaked out to the newspapers, and the courtroom was filled to overflowing.

Upon my arrival, I was dismayed to discover a large and unruly group of demonstrators gathered outside the courthouse, many waving signs and placards demanding that the dirty yellow devils be strung up from the nearest tree or, better still, be drawn and quartered, like in the good old days.

To my horror, I saw several people who had obviously read Foldger's article the previous evening. They carried signs denouncing me as a loose woman, a hussy, a tramp, and, God help me, even worse. Reminding myself that I was here for the sole purpose of defending my clients, I lifted my chin and, paying no heed to the angry catcalls and racial slurs, boldly led Sun Kin Lu through the rowdy throng and into the building.

In spite of all the commotion, the proceedings themselves were quickly concluded. Although I received a few sly looks from the assistant district attorney's table, the judge—a portly, humorless man whom I knew to be one of Papa's friends—put a vigorous stop to the murmurs and snickers directed at me from the spectators.

The two witnesses who claimed to have seen my clients near the Harrison Street Bridge on the night of Deacon Hume's murder dutifully testified. Notwithstanding my attempts to challenge their ability to identify Fan and Lee on such a dark night, the judge inevitably remanded the pair over for trial. Bail was denied.

What I found most disturbing were the vague insinuations coming from the assistant district attorney that there was a possibility Lee and Fan might also be linked to Nigel Logan's death. To allow sufficient time for the police to dredge up new evidence to support this charge, my clients' trial date was set for late the following spring.

As promised, Sun Kin Lu had brought with him a bag of dried meat and fish, enough I judged, to feed a dozen men. I stood patiently by while the guards removed every item from the burlap bag, holding each repugnant-looking piece up and trying, with deep belly laughs, to guess what it might be. To be fair, even I found it difficult to identify the dried foodstuff, some of the shapes resembling flattened rats, squid, pig's livers, and giant insects.

As one piece of dried meat and fish after the next was inspected and mocked, it was tossed with loud guffaws into the waste container. Sun's face grew progressively darker as this continued, until I feared he might lose control and explode. Good heavens, I thought in alarm. If he, too, were arrested, I would be forced to defend my Chinese interpreter, along with the two clients I already felt powerless to save!

When the guards finally finished, they left the room still joking about the disgusting-looking discards. It was pitiful to watch the disheartened expressions on the boys' faces, to see so many Oriental delicacies carried out with the trash. All that remained were a handful of grisly bits that would probably not amount to a single meal.

With Sun Kin Lu's help, I did my best to allay the young men's fears and confusion about what had just taken place in the incomprehensible white man's courtroom. I could tell by their faces that they understood little of what I said. In all honesty, I wasn't sure how much Sun had grasped, consequently it was easy to see why he had failed to pass the information on to my clients.

When Fan and Lee were finally taken back to their jail cells, I asked Sun to wait while I composed a note to Li Ying, explaining the outcome of the morning's proceedings. It was a disheartening missive. I even offered to return Li's generous retainer, since I felt I had done precious little to help his unfortunate countrymen.

Sealing the letter in an envelope I had brought with me for this purpose, I thanked the interpreter, then left the courthouse to make my way back to Sutter Street.

I was surprised to find Pierce waiting for me when I returned to my office. He and my downstairs neighbor, Fanny, were chatting in front of her millinery shop. The look of relief on Pierce's face at my arrival led me to believe that this was more than a strictly social call. I felt a stir of alarm, fearing that he and Fanny had read Foldger's article. Then, after studying their faces, I was relieved to realize that I was imagining trouble where it did not as yet exist.

"Ah, there you are, Sarah," said Fanny, gazing up at the tall man as if he were a Greek god. Was I imagining it, or did her eyelashes actually flutter? "You have kept poor Mr. Godfrey waiting for nearly half an hour."

"I was not aware that Mr. Godfrey intended to call upon me," I replied with composure. "If I had known, I could have informed him that I would be occupied at the courthouse this morning."

"You have a new case?" asked Pierce.

Before I could respond, Fanny said, "Our Sarah is representing those two unfortunate Chinese men who've been arrested in the Deacon Hume murder."

"You don't say." Pierce's dark eyebrows rose. Although he showed polite interest in my new clients, his expression clearly indicated that he wished to speak to me alone. "Why don't we go upstairs to your office, Sarah, and you can tell me all about it." He turned politely to Fanny. "I'm grateful for the pleasure of your company, Mrs. Goodman. I trust we will meet again soon."

To my astonishment, my sensible, middle-aged neighbor actually blushed. "I look forward to that, Mr. Godfrey. And next time you really must join me for a cup of coffee, and perhaps something fresh from the oven."

"I would be delighted," Pierce answered, smiling down at her with the full force of his considerable charm.

I would not have thought it possible, but the woman's grandmotherly face turned an even brighter shade of pink.

"Shame on you," I told him, unable to smother my laughter as we entered my office and I removed my wrap. "You've bewitched the poor woman. I'll never hear the end of it." I took a seat behind my desk. "Now, Pierce, what are you bursting to tell me?"

His look became serious. "Is that Tremaine girl really as good as you claim she is?"

This unexpected question took me aback. "You mean as a singer? Yes, she is. Why do you ask?"

"I have arranged an audition for her with Joseph Kreling at the Tivoli Opera House."

"Good heavens!" I stared at him in astonishment. "When?"

"That's the tricky part," he said, crossing one perfectly pressed pant leg over the other. "Kreling is going out of town this evening, and isn't sure when he'll be back in town. It has to be this afternoon, Sarah. No later than three o'clock."

"Three o'clock!" I parroted in surprise. I consulted the timepiece pinned to my shirtwaist. It was already well past the hour of noon. "I'm not sure if Melody is even at home, or how to reach her if she isn't."

I sat silently contemplating this for several moments. There was no guarantee that rushing to the Tremaine house would result in her parents' agreeing to the audition. In fact, from the comments they'd made the night of Faith's birthday dinner, it was far more likely they would refuse the girl this opportunity. The opportunity she had longed for since childhood.

Without further ado, I made up my mind. If I had anything to say about it, the girl was going to have her chance!

Bounding out of my chair, I reached for the wrap I had just removed, and crossed swiftly to the door.

"We must hurry, Pierce. There's no time to be lost."

CHAPTER TWENTY-ONE

Although I had never been inside the Tremaine house, I knew it was located on Harrison Street and Rincon Place, a mere two blocks from our own home. It was about the same vintage as ours, most likely dating from the early 1860s, and had been erected in the Italianate style, as had our own. Gerald Tremaine's residence was three stories high and had a mansard roof, that is, with two slopes on each of the four sides. A tall eucalyptus tree grew to the right of the house, while a lovely old cypress shaded the left. The surrounding grounds were well maintained, although the normally colorful flower beds had long since fallen dormant for the winter.

I was surprised to see Marco Ciatti, the handyman and gardener who helped Papa maintain our own yard, clearing out vegetation and weeds from beneath a row of overgrown bushes.

Catching sight of me, he politely tipped his cap, and gave me a jaunty smile. "*Buon giorno,* Miss Woolson. You look *deliziosa,* very nice this afternoon."

"Thank you, Marco," I replied, too intent on our mission to give much thought to the little Italian, or his opinions concerning my appearance.

"That man strikes me as a good deal too forward," Pierce commented, as we ascended the steps to the Tremaines' front door. "How do you know him?"

"Marco does odd jobs around the neighborhood," I told him, stopping as we reached the elaborate front door. "Do you think Melody's father will agree to the audition?"

"My hope is that he's not here," he said candidly. "That way, with any luck we may avoid having to ask his permission. If he challenges us later, we can truthfully explain that there was no time to seek his consent."

I gave Pierce a nod of agreement then, without allowing myself time for second thoughts, rang the bell. "To be honest," I said, leaning closer and speaking softly, "I think I would rather face Mr. Tremaine than his wife. She seems determined to marry the girl off at any cost. I'm sure that a career in the theater is not what she has in mind for her stepdaughter."

Before Pierce could reply, the door was opened by a man I assumed to be the butler.

"Good afternoon," I said. Reaching into my reticule, I handed the man my card. "Miss Sarah Woolson and Mr. Pierce Godfrey. We are here to see Miss Melody Tremaine, if she is in."

Solemnly, the man accepted my card and placed it on a silver salver sitting in readiness on a table by the door. "If you would care to wait in the parlor," he told us rather stiffly, "I shall ascertain if Miss Tremaine is here."

We entered the foyer, then after the butler had closed the door, followed him into an agreeable, west-facing room, pleasantly warm from the rays of sun which had finally made its first welcome appearance in several days. A lovely vase of fresh-cut flowers was arranged on a polished table, and two smaller flower vases were positioned about the cheerful room.

While we waited, I took the opportunity to examine the photographs which were displayed on the fireplace mantel. All of the pictures were of Reginald Tremaine's second wife, Faith, and their family. Although Melody and David were featured equally with the two offspring of his second marriage, I could find no photographs which might be of the twins' mother. Surely this was understandable, I told myself. Faith Tremaine would hardly care to be constantly reminded of her husband's first wife.

Over the fireplace hung a large oil portrait of the family, including all four children. Even in a painting, Melody's beauty was striking. The artist had skillfully captured her delicate innocence, while at the same time hinting at the promise of womanhood which was soon to blossom.

"She is beautiful, isn't she?" Pierce said, as if reading my mind. "If she possesses half the talent you've described, Joe Kreling will snap her up in a minute."

"*If* her parents agree to allow her to appear on the stage," I answered, not bothering to hide my skepticism. "I know this is what she wants but—"

I was cut off as the parlor door opened and Melody Tremaine swept into the room, closely followed by her brother David.

"Miss Woolson," she said, with a welcoming smile, "how very nice to see you again." Her lovely eyes went to Pierce, then widened in obvious admiration. "And this gentleman is . . . ?"

"Pierce Godfrey, Miss Tremaine," he said, bowing slightly and returning her smile. He held out a hand to the boy, saying, "You must be her brother, David. The likeness is remarkable."

The young man returned Pierce's shake politely enough, but I could see that he was puzzled by the older man's presence in their home. "Miss Woolson, Mr. Godfrey, please sit down. To what do we owe the honor of this visit?"

Pierce and I took seats on the sofa, while Melody and her brother sat in armchairs facing us. "Are your parents at home?" I asked, looking nervously to the door which remained open behind the twins. Somehow I must have betrayed my apprehension, because now even Melody looked perplexed.

"No, they're not," she answered, studying our faces curiously. "If you wish to see them, you'll have to return later this afternoon. Our stepmother will certainly be home by then. It is more difficult to say with our father. He sometimes remains at the store long after it has closed for the day."

"No, Miss Tremaine," said Pierce. "Actually, it is you we have come to see." He paused and looked at me, as if feeling it would be better if I explained the purpose of our visit.

"I was very impressed by your beautiful singing voice the evening you performed at our home, Melody," I told her. "So was my entire family. When we met for lunch the other day, you mentioned that you wished to pursue a career on the stage. Is that truly how you feel?"

The girl moved forward in her seat, enthusiasm causing her brilliant blue eyes to sparkle. "Yes, that is my fondest hope. I would love nothing better than to become a professional singer."

"Why are you asking these questions, Miss Woolson?" asked her brother, eyeing me suspiciously.

"Mr. Godfrey is acquainted with Mr. Joseph Kreling, the owner of the Tivoli Theater," I explained. "He has managed to arrange an audition for your sister this afternoon. Only if you would care to do it, Melody. And of course there is the matter of your parents. I received the impression that they might not approve of your performing in public."

"No, they would not," Melody responded gravely. "But they're not here to ask, are they?" she added, unknowingly parroting the very words Pierce had spoken only moments before.

Clapping her small hands in delight, she sprang out of her chair and fairly danced about the room, stopping only to bend down to kiss her brother on the cheek. "Oh, David, I can hardly believe it. This is the answer to our prayers. We must go. Oh, please, say that you agree."

The boy looked at Pierce cautiously. "With all respect, sir, we are not acquainted with you. And this is a very serious matter. I cannot allow my sister to do anything which might put her in harm's way, or tarnish her reputation."

"I assure you, young man, that if Miss Tremaine desires to attend the audition, it will not tarnish her reputation in any manner whatsoever. Miss Woolson and I will accompany her, as you may yourself, if you wish, and we will not allow her out of our sight."

The boy continued to look worried. "I'm not sure. I'm certain our father would not approve of a strange man taking my sister to—"

"What is going on in here?" came a voice from the doorway. Melody straightened and turned toward Major Zachariah Tremaine, as he entered the room. "May I inquire just where you are proposing to take my granddaughter, sir?"

Perhaps it was the man's upright bearing and air of authority that caused Pierce and I to rise from the sofa at his entrance. I noticed that David was already on his feet, and was regarding his grandfather with keen respect, as well as genuine fondness.

"This is Mr. Pierce Godfrey, Grandfather," David told him. "He has just informed us that he has arranged an audition for Melody at the Tivoli Opera House. This very afternoon."

"Yes, Grandpapa, it's true," exclaimed his sister, once again prancing about the room in unabashed pleasure. "Isn't it wonderful? Please, please, Grandpapa, say that it is all right with you if we go to the Tivoli. And say that you'll accompany us. You are so brave, I know your presence would lend me courage."

"My dear girl, calm down," the elderly man said, his pale eyes studying Pierce warily. "You say your name is Pierce Godfrey, sir, but I do not recall that we have met."

Pierce reached into his pocket and withdrew a business card, which he handed to the older gentleman. "My brother Leonard and I own Godfrey Shipping here in the city, sir. When Miss Woolson described your granddaughter's remarkable singing voice, I promised I would speak to my friend Joseph Kreling, who owns the Tivoli Opera House."

"I've heard of the fellow," said the major, his expression relaxing a bit as he examined the card. "And you say that he has actually agreed to hear Melody sing? Does that mean there is a possibility she might be asked to appear in his theater?"

"Yes, sir, that is exactly what will happen if he feels she's right for the stage," Pierce told him. "But only if she can audition for him this afternoon. He's leaving town this evening, and may be gone for some time. This is the only opportunity for her to sing for him until he returns to the city."

The old man spent several silent minutes considering this, while Melody fairly bounced up and down in front of him, her large blue eyes pleading for his approval. At last, he took the girl's hands in his and kissed her on the cheek.

"My darling Melody, how could I possibly deny you the chance to follow your dream. Of course, your father will more than likely never forgive me, but fortunately he's not here to forbid us, is he?"

He smiled broadly and gave the twins a mischievous wink. "As Major General Hooker said at the Battle of Lookout Mountain nearly twenty years ago, always take the offensive while the enemy is diverted. Right, bub and sis?

"Just let me get my coat and we'll be off."

The Tivoli Opera House was located on Eddy Street near Market, its second location since a twenty-two-year-old Joseph Kreling had opened its predecessor, the Tivoli Beer Gardens, a few years earlier. The Beer Gardens had proved to be so successful that Kreling and his brother, John—with the help of various other members of their industrious family—built the Opera House in 1879. The three-story white structure looked for all the world like a respectable private dwelling, welcoming one and all to some of the best entertainment to be had in the city. I had attended the "Tiv," as it was commonly referred to, several times myself, and had unfailingly enjoyed the experience.

It had changed a great deal during the two and a half years of its existence. When the Tivoli Opera House first opened, it had been set up as a cabaret-style hall with small galleries to either side of the auditorium. Configured in this manner, it had served beer, wine, and light refreshments. Its ever-growing popularity, however, resulted in an expansion of the stage, removal of the dining tables to make room for more conventional seating, and the installation of numerous new viewing boxes.

The "Tiv" could now accommodate up to sixteen hundred patrons, and had became one of the most frequented entertainment halls in San Francisco, especially given its reasonable ticket prices ranging from twenty-five to fifty cents. It was said that some patrons attended the Tivoli at least once a week, and it was acknowledged as an establishment where millionaires and workingmen alike could companionably rub shoulders.

We followed Pierce around to the stage-door entrance, where an older gentleman let us in. The man wore a stained ten-gallon hat perched above long, scraggly looking gray hair. He had spurs which clanked noisily on his boots as he walked, and a large cigar clenched tightly between yellowing teeth.

"This way," he instructed tersely, then waited for the five of us to enter before slamming the door closed behind us. Without speaking another word, he led us through a forest of backstage sets, furniture, pulleys, and other contraptions, to the front of the theater, where several men were talking in loud voices on the stage. So animated was their discussion, that they didn't seem to notice our arrival, until Pierce walked out of the wings to join them.

"I'm Pierce Godfrey," he said, instantly stilling the men's conversation. "We have an appointment to meet with Joe Kreling this afternoon."

The youngest of the three men turned and hopped lightly down from his perch on a tall wooden stool. He was rather short and had to tilt back his head to look up at Pierce, who towered over him.

"Sure, sure, I know who you are. Joe told me you'd likely be coming in around three." The man's lively brown eyes quickly scanned the rest of us, then came to a rest on me. "And you must be the young lady who has the voice of an angel."

I took a hasty step backward. "No, not I. I fear you would find my voice more akin to an ailing calf, than to an angel."

I reached for Melody's hand and drew the suddenly shy girl forward a few steps. "This is Melody Tremaine. She is the one who will be auditioning."

The young man's eyes gleamed with interest, as he took in the girl's peaches-and-cream complexion, her vibrant blue eyes, framed by a thick fan of lashes, and the mass of golden curls surrounding her delicate oval face.

"Well, well," he said in sincere appreciation. "If her voice comes anywhere close to matching her looks, we have ourselves a rare find. I'm Dick Raimie, by the way, Joe's assistant and general lackey. He had to leave town earlier than planned this afternoon, but he told me to listen to little miss nightingale here, and let him know what I think when he gets back to Frisco."

I grimaced at his use of this very unpopular nickname, unpopular, that is, with longtime residents of San Francisco. Individuals who unknowingly referred to our fair city by this nickname were instantly labeled ignoramuses and foreigners by any self-respecting native. Pointing this out to Mr. Raimie, however, would hardly facilitate Melody's audition, so I wisely remained silent.

"Mr. Kreling said he would be here today," said Pierce, sounding irritated. "We've gone to some trouble to bring Miss Tremaine to the theater. When do you expect him to return?"

"Sorry, Mr. Godfrey, but I have no idea. Could be a week, could be a month. Personal business, you see. No telling how long it will take to untangle things." He smiled cheerfully at Melody. "That doesn't mean you can't audition for me, Miss Tremaine. Joe puts a lot of store in my opinion."

Pierce continued to look perturbed as he turned to Melody. "It's up to you, Miss Tremaine. Would you like to sing now, or would you prefer to wait until Mr. Kreling returns to the city?"

A variety of emotions crossed the girl's face—excitement, apprehension, fear—but she hardly hesitated. She turned to the major. "It had better be now while I still have the courage, don't you think, Grandpapa? Who knows when Mr. Kreling will return? I could not bear the wait."

"I agree, my child," the elder Tremaine said, patting the hand she had reached out to him. "I think you should sing for Mr. Raimie. After that, we shall have to wait and see."

David, who had shyly hung back as the rest of us spoke to Dick Raimie, took his sister's arm. "Are you sure you want to go through with this, Mel? You don't have to if you're uncomfortable."

The girl stood on tiptoes and kissed her brother on the cheek. "But I want to do it, David. This is the chance I've been waiting for all my life. I must at least try to make a success of it."

"Good, then," the boy said with a reassuring smile. Hugging his sister, he encouraged, "Let her rip, sis. Once they hear you sing, they're going to be knocked for six!"

Dick Raimie was waving one of the two men he had been speaking with earlier over to the piano. "This is Wes Corbett, Miss Tremaine," he told Melody. "He'll be accompanying you on the piano. Did you bring your music?"

Melody looked horror-stricken. "No, I didn't. We left the house in such a hurry, it never crossed my mind."

"No problem," Mr. Corbett told her from the piano bench, then pointed to his head with a forefinger. "I've got hundreds of songs stored right here, miss. Just name the tune, and more than likely I can play it from memory."

Melody thought for a moment, then asked if he was familiar with Josephine's first solo from Mr. Gilbert and Mr. Sullivan's wonderful comic opera *H.M.S. Pinafore*.

"Nothing could be easier," Wes Corbett pronounced with a wide grin. "We did that very show here not two years ago. Now why don't you come over here and we'll decide what key is right for you."

Melody did as she was bade, and five minutes later she stood alone, appearing small and very vulnerable, on center stage of the Tivoli Opera House. The rest of us, including Dick Raimie, had taken seats in the audience. The second man Raimie had been conversing with before our arrival had hurried backstage and soon two limelight spotlights came on, illuminating the young girl from either side of the stage. She started nervously when they were lit, then smiled sheepishly, took a deep breath, and resumed her place before the footlights.

"Are you ready, dear?" Raimie called out to her from his seat.

Melody shielded her eyes against the glare of the spotlights to locate him in the audience, then somberly nodded her head. "Yes, Mr. Raimie, I'm ready."

I could just detect the slight shaking of the hands she held clasped to her breast, and thought she well might have added, "as ready as I shall ever be." Fortunately, this thought vanished the minute the piano started to play the introduction to Josephine's first solo, "Sorry Her Lot Who Loves Too Well," from *H.M.S. Pinafore.*

During this piano overture, Mr. Raimie behaved rather rudely, I thought, ignoring Melody and speaking in undertones to Major Tremaine, who was in the seat to his right. The instant she began to sing the first few measures, however, Raimie's head snapped up to the stage, and he stared at her in astonishment.

"Good Lord!" he gasped. "That girl has one almighty fine set of pipes."

Even I looked on in disbelief. If I had been impressed by the quality of her voice the first time I had heard it, this afternoon she literally took my breath away. Whether it was the superior acoustics of the Tivoli Opera House, the skill of Corbett's piano accompaniment, or just her innate stage presence, Melody Tremaine's small, delicate figure suddenly appeared larger than life. Her magnificent, perfectly pitched voice seemed to grow in clarity and richness until it filled the entire auditorium.

Everyone listened, captivated, until the end of the piece, then broke into ecstatic applause. Hearing the sound of clapping coming from the rear of the theater, I turned to see that two men had entered the hall from the lobby. At first, I failed to recognize either of them. Then, with a wave of shock, I realized that the taller of the two men was none other than Gerald Knight!

"What is it, Sarah?" asked Pierce in a low voice, seeming to sense my sudden rigidity. "Do you know those men?"

"Only one of them," I answered in a tight voice. "The man on the right is Gerald Knight, owner of the *Daily Journal* newspaper. I've had some unfortunate business dealings with him lately. What can he possibly be doing here?"

Dick Raimie had also spied the newcomers, and gave them a quick wave, before turning his attention back to Melody.

"That was first-rate, love," he called out to her. "What else can you sing for us? How's about 'The Hours Creep on Apace,' Josephine's ballad from the second act of *Pinafore*?"

"Yes, Mr. Raimie, I know that one," she replied, once again shielding her eyes against the bright lights and regarding him with a huge smile of relief now that her first song had been so enthusiastically received. "Is that all right with you, Mr. Corbett?" she asked the pianist. At his easy nod, she once again positioned herself center stage. This time she appeared far more confident and relaxed as she prepared to sing.

I was so disconcerted by seeing Gerald Knight—who, with the second man, had taken seats several rows behind us in the hall— that I hardly noticed Melody singing Josephine's second song from *Pinafore*. I was much too preoccupied wondering what the newspaperman was doing here.

Then I remembered Samuel telling me that Knight fancied himself a patron of the arts, especially the Tivoli Opera House. If he were one of Joe Kreling's financiers, then of course he would enjoy ready access to the theater whenever he cared to visit. What an inopportune coincidence, I thought, that it should be today.

Turning in my seat to catch a glimpse of him, I was taken aback by the way he was ogling Melody as she performed. His eyes were narrowed in chilling concentration as he followed her every gesture on the stage. His expression reminded me of a tomcat stalking a helpless mouse. Was he evaluating her as Brielle Bouchard's possible replacement as his mistress? I wondered with a sinking heart.

I was so lost in these troubling thoughts, that I was only recalled back to the present when everyone around me once again started applauding. Dick Raimie had bolted out of his seat and was dashing up the stairs and onto the stage, clapping wildly all the way. David and the major followed upon his heel.

"That was marvelous, just marvelous, Miss Tremaine," Raimie exclaimed, sandwiching her small hands between his own. "Joe will be thrilled to learn that we have uncovered such a beautiful rose in our own fair city. I shall send him a telegram this very afternoon."

Major Tremaine and David beamed with pride, as Melody was congratulated. Glancing back to where Gerald Knight had been sitting, I saw that he, too, was out of his chair and hurrying toward the stage, his companion following closely upon his heels.

"Mr. Knight," I called out after him. Either he didn't hear me, or was pretending that he had not, for he failed to so much as glance in my direction.

"Just what sort of business have you had with that man, Sarah?" asked Pierce, watching the owner of the *Daily Journal* as Raimie introduced him to the girl. "I saw your face when he walked into the theater. You looked as if you'd like to skewer him on the spot."

"He's a man—a *married* man—who fancies very young girls," I told him, my voice tight with fear. "And I don't like the way he's looking at Melody as if she's to be tonight's dessert."

"He must be a friend of the Krelings'," Pierce said, watching as Dick Raimie introduced the second man to the girl. "That's Joe's brother, John, with him. John Kreling is the Tivoli's coowner, although Joe makes most of the company's decisions."

I took hold of his arm, suddenly afraid I had made a terrible mistake allowing this audition to take place. The fascination I saw gleaming in Knight's eyes, as they traveled boldly from the tip of Melody's polished slippers, to the top of her curly gold-brown hair, was unmistakable. There was no doubt that he had made up his mind to possess this girl. Worse, the man exuded an air of confidence which made it clear that he was used to getting whatever his heart desired!

As we entered Pierce's carriage some minutes later, I saw that Melody's original excitement had been somewhat deflated since

Dick Raimie had informed her that she would still have to audition for Joe Kreling when he returned to town.

"He's solely responsible for the talent that appears on this stage," Raimie had told Pierce, when he complained that Joe had promised him a decision that afternoon. "I'm sorry, but those are Joe's rules, Mr. Godfrey. Sure as I am that he's going to love her, it would cost me my job to schedule Miss Tremaine to perform in the Opera House without the boss seeing her first."

Promising to let us know when Mr. Kreling was back in San Francisco, he hustled back inside the theater. As we settled into Pierce's carriage I spied movement in the doorway of an adjoining building. I realized with a jolt of alarm that Gerald Knight was watching us as we drove off. The predatory look on his face was frighteningly simple to read.

Feeling my face flood with sudden anger, I silently vowed that I would not allow that lecherous man to have his way. No matter what I had to do to prevent it, Gerald Knight could not be allowed to destroy another young girl's life the way he had ruined Brielle Bouchard's!

CHAPTER TWENTY-TWO

After a quick breakfast the next morning, Samuel and I shared a cab downtown, he to City Hall for a story he was writing, while I went on to the jail to visit my clients. During the drive, I brought my brother up to date on Melody Tremaine's successful audition at the Tivoli Opera House the day before.

"What a shame Joe Kreling wasn't there," he said. "Do you think her parents will allow her to audition again when he gets back in town?"

"I wish I knew. We were fortunate neither of them were at home yesterday afternoon. I know her grandfather is eager to see her sing for Mr. Kreling. He adores those twins, and I have the impression that he'd like to see them follow a path of their own choosing."

"Still, the Tremaines have the final say on the subject," he pointed out.

"I'm sure they realize that all too well," I said soberly.

"Don't sound so dejected, Sarah. Not every young woman has your spirit and determination."

"Or every young man, Ian Fearless," I teased, calling him by the pen name he used when writing his crime articles.

"Ugh. I wish you hadn't brought that up."

"Sorry, but I've been wondering what you plan to do about the position in Arthur Cunningham's law firm. It's a big decision."

He shook his head. "I've been looking over some of Father's law books. Heaven help me, I've been out of school too long." He gave a rueful smile. "You realize, of course, that I'm going to have to spend all my time studying if I'm actually going to take my bar exams in February."

"Well, if you decide to go through with it, let me help you. It'll be easier with two of us."

"Don't worry, Sarah," he said dryly. "If I actually agree to take the bloody exam I'm going to need all the help I can get!"

"Papa will be a good resource, too."

"Oh, no," he protested with a grimace. "I can't afford to let him see how hopelessly far I've fallen behind. Don't forget, he thinks I've been working as a part-time paralegal since law school."

"Have you actually done any work for Andrew Wayburn?" I asked, referring to his law school friend who passed his own bar examinations shortly after graduation.

"At first, yes. Then when Andy's father died and left him settled with a small fortune, he all but gave up his law practice. The scoundrel decided it was more fun to play than to work, although he did continue to let me use his name to explain the money I was earning as a crime reporter."

In an effort to change what was obviously an unwelcome subject, he inquired how preparations for Saturday night's Christmas party were coming along.

"I've managed to avoid most of the hullabaloo," he said with a chuckle. "Although Mama tagged me to decorate the tree with the popcorn and cranberry strings Tom and little Mandy made. And, of course, I placed the angel atop the tree."

"A task you've performed ever since you were ten years old," I pointed out. "Come on, Samuel, you can't fool me. I know how much you enjoy trimming the tree."

"You have to admit that it requires a certain keen eye for symmetry," he said with a smile. "I've already begun to train little

Tommy. At the rate he's growing he'll soon be tall enough to take over the job."

"Speaking of the party," I said, eyeing him curiously. "What lucky lady have you invited?" I find it difficult to keep up with my brother's active social life. I believe I've mentioned more than once that, as an extremely handsome bachelor, he enjoys great popularity with the young ladies in town.

"I've decided not to ask anyone. Actually, Catherine Butler and I are—well, let's just say that we've had a bit of a misunderstanding. I think it's best to allow her time to cool down."

I swallowed a smile. "I see."

"What about you? Have you invited a guest?"

I thought back to the kiss I'd shared with Robert several nights ago, and once again realized how much it had complicated my life. Weeks ago, when I'd first invited him to the dinner party, all had been as usual between us. Now I sensed he was as uncomfortable over the situation as I was. Perhaps too uncomfortable for him to attend? I wondered. If that was the case I determined I would not attempt to change his mind.

To my surprise, this thought brought about an immediate pang of regret. The idea of Robert sitting home alone, while our family celebrated the holiday with good cheer and good friends, bothered me more than I would have expected. The truth was, I truly did not want to see him alone for the holidays.

"Sarah?" Samuel said, nudging me with his shoulder. "Have you fallen asleep?"

"Sorry, I was thinking of something else. Actually, I asked Robert to the party some time ago."

"Have you now? And Mama has invited Pierce Godfrey."

I silently nodded, having no desire to voice my concerns about such a potentially volatile situation.

"Hmm," he said, giving me a teasing, sidelong look. "All things considered, it promises to be an interesting evening, don't you agree?"

When I reached city jail, I was unhappy to see that Fan Gow and Lee Yup's cell was as odiferous as it had been upon my initial visit. Once again the jailers had allowed the chamber pot to overflow with waste, and the air smelled positively foul. Sun Kin Lu, who had accompanied me into the jail, wrinkled his nose and hastily covered his mouth with a piece of cloth. I did not bother. I was so angry that I marched to the cell door and called out for the guard, demanding that he immediately empty the bucket.

"And wash it out with soap and water before you bring it back," I ordered. "How would you like to be forced to live in such filth?"

Grumbling beneath his breath, the sullen jailer shuffled unhurriedly over to the pail and picked it up. As he carried it across the cell, I thought I caught him mumbling the words "ain't like Johns are really human or nothin'," before he exited the cell, banging the door closed behind him.

Fan and Lee had sprung to their feet the moment Sun Kin Lu and I entered their cell, both indicating that I should take a seat on their respective cot. I smiled with a smidgen of reluctance, but for civility's sake chose the bunk closest to where I was standing. I noticed with relief that the bedding appeared a good deal cleaner than it had previously, and two rough wool blankets were neatly folded at the foot of each cot. I was thankful that at least these small comforts had been afforded the prisoners.

The purpose of today's call was more to reassure my clients that they had not been deserted, than to pass on news about their case, and Sun and I did not stay long. In an effort to lift the young men's spirits, I exuded more confidence than I felt. After yesterday's arraignment, I realized more clearly than ever that if I failed to locate the real killer there was little hope of proving my clients innocent.

If I'd felt discouraged upon entering Fan and Lee's cell, the guard I had berated for neglecting their chamber pot could not wait to pile on the agony upon our departure.

"I hear the coppers are gonna pin the murder of that science fellow onto those Johnnies of yours."

I swung around to face the jailer. "Do you have news about Mr. Logan's case?"

The unpleasant man smirked, no doubt delighted at having so thoroughly captured my attention. "Seems like the gents who found his body have changed their story about seein' only one man runnin' away from the scene. Now they're claimin' they mebbe saw two blokes hightailin' it outta there." His small eyes gleamed maliciously. "They say that mebbe it was a couple of Chinamen. *Your* Chinamen, I reckon."

He moved closer, and I had to hold my breath when I was assaulted by his foul breath. He gave me a leering wink. "Say, how's about you fixin' me up with one of them fine lady friends of yours from that cathouse I read about in the papers? I hear they know how to show a feller a mighty fine time."

Leaving the nasty guard roaring with laughter, I hurried off to locate the officer in charge. Without official verification that the disagreeable jailer was telling the truth about the new charge about to levied on my clients, I refused to believe a word he said.

I was in luck. My old friend Sergeant Jackson was on duty. The sergeant had been kind enough to help me with a former client, who had been incarcerated in this very jail during the Cliff House case several months ago. I knew I could count upon him to give me an honest answer.

"I'm afraid he's right, Miss Woolson," Jackson told me solemnly. "The police are planning to accuse your clients of Mr. Logan's murder, along with Mr. Hume's. I expect the official charge will come sometime this afternoon."

"But I spoke to the men who found Mr. Logan's body," I protested. "They assured me they saw only one man running from the bridge. And they said nothing to indicate the man was Chinese."

Sergeant Jackson's face was sympathetic. "I know, Miss Woolson, and I'm sorry. I've been to see those two Johnnies, and to tell the truth I feel a little sorry for them. I tried to ask them one or two questions, but they don't speak a word of English." He raised his shoulders fractionally, as if to emphasize the hopelessness of the situation. "I wish I could help you, I truly do. But if a witness changes his mind, well, there's not much we can do but take his word for it."

"Yes, I know," I said with a sigh. "The situation just keeps going from bad to worse. The next thing you know, they'll be accusing my clients of murdering Patrick O'Hara, as well. Even though they were locked up here in a cell at the time the poor young man was killed."

He smiled. "Well, at least you don't have to worry about that, Miss Woolson. We arrested a man this morning for O'Hara's death."

I looked at him, shocked. "You did what?"

"We arrested one of O'Hara's customers. Seems the Irish boy had become a bit too friendly with the man's wife. The powers that be figure that in a fit of rage, the fellow stabbed him to death with the ice pick. Not much of a mystery there, after all. We see that kind of thing all too often, I'm afraid."

"Has the man confessed to the killing?"

"Not yet, but the boys upstairs are working on it. He'll come clean sooner or later, you can be sure of that." He appeared to have second thoughts about these words, for he quickly added, "All legal, of course."

I exited city jail in a daze. If Patrick O'Hara had been murdered by a different villain than the one who killed Nigel Logan and Dieter Hume, then my theories were all wrong. In a way, I supposed it made more sense that the crimes were not connected. After all, Logan and Hume had been friends, had both attended the same dinner party the night of the first murder, and had both been beaten to death beneath the Harrison Street Bridge. Patrick O'Hara, on the other hand, had probably never met the first two victims, and had been stabbed to death with an ice pick inside an ice cream parlor.

Why, then, did this new arrest seem so wrong? I could not explain why I felt as I did, but I simply could not accept that a second killer had murdered the young Irishman; the pieces just would not fit together in my mind. I was going to have to give these latest developments some serious consideration.

I was mulling the situation over as I walked toward the public horsecar line, when I caught sight of a man about half a block ahead of me ducking inside a doorway. There was something about this movement that struck me as suspicious, almost furtive. I had only caught a quick glimpse of the figure, but I was certain it was Ozzie Foldger. The nerve of the man, I seethed. After the appalling article he had written the day before, the dreadful little reporter was still following me!

Hastening my step, I strode purposefully up the street until I reached the place where I thought I had glimpsed the man. It was a tobacconist's shop, and the door still stood wide open. Walking to the entrance, I looked inside and spied a short man, wearing a dark brown cap, ducking behind a display of cigars and chewing tobacco. It was the cowardly reporter, all right. Without hesitation, I marched inside the shop and directly over to the display.

"Mr. Foldger," I said, in a voice loud enough to command the attention of every man in the store. "Come out from behind that shelf immediately."

Instead of complying, he slipped around the end of the display, and out of my sight. I quickly followed and caught him up before he could slip outside and back onto the street.

"You are nothing but a spineless weasel, Ozzie Foldger," I exclaimed, catching him by the sleeve of his coat, and pulling him back inside the store proper. I noticed the clerk eyeing us in some alarm, while two or three customers stopped their shopping to see what the commotion was all about.

"How dare you follow me for over a week, spying on my every move. My father is right, you are the very worst example of exploitive journalism."

When the little sneak attempted to push by me and out the

door, I quickly blocked his way by placing myself between him and his only route of escape. In order to flee, he would be forced to physically knock me over.

"Hey," the clerk behind the counter said, "ain't you that reporter from the *Tattler*? The one who's always writing about some scandal or other?"

"He is, indeed," I informed the man, when a sulking Foldger declined to answer.

"He's the one who wrote about that woman attorney defending those two Chinamen," declared one of the shop patrons.

"Wait a minute," exclaimed his friend, who stood beside him holding a box of cigars. "That's you, isn't it?" He poked his friend on the shoulder and nodded at me. "You're the lady attorney. I've seen your picture in the paper."

"I'm sure you have," I said dryly. "However, you might want to take the time to learn more about the man writing the articles. Mr. Foldger, here, gives very little thought about whose reputation he ruins, even though the harm caused by his lies and innuendoes, once in print, often cannot be reversed. He invades people's privacy, then writes whatever twaddle he thinks will sell newspapers."

I drew closer to the despicable reporter. We were very nearly the same height, and I was able to stare him straight in the eye. The little worm squirmed uncomfortably, pulling his head back in an effort to avert my gaze. I took hold of his coat lapel, forcing him to meet my gaze.

"I am warning you, Ozzie Foldger," I told him in a low, resolute voice. "If I ever catch you following me again, I shall report you to the police. You might also want to keep in mind that I have three older brothers, each of whom is more than capable of teaching you a lesson you will never forget."

I threatened him with this, knowing full well that my eldest brother Frederick would turn and run at the first mention of a fight, and that my brother Charles, as a healer, would never join in. Unless I were in physical danger, even my brother Samuel—who was a skilled pugilist—would most likely claim I had gotten myself into the fix, and now I could get myself out of it. But I did have three brothers, and Ozzie had no need to know more than that.

I continued to stare into his small, squinty eyes for another minute, then released his lapel and stepped aside, leaving the doorway clear. Without a second's hesitation, Foldger bolted out of the tobacconist's shop and into the street.

As I watched him flee down the block, I heard an unexpected sound from behind me. Turning around, I realized that the clerk and his three customers were all applauding me!

I returned to my office so engrossed in my thoughts that I very nearly ran into Fanny, who must have been keeping watch for me from inside her shop. She brushed off my apologies, obviously eager to pass on an important message.

"That nice Mr. Godfrey was here about half an hour ago," she gushed. "I thought you might have gone to the jail before coming in this morning, so I told him you should arrive at any time. He said he would be back at noon to take you to lunch."

Fanny uttered these words with so much deference, you would have thought Pierce was taking me to lunch at the White House. I hid a smile, amazed that he had the ability to charm a woman of fifty, every bit as easily as girls in their teens.

"Thank you, Fanny," I said, wondering what could have prompted Pierce to visit my office. "As it happens, I did stop off at the jail."

Fanny eyed me anxiously. "What's happened, Sarah? You look as if you've received a shock of some kind. Why don't you come inside and I'll put the kettle on for tea. You can tell me all about it."

"Not right now, Fanny, but thank you for the offer," I declined with a distracted smile. "I need to spend some time alone before Pierce returns. I have some thinking to do."

"Oh, dear. That does sound grim." She raised salt-and-pepper eyebrows. "Are they still treating those poor Chinese boys like some sort of animals?" she asked indignantly.

I was surprised that she had touched so closely upon what had occurred at the jail. Once again, I was in awe of my neighbor's amazing perspicacity.

"Yes, unfortunately, they are. But, well, there's more, I'm afraid." I patted the hand she had rested on my shoulder. "I promise to tell you all about it, Fanny, as soon as I've made sense of it myself."

"You do that, dear." Her kind gray eyes were regarding me with concern. "And do enjoy your lunch with Mr. Godfrey. If anyone can brighten your day, it is certainly that man!"

Once upstairs, I removed my cloak and hat and sank wearily into the chair behind my desk. It was only ten thirty, yet I felt as if I had been hard at work for hours.

Mentally, I gave myself a little shake. For the time being, I had to forget Ozzie Foldger, his troubling article, and even Brielle Bouchard's predicament. I had two bewildered and frightened boys counting on me to save their lives, a huge responsibility which required all my attention.

It was hard to believe that the men who had found Nigel Logan had changed their story about the man they spied running away. Were they only now telling what they really saw that night? Or had Jackson's mysterious "boys upstairs" somehow persuaded them to alter their original statement?

For the next hour and a half, I went over every detail I knew concerning the first two murders. As was my habit when trying to organize my thoughts, I had taken out my notebook and was listing everything—no matter how insignificant—I could remember about the crimes. Because I could not totally accept that Patrick O'Hara had been murdered by a cuckold husband, and therefore was unconnected to the other two killings, I added his death to the list.

My jottings had extended to several pages by the time Pierce arrived at my office. As is often the case when I am preoccupied, I had paid little attention to the time and was surprised to realize that it was already noon.

Beneath his unbuttoned navy blue long coat, I could see that he was wearing a dark suit and white shirt, set off nicely by an elegant gray and blue cravat. His thick, ebony hair looked to be a bit longer than he usually wore it, but as always it was carefully groomed and combed back from a tanned face. Watching him walk with casual grace into my office, I could well understand how even sensible Fanny found him irresistible.

"Hard at work, I see," he said. He took off his hat, but did not remove his coat, or take a seat. Instead, he remained standing in front of my desk.

I put down my pencil and sighed. "I only wish you were right. Actually, I've accomplished very little." I straightened in my chair and smiled. "Fanny said that you would like to take me to lunch?"

"I would, indeed."

"Good, because I'm very hungry."

"Excellent." He helped me on with my wrap, which I removed from its customary hook on the coat tree, then started for the door.

We walked several blocks up Sutter Street to one of my favorite restaurants. Giuseppe's was not large but the food was good, and the service even better. It was not my custom to dawdle for hours over my midday meal, and I had found the waiters here to be speedy and reliable. It was possible to enjoy a full pasta meal, or an assortment of sandwiches with beer or wine, and be back to work in little more than an hour.

Pierce and I ordered, then without my having to ask, he explained the reason for his unexpected luncheon invitation.

"I've been to see the Tremaines," he said, in obvious irritation. "Melody's father flatly refuses to allow her to audition for Joe Kreling when he returns to town."

As this news was no more than I had expected, I simply shook my head and sighed. "I didn't think he would agree. If he or his wife had been at home yesterday, we would never have been allowed to take her to the Tivoli."

"I didn't see the girl, or Mrs. Tremaine. Just Melody's father. I'm afraid she's going to be very disappointed."

"Yes, she is." I thought back to how excited she had been the day before at the opportunity to audition, and how beautiful she had looked on the stage. "I doubt that Mr. Tremaine will use a great deal of tact when he tells his daughter that her singing career is over before it has even begun. And I fear she will not receive much sympathy from her stepmother."

"I've never met her mother, but I saw pictures of her in the drawing room yesterday afternoon. She looks to be an attractive woman, but hardly in the same class as Melody." He sat apparently lost in thought for a few moments. "You don't suppose Mrs. Tremaine opposes the girl's career because she's jealous of her stepdaughter's beauty and talent, do you?"

I smiled. "The thought has crossed my mind. It can't be easy for a second wife to be so outshone by her husband's first wife's daughter." Once again, I sighed. "I guess that is that, then. You did your best, Pierce. And Melody certainly proved she has the ability and charisma to enjoy a successful career on the stage."

Pierce breathed slowly in and out before responding. "I wish I could take Tremaine's pigheadedness as calmly as you, Sarah."

"You mistake acceptance for equanimity, Pierce. Don't forget I've met the man, and was forced to listen to his views on Melody's singing aspirations."

I thought back to the night of Faith's birthday dinner. "You know, I don't believe Reginald Tremaine understands his children very well, especially the twins. He's been so preoccupied with building his business, I think he's left much of their upbringing to nannies, and then to his second wife, Faith. I doubt that he has any true idea how much this means to Melody, or how devastated she'll be at his refusal to grant her her life's dream."

Pierce nodded his agreement. "You should have heard the man. He actually seemed surprised I'd gone to the trouble of scheduling

Melody's audition. He dismissed her ambition as if it were nothing more than a silly young girl's fantasy. Which, I might add, he made clear was beneath the family's dignity."

"I think he's proud of his daughter, and probably of her singing—but only as a pleasant after-dinner entertainment, or to show off in front of friends. The very idea that she might possess sufficient talent to perform outside the home is completely beyond his frame of reference."

"I feel sorry for the girl."

"Yes, I do, too. But there's little we can do about it. He is, after all, her father. Unless she cares deeply enough about a career to defy him when she comes of age, he retains the final word."

"Perhaps," he said thoughtfully, "perhaps not."

Before I could question this strange statement, the waiter arrived with our lunches and Pierce fell quiet.

Despite several attempts, I could not get him to discuss the matter further.

CHAPTER TWENTY-THREE

Despite my objections that I had no need for another evening dress, Mama had insisted I have a new gown made for our Christmas party. I was more than a little shocked when it arrived from the dressmaker Saturday morning, to discover several modifications to the design had been executed without my approval. The modest neckline I had chosen for the periwinkle-blue damassé silk-and-satin gown was now cut so low I feared I would be forced to stand bolt upright the entire evening or cause a scandal. Mama had also added—again without my knowledge—a full frill of cream-colored duchesse lace to circle the plunging décolletage, along with a train of cream brocaded satin. Neither of which, I'm sure I need not add, were my style. Investigating these changes, I discovered that Mama had requested them to be made the day after she invited Pierce to the soiree, with instructions to the dressmaker that the gown be delivered to our house the morning of the party, when it would be too late for me to object.

At least I could not complain about the way our ladies' maid, Hazel, dressed my hair. She was so rushed attending to Mama's and Celia's coiffures, as well as mine, that she was content to arrange my ebony locks into a simple cluster of curls atop my head, allowing the rest of my thick mane to hang in long tresses down my back. And for once she didn't argue with me about adorning my head with anything but a few sprigs of holiday flowers.

When I descended the stairs to help greet guests, my mind was in a turmoil. I had not seen or heard from Robert since the previous Tuesday evening when he, Samuel, George Lewis, and I discussed the recent spate of murders. Since then, I had vacillated over the wisdom of his attendance tonight. Given his illogical dislike for Pierce, I feared what might happen if he were forced to spend an entire evening with him in the same house. On the other hand, the thought of Robert sitting home alone in his dreary rooming house so close to Christmas made me feel heartless in the extreme.

I had no worries concerning Pierce's behavior; he would remain a gentleman however much Robert baited him. My hotheaded colleague, on the other hand, could be alarmingly unpredictable. If he precipitated a scene with Pierce during tonight's festivities, my mother would never forgive me.

It was Samuel's opinion that I was once again making mountains out of molehills. "They're grown men, Sarah," he'd said earlier that afternoon. "They know how to behave." I could only pray that he was right. Truly, my life at present was so full of life-and-death issues, I had no need for added complications, especially those of a romantic nature.

Celia and Charles came downstairs shortly after me. My sister-in-law looked lovely in a shaded emerald-green lampas gown, trimmed with faded gold satin. That she could look stylishly slender so soon after giving birth recently continued to amaze me.

I was relieved to have them by my side when the first guests to enter were my eldest brother Frederick—who is, to California's peril, a state senator—and his wife, Henrietta. Thankfully, they had left their unpleasant nine-year-old son, Freddy, at home. Unfortunately, they had brought their latest grievances concerning me with them.

"Sarah," my eldest brother began, as soon as they had turned over their wraps to our butler, Edis. "I cannot believe Mother permitted you to show yourself in public tonight. The papers are full of your peccadilloes. This time you have gone too far!"

My sister-in-law Henrietta was wearing a gown in a shade of pale green which was not at all flattering to her sallow complexion. I knew by the cut and the quality of the material that the dress was costly. Why, I wondered, did the unfortunate woman insist on spending so much money on clothes which so ill suited her?

"You seem determined to bring this family to ruin," she hissed, glancing around to ensure no other guests were close enough to overhear talk of her sister-in-law's latest scandal. "What possessed you to agree to defend yet another Chinaman? I would have thought you'd learned your lesson the last time you put us through such a humiliation. And to visit a—a—"

"A cathouse?" I offered serenely. "I believe that is how the *Tattler* described it. I must admit that I'm a bit surprised to learn that you have taken to reading the gossip journals."

It was rewarding to see Henrietta's pasty complexion turn an almost pleasant shade of pink. She sputtered in an effort to find words sufficiently rancorous to describe her moral outrage.

My brother beat her to it, making no attempt to lower his own voice. "I am going to demand that Father do something about your conduct, Sarah. You are sullying not only my reputation, but his as well. If you refuse to behave like a proper young woman and marry—supposing, of course, you can find a decent man willing to accept you—then you should be placed in a nunnery, or at the very least settled in the country where you can no longer bring shame upon the family's good name."

"Frederick! That is enough."

We all turned to find Papa standing in the hallway, angrily regarding his eldest son. Behind him, our mother was looking in acute embarrassment at some guests who had gathered behind my brother and sister-in-law, awaiting their turn to enter the house.

"We will discuss this later," Papa told Frederick in a low tone. He regarded me meaningfully. "I have not yet had an opportunity to speak to your sister, but rest assured, I will."

Assuming a welcoming smile, he brushed past us to greet the new arrivals. With a scathing look in my direction, Mama followed. Taking advantage of their preoccupation, I slipped quietly into the kitchen where, given the hectic activity going on in the room, I was hardly welcome.

After nearly tripping our Irish maid, Ina Corks, who was bustling out the door carrying a tray of hors d'oeuvres, I moved quickly out of the way. As I did, I spied our part-time gardener and handyman, Marco Ciatti, entering the kitchen from the back porch, a block of ice slung over his shoulder. Unable to tip his cap because of his heavy load, he nonetheless smiled cheerfully, and continued on into the scullery, where I presumed the ice would be cut or slivered depending on its intended use. Marco was frequently pressed into performing the odd chore here and there when our family entertained.

As I turned to leave the kitchen, I saw one of the maids attempting to tie Eddie Cooper's cravat. My mouth fell open at the sight of the young cabbie. He was so clean I hardly recognized him: face scrubbed, hands spotless, brown hair shining and neatly combed back from his face. Instead of his usual work clothes, the boy was attired in footman's dress livery, which, because it had been intended for another, taller young man who had canceled on us at the last moment, was far too large and hung loosely on his thin frame. Height, good looks, and a well-turned calf were the qualities most desired in a footman. Since Eddie had hardly any discernible calf muscles, I suggested to one of the maids that she use pins to fasten his white hose to his britches in order to hold them up.

Our family employed only one maid of all work, Ina Corks, a butler, a cook, and a ladies' maid. We had no full-time footmen or kitchen maids, but hired temporary servants whenever extra help was required. Eddie had initially seemed excited to be asked by

Mama to replace the missing footman. Now, the lad looked pale, frightened, and very nervous. Despite the maid's continued entreaties for him to remain still, Eddie could not stop fidgeting.

"Here, Sally," I said, "I'll take care of that."

"I'm not sure I kin do this, Miss Sarah," the boy told me anxiously.

"Of course you can, Eddie," I said, straightening his tie. "You look very handsome. Just try not to act as if you're about to face a hangman's noose. No one is going to bite you, I promise."

"But I ain't never done nothin' like this before," he said. "What if I make a mistake, or drop somethin'?"

"Just take your time and be careful. Remember to say 'yes, ma'am or sir,' and don't speak any more than is necessary. Cook will instruct you about which dishes to take out and where to place them on the table. I'm sure you're going to do just fine."

Giving Eddie a reassuring pat on the shoulder, I exited the kitchen and returned to the front foyer. I was in time to see Pierce entering the house. He was carrying a small, beautifully wrapped box, as well as a lovely selection of cut winter flowers. He handed the bouquet to Mama, but kept the box.

"These are absolutely lovely," I could hear her gushing. "Marie will put them in a vase." I was surprised to realize that my mother was actually blushing. I was beginning to suspect that no woman, regardless of her age, was impervious to the man's charm!

"Pierce, you weren't supposed to bring presents," I told him, after Mama turned to welcome more guests.

Without answering, he peered around, then leaned over and kissed me gently on the lips. When I started to protest, he raised his eyes, nodding toward the mistletoe hanging above our heads.

"It's an old Norse tradition, Sarah," he explained, his dark eyes twinkling. "You wouldn't want to risk bad luck by ignoring it, would you?"

"Given that it's a famous Norse tradition, of course not." To my surprise, I broke into laughter. It felt good, releasing me, if only for a brief time, from the heavy burden I felt resting upon my shoulders. "I'm happy to see you, Pierce, I truly am. But seriously, you weren't supposed to come bearing gifts."

"I believe it's still a free country," he said, and handed me the small gift box.

"Pierce, really, you—"

He placed a finger lightly over my lips. "Don't fuss, Sarah, just open the box."

Moving to a more private space behind the stairs, I duly opened my gift. Inside, lying on a bed of black velvet, was a pair of beautiful silver earrings that gracefully depicted a tiny Chinese figure dressed in intricate robes, and holding a branch of some kind.

"Pierce, these are exquisite," I said, moving out of our cubbyhole and holding them up to the light. "They look very old."

"According to a Chinese antique dealer I know in Hong Kong, they date back to the Ming Dynasty."

"The Ming—!" I stared at him, not sure I had heard him correctly. "But that means they could be more than two hundred years old."

"My friend claims that they probably date to the sixteenth century. The Chinese regard the peach tree as a symbol of longevity and springtime. The peach tree of the gods was said to bloom once every three thousand years, and then it bore the fruit of eternal life. They also believe it wards off evil influences. Your earrings depict the god of longevity emerging from within a peach."

"Pierce, I love them," I said, a bit overwhelmed. "But it really is too much."

"On the contrary," he said, laughing. "Given your penchant for chasing after murderers and other dangerous characters, I thought a charm that guaranteed long life, and warded off evil spirits in the bargain, was a very practical gift."

I started to protest again, then realized that I truly did love the earrings. "I'll cherish them always," I said quietly. "It was very kind of you to think of me."

His dark eyes became suddenly intense as he looked down at me. "Kindness has nothing to do with it, my dear Sarah. You're in my thoughts far more than I find comfortable."

I'm sure my face would have betrayed me, if the light had not been so dim in our little corner. In truth, my whole body felt unexpectedly warm, despite the chill air blowing in through the front door as more guests entered the house. I was startled out of this delightful reverie when I heard my mother's voice calling my name.

"I, ah, had better go," I stammered, feeling like an awkward schoolgirl.

He said nothing, but simply stood aside so that I might pass by him. As I did so, the front of my gown brushed against his chest, and he made a small sound in his throat. My eyes went to his face, but he already had his features under control. Swallowing hard, I quickly moved past him and out into the hall.

Standing at the door, looking embarrassed and out of place, was Robert. I reached him as he was handing his coat and hat to Edis. He was wearing the new suit I had helped him select two weeks ago, along with a colorful cravat which set off his rugged good looks, and was perfect for the holiday season. His thick, unruly red hair was, for the time being at least, combed neatly back from his forehead, and looked as if it had been drenched in pomade. I was mildly surprised to realize that he looked extremely handsome.

"Robert," I said, smiling as I reached the door. "I'm happy to see you. Please, come in out of the cold."

Upon entering, he happened to see the small jewelry box I still held in my hand. His dismay was evident.

"Sarah, you didn't say anything about gifts. I don't—That is, I didn't bring anything."

"Nor were you expected to, Robert." I started to place the box in one of the pockets I had the dressmaker include in all my business suits, then remembered that the formal gown I was wearing did not come equipped with such a handy appendage.

My mother seemed to understand my predicament and reached for the box. "I'll take care of this for you, my dear. Why don't you introduce Mr. Campbell to the rest of our guests and see that he receives some refreshment."

I readily agreed and, taking Robert by the arm, walked him into the front parlor where the Christmas tree stood, and champagne, wine, and fruit punch were being circulated by several maids and our "footman," Eddie. The boy was carrying a tray of champagne with such care and deliberation, you would have thought his life depended upon safely navigating it through the room.

"Good heavens," Robert exclaimed, staring at the boy in considerable surprise. "Is that Eddie?"

"It is, indeed," I answered, experiencing a feeling of pride. "He cleans up rather well, doesn't he?"

"Amazing," said Robert. "Now, if he just doesn't open his mouth all may be well."

Before I could reply, Pierce suddenly appeared, smiling as he blocked our forward progress into the room.

"Good evening, Robert," he said politely, holding out his hand.

Almost reluctantly, Robert grasped the other man's hand and shook it. "Godfrey," he acknowledged, his tone falling just short of sounding rude. "I should have known you'd be here."

"I'm glad I didn't disappoint you then," Pierce said.

Robert drew breath, no doubt to say something offensive, when I spoke first.

"Robert, this will not do. I trust you can bury your grievances against Pierce, whatever they may be, for I have no idea, and get along at least for this one evening. Please remember, we are here to celebrate the Christmas holiday."

Robert continued to stare at Pierce for another long minute, then transferred his gaze to me.

"I apologize, Sarah," he said evenly. "You are quite right, this is not an evening to quarrel." He turned to Pierce, even managing a weak smile. "What do you say, Godfrey, shall we find some refreshment? I see yon lad has a tray of champagne. We should probably commandeer a glass before he trips over his own feet and drops the whole kit and caboodle."

I was giving an inward sigh of relief, when I heard familiar voices coming from the foyer. I moved into the hall to see that the Tremaines had arrived, in company with the Reverend Mayfield. They were being greeted by Celia and my brother Charles.

Except for the two youngest children, the entire family had come, just as they had for Faith's birthday dinner. Reginald Tremaine and his wife, Faith, seemed in good spirits, while Major Tremaine appeared a bit subdued. David and his sister Melody—who looked lovely in a dark pink gown and dainty pink slippers—were also quiet as they handed Edis their coats, and I noticed that Melody went out of her way not to look at either parent. Obviously, she was upset with her father and stepmother for not allowing her to audition for Joseph Kreling. Judging from the looks Major Tremaine was directing at his son, it was clear that he shared his granddaughter's disappointment.

"Good evening," I said, greeting the new arrivals. "Major Tremaine, Mr. and Mrs. Tremaine, Reverend Mayfield, I'm so pleased you could come. It's good to see you, Melody, David."

"We're delighted to have been asked," the younger Mr. Tremaine said, looking past me to the party, which by now was well under way.

"Miss Woolson," said the rector, smiling at me. "It is very nice to see you again. I must tell you once more how much I appreciated you and your brother visiting me the day poor Deacon Hume was—" He came to an awkward stop, as if he could not bring himself to say the dreaded word.

"Yes, Reverend Mayfield," I said quickly. "It was a most lamentable day. I'm happy if Samuel and I were able to offer you some small comfort."

"Not small, Miss Woolson," he protested. "No, no, indeed not. It was most kind of you both. Unusual, I assure you, for young people to take the trouble to pay a visit at such a trying time."

"Why don't Charles and I take you inside?" Celia said to the pastor. With a gracious nod, she included Mr. and Mrs. Tremaine in this invitation. "There are some people I think you would enjoy meeting."

When they left, Major Tremaine, Melody, and David remained behind. I led the way down the hall and into the library, closing the door behind us.

"Mr. Godfrey tells me that your parents refuse to allow you to audition for Mr. Kreling," I said. "I'm truly sorry, Melody."

Not surprisingly, the girl looked crestfallen. "I told Father I was willing to perform under a different name. No one need know that his daughter was singing on the stage. He just laughed and said I was being silly. He told me to put the idea out of my mind, that the theater was a fantasy world, not for real people with a standing to uphold in the community."

"He assumes it is just a passing fancy," David put in. "He can't imagine Melody is serious about pursuing a career. Grandpapa tried to get Father to change his mind, but it made no difference. He simply won't listen."

Major Tremaine sighed. "I did try, but—" He paused, then went on, "Please don't judge my son too harshly, Miss Woolson. He and Faith have the girl's best interests at heart. I'm an old fool, and much too fond of these youngsters to tell them no, when that's what I probably should be saying." He smiled affectionately at the twins. "My son says I've hopelessly spoiled the two of you, and he's probably right."

"No, Grandpapa, you haven't," David said. "Sometimes you are the only one who seems to understand."

"He's right," said Melody. "David and I will never forget all you've done for us."

There was a knock on the door, and my mother peered inside. "There you are, Sarah." She smiled at Major Tremaine and the twins. "What are you doing keeping our guests all to yourself? Please, Major, children, come and enjoy some refreshments."

Mama ushered us back out into the hall toward the front parlor. As we walked, she whispered, "Sarah, I am counting on you to circulate. You are a member of this family, and I expect you to do your part to make tonight a success." She gave me a look that brooked no argument. "Now, please, move about and be sociable."

D inner was served an hour later. Since it was a buffet, Mama and Celia had carefully selected a bill of fare which could be easily eaten while standing. I obeyed Mama's instructions and circulated, ensuring that everyone had what they required for supper, including the proper silverware and drinks.

Several people looked at me as if amazed that I had the nerve to show my face after Ozzie Foldger's article. And of course Frederick and Henrietta missed no opportunity to favor me with a censorious glare. On the whole, though, the evening seemed to be going smoothly.

"Has Papa said anything to you about the article in last Tuesday's *Tattler?*" Samuel said, catching up with me as I sought a moment's respite in the back parlor. "I can't imagine that he hasn't heard about it by now."

"Oh, he's heard," I said darkly. "And he has promised to discuss the matter with me later. I'm just surprised the story hasn't been picked up by other dailies."

"I gather that you haven't heard the news, then," my brother said with a mysterious smile.

"What news?"

"Only that our good friend Ozzie Foldger is being sued by a state senator for slander."

"Considering the gossip he reports, I'm not surprised," I said. "But what does that have to do with my visit to Madam Valentine's parlor house?"

"For one thing, the senator is demanding an investigation into other articles that parasite has written, claiming that Foldger makes a habit of printing rumors without first proving their veracity. Which answers your question as to why the city's more reputable newspapers hesitated to pick up your story."

"Good heavens," was all I could think to say. "That was a piece of good fortune."

"Even more fortunate," Samuel continued with a broad smile, "is that Madam Valentine publicly denied Foldger's assertion that you'd ever visited her establishment."

"Bravo for Matilda Abernathy," I exclaimed, wishing the woman were within my reach right now so I might kiss her out of gratitude. "Fanny said she was known for her discretion."

"And you can count your lucky stars that she is," said Papa, joining us as we talked in the back parlor. "Not that you deserve it, my girl, but it seems you've dodged yet another bullet."

"I went to the parlor house to see my client, Brielle Bouchard, Papa," I explained. "She and her baby have been staying there since Gerald Knight forced her to leave the house on Pacific Avenue."

"I gathered as much." Papa regarded me from beneath somewhat shaggy, salt-and-pepper eyebrows. "Regardless of the reason you went there, Sarah, you should have considered the consequences if you were seen. You were lucky this time. In the future, you may have to pay a much higher price for such indiscretion."

After Papa left us to return to his duties as host, Samuel let out a long sigh. "I wish he would as easily let me off the hook."

I studied his face. "Have you decided what you're going to do yet?"

He shook his head. "No, but I did sign up to take the bar exams in February. I can always change my mind."

"Samuel, you're just postponing the inevitable. Why don't you simply tell Papa how you really feel?"

He gave a little shudder. "I will when the time is right. Sometime after the holidays I'll make my decision."

I sighed. "You have to do what you think best. I just don't see that putting it off is going to make it any easier."

He smiled and kissed me on the cheek. "You're such a fighter, little sister. Why wasn't I blessed with some of your courage?"

Just then I caught Mama's meaningful glance from the hallway, and I left my brother to resume circulating among our guests. Every time I spied Pierce, he seemed to be surrounded by a gaggle of silly young women, all of them looking up at him as if he were some kind of Greek god come down to earth for them to worship. I found it disgusting!

I noticed a goodly number of women were also drawn to Robert, but instead of taking the attention gracefully as did Pierce, he seemed to find it highly unsettling. His craggy face retained a permanent flush, and he regarded the women much as a sailor might view a school of hungry sharks. Finally taking pity on him, I came to his rescue and led him to a quiet spot off the dining room where he might eat his dinner in peace.

As far as I could tell, everyone seemed to be having a good time. After all our hard work the house truly did look festive. The tree twinkled merrily with dozens of small lit candles, and our mostly handmade decorations added just the right touch. As usual, Cook had outdone herself with the food. Although I'd had little opportunity to do more than try a bit of this and that on my way past the buffet tables.

Several times I spied Eddie passing through the rooms, bearing trays of drinks and other refreshments. His thin face was screwed into such a look of fierce concentration, that it was all I could do not to laugh. Poor Eddie, as a footman the boy was truly a fish out of water. His livery was so large, I feared his trousers might slide down his narrow hips at any moment and onto his ankles. More than once I tried to straighten his tie, which refused to remain in place, but from the way he squirmed you would have thought I was trying to strangle him.

I noticed that Melody ate very little and did almost no socializing, although several young men attempted to engage her in conversation. As ever, David hardly left her side, but his attempts to make her laugh and eat more dinner mostly failed.

Her father and stepmother appeared to be enjoying the evening enormously. Earlier, I saw that Mrs. Tremaine seemed to have caught the fancy of two young gentlemen, who were entertaining her with stories of their recent trip to France. She was basking in the attention, laughing at their jokes and batting her eyes coyly when they paid her a compliment.

From the bits of conversation I caught in passing, Mr. Tremaine spent time discussing the current state of men's retail with a group of like-minded gentlemen. Throughout the evening, I noticed the Major wandering from one group to another, although he seemed to keep a close eye on Melody and David. His distracted expression puzzled me. I received the impression that something was bothering him, but could not think of a subtle way to inquire what it was.

For some reason his mood made me think of the dinner party the Tremaines had held just two weeks ago, the night Nigel Logan was killed. I glanced around at our guests. Was the murderer here? I wondered with a little shiver. Were we unknowingly playing host to a monster who had viciously murdered three people in the past two weeks?

I wished I knew who had been at the Tremaines' dinner. A number of tonight's guests belonged to our church; in all likelihood they had been invited to celebrate their rector's twenty-fifth ordination anniversary. Could one of them have been so provoked by Nigel Logan's defense of Charles Darwin's evolution theory that they had bludgeoned two men to death? If so, how did Patrick O'Hara fit into that picture? He was Roman Catholic. The chances of him being acquainted with members of our church—except those who might frequent the ice cream parlor—were slim.

And what if the police were right after all, and O'Hara's murder had nothing to do with Logan's and Hume's deaths? I was still convinced that my two young clients were innocent of wrongdoing, but what if the first two victims had been killed by thieves, or other hoodlums?

I was still going around in circles and getting nowhere, when Pierce came over and took me aside.

"I'd like you to do me a favor and ask Melody to sing," he said quietly. "All evening she's been drifting about as if she just lost her best friend. I thought performing might cheer her up. And David, as well. He's hardly left her since they arrived."

I looked at him curiously. "Of course, I'll be happy to ask her. But why do I have the feeling there's more to this request than meets the eye? You've got a peculiar look on your face."

I followed his gaze and saw that he was looking at Melody as she sat in a chair to one side of the parlor. Her brother was standing stiffly behind her. Both of them appeared uncomfortable and out of place.

"Let's just say there's more than one way to skin a cat."

I looked at him, confused. "That's a strange thing to say. Whatever do you mean?"

Instead of explaining, he gave me one of his enigmatic smiles, then went to talk to some men gathered in front of the fireplace. What was going on? I wondered. Why was he suddenly so eager to have Melody sing?

The impromptu performance was soon arranged, although Melody did not appear overly enthusiastic about the request. Marco was called out from the kitchen to help Samuel position the piano so that it could be better seen by everyone, and they provided chairs so that most of the ladies could sit. When all was ready, Mama announced that we were in for a wonderful treat; young Melody Tremaine had agreed to entertain us with one or two songs.

I felt a movement from behind, and turned to find that Robert had joined me. A moment later, Pierce appeared to stand to my other side. Robert nodded to him, but thankfully held his tongue. Pierce gave my hand a little squeeze as Melody walked to the piano, gracefully arranged her skirt, then took a seat on the bench.

When she was settled, and without saying a word to her audience concerning what she planned to sing, Melody began to play. As before, she became immediately engrossed in her music, and I again had the impression that she had escaped to a place exclusively her own. The few conversations still going on in the room quickly stilled as she began to sing the first measures of a popular song.

Looking around at the rapt faces watching the girl, I was overcome by a sudden sense of sadness. She was so exquisite and so talented, I could not help but bemoan the fact that, because of her father's stubborn lack of understanding, her music would be lost to the world. Couldn't he hear the magic her agile fingers coaxed from the piano, and the glorious voice that issued from her slender throat? How could he deny the girl the life she was surely meant to follow?

Melody had just begun a second song when I heard the front door open and the murmur of Edis's voice. Pierce instantly left my side and moved into the foyer.

When I turned to see who had arrived so late in the evening, my mouth fell open in shock.

Very quietly, Pierce was directing two men into the front parlor. The first gentleman was a stranger to me, but I recognized the second man all too well.

It was Gerald Knight!

CHAPTER TWENTY-FOUR

I stopped Pierce before he could follow the latecomers inside. "What is Gerald Knight doing here?" I demanded. "He is the last person I would invite into this house."

"I didn't invite him, Sarah," Pierce answered softly. "He came with Kreling."

"Kreling?" I repeated. "You mean the man with him is Joseph Kreling? The owner of the Tivoli Opera House?"

"Yes."

"But I thought he was out of town."

"He was, but when the Tremaines refused to allow Melody to audition again I sent him a telegram saying this might be his only opportunity to hear the girl sing. He cut his trip short and returned to San Francisco this afternoon."

"What makes you think that having Kreling listen to Melody tonight will change her parents' minds about her pursuing a musical career?"

"I reasoned that if they saw her perform in front of an audience, they might realize how talented she is. And if Joe liked her, which I was sure he would, I hoped they might be swayed by the opinion of a professional."

"What is it, Sarah?" Robert had come up behind me. "Is God-frey bothering you?"

"No, Robert," I answered, giving him a pointed look to behave. "It appears that we have an uninvited guest. Pierce and I are trying to decide what to do about it."

Robert studied the people in the parlor. "Who is the intruder?"

"Do you see those men who just came in? The taller of the two is Gerald Knight, Brielle Bouchard's ex-lover."

"What? You mean the cad who threw the poor girl out onto the street when he found out she was carrying his child?" Robert's face screwed up in fury. "Come, Godfrey, let's show the blackguard what it feels like to be tossed out like so much rubbish!"

"Robert, wait! And please lower your voice." I grabbed hold of his arm and pulled him back from the parlor door. "Mama will have my head if we create a scene. She has planned this party for weeks. We have to think this through calmly."

"Why?" Robert persisted, but in a slightly lower volume. His large hands hung clenched at his sides, as if itching to wring the newspaperman's neck. "If your mother knew who this man was and what he has done, she'd be the first person to throw him out on his ear."

"Well, I'm not going to tell her. And neither are you." I thought about our options. Robert was right, we had to get Gerald Knight out of this house. But without creating a commotion. "For now, all we can do is to keep a close eye on Knight. Under no circumstances is he to be left alone with Melody."

Before either man could voice an opinion, or an objection, to this plan, Samuel came out of the parlor to join us in the hallway. He looked disturbed, and not a little confused. "I must be seeing things. Are you aware of who just walked into this house? I had no idea Gerald Knight had been invited tonight."

"He wasn't," I replied, moving even farther away from the parlor door, so there would be less chance of our being overheard. "Pierce asked Joseph Kreling here tonight so that he could hear Melody sing.

Evidently, Knight somehow found out about it and invited himself along."

"Because of his fascination with the girl," Samuel said, obviously remembering what I had told him about Knight's attraction to Melody at the Tivoli.

"We're trying to think of some way to uninvite him," Robert said, his expression still resembling a thundercloud.

"Perhaps when Melody is finished performing, we might try to escort Knight out without creating a fuss," I offered, although with little real hope.

Samuel looked skeptical. "You don't know that man, if you think he's going to leave quietly, Sarah. Gerald Knight is used to getting what he wants." He glanced back into the parlor, where Melody was holding her audience mesmerized. Except for her glorious voice filling the room, you could have heard a pin drop. "And judging from the way he's ogling the girl, I'd say you were right about his wanting Melody Tremaine. I seriously doubt that he's going to go just because you ask him to."

"Then what do you suggest?" asked Robert. "I'll be more than happy to see him out the door, whether he cares to leave or not."

"Robert, please," I said. "That won't solve anything."

My eyes went back to Melody and I noticed moisture glistening in her lovely eyes. The song she was currently performing was a ballad about two star-crossed lovers, but I did not think that was what had brought her close to tears. I suspected the mere act of singing in front of such an appreciative audience served to underscore her disappointment at being denied her lifelong dream. I prayed I would be proven wrong, but I seriously doubted that Joseph Kreling would be able to change the Tremaines' minds.

Her brother David was standing to the side of the piano, watching his sister sing in the same adoring way he had the night of Faith's birthday dinner. I also noticed that he kept massaging his temple, much as he had done last weekend when we had sought shelter from the storm and enjoyed our impromptu lunch. I wondered if he was suffering another attack of the sick headaches he was evidently prone to. The poor boy. How sad if he were forced to endure one tonight.

The parlor suddenly erupted in applause, and I realized Melody had finished singing.

"Just keep Gerald Knight away from her," I told Samuel, Robert, and Pierce, then started into the parlor in an effort to reach the girl before the newspaperman.

This proved to be more difficult than I had anticipated. Guests were giving the girl a standing ovation, and blocked my efforts to move through the room. Melody hardly seemed to notice the many accolades. Tears were coursing down her pale face as she rose from the piano bench. To my alarm, I saw Gerald Knight approach her, lending her a steadying arm when she appeared to trip on her skirts.

I hastened my step, but it was difficult pushing through people without being rude. And of course the train Mama had insisted on adding to my dress made it challenging to walk more than a few inches without someone stepping on it. Several guests stopped me to inquire about the beautiful young girl with the marvelous voice. Ironically, a few even went so far as to declare that a talent like hers belonged on the stage!

Pierce made better progress than I did, and I saw him introducing Joseph Kreling to Mr. and Mrs. Tremaine. Major Tremaine stood with his son and Faith, and was beaming with pride as he shook Kreling's hand. Melody's parents, on the other hand, looked more affronted than honored when the theater impresario praised their daughter's talent.

"You own the Tivoli Opera House?" I heard Reginald Tremaine say as I drew closer. "But I don't understand why you're here. We have informed our daughter that a career on the stage is out of the question. I'm afraid you have wasted your time coming here this evening, Mr. Kreling."

"Come now, Mr. Tremaine," Kreling said, turning on considerable charm. The young man wasn't tall or particularly imposing, but I could see why he had achieved so much success in his brief twenty-six years. He had the sort of face people naturally trusted, along with more than his fair share of charisma. His brown eyes were focused and sparkled with sincerity. Despite her objections to Melody's pursuing a career, it was obvious that Faith Tremaine was taken with the young man.

"I can see where Miss Tremaine gets her beauty," Kreling said, giving the woman an admiring smile. "But surely you must be her sister. You look far too young to be the girl's mother."

Faith blushed prettily. "Actually, I am her stepmother, Mr. Kreling. But she is as close to my heart as is my own daughter." She actually fluttered her eyelashes at him. "I married quite young, you see, but I have raised Melody since she was a small child."

"Then you are much to be commended, my dear lady," Kreling said. "Not every bride would dedicate herself so selflessly to the care of a stepchild."

"Stepchildren," Faith corrected, with a coquettish smile. "Melody has a twin brother, David."

"Does she?" Kreling fawned. "Then you are truly to be admired as a gem among women."

I could stomach no more of this twaddle. With many apologies and a contrived smile, I made my way more briskly through the crowd of guests. When I finally reached the piano, however, Melody was nowhere in sight.

Standing on tiptoes, I surveyed the room, but could see no sign of the girl. Nor, I thought with growing unease, could I see Gerald Knight! Spying Eddie coming through the parlor with a tray of coffee, I beckoned him over.

"Have you seen the young lady who was just singing and playing the piano?" I asked him.

"No, but I wish I had," he answered with awestruck eyes. "She's a real looker, ain't she?"

"She's a very attractive young lady," I agreed. "Please tell me at once if you should see her."

"I'll do that, Miss Sarah," the boy said cheerfully.

"Oh, and Eddie," I said as he turned to leave. "When you get a chance, pull up your trousers. They're sagging."

"Did you speak to her?" Samuel asked as I left the parlor.

"No. She was talking with Gerald Knight, but they left the room before I could reach her."

"Where did they go?"

"I wish I knew." I could not hide my concern, and I was certain from my brother's expression that he was equally worried. "Eddie hasn't seen her, either."

"I caught a glimpse of Kreling doing his utmost to charm her parents," Samuel observed. "Mrs. Tremaine appears quite impressed by the man."

"I noticed," I said. "But I doubt if anything he says will change their minds."

"You don't suppose Knight took her off somewhere?" he said with fresh concern. "Surely she wouldn't leave the house with a strange man."

"I should hope not," I said, but had to repress a shiver of fear. In her present state of mind I had no idea what the girl might or might not do.

"Then where is she? Have you seen David? He's usually hovering about somewhere near his sister."

"If he's with Melody, then I'm sure she's safe," I said, taking comfort in this thought. "He would never allow anyone to harm her."

We were still standing there, trying to decide where to search next, when Pierce and Robert joined us.

"I wish now that I had taken what you said about Knight more seriously, Sarah." Pierce appeared more worried than I'd seen him. "I'm beginning to regret that I ever hatched up this little scheme. If I've placed that poor girl in danger I'll never forgive myself."

"She's seventeen," said Samuel unexpectedly.

"What?" Pierce and I asked in unison.

"Wasn't that Brielle Bouchard's age when she became Knight's mistress?" my brother asked.

"Dear God, yes," I replied, panic rising in my throat. "Come, let's spread out and look for her."

Samuel headed toward the front door, obviously to ensure that the girl really was too smart to leave the house with a strange man. Pierce entered the dining room and Robert went to check the parlor again, as well as the sitting room.

For my part, I went to the kitchen to see if any of the servants had seen the girl. Although it was mid-December, the room was still uncommonly hot, due to all the preparation for tonight's party. I found Cook sitting on a straight-backed chair fanning herself with a copy of yesterday's newspaper.

"Mrs. Polin, I was wondering if you, or any of the staff, have seen a very pretty young girl wearing a dark pink dress?"

"You mean the poor little thing who came running through here crying her eyes out?" Mrs. Polin nodded toward the door leading out to the back porch. "Far as I know, she's still out there. Probably still crying, too. She looked that upset."

I crossed the kitchen and went out onto the porch. Heedless of her gown, Melody was sitting on the top step leading down to the garden sobbing into her hands. I sat down beside her.

"What is it, Melody?" I asked softly.

She shook her head, trying to control her tears, then looked up from her hands. "Mr. Knight. He—" She hiccupped. "He wants me to go against my father's wishes and appear on the stage. He—he said he would take care of me, that I need never again worry about my future. Then he—" She drew a ragged breath and wiped at her tears with a lacy white handkerchief.

"He what, Melody? What did Mr. Knight do to you?"

"I hardly know how to tell you, Miss Woolson. It was so unexpected, and vulgar. One minute we were talking quietly, then suddenly he—he pulled me into his arms and kissed me."

"Dear Lord," I exclaimed.

"I'm afraid that is not all," she went on, lowering her face in obvious embarrassment. "He—Oh, Miss Woolson, then he placed one of his hands on my—my bosom!" Once again she began crying. "I—I thought he was a gentleman."

"Gerald Knight is no gentleman, my dear," I told her through gritted teeth. "Indeed, he is far from it." I put an arm around the girl's shaking shoulders. "If you are ever unfortunate enough to encounter that man again, you must ensure that you are not left alone with him."

"I never want to see him again," the girl said through her tears.

"I sincerely hope you never do."

I heard the sound of running footsteps, and a moment later the back door flew open and Eddie bolted outside.

"Come quick, Miss Sarah," he shouted. "There's a man hurt. His head's cut plum open and there's blood all over the place."

I jumped up from my seat on the stairs. "Melody, you stay here," I told her. "Take me to the injured man, Eddie. Quickly!"

"I heard a god-awful ruckus comin' from that room over there," he threw over his shoulder as he ran. "I looked in to see what was goin' on, and I seen this gent lyin' on the floor with his head bashed in."

The room he was referring to turned out to be the library. Opening the door, I spied Gerald Knight sprawled on the carpet in front of the fireplace. Papa's bronze bust of Abraham Lincoln was lying on its side by his crushed head.

I was so shocked by the sight of the newspaperman, that it was a moment or two before I saw Major Tremaine kneeling beside Knight's prone figure. His hands and suit trousers were covered in blood.

"Major, what has happened?" I started to kneel down beside the elderly man, but he held up a hand to stop me.

"There is nothing you can do for him, Miss Woolson," he said somberly, his face nearly as white as the man lying before him. "He is beyond human help."

"But—how did it—?"

"It was an accident," he told me, placing a hand on a nearby chair to aid him in rising to his feet. I noticed, as if in a dream, the bloody handprint he left on the chair cushion. "I came in here several minutes ago to find this man fondling my granddaughter. When I pushed him away from her, he crashed against the fireplace and the bronze bust fell onto his head."

My eyes went to the mantel, which was at least a foot lower than Knight's six feet plus height. I vaguely realized that I must be in some kind of shock, yet I could not visualize how such an accident might occur. Even if by some chance the bust had fallen on Knight, it most likely would have hit his shoulder, not his head. And never with the force necessary to inflict the kind of damage he had sustained.

I turned back to the door to find Eddie staring at the body with a mixture of alarm and fascination.

"Eddie, get my brother Charles," I told him. "And tell him to bring his medical bag. Hurry, please!"

With some effort the boy tore his eyes off the body, then turned and fled, slamming the door shut behind him.

"Major," I said, regarding the elderly man steadily. "Tell me the truth. What really happened here? Gerald Knight surely did not meet his death the way you described it."

"My head!" cried a voice from behind the Major. "Oh, God, my head."

I looked across the room and for the first time realized that someone was standing where the spill of light from the overhead gasolier did not quite reach. It was young David Tremaine.

"David," I called out. "What's the matter? Are you suffering one of your sick headaches?"

"Leave him be," the Major said rather sharply. "I am bringing him home and will see that he takes his medicine. It's the only way he'll obtain relief."

"Wait," I said, as he moved to help the boy. "First you must tell me how Gerald Knight died. How he *really* died."

"He was just like all the others," David said, his face contorted in pain. "They all wanted to take Melody away from me. I—I couldn't let them."

"David. Be quiet!" Major Tremaine commanded. "You are ill. You don't know what you're saying."

I stared at the elderly man and his grandson, and suddenly I saw what I had been missing for the past two weeks. Everything seemed

321

to shift in my mind, then neatly click into place. The mystery surrounding the three murders—four murders now—became tragically clear.

"You killed them, David," I said quietly. "That was what Nigel Logan, Dieter Hume, and Patrick O'Hara had in common: All three men had been attracted to Melody. You feared they would convince her to leave you, and you could not allow that to happen."

"It's always been Melody and me," the boy cried, still holding his head. "Can't let anyone come between us."

"You even murdered a man you admired," I said. The words rushed from my lips, but my mind was still struggling to accept their truth. "It must have been very hard for you to kill Mr. Logan."

"He was the first," David said, his eyes becoming glassy with pain. "I liked Nigel. But—but I could see he was in love with Melody."

"David, that is enough!" Major Tremaine had reached his grandson and was leading him toward the door. "I must take him home, Miss Woolson. The boy is unwell, you must see that."

"I see everything now, Major Tremaine. I know how much you love the boy, but you cannot protect him. These senseless killings must stop."

He stood still and looked at me. The despair written on his face was so heart-wrenching it robbed me of breath.

"Melody must never hear of this," he said, his voice ragged. "It would kill her. She adores her brother. She can never know that, because of her, he took the lives of four men."

His eyes burned into mine, pleading for me to understand. "I am the one who murdered those men, just as I killed Gerald Knight here in your library. That must be the story told to the police. Please, Miss Woolson, promise me that you will never tell anyone what—what really happened."

He looked with great affection at his grandson, using his fingers to stroke the hair out of the boy's face. David seemed very small, almost like a child, wrapped in his grandfather's protective arms.

"I should have acted sooner," the old man said. "Ever since the

O'Hara boy's death I suspected that David might be involved in—" He choked, and I could see he was fighting back tears. "But I didn't—I couldn't believe it." With an effort, he pulled himself together. "There will be no more murders, Miss Woolson, I promise you. Just, please, leave poor David out of it."

I did not immediately answer. What he was asking me to do went against all my principles, as well as my integrity as an attorney. I was an officer of the court, sworn to uphold the law. And yet, was the truth more important than a young girl's life? I believed the old man when he promised there would be no more murders. Wasn't that the important thing? He was willing to irreparably tarnish a lifetime of distinguished service to his country in order to save his beloved grandchildren. What purpose would be achieved if I put the lie to this last sacrifice by a brave soldier?

I sighed, and my heart felt heavy in my chest. "Yes, Major, I agree. I will give you an hour."

He smiled wanly at me as he reached the door. "Thank you, Miss Woolson. It is the right thing to do."

Only moments after Major Tremaine led his grandson out of the room, Charles burst into the library, closely followed by Samuel, Robert, and Pierce. My mother came to the door, but was quietly turned away by my colleague.

"It is best if you don't come in, Mrs. Woolson," the Scot told her. "There has been an accident. A man is dead."

"Oh, dear Lord," I heard her exclaim, but she did not press Robert to enter the library. "Who—who is it?"

"I don't believe he was invited," Robert told her. "I doubt that you know him."

"Heaven help us!" Mama's voice was thin and cracking in distress. "Whatever shall I tell my guests?"

"Tell them there has been an accident," I said, going to her at the door. "It would probably be best if they didn't leave until the police arrive."

Before I could close the door on my mother's retreating back, Papa entered the room.

"What has happened—? Oh, my God!" He stood just inside the library door, staring at the dead man on the floor. "Who is he? Is he—dead?"

"It's Gerald Knight," Samuel answered. "He owns, *owned,* the *Daily Journal.*"

Papa looked at his youngest son in confusion, then turned his attention to me. "Gerald Knight? Isn't that the man you were telling me about, Sarah? The one who kept the girl on Pacific Avenue?"

I nodded.

"Well, what in tarnation is he doing here? I don't remember your mother inviting him. And how in God's name did he end up like that?"

"He wasn't invited," I explained. "He accompanied Joseph Kreling, owner of the Tivoli Opera House."

"Yes, I met Kreling after Miss Tremaine sang. I wasn't introduced to this fellow."

"No, he left right after Melody finished performing," I told him.

Before my father could question me further, my brother Charles rose to his feet. He was shaking his head. "He's gone. He must have died almost instantly." He looked at me. "Sarah, do you know who did this?"

I attempted to remain as close to the truth as possible. "Major Tremaine was in the library when it happened. He claimed it was an accident."

All four men looked at the bronze bust on the floor, then at me. "How in hell can this be an accident, Sarah?" Samuel asked. "Are you telling us Lincoln's bust flew off the mantel all on its own and attacked Knight? There is no way it simply fell on his head, unless he was crawling around on all fours beneath it."

"I'm only relating what the Major said," I told him, endeavoring to keep my face blank. "It's up to the police to determine if they believe him or not."

"Sarah," said Robert, "what are you holding back? I know that look on your face all too well."

"You're always telling me to leave these matters to the police,"

I answered quietly. "Well, you should be happy, for that is exactly what I intend to do."

After the police arrived and I had given them my statement, I threw on a shawl and slipped out of the house, making my way to the Tremaine home on Harrison Street and Rincon Place. Reginald and Faith, along with Melody and the rest of our guests, were still being questioned by George Lewis and a lieutenant who had been assigned to the case. I had not asked anyone to accompany me. In fact, I had told no one I was going out. My father and Samuel—and probably Robert and Pierce, as well—would have insisted on accompanying me. However, this was something I felt I must do on my own.

It was well after midnight when I knocked on the Tremaines' door. The twins' young brother and sister would have long since been put to bed, but surely at least one of the servants would still be awake. It was customary for a member of the household staff to stay up until the family returned after an evening out.

When I knocked a second time, the door was opened by a surprised-looking butler. "Yes, miss?" he said, obviously not sure what to say to a young woman who was out and about apparently on her own at that hour of night.

"I know it's very late," I told the man, "but it is urgent that I see Major Tremaine. I believe he is expecting me."

"If he is," the butler said doubtfully, "he failed to inform me, miss. I suggest that you return tomorrow at a more civilized hour."

I was sorely tempted to take the man's advice and allow circumstances to reveal themselves in their own time. But that would be cowardly. In my heart, I was sure I knew what the Major planned, and I could not bear to think of Melody or one of the younger children making the discovery. If I was wrong, my only sin would be disturbing an old man's sleep.

Having made up my mind, I rudely pushed my way past the butler and started up the stairs. The poor man was so shocked that it was several moments before he gathered his wits and followed upon my heel.

"Miss, you cannot barge in here like this," he sputtered, hurrying up the stairs behind me. "Please leave this house at once!"

The man was a bit overweight, and he was breathing heavily when we reached the second-floor landing.

"I can open every door on this floor," I told him, starting down the dimly lit hall. "Or you can point out the Major's bedroom. I would prefer not to wake the children, or their nanny, but it is your choice."

To prove my point, I gave a little knock, then opened the first door to the right of the landing. The room was dark, but I could make out enough detail from the faint spill of light coming from the hall, to see that it was a very feminine room, probably Melody's. I closed the door and proceeded on to the next.

"Wait, miss, please," the butler pleaded. "You will wake the entire household."

"Then show me which room belongs to the Major," I retorted, knocking on the second door and throwing it open.

It, too, was decorated in feminine colors, with a good deal of lace and a number of dolls piled high in a basket by a wall. I could just see a small form curled up beneath the covers in the room's only bed. This must be little Carolyn's room, I surmised.

I was about to try the third room, when the butler came up behind me, clearly at a loss as to what to do with this crazy woman who had invaded his well-ordered house.

"Miss, wait," he cried out, as I raised my hand to knock. "The Major's room is the last one on the opposite side of the hall. Although what he will think of a strange woman entering his bedchamber at this time of night, I cannot imagine. Won't you please leave off this business until tomorrow?"

"I am truly sorry," I said, wishing with all my heart that I could do just that. "But it cannot wait."

With a great deal of apprehension, I approached the room the butler had pointed out as belonging to Major Tremaine. Light from the few gas lamps fitted upon the walls was more faint at this end of the corridor, and I slowed my step. It pains me to admit to such weakness, but my heart was pounding so hard in my chest I was surprised it was not audible to the butler.

I looked back to where he stood midway down the corridor. He probably wanted to be well out of shouting range, if the Major objected to his allowing a madwoman to assault his bedroom

"Would you please accompany me?" I asked him, angry that I felt obliged to request the man's help. "I—I know this is very irregular, but I would appreciate having you by my side."

The butler appeared taken aback by this request, but he reluctantly came to stand behind me as I knocked softly on the Major's door. When there was no response, I pushed it open. The first thing I noticed was a strong odor permeating the air. I was at a loss to identify the smell, but the butler recognized it at once.

"That's cordite."

"You mean from a gun?"

"Yes, miss. A gun that has recently been fired."

His reply sent shivers racing down my spine. The room was dark and silent. I listened, but could detect no sound, not even of breathing. All was ominously quiet.

With great force of will, I made my way with slow reluctance across the room to the bed. When I was closer, I could see the figure of a man partially propped up by pillows. Even in the dim light it was obvious that his body had slumped to the side at an awkward angle. I could make out something shiny on the white pillows. Tentatively, I reached out a hand and touched the substance. My fingers came away wet and sticky. I was sure it was blood.

"Is he—?" The man's voice behind me was none too steady.

"What is your name?" I asked, fighting to keep my voice steady.

"Arlott, miss."

"Arlott, would you please fetch some candles? I think Major Tremaine may be in need of medical assistance."

The butler needed no further urging to flee from the room. He returned in no more than five minutes, carrying a candelabrum which clearly illuminated the poor Major's inert body on the bed. I experienced a moment's light-headedness to see so much blood, not only on the bed coverings, but on the walls and floors. The Major had obviously shot himself through the head with what I took to be an old service revolver.

"Dear Lord," the butler gasped, clapping his free hand to his mouth.

Taking hold of my emotions, I forced myself to look around the room. Atop the Major's bureau I spied a white envelope. I assumed it was a suicide note, and very probably a confession accusing himself of the four Rincon Hill murders.

"Before we notify the police," I told the butler, "please show me to young David's room."

"Oh, miss, you don't think something terrible has happened to the boy, as well?"

His hand began to shake so badly I took the candelabrum from him. "Would you please lead the way to David's room?"

The boy's room was several doors down the hall from his grand-father's. When we reached it, the butler fell in behind me, obviously not wishing to enter first. I took a deep breath and opened the door.

David's room, too, was ominously quiet. Even as I entered, I could make out his still form lying beneath the bed coverings. Holding up the candelabrum, I saw that he looked quite peaceful; it would be easy to assume he was just sleeping. But of course he wasn't. An empty bottle of laudanum sat on a bedside table. Just to be certain, I placed my fingers on his neck, searching for a pulse. There was none.

I continued to study the boy's serene face for several minutes. He looked so young and so very handsome. I had become acquainted with David and the Major less than two weeks ago, yet in that time I had grown to know something of their feelings, of the kind of people they were inside. It seemed impossible that he and his grand-father could be in my life and then gone within the space of ten short days. What had snapped in this poor boy's head that he felt compelled to kill every man who seemed even casually interested in his sister? Perhaps some bonds between people could be too strong, I thought, too unyielding not to eventually lead to tragedy.

I handed the candelabrum back to the butler. "Would you please escort me to the front door, and then return to keep watch over David and the Major until I come back with the police? Mr. and Mrs. Tremaine are still at my home and they will need to be informed." I swallowed hard, fighting back tears. "As will David's sister, Melody."

"Miss Melody will be devastated," he said miserably. "I cannot imagine how she will manage without her brother."

"It will be very difficult, especially at first," I said wearily as we descended the stairs. "But unless I am mistaken, that young woman is made of stronger stuff than we imagine. I have every confidence that she will survive."

CHAPTER TWENTY-FIVE

New Year's Day was cold and damp, an inauspicious beginning for 1882. It had been two weeks since David's and Major Tremaine's deaths, but the shock of that night still cast a long shadow on everyone involved. The authorities seemed satisfied by the Major's confession, and reluctantly freed my clients, as well as the suspect in Patrick O'Hara's case. Young David was deemed to have died from an accidental overdose of laudanum, taken to relieve the pain of a migraine headache.

Melody Tremaine left her room only long enough to lay her beloved brother to rest. Since then, she had remained isolated and inconsolable. Joseph Kreling, with a little help from Faith Tremaine—who had become one of his steadfast admirers—had finally convinced Reginald to allow his daughter to appear at the Tivoli Opera House for a limited engagement. At the end of one month, all parties involved would revisit the contract, based upon the girl's success and her continuing desire to pursue a career on the stage. Although Melody was too heartbroken to appreciate this victory so close to her brother's death, I had faith that music would, in the end, be her salvation.

Interestingly, Madam Valentine wrote to thank me for the publicity I had inadvertently generated for her brothel thanks to Ozzie

Foldger's article. It seems that an unflattering exposé for one individual can be an excellent advertisement for another. Even though the famous madam publicly denied my presence at her parlor house, she privately admitted that business had never been so brisk!

Perhaps the most unexpected, and certainly the nicest, surprise to come out of the tragic happenings on Rincon Hill was Mrs. Lily Knight's generosity toward her husband's mistress. It seemed the visit Brielle and I paid to Gerald Knight's newspaper had not been in vain after all. According to Mrs. Knight's attorney, Brielle Bouchard and her small daughter were to receive, all expenses paid, a small apartment on Union Street near Washington Square, where the child might spend happy hours frolicking in the park. Although I doubt it was part of the widow's plan, Brielle's new home would also be within blocks of Madam Valentine's parlor house on Montgomery Street. Very handy, according to the former Matilda Abernathy, for visiting little Emma, who had become the darling of the brothel.

A few days after Christmas, Pierce fulfilled his promise to take Eddie aboard one of his ships for a grand tour. The day was clear and warmer than usual for that time of year; perfect weather for an afternoon on the Bay. Pierce chose a large, four-masted schooner, a powerful ship that regularly made the voyage from San Francisco to the Orient. To Eddie's delight, Pierce even arranged for a picnic lunch to be brought up from the galley. After showing the boy every nook and cranny on the ship, demonstrating how the sails were rigged, giving him a turn at the wheel, and answering a seemingly endless stream of questions, we finally called it a day as the sun began to set.

Riding home in Pierce's carriage, the lad seriously reconsidered his ambition to become a crime reporter like Mr. Samuel, in favor of a life on the sea.

"I reckon you got the beatenest job a body could have, Mr. Godfrey," the boy declared, the fire of adventure blazing brightly in his eyes. "A feller could go like greased lightning on a ship like that."

"He could indeed, Eddie," Pierce said, covering a smile. He gave me a significant look. "I've been trying for some time to talk a friend of mine into just such a life."

"Well, if he don't hanker to join you, then he ain't worth shucks," the boy pronounced, appearing incredulous that any sane man might reject such a grand offer.

"My thoughts exactly," Pierce agreed, but he wasn't speaking to Eddie. His eyes remained fixed on me.

To Mama's delight, I saw Pierce once or twice between Christmas and New Year's. We dined together on New Year's Eve, and then took in a play recently opened at the Baldwin Theater. The play was undoubtedly entertaining, but to be honest I saw little of it. Pierce's presence in the next seat was too distracting. I had worn the exquisite silver earrings he had given me for Christmas, and he used them as an excuse to kiss me behind each ear. I did my utmost not to reveal how this caused my pulse to race, but judging from his expression I do not believe I was entirely successful.

"I have enjoyed our time together immensely, Sarah," he said, as his carriage pulled up in front of my house. "I'm leaving for Hong Kong in a couple of days. From there, who knows?" His voice grew very soft. "My offer still stands, my dear. I would love to have you by my side. It would be an amazing adventure."

"You make it sound so wonderful," I replied, and it was nothing less than the truth. Part of me longed to join Pierce on the deck of his ship, bound for lands I had only read about in books. He made it appear so real I could almost smell the sea air and feel the ocean winds in my hair. I thought back to the week before when Eddie and I had spent such a delightful day on the schooner, and wondered what it would be like to sail aboard such a ship to China, Japan, or India.

"At least this time you're considering it," he said, when I didn't immediately answer.

"How can I not? As Eddie said, anyone who wouldn't jump at the chance isn't worth shucks. But—"

"But what? Just think, my darling, we'd be free to explore all the wonders of the world."

For a moment, I allowed myself to imagine what it might be like to lead the life of an adventurer. There would be no one to satisfy but ourselves, no arbitrary strictures of society to adhere to, just the blessed freedom to go wherever we pleased and do whatever suited us.

Then again, freedom always came at a price, I reminded myself. How would I feel after ten or twenty years spent enjoying a life of such self-indulgence, without ever accomplishing the dreams I had vowed to achieve? And how long would it take before I tired of the weeks, even months, I'd be forced to spend aboard a ship? Could my affection for Pierce survive such unremitting intimacy? And what about his feelings toward me? When all was said and done, would familiarity breed love or contempt?

"I don't like that expression on your face," Pierce said. "You look entirely too solemn."

"I can't do it, my dear," I said with true regret. "I don't doubt that it would be great fun for a while, but then I would surely begin to miss my work. I've dedicated my entire adult life to the law. I'd feel incomplete without it, like only half a person."

"Are you so certain about that?" He placed his hands on my shoulders, gently turning me in my seat until he could look into my eyes. "Marry me, Sarah. Marry me and we'll sail to Hong Kong for our honeymoon. Then you can decide how you feel about such a life."

"What will we do if I decide that it isn't for me? As your wife, it will be my duty to follow you whether it's what I desire or not."

"In that case I could stay here in San Francisco and run the company. Leonard could attend to our affairs in the Orient."

"That's very good of you to offer, Pierce, but then we would both be unhappy, you for giving up the life you love, and me for forcing you to do so." I sighed. "No, it's better this way. We can remain good friends and still be free to follow our own paths in life."

He studied my face as if he were memorizing my features. "The reasons I fell in love with you are the very ones that are keeping us apart. You're beautiful, intelligent, dedicated, all the qualities I most admire in a woman." He sighed. "You're one of a kind, my darling."

There was a catch in my throat as I whispered, "I don't know what to say, Pierce. You must know how much I admire you."

"Admire, but not love." His voice was soft and held an edge of sadness. "There's a world of difference between those two small words."

His hands cupped my face and suddenly his lips were on mine, gently at first, then with more urgency. As if driven by a will of their own, my lips responded with an intensity that shocked me, as did other unexpected sensations stirring my body. This involuntary response caused me a moment's panic, and I pushed against his chest with my hands. Reluctantly, he broke off the embrace, leaving me breathless and confused.

"Pierce, please, I—"

Once again his lips touched mine, this time with a tenderness that left me weak. "You say you admire me, but I think your lips care rather more for me than that."

When I once again tried to speak, he said, "No, darling, don't say anything. We'll see how your lips feel about me when I return from my next voyage. I'm beginning to think that admiration isn't such a bad place to start, after all."

We invited Robert to join us for our New Year's Day dinner. As usual, he was a bit uncomfortable in my father's presence, obviously unable to forget that Horace Woolson was a superior court judge for the county of San Francisco. As the meal progressed, however, my colleague began to relax, and toward the end he was actually enjoying Papa's company.

There was a new painting hanging in our dining room, a late seventeenth-century ink and colors on silk of a beautiful peony. It was a gift from Li Ying, delivered to our house on Christmas Day. The peony, he explained, was regarded by the Chinese as being a symbol of feminine beauty, which he insisted—to my embarrassment—I possessed in abundance.

The remainder of the note expressed his gratitude for my securing the release of his two young countrymen, and forbade me to return the retainer I received upon my visit to his home. The end of the missive read:

> *Once again you place too small a value on your dedication to champion all races, creeds, and genders with equal courage and resolve. This is a rare quality, indeed, and much to be prized. I am yet again in your debt.*
>
> *I look forward with much anticipation to our next visit.*

As was his custom, there was no signature or return address affixed to the letter.

Mama had the painting hung above the dining room buffet, where the stunning antique Chinese tea service Li had given me following the Russian Hill affair was displayed. Papa had remarked that if I continued to represent Li Ying and his countrymen, we might one day be able to dedicate an entire room to Chinese artifacts!

After a fine dinner of mulligatawny soup, fried codfish, Papa's favorite fried oysters, roast lamb, roast turkey, vegetables, fruit, cheese, and a wide selection of desserts, we sat about the table, satiated and content.

"Shall we take coffee in the parlor?" Mama inquired, pleased to be surrounded by her entire family.

There were nine of us, including Robert, sitting around the table: Mama, Papa, Samuel, Charles, Celia, and myself. Even my eldest brother, Frederick, and his wife, Henrietta, were in attendance.

"In a moment, my dear," replied my father. He turned to his youngest son. "Well, Mr. Fearless, I see that you've signed up to take your bar examinations next month."

"I have indeed, Father," Samuel replied with a smile, then stopped short, belatedly registering what Papa had just said. He tried to arrange his features into the innocent façade he was so good at assuming, but this time he failed miserably. "Mr. Fearless? Why—why ever would you call me that?"

Papa looked at him with steely eyes. "I'm sorry if I got it wrong, Ian. I thought that was the name you use in journalistic circles."

Everyone but Robert and I stared at Samuel in disbelief.

"Samuel," Mama exclaimed in distress. "Why didn't you tell us?"

"I thought you worked as a paralegal," Frederick said. "And who is Ian Fearless?"

"Evidently, your brother Samuel writes true crime stories under that pseudonym," Papa explained, his eyes never leaving his youngest son's face. "I hear that they appear frequently in a number of San Francisco newspapers."

"Good heavens," said my brother Charles. "I've read a few of Fearless's articles, and found them rather good. So they were written by you, Samuel? Well, I'll be dashed!"

Henrietta was regarding Samuel as if he had suddenly transformed into a two-headed serpent. "This is really too much! It is bad enough we are forced to put up with Sarah's antics, but a reporter in the family? No, that is going too far. It is not to be tolerated."

"I rather think we've been unknowingly tolerating it for the past five years, Henrietta," Papa informed his daughter-in-law. "What do you have to say for yourself, Samuel?"

My brother's face had turned a sickly puce color. "How did you find out?" he asked Papa, his tone none too steady.

"A better question might be why I didn't find out about it sooner," Papa replied. "Apparently, I am one of the last people in the city to learn that my youngest son has a secret identity. When were you planning on telling me the truth, son? Before or after I succeeded in making a complete fool of myself in front of Arthur Cunningham?"

I had never seen Samuel look so mortified. "I . . . that is, I planned on telling you after the holidays."

"Does that mean you've come to your senses, then, and will enter Cunningham's firm after you've passed your bar exams?" Papa demanded. "You *did* sign up to take them, didn't you, Samuel? Or is that yet another of your lies?"

"No, Father, I did sign up to take them in February," Samuel told him. "I've been, ah, studying a good deal to get ready."

"I imagine you have, if you haven't opened a law book in over five years," Papa told him. Frederick started to say something, but Papa motioned him to hold his tongue. "This is between Samuel and me, although I thought the rest of the family had a right to know. Since I'm sure you must already be aware of the situation, Mr. Campbell—as well as you, Sarah—I saw no reason not to address the matter openly."

Robert nodded, but wisely kept silent. I thought my mother, Charles, and Celia looked intrigued by this revelation, while Frederick and Henrietta appeared scandalized.

"All right, son," Papa went on. "Let's get down to brass tacks. If you've been working as a crime reporter for five years, you must find something to like about the job—although I cannot imagine what it could be. Are you going to squander your education and spend your life appealing to prurient public curiosity? Or will you take the position with Cunningham and Brill?"

Samuel looked uncertain, an expression that seemed oddly out of place on his face, given his usual self-confidence.

"Papa, he's a talented reporter," I said after an awkward silence. "Moreover, it's a job he loves. He's only kept it a secret because of your low opinion of journalists."

"A very sound opinion, too," put in Frederick. "I cannot believe you've been writing this drivel since you graduated from law school."

To my surprise, Robert cleared his throat and said, "It's hardly drivel, Senator Woolson. Sarah is right, Samuel is an accomplished writer."

Frederick regarded my colleague with ill-disguised derision. "I hardly think it is your place to comment, Mr. Campbell. As my father said, it is a family matter."

Robert's face reddened. When he spoke I noticed his Scottish burr had become considerably more pronounced. "I appreciate that, Senator. However, I cannot sit here tamely holding my tongue while Samuel is disrespected. I agree with many of your father's concerns about popular journalism, but believe me, your brother is far and away the most accomplished and respected reporter in this city. Not only that, but I consider him to be a good friend." As if suddenly aware that he had everyone's attention—and that, moreover, he was verbally dueling with a state senator—Robert sputtered into uncomfortable silence.

Samuel gave him a grateful smile. "Thank you, Robert. I'm not sure I deserve such praise, but I'm indebted to you for saying it."

"I agree, Father," said Charles. "Samuel's stories are first-rate."

Celia kissed her husband's cheek and smiled at Samuel. "I haven't read them myself, but I'm sure they're quite excellent."

Frederick looked as if he were about to burst. "Of all the preposterous—"

"Frederick, please," Papa interrupted, then turned back to Samuel. "It seems you have a number of staunch supporters, son. But I want to hear the decision from you. What is it to be? How do you intend to earn your livelihood—the law, or journalism?"

Samuel looked from me to Robert, then to Charles and Celia. Even Mama was smiling at him, clearly ready to accept whatever path he chose.

"I want to continue working as a journalist, Father. I don't think I could bear sitting in a stuffy office all day dealing with people's legal problems. Being a reporter is exciting and fulfilling. I can't imagine doing anything else with my life."

Papa did not immediately respond, but sat studying his son as if truly seeing him for the first time. After several long moments, he sighed. "I'll not force you to do something you would hate just to please me," he said quietly. "I admit that I'm disappointed, and I still hope you'll change your mind, but in the end it's your choice. But writing for a newspaper—" He could not hide his displeasure.

"He's also writing a book, Papa," I put in, knowing that he would find this a more acceptable endeavor than journalism. "Samuel is writing a book about crime in San Francisco since the Gold Rush days."

"Oh, Samuel," said Mama, looking pleased. "Are you really?"

Papa eyed Samuel speculatively, then shook his head in resignation. "All right, son, you win. It seems we're to have a writer in the family whether we care to have one or not."

"Look at it this way," said Samuel, a smile of obvious relief lighting his handsome face. "We already have a judge, a lawyer, a state senator, and a doctor. Why not a writer? Just to balance things out in the family."

Thank you for coming to Samuel's defense earlier, Robert," I said, walking him to the door.

It was nearing ten o'clock, and the night had turned cold, yet I felt an agreeable warmth remembering the brave way Robert had stood up to a state senator and a superior court judge. What the gruff Scot lacked in social niceties, he more than made up for in staunch loyalty to his friends.

Standing in the open door, he turned up his coat collar and donned his hat. "Samuel is a fine writer. I thought your father should know."

"As well as Frederick," I said, smiling. "Did you see his face when you told him Samuel was the most respected reporter in town? You were wonderful."

Although the foyer was dimly lit, I thought I saw him flush at this praise. "Samuel looks as if a huge weight has been lifted off his shoulders."

"He's been dreading this day for five years. I'm grateful you were here to help support him. And I think my mother is secretly pleased. She did a bit of writing herself in her younger years."

"She did? That must be where Samuel gets his talent."

He seemed about to say something else, then looked up above my head. With a broad smile, he leaned down and kissed me.

"The mistletoe," he said when I regarded him in surprise. "There's some hanging above the door. You must have forgotten to take it down after the Christmas party."

"Oh," I said, following his gaze. "It's an old Norse tradition, you know. Someone told me that it's bad luck to ignore the custom."

"Really," he said with a smile. "Well, then, I think it's a good idea to try it again, don't you? Just in case we didn't get it quite right the first time."

I returned his smile. "Yes, the Norse are usually very accurate about this sort of thing."

And standing on my tiptoes, I reached up and kissed him.

Just in case.